The Reddening

Books by
Adam L. G. Nevill

Novels

Banquet for the Damned

Apartment 16

The Ritual

Last Days

House of Small Shadows

No One Gets Out Alive

Lost Girl

Under a Watchful Eye

The Reddening

Collections

Some Will Not Sleep

Hasty for the Dark

The Reddening

Adam L. G. Nevill

Ritual Limited
Devon, England
MMXIX

The Reddening

by Adam L. G. Nevill

Published by
Ritual Limited
Devon, England
MMXIX
www.adamlgnevill.com

Dust jacket and cover design by Simon Nevill
Cover artwork by Samuel Araya
Text Design by The Dead Good Design Company Limited
Ritual Limited logo by Moonring Art Design
Printed and bound by Amazon KDP
ISBN 978-1-9160941-1-6

For Will Tenant, David Bruckner, Joe Barton,
Richard Holmes, Keith Thompson, all at Imaginarium,
and the cast, crew and post-production team of *The Ritual*.
You took the last old god of the woods by the horns.

'They were the first fossil teeth I had ever seen, and as I laid my hands on them, relics of extinct races and witnesses of an order of things which passed away with them, I shrank back involuntarily . . . I am not ashamed to own that in the presence of these remains I felt more of awe than joy.'

Father John MacEnery (on his discovery of prehistoric artefacts in Kent's Cavern, South Devon, 1825).

Origins

I

On the coming darkness, stepping off the stony cliff path and into thin air did not seem unfeasible. Andy too easily composed the only headline he'd ever make, post-mortem. *Body recovered in harbour . . .*

A mere glance down and he sensed the potential for a terrible skittering of his feet. The earth rolling marbles beneath his boots before the sickening plummet tingled his sphincter. Over he'd go, snatching, thumping, scraping onto spumes of foam in the din of water that smashed the slate teeth of the shoreline two hundred feet below.

Or would he drop silently, without fuss? He pictured an egg breaking on the side of a ceramic bowl and winced.

Even though little had been marked or signposted across the last five miles to offer an escape from the coast path, remaining on it was too dangerous. The further he'd ventured the more remote and hostile the cast of the land, so unlike the lush, near-tropical sections around Torbay, or the long, open reaches of South Hams.

Heather now bearded the slate and shale at the top of the cliffs, producing a vast rust and grey stonescape that suggested Scotland or the South Island of New Zealand, not what he expected to find in South Devon.

Since the first coves of the morning, north of Divilmouth, he'd walked the edge of an unceasing undulation of mostly bare, hilly farmland. Distant copses had occasionally sprouted on higher ground, the silhouettes of the trees seemingly silent and still with anticipation, like warriors watching on horseback in old Westerns.

Earlier, closer to Divilmouth harbour, it had been the vista of an enormous aquamarine sea that had lulled him into complacency. Nothing could go wrong beside water so achingly beautiful. But beauty doesn't last. That stretch of the coast was a long way behind him now and he'd not seen another walker since. Only a paraglider had offered any human contact. That was at midday and he'd been packing up when Andy stopped for lunch, three hours gone. The man had called the hills 'the cardiacs'.

Those hills.

Rendered clumsy with fatigue by late afternoon, what remained of his body's depleted stamina tinkled inside a near-empty tank. Andy couldn't even recall how many rocky hillsides or rough stone steps he'd struggled up. Maybe four, but they'd all looked similar and in his memory had fused into one tortuous travail. Descending the slopes had pressed his toenails into their cuticles: he'd not trimmed his nails before wearing new hiking boots and was close to limping.

There had been no mention of so many hills in his guidebook, a publication aimed at those with more local knowledge than he possessed. Although it had let him down on each walk so far, he'd wanted to get his money's worth so had persevered with *Spectacular Walks on the South West Coast Path: South Devon.* But what if he'd been elderly? The numerous steep rises would burst hearts.

Forty minutes for lunch at midday was also a stupid decision. As were the hours he'd spent exploring the first three coves at ten. His one litre of water was long gone. *This is how people get into trouble.* The tone of his head-voice was now his dad's.

Time.

The atmospherics served as a premonition of how dark it would soon be. To get out of the situation safely he'd need every minute of the one hour of remaining sunlight. Then another hour of half-light to find the car.

Andy looked up, imploringly, at the light situation. Cloud had tarnished the sky metallic, giving the sea an appearance of liquid steel. In one circular portion of the iron cumulus, light splintered to produce the sulfur and mercury of a Turner seascape. Far out at sea, one great shaft of concentrated sunlight struck the water, producing a white-gold disc too blinding to look into.

But definition along the cliff edge was growing vague. Greens, blues and reds were being extracted from the earth. He pictured himself reduced to a tiny figure in a dark aerial photograph, the surface murky with dust.

Wind with cold pins began to sheet off the sea, shivering his flesh. Perspiration beneath his fleece transformed into a second skin of frost, covering his back, groin and forehead. For all the protection it offered, his thin woollen hat might have been a Christmas crown made from tissue paper.

The latest edition to the new script was rain. The white horizon was blackening. *If you get wet in a cold wind . . . Shit going wrong just builds.* He could no longer use the GPS on his phone either: he'd run the battery down by taking pictures to show his wife.

Anticipation of a temperature plummet at nightfall tightened the tourniquet of concern further, squeezing his thoughts into choices measurable on a three-fingered hand.

Should he go back to where he had a vague memory of a path heading inland, in the direction of a Land Trust property? He guessed that route promised to be a death march uphill into the interior. Then he'd have to locate the house. *Would it be open off-season?* Those places usually closed at five anyway. *Or was it six?*

Or should he just press on for his original goal, the nature reserve at Brickburgh? He'd intended to cut inland from there on the sole track his map noted: a route that would eventually circle back and deliver him to the small Access Countryside car park where he'd left his Volvo at nine that morning.

Though it was the best option for locating the car, the Brickburgh route would surely involve over an hour on the hilly coastal path in dimming light and intensifying cold. So Andy ruled it out almost as soon as he mooted the notion. A glance at the beach below pulled his eyes to the steep shale hills that buttressed the shore. The map helpfully indicated that two more beaches would follow that one too. There wasn't sufficient light remaining to make agonisingly slow progress up three more *cardiacs*.

For the first time in years, he felt tearful.

A third option involved a yomp directly inland from Slagcombe Sands, around the wetland and up the valley. But a glance in that direction invited the question: what awaited at the summit? A bloody fence? It'd take him an hour to get up there too, the final hour of daylight. There was no street lighting out here. No prospect of electric light save from a few remote farms dotted about the hills. He'd seen a couple of dejected buildings earlier, perched atop the valleys. But distant yellow windows wouldn't illumine where he placed his feet on uneven ground. He'd already lost his balance and fallen twice in daylight.

There were options, or diminishing choices made in desperation. None were satisfactory.

He was not an experienced walker. At Christmas, as a means of keeping fit, he'd made his rambling debut. This was walk six in two months but the first on the wilder stretch of the coast path.

Self-loathing added to a fearful mix of incomplete thoughts. The day had no room for another bad decision: no about-turns, retracings or hunkering down in the wind to beseech the map that he could barely see without reading glasses. The last few times he'd returned the book to his pocket, he'd already forgotten what he'd just looked at: cold-wind dementia.

Option one: the Land Trust property.

Head down, his mouth a rictus, he meandered up a slope parallel to the direction he'd just walked. The period building would be on a road, somewhere inland, behind this section of the path. *It must be.* There might be a phone. He'd have to reach it cross-country, across fields.

So turn around, twat, and walk until the darkness swallows you . . .

A dining room. Two figures sitting upright at a table. Painted red from their hairlines to the soles of their bare feet, their torsos and limbs oiled to a dull sheen. Not speaking, their eyes closed. Perhaps deep in the concentration of prayer and giving thanks for what they were about to receive: those bruised slabs of meat, wet and heavy upon their white plates. A fare not shocking Andy as much as the couple's appearance. To come so far and be confronted by *this*? He feared that fate had marked this day out for horror.

Prior to this revelation, he'd walked inland from the coastal path for a couple of hours, moving west on a muddy groove rutted by hooves in black soil caked with dung. The odour of animal waste had become a permanent stain on his sinuses. He'd persevered and followed the crease for ninety minutes until the lit windows of a building had become visible atop a ridge.

As he trudged to the isolated house, the last vestiges of sunlight had dissolved into a sky of iron. The iron had subsequently faded to coal, his eyes filling with pitch. He'd stumbled through night-sodden fields and talked out loud to suppress panic. Blind to the world's forms from his waist to his feet, he'd crashed through hedges and fallen down the sides of stone walls, snagged himself on fences he'd only seen when bent over them. Pawing his way over a gate, he'd scraped a thigh. That whole leg was now wet and his waterproof trousers were stuck to stinging flesh. Both knees were bruised.

Sometimes his feet had crunched stone chippings, sometimes grass. Sometimes he'd slid in mud; often he'd skated through dung. His hands were chilled to claws black with dirt. Blood from his nails had adhered the wool of his socks to his toes. Rain had made his jacket twice as heavy. But he'd continued, staggering about a lumpy land without light, aiming his lurching at a far-off row of yellow squares: window-shapes that had been distant for hours, embedded within buildings indistinguishable from the void their lights pin-pricked. A lighthouse for a careless rambler. A farm enclosed by barbed wire.

As he'd arrived, the big hand on the luminous face of his watch had clicked past seven, the hour his wife would start to worry.

He'd then passed between outbuildings, his feet sliding through putrescence, the stench of fresher faeces drifting from underfoot to seep brain-deep, swinish with nitrates, shortening his breath.

He'd even heard a deep cough in the nearest night-smudged building, followed by two more cries, as if the beasts within had acknowledged his trespass through their sleep. Unlit barns? He'd only sensed solid structures rather than identified what they were, but the glowing windows of the farmhouse had gradually enlarged. And then he'd been standing outside a long room: a combination kitchen and dining room.

By that time, any shame he felt about banging on a stranger's door at so late an hour had evaporated. Human intervention in his plight had become necessary.

And then he'd seen *them* through the window. The people. The red people. Naked red people. A woman and a man, their true age obscured by the dark pigment encrusting their faces. Had they wiped each other red with blood-caked hands before sitting down to eat?

They didn't make sense, and while lost in the dark Andy couldn't imagine anything he'd rather not have seen through the windows of a stranger's house.

Dizzy with shock, he turned to sneak away. His intention was to move silently round the building to the enigmatic front, where he'd creep away on whatever metalled surface he could place his bemired boots upon. But when the toe of his boot struck an object that refused to move, his hopes for a silent escape came off the table.

Solid, immobile and unseen, the shape responded with a dull *thunk*, transmitting a tremor to his knee. His body continued while the foot remained rooted. Falling forwards, he thrust out a hand, striking the very window that had so recently promised salvation.

Second leg swinging wide, he just kept to his feet and righted his spine. As the hot-cold sensation preceding the fall wilted, he peered back at the scene he'd surely disturbed.

He had.

The two figures remained seated but their horribly white eyes had widened to stare right at him. Big eyes that contained as much surprise as his own.

When the bulky male figure rose from its chair and pointed at his face, Andy stumbled and fell about in the darkness of the yard.

Within moments the sound of a door latch chimed through the cold. And under the roar of his breath, the trespasser whimpered.

2

Later that year.

*B*ones seeped from the cliff's freshest wound. A few lay scattered about Matt's feet. Like fallen columns from an ancient temple, two great plinths of rock had separated from the cliff-face and cracked apart on impact with the sand. He imagined the wet thud they'd once made in the tiny cove.

Moving his gaze from the fissure above his tousled red head to the grey shore, he tracked the path of fallen debris: broken limestone resembling a frozen river, the furthest extent of the rock-fall hurling rubble across the pebbles and into the sea. The cliff must have collapsed within the last week, so how long had those bones been embedded in the rocks? Were the darker pieces all bone fragments? *Animal or human?* Maybe even fossils?

He decided to collect as many of the more interesting bits as possible before the tide took them away: the same tide that had eroded a notch in the cliff's foot and written collapse into its future. The new spring tide would rise higher with a full moon, suck at the landslip and reclaim the relics.

Thirty years of coastal erosion in one month of continual storms were responsible for this avalanche, the sea's perpetual rage unrecognisable in this part of South Devon. So recently had these blue skies blackened with fury and the aquamarine waters darkened to grey before spitting great briny gouts, day and night and for weeks, right into any face turned seaward.

Much had been smashed apart in South Devon. Comprising no fewer than thirteen hurricanes, the sea's maelstrom had surged over walls, bent iron railings and train tracks, battered harbours and fishing boats into fragments, torn down holiday lets from Plymouth to Dawlish and even shrugged off the cliff's heavy coats. What had been relied upon to be benign, sheltering and gentle had reverted to assault.

Over now, the weather-front spent, the sea assumed a sheepish, remorseful character. But the towns remained shaken and their people subdued, bruised at a deep psychological level. No one trusted the sea. They wouldn't for a while. For those who lived beside the coves and the long red beaches of the towns further north, it would take time and forgetfulness to rehabilitate the old bond.

On hands and knees, Matt climbed into the stones and into the bones. He'd seen the fissure two hundred metres up while paragliding in air cold enough to bite through his face mask and purple his skin.

Conditions for gliding had been good and he'd reverse-launched from a beauty spot intended for coast-path walkers. In seconds, a high easterly headwind charging off the sea had raised him from standing on his feet to sitting in thin air. As soon as his wing had flapped, risen over his head and inflated, he'd been aloft, his stomach momentarily loosening like it was too big and on the outside of his body, before tightening to a closed fist inside a physique rendered frail. Up through the atmosphere he'd risen, alone and dwarfed by an immensity of sky.

Seated in his harness, he'd looked to the green water turning milky turquoise in one great stripe of sea. Further out the waters were stained a bitter Atlantic blue, finally turning indigo and sparkling silver, the distant horizon rimmed with white fire.

When he glanced back, the land lost the ramparts of natural obstruction at ground level and appeared flatter.

No matter how many times he'd looked down upon this earth from altitude, the sight of how Brickburgh was revealed anew always startled him. A velvet fuzz of grass scarred white by tracks and roads. Trees imitating broccoli. Rocks at the shore lumpen and necrotic. Cloud shadows wafting like ghosts wearing actual sheets. Grey farm buildings imitating the hard Lego bricks that found the arch of his foot and cramped his toes to claws when his son stayed for the weekend.

A column of air had spiralled from the sun-warmed cliff-face and he'd stepped into the invisible, muscular core of a powerful thermal. *Get it wrong, drop into the sea and you're dead.* His mate, Bill, had told him that when he started Matt off, a long time ago. Matt had been piloting his glider up and down the coastal area for six years.

The cliff-fall was two kilometres east of where he'd launched and where he'd watched the earth re-form into an aerial photo. Cliffs that were a part of ancient South Devon. Most of them forged from dark volcanics and shales, forming a mosaic with the regal purple, the rust and brassy pigments of Devonian slates: rocks minted 400 million years before, when this part of the earth was under a sea positioned south of the equator. His own county had given its name to that era in the earth's long history: the Devonian, when its rocks were smelted in ancient elemental forges of fire, steam and pressure, raging beneath oceans now extinct.

But the fissure that had released the bones appeared in a strip of different stone. That rent gaped in the farthest southerly reach of the ancient limestone, once heavily quarried by the Victorians: a compression of prehistoric reefs and algae, seamed with the rusty blood of haematite. Mining had reshaped the peninsulas to resemble the prows of vast ships and it was beyond the last bow that Matt now gingerly picked his way.

Eying the new cliff edge above him, at the rear of the gouge, he could see that a corresponding section of the coast path had vanished. On either side of the collapse, the new cliffs leaned forward, chins out. It didn't look stable.

Gotta be quick.

The top layer of rubble was loose and the first bone he'd found he'd mistaken for a piece of waterlogged wood, until a closer scrutiny revealed a splintered end. In cross-section the inside of the fragment resembled desiccated coral, or the inside of a sea sponge: animal bone that had once held marrow. *Possibly a rib from a farm animal?*

Most of the hilly coastal land was used for grazing. All around Brickburgh, herds of Black Welsh Mountain sheep roamed. Slow-moving ensembles of ebony ponies also drifted close to the coast path. But the bone's brittleness and mahogany to coal-black colouring suggested age. And perhaps a great age, thwarting his theory of sheep tumbling from the cliff before their remains weathered above the sea.

Nearby, another bone was lighter in colour and camouflaged amongst pebbles, driftwood and chunks of haematite. The object's shape assured him that he was holding a portion of a jaw; the fragment's dimensions suggested it must once have belonged to a beast no longer indigenous to the British Isles. Three teeth remained. The most prominent tooth was worn, striated with capillary-sized cracks, and resembled an incisor the size of his thumb. A tooth compelling Matt to examine the ground about his knees more closely.

He'd seen the remains of the great scimitar cats in the museum in Torquay, their bones chiselled out of limestone at Kent's Cavern further down the coast: the very limestone that ended here, in Brickburgh.

Matt moved higher, through the rubble, filling his pockets with what might have been bird bones or the metatarsals of land animals, until he paused to inspect two larger objects, longer bones distinguished by heavy scores and cuts. They'd been worked at the top too: holes were bored into the flaring ends before the shaft concluded in a ball-joint for the hip or shoulder of an animal.

He knew other caves discovered in Devon's limestone had contained multiple entrances that weather and the movements of the earth had buried with rubble. Evidence of prehistoric animals and early man had been found in many of them. It was feasible that a cave might yet lie undiscovered.

Matt's breath caught with excitement. Sweat replenished itself beneath his waterproofs and cooled.

Jesus wept.

If there was a cave behind that crack and he discovered it, would they name it after him? No one could have spotted the fissure, unless they'd been hugging the shore in a kayak or seen it from the air. During the storms, the sea had been too rough for shipping, let alone pleasure craft. A giant freighter had even beached at Divilmouth. Not even the most extreme paraglider would have considered flying in that weather and he didn't know anyone else who flew this section. It was too dangerous.

So who should he tell first? The police? *Didn't seem right.* No, the council. *Maybe.* Or the Land Trust, who managed the public areas around the towns and farmland? *Probably them.*

The crack itself was only a foot wide and whatever lay beyond remained pitch dark. Maybe the inner space had seen no light for tens of thousands of years.

As he drew close to the fissure, he slowed, reminded of an orifice: bloodlike stains in the haematite issuing a sense of fleshy inner walls, moist and intersected by the pale bone of limestone.

His thoughts turning unpleasant, his comparison switched from ideas of a cliff vulva to those of a horrible head wound. An analogy immediately reinforced by what he recognised as the top of a skull in the debris around his knees. Matt shivered.

Mottled and tanned brown-black, the object sat upside down and formed a cup, like one half of an Easter egg his son had broken apart to retrieve a little bag of sweets. One half of a leathery egg with a jagged rim of spikes around the broken side. But the frontal and parietal bones were intact and still joined.

The bone was almost weightless and the exterior was also deeply grooved and scored as if scratched by stones or an implement. And if it was human, it appeared that the entire crown of this skull, from just above the eyebrows, had been roughly chiselled free.

Carefully, Matt slipped the fragment inside his rucksack and folded his spare hoodie around the object. He didn't want it crushed under a stampede of rubberneckers when word broke. That is, if this was important. Everyone had bigger things to consider these days: unemployment, a collapsing health system, the price of food, the terrible economy, a plummeting pound, the unpredictable climate, the strikes, unrest. No one might give a damn about a cave full of old bones.

At the mouth of the fissure he turned his smartphone into a torch and shone it inside the crevice, again wondering when light had last fallen inside this cave, because that is what this was: *a cave.*

Across the reddish floor he could see more bones, scattered as the fissure extended into a damp funnel with a low ceiling. At the furthest reach of light the ceiling met a tumble of rock. A restricted space, and nothing tempted him to push inside, his chest compressing at the very idea.

Instead, he extended his arm and shoulder into the hole to retrieve what resembled another bone with an odd shape.

Sitting back on his heels, he held the fragment in better light and gently brushed the sides with a thumb. *Bone*: and he could see where it had been snapped from a longer appendage, upon which the legs of the carven figure may once have been attached.

The creature's torso suggested a heavily-breasted woman with wide hips. Part of one arm had been fashioned, the other side was damaged. But if that was a head then it was the head of an animal. A dog, he thought: a hound thing with a boxy muzzle. In fact, the carving was intricate enough to suggest indents for tiny eyes. *This* had been made by human hands.

When Matt returned his scrutiny to the darkness of the fissure, his mind leaped into awe at what he held.

Behind his shoulders, the sea rushed in and slapped the pebbles. It then withdrew in a susurration across the stony shore as it had done for tens of thousands of years before this very moment.

Later, when questioned, he would struggle to articulate how he'd felt with the dog-headed thing within his hands. But he did offer, to anyone to whom he told his story, that he'd never felt as insignificant. Tiny, an irrelevant witness and a mere speck upon a great tide of time that surged ever forward. A tide upon which he too would be extinguished: the spark of all he was doused in less than a cosmic moment, just as the mind that had occupied the skull in his bag had been extinguished so many years before.

3

Two weeks later.

$\mathcal{S}$helly couldn't decide if their campsite possessed a single redeeming feature.

The landscape was all that Greg had promised: it was open, wild, hewn from steep valleys, framed by great vistas of sky and sea, and uninhabited. Though the land must have been more hospitable once and even crowded with trees before deforestation had left it barren. There had been a lot of mining here, a long time ago: Greg had said so. But despite man's devastations nothing appeared tamed. *Here* all remained intimidating and was as wild as it had been before, but in a different way to her eye: *here* was mistreated and feral, not healthily wild.

But by the second day of the trip, what really exceeded her considerable physical discomforts from the hike, followed by a sleepless night in the tent, was a curious, persistent murmur of anxiety: an enduring unease not dissimilar to mild vertigo combined with an apprehension akin to trespassing with confident friends, while secretly wishing that you weren't.

Maybe the strange emptiness of the land was troubling Shelly, or the paucity of colour accounted for the dissonance, the sheer relentlessness of the tones that she associated with camouflage. Whatever the cause, she'd remained unable to read the land about herself adequately, to acclimatise or orientate.

She must have moved too far from the familiar because her imagination had additionally been lured into epochal considerations she'd not entertained since childhood. Too clear here were reminders that she was a mite on a great chunk of rock, one formed by distant and monumental collisions and processes in deep space, occurring billions of years before. Awareness of the great absences above the inert earth and the vast, unbroken stretch of empty water unto the horizon seemed to intensify her loneliness while making her strangely fearful.

More discomforting still was the notion that this place and this planet were part of some divine plan and that her belittlement here was both intended and punitive.

Perhaps her feelings had inspired a growing suspicion, too, that their campsite was being observed from the top of the steep valley.

From the corner of her eye, the trees suggested figures that only became stationary when you looked at them directly. They seemed to alter their positions when she wasn't looking. And though this odd perspective was caused by her movements below, the imagined manoeuvres above were hard to disregard.

Hardest of all to judge were the distances around the tent. The top of the valley didn't appear far away and yet she was only too aware of how long it had taken them to descend just one side. In her memory, the very coast path they'd walked to get here had additionally greyed into mist as if swallowing the world they'd known. A unique set of perspectives – and Greg's enthusiasm for the valley had only served to increase her estrangement.

To even reach Slagcombe they'd crossed two similar beaches to the one they'd camped behind, all three formed from boulders rolled down by waters draining through valleys across millennia. At each beach the sand between the rocks was as dark as emery cloth. Neither of the first two beaches had offered car parks or public access by road, but at least they were closer to Divilmouth. Shelly had wondered out loud if they'd needed to walk any further, as the first pair of shorelines were empty enough for their purposes.

But Greg had described those beaches as 'too popular'. Once or twice before he'd seen a few fishermen use them. And because of what a local man had recently found in a hole inside a cliff near Slagcombe, even it would soon be 'fenced off' and 'full of twats'.

Sometime during their stay, Greg intended to find the hole that had been in the papers.

More of these vast stretches of rubbly beaches lay ahead of them too, in the direction of Brickburgh. In Shelly's imagination they were all more of the same thing, rugged and inhospitable.

They'd subsequently spent their first night at least seven miles from Divilmouth harbour. And except for hearing the distant grunt of a motorbike and seeing the drifting, luminous orange flag of a paraglider, they'd had no reminders of their own species. It was to be just the two of them for two nights: their tent beside the beach under an open sky.

A chilly breeze scoured from the sea again, blowing her hair into a tangle and prickling her pale, untrained body. From arrival, she'd stayed huddled inside her fleece and Gortex jacket, while occupying the sole fold-out chair that Greg had humped all the way from Divilmouth.

At least a big fire had been promised to add some much-needed colour and warmth to the excursion and its fulfilment was well underway. Where the wetland at the foot of the valley met the stony shore, Greg was building the pyre. He was going to cook on it: tinned sausages that would be slipped between open buns. Shelly watched her man toil, beyond the impossibly flat water of the marsh that glimmered like a huge pane of broken glass. Reeds the colour of wheat obscured much of the surface. Brightly coloured waterfowl continually flew over their tent.

And now *they* were back again, the stinking black rams. Their shit was everywhere. Shelly watched the group of black lumps moving down the valley sides towards the tent.

Shortly after their arrival, the previous afternoon, the sheep had descended and occupied the grass around their tent, a welcoming committee content to stare and crap. At first she and Greg had laughed, thinking the arrival of the animals an exciting addition to their weekend adventure in the wild. But it hadn't taken long for the unbroken gazing of so many amber eyes, bisected by a horizontal black slit, to unnerve her: a stolid watching presence increasing their exposure at the foot of the valley, the intense, unreadable eyes embellishing her suspicions that other eyes, higher up the slopes, were also observing them just as keenly.

Shelly wondered who owned the sheep. There were farms inland and a Land Trust house that was too far to reach, all uphill from the beach. Perhaps the sheep expected her to feed them. Their fleeces were matted with dung, their nostrils encrusted with snot, their presence a fitting epitaph to the 'romantic' weekend. She needed Greg to shoo them away.

'What?' she asked the one nearest the tent, but the ram stared, unblinking. 'Piss off!' she hissed. 'You actually stink of shit.' As if to mock her, the animal released a stream of black balls from its tangled backside.

She would ignore them. She had far bigger things to worry about. The row at first light had been far worse than the annoyance of random sheep and the cold. The tense, spitting exchange still echoed through her thoughts. Greg had even said, 'Never again.' She'd responded with, 'It's shit, Greg. Shit. It even stinks of shit. It's all round the tent in case we needed convincing. I didn't sleep at all and I'm freezing. I can't get warm. Divilmouth calling, mate.'

He'd paled at her outburst, called her 'ball-ache' and walked off to see the quarry.

She'd only seen him get that angry with her twice in six years. *Ball-ache.* Once Greg lost it he could take days to return to himself. They had another night to get through and the sulking was now wearying and wearing them both down.

Shelly stood up. Her knee joints ached from being stationary for too long in the cold. Stumbling about to ease the stiffness and to get a better sense of what Greg was up to, she moved away from the sheep.

As she did so, her enduring sense of a distant scrutiny found a startling definition and confirmation. A human figure was now standing at the top of the southern slope of the valley.

At first glance, she hoped the form was one of the odd-looking trees in her peripheral vision: bereft of leafage and made skeletal by the wind. But a closer scrutiny confirmed that it was indeed a person up there, because the thin figure, silhouetted against the ashen sky, was moving its arms. It was raising something into the air.

Shelly heard a note. A single piped note.

They weren't trespassing. The shoreline was public land managed by the Land Trust. You weren't supposed to light fires but 'Who'd ever know?' Greg had said.

Another note wavered behind her, from a distance. Shelly turned and spotted a second figure. What sunlight seeped through the clouds no longer smarted her eyes and she saw this piper more clearly than its partner: a man standing on the ridge, thin, scruffy-haired and blowing into a flute or pipe. He was naked too: she caught the hint of dangle at his groin. Across the valley his note was matched.

There was fresh movement behind the tent. Another four rams had made their way to the campsite as if directed downwards by these distant shepherds.

Shelly raised her eyes towards the inner depth of the valley and identified an additional trio of the spindly human silhouettes. They were also naked; it's why they all appeared so slight. What she didn't understand was why their skin was so dark.

Five of them now.

She called out to Greg. The wind buffeting up the valley from the sea prevented her voice extending much further than her lips.

She edged towards the wetland. If she walked at an angle she'd skirt the boundary of reeds and pick up the track that led to the shore.

She hadn't gone far but couldn't resist another look up the valley. The numbers of their visitors had swollen in mere seconds; the new arrivals were also now moving down the valley sides.

Shelly estimated that within a few moments a dozen of these figures had appeared, all now possessing a sinister inexorability in their unhurried descent. Equally distributed across the slopes of the valley and in the ravine flowing from the summit, *they* walked. The beach or their tent appeared to be the destination.

Her thoughts scratched about trying to fathom whether the situation called for hilarity or caution, fight or flight. A spurt of adrenalin made her lighter on her toes. She stumbled, jittery, knees clumping together. Her feet required her full attention and without that resource she skidded on the moist grass, ploughing dung. 'Greg!'

He hadn't heard and continued to roll a large stone across the pebbles towards the fire pit.

'Greg! Greg!'

That he heard. He looked up, his body still bent over. Shelly pointed to the slopes. 'We got company!'

She returned her eyes to the slopes. The naked people continued to observe their careful side-steps. Easier to see those on the northern slope now and in the low light their bare skin issued a scarlet sheen. *Red.* The people were painted red. *Red people. Naked red people.* And what had they done to their hair? That wasn't right, having it all tufted and clawed out from the sides where it glistened.

Most of them gripped *something* in their hands: small black objects. One of the men held what might have been a staff or spear. Two others carried the thin pipes she'd heard. *They've come out of time.*

Shelly turned to Greg for confirmation that these people were actually there and that this was actually happening. He'd stood up straighter to see over the wetland's reeds, shielding his eyes to survey the visitors.

Anxiety increased a pricking of Shelly's nerves. If she wasn't careful, fear would soon take hold of her throat and make her voice warble. She couldn't show that she was frightened. She had a notion that looking afraid would be a bad idea. She'd not run either, she'd walk normally.

Picking her way across the uneven ground and the slippery grassy mounds was slow going, comic even, slapstick slow, and she soon regretted the decision not to run. To circle the marsh and get to Greg on the beach, she'd need to make the track traversing the southern side of the valley. By moving so slowly, she'd now meet the naked red people descending the slope over there. They'd reach the track first.

Shelly stopped and acknowledged why she'd not run: she feared that *they* would too, towards her.

'Greg! Hurry!'

Greg was still on the rocky shore, slowly making his way to where the marsh turned into a stream, embedded with smooth boulders. Upon his distant pale oval of a face Shelly read his confusion. Tension had thinned his mouth to a slit. 'Shell!' he called.

On came the red people, without pause, fastidious in their exodus from the hillsides. Even though there were wide gaps within their ranks they were incrementally forming a tighter semi-circle as they neared the shore. Shelly was becoming trapped behind the wetland within a shortening necklace of naked people.

Far off, at the head of the valley, two of the group had remained behind. One was sitting down, which was odd, but Shelly lacked the clarity of mind to scrutinise what the distant form sat upon. The second figure was standing and had raised thin arms. All that differed between those that were approaching their tent and the couple who'd remained behind was the heads. At a distance, the heads of the couple at the top of the valley were out of proportion to their bodies: were too large, misshapen.

'Greg!'

A childish urge ushered her back towards the tent as if the campsite possessed a private domestic boundary that wouldn't be crossed or invaded by the insistent visitors. She wasn't thinking straight and knew it.

Like the rams. They just came. At you. Just came, from up there, out of the land. Then they're here, around you.

The idea was simple and it horrified her, as did the faces of the figures as they drew closer: all red, the eyes and teeth too white. Their expressions alone collapsed her resolve and her hope that it was all a jape. These people were angry. No, they were more than angry: they were enraged. Excited too, because they abruptly made a terrible noise. All of them started to howl and ululate like angry apes, a commotion intimating that the restraint they had used in their orderly descent was about to conclude.

The pair at the valley summit with the malformed heads had incited the chorus by issuing faint, high-pitched shrieks that had warbled into a horrible skirl. When the sound had pierced the valley their confederates had immediately taken up the cry.

When Shelly identified what the red people were clutching in their fists, she wanted to sit down in protest at being intimidated. *Black stones.* Rocks that tapered into points.

'Get here! Greg! Greg!'

As she looked desperately in her boyfriend's direction, her vision suffered a marginal judder. From the waist up he was visible over the furry tips of the reeds. He was running from the shore to their camp.

Ahead of him, a few of the red people had stopped as if to greet him on the beach path they'd already reached. Their tatty, greased heads and scarlet faces seemed more monstrous as they grinned and shrieked excitedly at his approach. There were four. He'd never get through them.

'Oh Jesus,' Shelly said to herself and to the unhearing universe of air and stone and sea that surrounded her. 'Jesus Christ.'

She'd waited too long to act and only now was she running at the nearest gap between the two red things closest to her: women with grimacing faces. Both were elderly, their breasts strangely plump and shiny beneath stringy throats.

But where did she go if she made it between them? *Up there? Up the sides of the valley?* Already the left side of her chest felt as if an ice cube was lodged in a lung: she wouldn't get far and wasn't fit enough to do more than crawl that slope.

Without any alteration in pace, the two women nearest to her moved together and narrowed the parting.

Shelly stopped running, turned, looked for another route through the enclosing corral of red figures. She ran for a space at ninety degrees to her previous course.

No sooner had she set this course when a heavily bearded man, his facial hair entirely soaked in what might have been blood, simply stepped closer to his neighbour and annulled that option.

Shelly adjusted her course again and ran for the other side of the valley. As if reading her mind, two of the red people sauntered inwards at her and sealed that route.

The wetland. That was behind her now. She might make it. *Into the water. Wade in. Harder for them to get to you in there.*

Shelly screamed, a reaction to Greg's raised voice behind her. He'd just shouted, 'What? What do you want?'

Above her rapid, noisy breathing, she heard the scuffling of bare feet on the stony track signalling a commotion, about thirty metres distant, where Greg was.

She looked there but no longer saw Greg. She could only make out the oiled torsos and spiky heads of the howling red people, standing where she'd last seen her boyfriend.

Amidst the reeds of the wetland, their stained arms rose and fell, rose and fell at whatever tried to tear itself from between them. *Greg.*

They hammered at her boyfriend. He'd fallen and the red people had quickly formed a circle to smash their rocks into his body. The sound Shelly heard was akin to the beating of a drum filled with wet sand. *Dunk. Thud. Dunk. Thud.*

Her will to run died. A whiteout of shock and bewilderment bent her at the waist so she could be sick.

Ducks flew overhead. Dusty wings flapped amidst honking cries of alarm.

Dunk. Thud. Dunk. Thud.

Oh, God. Leave him. Please leave him . . . Don't you think he's had enough? She wanted to say this but there was no air inside her body. She sobbed breathlessly.

Dunk. Thud. Dunk. Thud.

Arcs of dark liquid were flung into the air from the tips of many red hands, like suds cast from wet tools. The red arms went up and down, up and down. The flapping commotion of the water fowls dimmed and the noise of multiple pairs of bare feet slapping the turf drew nearer to her. She closed her eyes, then opened them.

Standing upright, her arms loose and weak at her sides, her nose running freely, she watched the red people close. Mouths open and howling: here a filling, there a gap, purple tongues, black nostrils. Eyes too big: wild like animals.

A moment of strange calm came upon her then: a warmth spread through her muscles. 'No.' Her final word.

The red people took her down to the wet grass and began tugging her into position.

She wanted the first raised rock to knock her out so that she wouldn't feel the impact of the other five. It didn't.

4

Two years later.

'can assure you, in my field, no prehistorical site in the British Isles has been the cause of so much excitement. The extraordinary finds at the Brickburgh cave far exceed the combined riches discovered at Boxgrove, Creswell, Swanscombe and Gough's Cave.'

Katrine arrived at the press conference late. For a few seconds the room was a blur of lights, unsmiling faces, tight rows of chairs upholstered in red to match the hotel's furnishings. Even the carpet was obscured by the equipment bags, studio lights, cables and camera equipment littering the floor. There was barely enough room for national press; local was squeezed at the rear, the closeness of the air and its temperature already reaching stifling in the conference room.

Damp all over and stressed, angry at herself, she sat at the back. *Journalist misses press conference for the biggest local news story of her lifetime.*

Unable to park anywhere near the hotel, she'd hobbled in heels through town to get to where the press had assembled to brief the world. She'd seen Euronews and CNN Europe's logos on the vans parked outside the hotel. Her press pack was on the floor. She picked it up and started her recorder. The speaker continued.

'We know that the cavern was used thirteen thousand years ago, and for around one thousand years. The semipermanence of the occupation being *the* most crucial element.

'As with other European sites, our cave was used by Late Upper Palaeolithic people. Creswellian hunter-gatherers. They'd been returning to various parts of Britain from France, Belgium and the Netherlands, during warmer spells in Europe's climate. A relatively brief thawing before another cold period, the Younger Dryas, that ensued in 12,800 BC, when most of Britain would have been covered by an ice-sheet, the South West a bitterly cold tundra.

'To get here these people would have crossed a great land bridge known as Doggerland, now submerged beneath the North Sea.'

For a journalist, Katrine was terrible with names, dates and figures, though she never forgot a face. The speaker was a leading palaeontologist from the Natural History Museum in London. She'd seen him interviewed on national news during the first two years of the excavation in Brickburgh. Her local monthly, *Devon Life and Style*, would dedicate a pull-out supplement to the revelations he offered today: the most significant press conference yet from the dig's management.

'But this is the only British site that signifies a formal occupation, including burials across centuries.' The speaker paused as if to allow the weight of that fact to sink upon his audience.

A few people were taking notes. Glazed expressions or contrived looks of anticipation accounted for the greater number of faces in her line of sight.

The speaker looked past the journalists from the London networks and towards the back as if to appeal for some local enthusiasm. None was forthcoming. A camera flashed.

He had his work cut out. Considering the current state of the world and its weekly upheavals, Kat questioned for how long this story would run beyond specialist pages and presses.

'We also know what the Brickburgh community hunted and ate.'

Kat suppressed a yawn. Her eyes watered, blurred, then cleared.

On-screen: a picture of a grassland, bordered by marshes

and small trees. A wide, flat landscape inhabited by wild horses, red deer, antelopes, some kind of giant ox, what looked like grouse, a solitary badger. A pack of wolves watched the game expectantly from one side of the illustration. Opposite the wolf pack, standing beside a marsh, a group of bearded men were poised, their muscular bodies part-covered in animal skins. Rough leathery faces crowned by tangled hair watched the centrepiece of the picture: a woolly mammoth. Spears were readied.

Were mammoths down here? Kat wondered and felt her interest increase, though not by much. It dropped a notch again when the professor presented the next photograph, which featured a tray filled with flint tools, carved spear blades and points. Notched spikes bore the caption: 'Shinbones of arctic hares'.

'We've removed five hundred tons of debris so far, and over two thousand items of worked bone and flint. The flint came from Wiltshire . . .'

Katrine's feet ached and throbbed. She wished she'd worn jeans and trainers. Several women had done so, including the loathsome Vicky from *Devon Tribune*, one row in front. Much like her own publication, the *Tribune* was 95 per cent advertorial masquerading as news. But other than Kat, only the female journalists from the big networks were attired in suits and heels and lavishly made up. Those higher-profile journalists would interview the visiting experts for the networks, one-on-one: women who exuded a cultivated indifference to everyone sitting behind them. Their heads even appeared to be enhanced by a celestial halo created by camera lights. A set-up that produced the near-unbearable contained heat.

Katrine removed her suit jacket but didn't feel any cooler and wanted to strip down to her bra. Her tights were laddered up the back of one calf. As she'd run from the car, a tiny burr of leather in the heel of one of her new shoes had rubbed a foot raw and fired white striations up her hose to the left knee. She wanted to pinch herself, hard.

'From analysing nitrogen isotopes in the wealth of the recovered human remains, we know that the people using this cave maintained a diet that was very high in animal protein. They were towards the top of the meat-eating food chain. Only wolves should have been competing with them for game. The cave lions had been gone for fifteen thousand years.

'These people mostly ate giant oxen, deer, elk, horse meat and the occasional cave bear. We also speculate that domesticated wolves assisted their hunting. But . . . well, there was another reason why we called this conference before luncheon.'

Luncheon? Just bloody call it lunchtime. Katrine suppressed a flicker of class rage and refocused her attention on the next slide that appeared on-screen: a photograph of a trench filled with hundreds if not thousands of bones, in all shapes and sizes.

The charnel house was lit by powerful lights mounted on metal stands at the head and foot of the long gutter. From the pit, the macabre grimaces of incomplete human skulls drew the eye. Jawless, they peered over the surrounding bones at what may have been the first living human faces to gape about the cave in twelve millennia.

'A bank of sediment on the south side of the cave that survived the cliff-fall contained over five thousand individual animal and human bones, interred together. So we can be certain that this cave was associated with sustained butchery, operating at recurring intervals across a thousand years.

'From the wear on the bone awls and flint scrapers recovered from this level of the site, we know what created the myriad cuts and scratches on the examined bones. And what took place here was a great deal of skinning, filleting and dismemberment, as well as the stripping of tougher tendons from carcasses, perhaps to manufacture rope or even thread . . . on *all* of the remains.'

Katrine's spine tensed. *What's he saying? Did they . . .*

A camera flashed at the front. The rustling in the room ceased.

The speaker raised his voice as if his throat were dry.

'In this phase of the excavation, the process mimicked the purpose of a police forensic team at a crime scene. Or that of the United Nations inspecting the evidence of war crimes. You see, the teeth marks on most of the examined bones are unmistakably human.

'For a settlement with a carnivorous diet, we cannot fathom why cannibalism occurred on this scale when other food sources appeared to be plentiful. Or perhaps there was a scarcity of food at the climax of the Last Glacial Interstadial to account for this behaviour. But, between glaciations, the inhabitants of the Brickburgh caves were engaged in a systematic, industrialised practice of nutritional cannibalism.'

Murmurs gathered momentum the length and breadth of the room: indistinguishable mutters as if the journalists were talking into their lapels, afraid of being heard. Only the blonde heads of the A-listers up front appeared more alert at this whiff of blood in the air.

The whispering continued until the speaker finished drinking from a glass of water and cleared his throat. 'To make absolutely certain that we were looking at interpersonal trauma within this community, an extensive forensic investigation was carried out by our colleagues at several British universities. This established a more precise idea of how these people died. From an eventual assemblage of single body parts, and from the angle of the cuts in neck vertebrae, we were able to ascertain that nearly all of the victims were decapitated while lying face-down.

'The removal of the heads probably occurred after death. Other bones matched to the same skulls, particularly the ribs, revealed scars resulting from violent blows, caused by spear points or blunt trauma from hand-axes' – the speaker paused '– occurring prior to the remains being butchered and processed for food.'

Kat guessed it was one thing to know this and another to articulate it in public.

'But whether we examined the remains of human or

horse, elk or ox, the same tools were used in these distasteful preparations. For example, we know that a bone tool resembling a spatula was inserted into the mouth to break the jaws free of the skull, in order to make the softer tissues in the mandibles accessible for consumption. And we can be fairly certain that the facial features, the eyes, lips, ears, noses and even the tongues were defleshed. Cut and scraped away carefully, along with the muscles surrounding the skull on the brow and at the sides and rear of the head.

'This technique is consistent with the processing of animals for food at this time across Europe. From a close scrutiny of the cuts impressed into the skull bones we can even establish the actual angle at which the individual's heads were held by one hand, while a second hand operated a sharp tool to remove the flesh and soft organs from the exterior.

'Rather gruesome, I'm afraid. It may even be upsetting for your readers and viewers. But we must remember, despite our sensibilities in the civilised world, that our species has resorted to cannibalism throughout its history. Even in recent history in some parts of the world.

'But the evidence from the Brickburgh caves chiefly indicates that there was no difference between the preparation and consumption of animal and human carcasses. Here butchery found an equivalency between man and beast that we've not witnessed since the twentieth century in Russia and North Korea.

'We must remember that the brain, bone marrow and the soft body tissues all contained an important nutritional value in cold uncultivated environments. These food resources were extracted from the broken bones by gnawing and chewing actions that we've matched to human teeth. So these human remains were not scavenged by other animals.

'So far, we have assembled the mostly complete remains of two hundred and seventy-six people who died and were processed in this way. The eldest appears to be a forty-three-year-old male who was suffering from what must have been very painful gums, infected by a tooth abscess. But neither women or children were spared. The youngest victim was three and appeared to be perfectly healthy at the time of death.'

A woman towards the middle of the room stood up, apologised to those at her side and left the room through a side door. Even Katrine wanted to shout, *Bastards!*

'This trench became, in effect, a rubbish tip, or landfill, for the discards or unused materials from the community's food supply. Interestingly, we also uncovered evidence of a twelve-metre-long hearth, close to the entrance of the cave, but the human remains do not appear to have been cooked.'

Attention was rapt: Kat would have heard a metatarsal drop inside the room.

'The crafting of many of the human skulls at the Brickburgh site, as a domestic and cultural centre, is also extraordinary. We've observed an identical usage of the human skull in Gough's Cave in Somerset, but not on this scale. As I've mentioned, some of these victims were carefully scalped. Score marks on the skull bone are consistent with this procedure. And in twenty instances, a sharp hammerstone was used to chip away the top of the skull.

'The cranial vault of some victims was of particular importance to this community. The upper part of human heads was often scraped and cleaned before being worked into what has been called a Magdalenian "skull-cup". We know in more recent cultures that such containers were used to carry liquids and as drinking bowls for ritualistic purposes.'

Upon the screen what looked like an ancient but intact pottery bowl appeared. Mottled on the outside like a dark hen's egg, with visible impressions of tributaries across the inner surface, where blood vessels had once supplied a living, thinking, feeling brain.

Kat wouldn't have guessed it was the top of a human head if she hadn't been told. And now she'd seen it, and learned of how a human form was reduced to a cup and a pile of chewed bones, she wished she hadn't. For her feature, the details of the butchery and cannibalism would have to be toned down and reduced to bare hints. She knew her editor, Sheila, wouldn't print most of what had been shared with the press today. Their readership was predominantly elderly, affluent and conservative.

Considering the heat and lack of oxygen, Katrine didn't judge the younger woman, sitting three rows down, who at first seemed to be coughing with her head bowed. But when the barking girl was identified by two self-conscious hotel stewards, standing at the side of the room, they soon plucked her out of the seating and led her from the conference. The woman had been sick, probably into a coffee beaker. One of the stewards held a paper cup at an arm's length. Katrine held her breath.

'But moving on from the unpleasant evidence of how this early culture sustained itself in a harsh environment, I'd like to share some of the rich evidence suggesting that a sophisticated culture coexisted. One fully immersed in its own religious rites and practices. A community that also skilfully produced some very affecting art, artefacts and funerary rites that demonstrate a great reverence for *some of* their dead.'

The speaker couldn't get the skull-cup off the screen fast enough. A few journalists were already whispering into phones as if they'd received a scoop, and Kat guessed the evidence of cannibalism would be exactly that for the tabloids. She could even supply their headline: *Cannibal Holocaust: The Prequel.*

Two arms were raised near the front, which encouraged the rising of a dozen more. Two hands clicked fingers.

'We'll have a Q&A at the end of the presentation,' the speaker said with a smile. 'I'd first like to share evidence of these exquisite burials. Twelve in total, recovered in the section of the site excavated so far.'

The new slide featured an intact human skeleton lying in a dusty recess on the floor of the cave. The bones had been carefully exhumed and brushed clean by the archaeologists.

'Deeper inside the cave and interred within what we've been calling the "false floor", we've uncovered the remains of twelve humans, all female and all aged between thirty-seven and forty-eight.

'Their remains are in an excellent state of preservation. We can see that each individual was carefully placed in a nest and surrounded with a range of remarkable grave goods. Some of this material's manufacture dates from at least twenty thousand years earlier. So artefacts were being reused. The occupants of the graves have become known, on-site, as The Red Queens of Brickburgh.'

As soon as the speaker uttered the regal title every journalist in the room bowed to make a note.

'We've arrived at this term because each corpse must have been painted with iron oxide, a red pigment extracted from local stone. It would have been processed into a dye by these people. Ample vestiges of this haematite have been recovered from each nest. These interments were ritualised.

'We've also recovered a variety of animal skulls from each grave. Objects that must have offered a special significance to these individuals, perhaps even a spiritual status.

'The first queen uncovered still held the preserved skull of a hyena, *Crocuta crocuta*, and a relic at least twenty thousand years older than she was. An animal that was once the size of a modern African lion. This might have been rediscovered within the cave, or even brought here by the group as they transported their culture into the area.

'The other queens were also buried with skulls, though of wolves in nine cases, an animal indigenous at the time. Interestingly, one of the queens was interred with the much older skull of a giant cave lion, *Panthera spelaea*, once endemic to this area. Another held the skull of the scimitar cat, *Homotherini*. That species went extinct around the time the cave was abandoned at the onset of the Younger Dryas.

'This burial practice and culture are similar to what has been found at various German sites. And as with those continental burials, at Brickburgh we also uncovered a large number of manmade grave goods. Carven images and simple but beautiful musical instruments.

'And make no mistake, this is figurative art. Each of the flutes was carved from swan wing bones, the longest being forty centimetres in length, the smallest six centimetres. Each instrument has been inscribed with precise and quite sensual images of water birds.'

A fresh slide on-screen revealed a pair of hands, clad in rubber gloves, gently holding a smooth length of what looked like a pipe of hollowed wood.

'There was once music in this cave. Perhaps music was incorporated into ceremonies, ritual practices. Maybe it was simply a source of pleasure and bonding in hard times. We can only speculate.

'Of the carven artefacts, we know that most were crafted and worked out of mammoth bone. And most of the carven images appear to be representative of the human female, though the heads of these figures are animal. Hyenas, giant cats, dogs or wolves, we think. But there has been some decay and most of the recovered pieces appear incomplete. They may once have been attached to wooden staves, since decomposed.'

The carvings on-screen were upright, straight-backed. All missed hands and feet, their abdomens tapered to spikes, but the tiny, blockish spurs of animal ears were unmistakable. Well-proportioned, even elegant figures, but transmitting a distinctly bestial character to Kat. She found the shape and posture of the artefacts subtly aggressive, the worn but barking faces grotesque, even mad with a horrible delight.

'The last item of great interest that I will share today is this exquisite larger figurine of a woman's body. This item, however, was constructed out of baked clay and mirrors similar Venus figurines that have been recovered from all over Europe from earlier Cro-Magnon sites. Again, we date this figure's manufacture at around 30,000 BC, some fifteen thousand years before a revival of its significance by this community.'

Despite the long, sensual curves, Katrine would not have described the black object as 'exquisite'. A torso missing its head and feet occupied the screen. Suspended against a white background its dark breasts were outsized, pendulous, perhaps suggesting a heaviness with milk. The hips and buttocks were given prominence from the rear and rendered lifelike.

'A tribute, perhaps, to fertility and the continuance of human life.'

Or its flux and the prolonging of brutality.

Kat disliked the turn in her thoughts, inevitable whenever she was exposed to the gruesome details of human history.

Inside the hot room her skin cooled. She closed her eyes and her mind immediately became busy with what had just leered from the screen.

The speaker called for questions.

Can I go now?

When that red earth of Brickburgh yawned and revealed its horrors to the archaeologists, Kat was living north of Divilmouth, on the periphery of the affected area. Tucked away in Moorbridge, in her two-bedroom cottage on Kiln Lane, she'd observed the transformative power that spread from the lightless mausoleum to the nearest harbours.

The discovery of the first cave made headlines, locally and nationally, for a while, and perpetually in academic and scientific journals that fewer eyes read. But two years after a paraglider spotted a crack in a cliff-face in South Devon, the initial excitement was eclipsed into insignificance by a greater fascination about *what* had been found inside the cave.

The piles of ghastly, rusticated artefacts extracted from within that cold, pitch-black tomb possessed a unique reach and enduring resonance internationally. Such discoveries generated stories and theories and revisions of what was known about early man. And these speculations, both academic and Fortean, did not quickly fade nor slow. The caves became the biggest deal in living memory for the harbour towns of Brickburgh and Divilmouth.

In Brickburgh, an ailing, deprived fishing port that had lost out to Brixham's rise further north, she'd watched the reawakening of a town all but abandoned after the last quarry had closed in the Fifties.

Further south in the affluent enclave of gleaming yachts and white-walled dream houses that comprised Divilmouth, the air of the caves settled over the town like an enchanted whisper of even more gold than it already possessed.

After the first exhibition that toured the British Isles and Europe, in Divilmouth and Brickburgh it appeared as if every hotel, inn, guesthouse, B&B, ice-cream parlour, gift shop and fish and chip restaurant swelled with a horde of new faces, while each ferry, car park and narrow rural road rumbled anew with vehicles from elsewhere.

As if the caves had called out with some silent, summoning dog whistle, tourists from all over the world appeared again to startle the amiable, taciturn and undemonstrative outer reaches of South Devon. *We're on the map. Change is coming.* That seemed to be the message, the belief, the impetus. And for a time down there, anything had seemed possible. Even out in Brickburgh's purposeless, ailing satellite, Redhill – that tired grey village, hanging on amidst the last working farms – the renewal that none had ever thought possible began.

Kat saw the holiday accommodation near the harbours refurbished, the empty shop units find new tenants, the widening of roads, the council's dispensing of development grants, the resurrection of ancient and dimly remembered festivals and the arrival of a celebrity chef to open a fish restaurant. Even the odd cruise ship was occasionally seen on the horizon, slowly passing what had come to be known as 'The Cannibal Coast'.

But the most noticeable changes all occurred some distance from the actual caves. Across the twelve square miles of hilly land surrounding the caves and where the sea's mists smothered the coastal combes, things remained resolutely agricultural, as they had done long before the old quarries first opened and long after they'd closed.

There were a few hiker trails out Redhill way and they proved too difficult for guided tours to take hold. The farmers, as if forming some ancient guardianship of the land, had tended to renew and heighten their border fences and pretty much carry on as they had done for some time. A ring of wagons around the caves.

But what Kat recalled most about this time of discovery and potential was the night that followed the press conference in Plymouth.

To her mind it seemed – and this was a mind that went to great lengths to protect itself from the madding crowds it had once known in London – her own past had been strangely exposed by the excavation and her imagination infected by what had been exhumed from those caves.

A cold stone bed lined with bones.

A collapsed human skeleton scattered about the crumbling skull of a hyena. Thin arms hugging the mottled and fearsome head.

Red queen.

Crocuta crocuta.

Not fully asleep, nor properly awake, but between the two states, Kat's thoughts had drifted through an edit of the day's events. They always did. Like having a television show on fast forward, she'd paused her recall to trigger imaginary interactions: how things could have gone, should have gone, *would have gone if* . . . And through that dark, ruddy ether of her mind's deep space, these *other things*, the images, had reappeared and defined themselves.

Snout raised and seemingly wet, the head alert, a jackal-headed figure of bone had rotated behind her eyes. The erect, footless image had even summoned the distant cacophony of a canine skirmish from the caverns of her mind.

This had segued into another scene of an indistinct herd of immense beasts, in which a powerful animal had been pulled by the throat to its lumpy knees and then onto its dusty side with a thump that had shaken the frozen earth beneath where . . . *she lay?*

The felled beast was then hastily opened by a scrum of busy black heads.

Snarling becoming laughter . . .

A dirty hand, holding a black stone, carving flesh from a human face as if it were preparing fish.

That final imagining had snapped her fully awake. She'd assumed that she'd been asleep and only dreaming, though the nightmare had seemed too vivid for that. There had been a sinking into a smothering darkness just before her nightmare: the sensation of physically dropping away from the room, her bed. Then had come the sensation of a missed step and a sinking into an inner abyss where that bestial head, carved into stone, had grinned and turned. But the *defleshing . . .*

She'd sat up. *Defleshing, nutritional cannibalism*: such terms had not been part of her awareness when she'd stepped inside that day's press conference. Her vocabulary had acquired a new vernacular of brutality and bloodshed.

A few moments staring at the newly decorated bedroom ceiling, to clear her mind of such a noisome infestation, had been required.

No doubt, a discolouration of her imagination had occurred that day in Plymouth: a taint, reanimating memories of what she'd seen in the PowerPoint presentation, had transformed into these dreamy scenes of her own making. But her curiosity had stopped short of asking how the visions had distinguished themselves by becoming clearer than dreams should be.

On awaking from the first bad dream, she'd noted the bedroom lights were still on. She and Steve had both been too tired to turn them off after a more intense sexual collision than they usually enjoyed.

Steve's slender back had been turned to her. In post-coital slumber his breathing had been muffled yet deep.

Her boyfriend had been eager to get her into bed after he'd found her dressed in a suit and heels that afternoon.

She'd smiled at that. An outfit she'd rarely worn since leaving London years before: a part of her wardrobe she rarely excavated. But the suit and its accessories had stimulated his libido as if she'd become another woman, a new lover.

And maybe it had been her clothes that had also awoken her reminiscences of the brightly lit-up parts of her former but abandoned life in the capital? A chapter she'd only dared skim-read since moving to South Devon, before swiftly closing that particular book.

She'd quit a career at its peak. But that wasn't even half the story and regret was deceptive because what caused regret was never the whole story. But at the press conference, her old uniform had swiftly become a high-maintenance encumbrance with bad memories stitched into the seams. There'd been a reopening of personal tombs that she'd locked away inside the false floor of her own mind: the falls and disgraces. Thoughts of her ex, Graham, were the most insidious recollections of all. As a result, she'd remained irritable for the duration of her journey home, even grinding her teeth as she always did when she thought of him.

What Kat usually remembered from her past in London was a lingering sinus condition with headaches akin to bullet wounds, the ethanol withdrawals, forgetting to eat, not sleeping then sleeping for twenty hours, her mind and mouth firing as fast as a computer processor, then crashing and stuttering lethargically like a shitty broadband connection for far longer. And being so weary. So tired, bone deep, soul deep.

But at least for a while, the sex with Steve had expelled the foul images of the cave and of Graham that she'd brought home with her. Though to be of any use the following day, Kat had known how badly she'd needed to sleep. She'd closed her eyes and tried to get back to sleep and passed out a second time, in a manner akin to being sucked into the darkness beneath her bed. And her dreams had quickly filled with other curious things.

A stone axe, shaped like a pendulum, near-purple in the thin light of memory. Knapped to produce sharp edges.

The toothy spike of a bone awl.

Thin notes from a flute fashioned from bone. A reedy lightness, beautiful and ethereal and filling a smoke-filled darkness.

Music that summoned skeletal human faces, the tops of their heads chipped away like egg shells . . .

The perforated bone of a wolf's head mounted upon human form . . .

Her running, then falling, as if one leg was shorter than the other, into a cave, into the void. Dropping into the false floor . . .

A bulbous Venus. Smooth clay turning as if on a carousel, round and round. Curves and raised contours catching red firelight . . .

A voice in the darkness, the gibbering of a man . . . or was it a dog?

A wet thud . . . the sucking of soft tissue . . .

Kat had sat bolt upright at that point, breathing quickly, bilious with nausea, the echo of the heavy thud resounding. From where did the sound originate? She'd been sure it had arisen from inside the cottage. Not a noise she'd have created herself or could have attributed to anything but murder.

She'd glanced at Steve and wondered whether to wake him. She'd not wanted to be alone after the second nightmare.

But once brighter, waking thoughts had banished the resonance of the wet thump, she'd climbed out of bed. After dousing the bedroom lights, she'd gone down the narrow stairs to the ground floor.

The cottage had once been the home of a quarryman and his large family, a hundred years gone. *The past was all around.* And wouldn't local history now make her more aware of itself? *Bad memories never died. They only blurred, became smooth and heavy and not so spiky and sharp.*

The small building had been her sanctuary for a few years. Two-up, two-down, with a front door that opened onto a lane that ran to the shops in Ivycombe: a home purchased from the sale of a one-bedroom flat in a depressing area of London, at a time in her life when she'd given up any hope of ever living in an actual house again with two storeys and a garden.

Her home was brightened by electricity, not kerosene or coal or wood. Magnolia coated the walls of the warm, centrally heated building. A wide-screen television dominated the cosy living area and she'd turned that on to rebury her upsetting dreams. *Had the other journalists shared her lurid thoughts?*

Kat had soon looked to the curtains and pondered what really surrounded her home: would the landscape henceforth only remind her of what had once roamed these valleys and of what had been done beneath them? Was her *funny turn* going to become permanent?

Butchery.

Processing.

How far away were the caves from her front door? Six or seven miles, she'd estimated, and situated in a place she didn't know well: all that empty space surrounding Brickburgh harbour. She only ever drove through it to get somewhere else.

Why would she go there? No one did. What was there? Farmland. Redhill, a dying village. Fields carpeting the rank spaces beneath the earth, filled with the chewed evidence of industrialised murder: the grimy fragments hidden for thousands of years but exhibited anew in her sleep.

She'd pushed back at an early-hour dread that there were no longer any solutions to the worst places and the worst kinds of human behaviour. She'd never ordinarily entertain such thoughts, but the early morning news had been sufficient indication that such desperate times thrived once more, were always striving to reappear and not only beyond the borders of the first world. An exposure to the bloodiest episodes of human prehistory would make anyone dream the way she had done. *Surely?*

Kat had turned the television off and in the sudden vacuum of silence had briefly warmed with gratitude that she was having her time then: in a home that wasn't a damp cave, inhabited with reddened flesh and dirty teeth within crude faces, where the black air must have reeked of carrion, and skeins of smoke been backlit by flickers of firelight.

Filthy hands, slippery with the fluids of what was stuffed inside bearded mouths.

In her imagination, the elegant modern room around the sofa briefly recast itself as stained and streaked with charcoal. She'd winced at that, wanting to punch her own face to knock it out of her head. She'd just seen it all too, hadn't she, when asleep? *How did those things get inside you and display themselves with such vigour?*

Kat had willed herself to think of something else. Wrapping herself tightly within her gown, she'd curled up on the sofa and flicked through the local paper.

Close to 3 a.m. she'd thought of her need to redraft her feature first thing. It was to be followed by five hours' work in the press office of the arts centre, at the Land Trust offices in Totnes, where she worked part-time. And the longer she'd stayed awake the more she'd also yearned for the sweet-sour taste of cold white wine.

That was a reckless compulsion: momentary. Easier than ever to ignore, to wait out and let go. Kat hadn't attended a meeting or called a sponsor in three years. She'd not felt the need.

She'd padded into the tiny kitchen and sipped from a glass of water. Washed some crockery, checked the door locks, made sure the oven rings were turned off. Only then had she returned to bed.

Sleep had returned as her wariness of it subsided. But sleep had again brought pictures and frantic motions of spiky shadows on red walls of rock. That third time, there had been screams too and children had wept.

She'd awoken a third time and stayed awake until sunrise, stricken with a crazy notion, the kind of idea that appears in the early hours, that when so many old bones are disinterred from the earth, things were never going to be the same again in that place.

Excavations

5

Two years later.

ecordings made by her dead brother were one click away. Lincoln had been gone six years.

In Helene's bedroom, the laptop screen cast the sole illumination. Next door, her daughter had finally succumbed to sleep. Each evening the pressure to make meaningful use of mum-time quickly transformed into anxiety, undermining the very possibility of relaxing. How determined little Valda was to occupy those last two hours of her day. She'd never been a child that could be alone for long.

At last, in the warm, dark silence about her bed, the residual static of irritation generated by the nightly struggle to settle Valda prickled less. Pebbles of tension eroded to sand in her neck, back and shoulders. A second glass of wine unclenched her mind. Only the ghost of a grimace remained as a trace behind her face, a fading mask. No longer committed to domestic and maternal tasks, Helene yawned. Most evenings her eyelids dropped and locked up shop before ten.

Partly from anger at Lincoln for taking his own life, Helene had never played the discs spread out on the duvet. She'd been the only person available to empty her brother's disorderly flat in Worcester, six years before. She'd found the recordings inside a plastic box with 'SonicGeo' written on the lid.

With the exception of smoking skunk and experimenting with legal highs inside his grubby one-bedroom nest above a bookie's in Worcester, Lincoln's sole and final obsession, as far as she knew, had been the recording of ambient subterranean sounds.

Through the concluding year of his life, the search for these curious noises had returned the excitement of childhood to her brother, until he'd jumped from the Severn Bridge. He'd only been thirty.

When the police located his car near the bridge they'd assumed the obvious. His camping gear had been stuffed inside the boot. There had been no note, which was odd, and Lincoln's body was never found. But bodies weren't always recovered when people jumped from that bridge, the police had told her and her mum.

In the garage of her little town house in Walsall, provided by a housing association, Helene had kept her brother's effects: boxes of books, comics, the strange music and weird horror films, his worn camping equipment, the recording devices found in his car and a box of compact discs no doubt crackling with weird sounds. All of it had been shrouded in polythene for six years.

At the time of his death, Helene had been too worried and preoccupied with a difficult pregnancy to go through his things, and her rage at her younger brother for ending his life had sustained itself until the last five minutes of his funeral. Only then, in the front row of pews, had a powerful sense of him come upon her. An inexplicable but comforting sensation, perhaps it even belied the madness of her grief.

She'd given birth for the first time four days after the funeral. There had been no capacity for mourning since and his possessions had remained a symbol of waste: a testament to his downward spiral, maybe even contributing factors to wherever his head had been at the end.

Caring for Valda had been the only thing keeping her and her mother upright ever since.

At the time Lincoln went missing, mishap and misfortune

had maintained an insidious habit of taking over her family: a momentum that gathered pace until there'd seemed no bottom to their woes. Only one year after her dad passed from prostate cancer and her mother's diabetes and arthritis flared to disabling levels, Lincoln had gone and done *that*. Inflicted more tragedy upon them. She'd never imagined that her anger at him could have served as so sturdy a mast amidst grief's storm.

While she'd been swollen, suffering abdominal agony with pre-eclampsia and back pain so severe she could barely stand straight most days, Lincoln had jumped from a bridge. Weeks away from becoming an uncle – an idea that had thrilled him – he'd taken his own life. As Valda's uncle he'd have adopted a major role too because Helene would have made her younger brother take one. They'd needed him to be around: her and her baby and their old mum.

Helene had returned to work when Valda was three. That arrangement, even when assisted by her mother, a childminder and fifteen free hours at a nursery, had hardly been easier to manage than being at home alone with a child for the preceding three years. But now Valda was showing a greater tendency towards independent play and developing a better awareness of personal safety, Helene had found herself thinking about Lincoln far more than at any time since he'd died.

The postponement of recognising that he was truly gone had never helped. The idea that he was still around was always hard to suppress: him being out there, *somewhere*, awaiting another fixation or obsession with a new group of people, or a preoccupation with a peculiar hobby. Even without his emails or texts for six years, she'd a hunch that he'd still come back when he was ready, like he'd always done.

Lincoln had yet to return.

His final recording was dated two weeks before he'd vanished and was made around the last time she'd heard from him. He'd sent an email too, which she'd since copied into a Word document:

Going back to Devon, Sisco, then I promise to check in with Ma. Have some amazing recordings from South Dartmoor and Brickburgh. Going back for more.
A website, GaiaCries, are going to post my collection. The best bits. I'm getting an album on there! An album! This stuff is so freaky they thought I'd faked it. It's better than anything I've heard on their site, recorded in all those train tunnels, nuclear bunkers and disused mines.
Think I'm only happy inside a tent too, Sisco. I have been in a state of ecstasy and awe in Brickburgh all summer. And no, it's not only down to the weed ;-)
Have uploaded some stuff for you to play to the baby – seals in a cove [here].
Promise I'll call mum.
Lin xxxxxxx

Mooching online, Helene had found GaiaCries, a website for investigators of the earth's ambient soundtracks. A forum for contributors who set up field labs and recorded subterranean noises in a range of uninhabited places: sound files made in disused urban structures, industrial complexes and the few wild places remaining on earth. There were even listings for Chernobyl and Area 51.

Down in the dark, forgotten places, the unobserved mines and tunnels, empty shafts, extinct volcanoes and caves at low tide, it seemed there was a surprising amount of sound produced by the earth's shiftings or piped from the rusting monoliths discarded by man's exploitations. Accidental performances with melody absent, rhythm obscure and unintended, the instruments utterly indifferent to an audience.

To punish herself, Helene recalled her own uninterest when her brother first enthused about his recordings. At their mum's house, in the spring of his final year, he'd jabbered breathlessly to her about his endeavours and produced a collection of wires and tiny black boxes from his greasy rucksack. Underwhelmed and frustrated with his inability to get his act together, she'd barely glanced at his equipment.

Lincoln had always sought her approval for his enthusiasms but she'd never offered even feigned interest. His attempts at making strange electronic music amidst a cloud of cannabis smoke had instinctively evoked a competitive resistance. Her hardwired habit of rejecting the past, her hometown and the very life that she was more or less trapped inside now, had prevented her from *seeing* her brother up close as a young man. Her final act to her sibling had been to hurt him with indifference.

She'd always pushed him away. She'd never encouraged him, nor stopped criticising him. And for that she disliked herself far more than she disliked herself for a myriad other reasons.

The link in Lincoln's final email had led to cloud storage. She'd checked it at the time of the funeral. But there'd been no file of 'seals in a cove'. Her brother had deleted every file, emptying the account the day before he'd jumped from the Severn Bridge.

Despite a terrifying recklessness with MDMA, at least Lincoln had seemed energised and happy in his final year. And that was all she and her mum had clung to. Only he couldn't have been happy. It must have been evidence of a bipolar mania.

There'd not been much else to salvage from his life. Her brother had been rat-shit poor at the end with only £170 in a bank account and an unpaid credit card debt of £10,000.

She'd never known anyone work so many terrible jobs and give up so many terrible jobs as Lincoln had done, often quitting a position in less than an hour. He'd once recounted how, one Christmas, he couldn't pass through the main doors of a warehouse on his first day of temporary work. He'd described the experience in typical fashion: 'a strange force' had filled him with a 'paralysing dread' and he'd known that a 'part of his soul would die on the other side of the metal roller doors'. He'd walked home in the rain, made poached eggs on toast and returned to bed to eat them.

Little brother.

Helene smiled and wiped the first tears from her eyes. The turn in her thoughts shuffled memories uncollected for decades: his freckled face, a cowlick of hair sticking up on his crown, his cockerel's comb, a boy, grinning, wearing a patterned jumper knitted by Nan. A brown and orangey haze to that photograph. Not even a proper memory but a picture in Mum's leatherette photo album.

But never a boy who'd stayed upset for long: that she remembered without recourse to family photographs. When they were kids she'd regularly been mean to him but he'd always come back to her, his tear-sodden eyes doleful with a hope that his older sister would become receptive to his prancing, restless antics once more. And how she'd made him cry was unbearable now. *That little boy.* Why must she remember that?

As if it were a heavy, cold stone, remorse pressed her heart. Her pained love for her brother suddenly transmuted into a yearning for the child in the next room. The need for her own choked her and she vowed to never hurt her daughter's feelings, never discourage her, never allow herself to transfer her frustration, her resentment, or to get too angry.

Helene stopped crying. She pushed at the painful memories until they sank through the floor of her mind. She slipped a disc inside her laptop and braced herself for the sound of his voice. Messily scrawled on the disc was a title: 'Divilmouth: Crevice above Wheel Cove & Crevice in cliffs @ Ore Cove'.

Lincoln's voice never materialised. A mercy, but whatever he'd recorded was faint. She adjusted the volume, slipped on headphones and only then did the sound of the sea, foaming over rocks, rush inside her ears.

Eyes closed, she listened to the water's swishing entrance and its withdrawal from an enclosed space. Nothing else existed. The rhythm was soothing.

Helene changed the disc. She selected: 'Cliff cave. Whaleham Point'. The disc was labelled with a star and exclamation mark, classifying a priority that was lost on her.

This recording contained a rumbling reminiscent of thunder. The piece was six minutes long but at two minutes the soundscape altered and she was reminded of air passing through a pipe. Not music, no notes, but a continuous funnelling of air through a narrow aperture: perhaps a recording from a subterranean crevice where he'd stuck a microphone. It made her feel cold.

When close to ejecting the disc, her head abruptly cocked alert at the sound of a distant voice, or voices.

Yes, what might have been a small crowd emerged, their speech muffled by distance and by the flow of air in the foreground. She increased the volume but no words or individual voices became discernible: the mumble remained a crowd, passing away.

Air rising underground might mimic voices.

Thunder returned to the background. Maybe an earth movement had caused the rumble. Without visuals or an explanation, anything could become something within a stimulated imagination. And yet she received her first intimation of why her brother was so fascinated with 'SonicGeo': how natural sounds extracted from an environment acted upon the mind, creating a mysterious sense of unobserved activity inside an uninhabited place. Lincoln would also have been stoned when he'd played these back.

The rhythmic thump of something solid against a hollow object replaced the thunder: a sound that encouraged her to picture a wooden vessel being struck. Then she imagined that something harder and denser than wood was being hit, like a hollow rock.

The recording ended.

Helene inserted a third disc into her machine: one marked by a star and three exclamation marks after the title: 'Second Cove at Whaleham Point'.

Complete silence.

She checked the clip's duration on the audio player's graphic: two minutes remaining. But she was still hearing nothing at twenty seconds and was about to stop the segment when an exhalation made her start. A tiny cough preceded absolute silence that resumed for another twenty seconds.

An animal?

At forty-six seconds, the sound of trickling water was unmistakable. The water may have been trickling over the rocks of what she presumed was the cove of the disc's title. It was unceasing for fifteen seconds before the running liquid was joined by another cough, this one in the distance.

Only when she heard an infant crying, a noise she was highly attuned to, did Helene sit upright and rewind the recording. She slipped off the headphones to make sure that it wasn't Valda next door. No, the cry had been on the recording.

She replayed that part of the track. There it was again, behind the sound of running water. Though surely that was the cry of a bird or an animal near the crevice, or inside it? *But, God, that had sounded just like a child.* The clip finished.

Helene exchanged the CD for a fourth disc: 'Slagcombe Sands & inside cliff crevice/cave @ Whaleham Point'. This one had also been festooned with stars and exclamation marks.

The recording had been edited and began with an audio commotion: a sequence of sounds expanding her imagination into the image of a pebble rolling around a stone bowl, continuously. That's what the noise made her think of: a dry pebble, small and smooth, circling the curved interior of a bowl. This continued until a word appeared inside her headphones.

Or almost a word: *crom-creel-hhom.* That was how she imagined it being spelled phonetically. The word was followed by the suggestion of a large throat swallowing.

And again, wind travelled through a hollow pipe. No notes, but a noise similar to Valda enclosing a tube with her lips and blowing through it. Only this was a thin continuous hush of air: one that grew until it filled her headphones, right before the soundfile abruptly ended.

Helene checked her watch. Getting on now but she no longer felt tired. Instead, she was intrigued, even unnerved.

She picked up the final compact disc, entitled: 'Redstone Crossroads. Quarry on Farmland'. The labelling was embellished with the subtitle 'Money shot'. This was Lincoln's last recording and he'd made it two weeks before he disappeared. Helene moved her fingertips over the surface of the disc in the place her brother's hand would have rested as he'd written the title.

The soundfile began with water trickling at some distance from the microphone, continuing until it was broken at sixteen seconds by a disturbance that might have issued from an animal. A kind of rumbling and lowing. Moments later, when the noise was repeated, she equated the sound to a man groaning. Though surely the reverberation was too deep for a man, the sound originating from a much larger chest capacity. *Maybe a cow or bull?*

A fresh groan lengthened before being abruptly choked off by a *bark*. So something that was not a man, but maybe a farm animal or wild animal, had been drawn to the water and had issued the noises?

Helene replayed the segment but the noise still suggested that it might possess both human and animal origins. Before she could consider this further, from out of the watery distance the infant's cry reissued. Only this time the wail was smothered by a pig-like grunt in the foreground, near the microphone.

A bellow followed, coughed with force from a muscular throat. And again she thought of a bull.

The juvenile cries drifted nearer the microphone. *An animal imitating a child?*

A rattle deep in a phlegm-filled throat.

A savage feline hiss.

Whatever Lincoln had recorded had been angry.

Again, the hiss. *Might that be a great cat?*

A rumbling growl, emerging from the pit of a large stomach.

A fox? A badger? But even when agitated, Helene couldn't readily imagine those creatures being responsible for these noises. Though how would she know? She was no expert on wildlife.

When the growling ceased, silence ensued, bringing her more relief than she was comfortable acknowledging.

She suspected she might have been caught out by a practical joke played by her dead brother. But as these were the last sounds he'd ever recorded, before leaping to his death from a bridge, his excitable, confused states of mind and drug use found an abrupt, momentary connection in his sister's thoughts: a sudden synthesis occurring between a sense of her brother and the horrid recordings, as if a fatal inevitability had always shadowed his experimental attitude to life.

The clip petered to its conclusion but was far from done with her. From the middle distance the microphone picked up more of the animals, because there must have been more than one contributor and these creatures were really distressed. Gut-deep rumbles ascended into sharp, pained bleats, as if expelled from the muzzles of awful, oversized lambs.

And yet was that not the snarly yipping of a dog or a fox that she was hearing too? Though surely nothing so small could posses such a powerful range of cries.

The cacophony grew, the intensification matched by her certainty that the cries possessed no possible origin inside human throats. This section of the recording effortlessly created an accompanying mental imagery: of brawny, monstrous shapes skittering and fighting within darkness, perhaps after detecting a man's scent on the intrusive equipment buried inside their cave.

Helene reached for the volume control as a series of swinish bleats descended to a resumption of a growling behind closed jaws. Large jaws. And what kind of mouth was she now imagining, with black lips quivering as it emitted that snarl? An idea of yellow-brown teeth and discoloured gums, so horribly moist, snapped at her nerves.

Helene thought of pit-bull dogs. Idiotic teenage boys on the estate were dragged about the local park behind them. How quickly she'd sweep Valda off her feet at the first sighting of the dogs, while their juvenile escorts would cry, 'Y'all right, she loves kids.' So maybe her brother had recorded, at a remote location in Devon, a wild or rabid dog?

Didn't people holiday, keep second homes and caravans and make ice cream down there? Had these noises occurred in Equatorial Africa, she'd have found the recordings far easier to accept than their actual origins in Devon. Lincoln's recordings were absurdly incongruous with what she knew of the place, which also wasn't much, admittedly.

Without warning, a high-pitched *laugh* erupted from the glottal medley.

Helene flinched.

It resembled gibberish uttered by a madman, or a shriek from an exotic animal that only sounded as if words existed within the cry. How would she ever know? But as the noises became increasingly apelike, the cries appeared to her ears too cruelly amused for a creature lacking human intelligence.

Mercifully, the 'laugh' dwindled, until only a trickling of water remained inside her headphones. When the clip fizzed to white noise she was sure she'd never play the recording again, nor any of the other discs from Lincoln's box.

Helene left her room, walked across the landing and sat in the doorway of Valda's room to watch her daughter sleep.

6

Two weeks later.

*D*id you walk here, little brother? And here? There too?
Did your scruffy hiking boots stand upon this spot? Did
you crouch and take in this view? Did the sea breeze
ruffle your red hair?

Google Maps, a walkers' guidebook and the scribbles on
the CDs had enabled Helene to identify the inlets where her
brother recorded the weird soundfiles. At first light, she found
the first two sites.

Each unremarkable cove had been near Divilmouth
harbour, where she was staying, and each rugged aperture
between the sea and forested cliff-sides had contained a
plethora of crevices and fissures. Inside a couple of those her
brother's microphones must have picked up the sighs and
grumbles and the tinkling of hidden streams inside the earth.

A good seven-mile hike had then stretched ahead of her to
Whaleham Point, the site of his penultimate recording. Inland
from there, near a farm at Redstone Cross, he'd captured the
nightmarish animal cries recorded in his final SonicGeo clip.
Those were the last two sites she planned to visit: curious
monuments to the summer before his smile vanished from
this life.

Save the bridge near Bristol, which she never wanted to
see, only those places significant to him at the end interested
her. There was no time for Dartmoor, a place he'd explored

for ten months before Brickburgh. But right here, during his final few weeks alive, her little brother had seemed happy and enthused while living out of his tent and scrabbling round these cliffs.

And yet, his inner life at that time remained as alien to her as the darkness inside the caves he'd explored alone: as much of a mystery as the strange subterranean songs that had called him here.

She'd come to better understand him at the end and to decipher what he'd been doing with such enthusiasm. But mostly, she'd come to bid him farewell, as she had failed to do six years before.

Four days at the coast was all she could give him, with two consumed travelling between Devon and Walsall. As every hour had to count she'd lit out early. Knowing that it was probably going to be an emotional day, she'd also braced herself mentally and counted the empty coast path ahead of her as a blessing. She didn't want anyone to see her talking to herself or crying. It was hard to cry at home because of Valda and she'd not had a single day apart from her daughter in six years.

Walking from Divilmouth, she'd been struck by how the land changed, the difficulty of moving through it increasing rapidly. Twelve or so miles might have separated the two harbours, though, had someone shown her two sets of photographs of the coastline, one set near Divilmouth and the second set near Brickburgh, and claimed that the two sets had been taken in different countries, she'd have believed them.

The land corralling Divilmouth's harbour and its ranks of millionaires' yachts was made soft and green by great capes of fir trees. The place reminded her of Switzerland, but also the tropics: pines in woods interchanging with lush palms in private gardens. A town built into cliffs and hills festooned with enormous, beautiful houses, arranged in curving rows above the mouth of a broad, glittering estuary: the sands the colour of unbleached sugar, the residents' yachts moored below their mansions. Boats upright and gleaming like a regiment of royal cavalry, their lances vertical and white. It's why she'd chosen to stay there.

Initially enchanted as she'd surveyed the harbour, when she'd had time to dwell on the matching lavish lifestyles of the residents she'd become deferential, before eventually feeling excluded. She'd also wondered, when these yachts had sailed along the coast in the past, if any of them had spotted Lincoln's little tent in one of the valleys or combes, the thin nylon walls shuddering from an exposure to the winds that now buffeted her.

Once clear of Divilmouth, Lincoln's final expedition had taken him, as it now took her, up and down a hilly collar of farmland above a serrated shoreline: a place almost bereft of human habitation for miles beyond a handful of farms and one Land Trust property. Above the sea the continuous range of mountainous mounds might have been the barrows of forgotten gods.

The surface had been wind-flayed into long, coarse wheat-like grass and brittle red heather, roamed by black sheep and small herds of jet ponies. Thorny hedges and black trees divided the turf into a patchwork eiderdown. Valleys emptied streams onto gunmetal sands. Crude faces, roughly hewn from dark volcanic rock, glowered over the empty gouges of coves that required ropes to reach.

When she was long clear of the yachts and big white mansions of Divilmouth, even the water below her boots on the coast path had looked unsafe for swimming. When cloud from the moors drifted west, the colour of the sea transformed from the turquoise of Aztec jewellery to slate.

She'd passed two ancient kilns, each covered in ivy, a cement gun emplacement from the Second World War and an abandoned cider mill. All were in ruins. Old, ravaged and scarred, but a land no longer interfered with.

Halfway between the harbours as she neared Whaleham Point, the sense of solitude before such a vast sky and sea had been intense enough to trigger flurries of panic.

How had her brother withstood it? Spending week after week here alone? Or had he shared the remote landscape with a companion? But who? Not Vicky, the young woman he'd been seeing in a long and fractious relationship. A sullen, possessive girl with a round face who'd attended his funeral and been overly conscious of what she'd looked like. Which impelled Helene to ponder how much kindness her brother had been shown by the girls in his life, including her.

She'd rushed into adulthood and away from home, powered by self-importance and a slow-burning humiliation about her origins. Nothing had worked out: her face had never been a fit in the places she'd tried to fit herself into, opportunities had been scarce, wages low, lovers immature or incompatible. Worn out, she'd eventually dragged herself home and briefly hooked up with an old boyfriend who'd always been kind. Mitch. And become pregnant within two months. He lived in Australia now and they had little contact beyond bank transfers. He'd shown no interest in Valda.

As she walked up a slope to a distant bench perched near the cliff edge, her thoughts ambled to the question of her brother's untroubled veneer and its incompatibility with the manner in which he'd ended himself. According to their mother, the easygoing persona Lincoln had adopted in his teens, the mask, had lasted until his death. *Chilled*: that's how people had described Lincoln. He'd even been optimistic about his future, despite all the evidence that he'd nothing to be optimistic about. This confounded Helene. Her brother had been a hippy trapped in the wrong chapter of history, *but to take your own life* . . .

At the top of the hill she could barely breathe from the exertion of her ascent but her brother seemed to fill her, briefly yet frantically, as if his very spirit struggled for her attention: a sense of him that was too fleeting for her to relish before it passed as quickly as an arresting dream that she couldn't claw back upon waking.

Tired and becoming tearful, she sat on the wooden bench above Slagcombe Sands. Across the beach, the mossy claw of

Whaleham Point reared; gulls circled the limestone spur like pieces of litter caught in an eddy of wind.

Somewhere over there Lincoln had recorded the curious piping and the crying infant sounds. Inland, up in those stark hills that Helene turned her gaze upon, he'd then recorded the awful screaming of the fighting animals in an old quarry.

The merest echo in her memory of those terrible cries made her wish she were not alone. She suddenly wanted to see a walker; even one in the distance would do.

And where was this famous dig, the cave filled with bones that had been discovered the year after Lincoln passed? This coastline didn't look celebrated. Nothing was marked. But she was not surprised that the cave had been discovered relatively recently. There was nothing to draw a crowd here and it was dangerous for walkers.

The sight of a distant cove, directly beneath her toes, made her dizzy. Uncomfortably exposed to the vastness of the air and sea, she almost felt compelled to be drawn forward and over the edge. Gravity itself seemed different here, altered: combining with the gusts of wind it seemed to move up and down in bands that made her too light on her feet.

Lincoln used to say he suffered vertigo merely from peering up at tall buildings from the ground. Not once had he mentioned bridges to her or their mother. His choice of exit from his life made no sense; the sheer improbability of it had always made her feel distant from his death. Going out like that just wasn't Lincoln. *But what do we really know of anyone?*

Helene left the bench, her legs stiff. Even in such an open, uncluttered space her thoughts confined her. Despite her fitness from years of swimming, she had less energy here. A late winter cold was trapped by the rock and bit more keenly when up so high.

She looked down to Slagcombe Sands, a gritty shoreline fringed with ferns and a wetland filled with reeds that reminded her of sun-bleached wheat. *Where the baby cried.* 'Slagcombe Sands. Inside cliffs @ Whaleham Point'. So maybe he'd installed his microphones in the distant dark hollows and slits that she could see at the foot of gnarled Whaleham Spur. With the wind slapping his head and the sea's tumult crashing inside his ears, he must have implanted a listening device inside one of those caves at low tide. His older sister's respect for her brother increased tenfold.

And at that moment, out of the very land and water, came a piercing light. Not a warm, golden light, nor the soft seaside light of Torbay that she'd driven through to reach the guesthouse in Divilmouth. Nor was it similar to the bitter white light of the north she'd known as a student in Lancashire. The light here was white-silver and pewter, like it marked a passage into another world or time. At its most concentrated and brightest, where spikes of sunlight pierced the cloud canopy, the light struck the battleship grey of the sea like a welding torch, becoming too strong to look into with unprotected eyes.

So there was magic here and beauty. Amidst her discomforts she managed to acknowledge this. This place was not idyllic, but here was a raw and wild beauty, one that inspired *awe*. Lincoln had used that very word. Here, right here, he'd found something special.

As soon as it appeared, the brief, silvery glare out at sea was swallowed by cloud.

The wind and sky changed everything, constantly: the colours, the temperature, the light and her perspective of how far she'd come and how far she had to walk.

Having recovered from the recent ascent, Helene made her way down to the beach.

'Nah, you can't get through here. University's here most of the time, on the dig. They don't want no one nicking souvenirs, so can't let you in, sorry.'

The portly security guard wore a luminous yellow jacket, its vibrancy at odds with his glum, bored face. To escape the cold, he was sitting inside a portable caravan at the entrance of a fenced paddock, above the caves.

'You gotta go round. Up that track, then down the other side of the fence. Over there. You see it on the other side? That's where the coast path starts again. Or you follow the road to Brickburgh that we use. Only other way out.'

Helene hadn't lingered. She'd disliked the way the guard had looked her up and down with a grinning over-familiarity. She'd walked away before the attention had turned suggestive, though not before establishing that the excavation was on the northern side of Whaleham Point, the cave located in the cliffs and not visible from the direction she'd travelled.

Online, she'd seen pictures of archaeologists entering the caves, accessing the site by a ladder and ropes, or up from the sea at low tide. Every local website she'd checked had linked to the dig and she'd been surprised to discover work was continuing into a fifth year. The archaeologists were still making finds in deeper sections of the limestone's secret hollows. There was another exhibition running in Exeter for a month, before the newer artefacts toured the country. If she had time tomorrow she would go: maybe first thing before she drove home.

But when Helene reached the security fence, what startled her to a standstill was the realisation of how close Lincoln had camped to the Brickburgh dig. During his final fortnight alive and while making his penultimate recordings, her brother had planted his devices around the dig site. Throughout an entire summer six years before, her little brother had been recording on the side of Whaleham Point opposite to where archaeologists were now clawing out the earth to find so many long-hidden bones. Had her brother returned the following winter, after the cliff-fall, he might have discovered the cave. And had he done so, his life would surely have followed a different path.

Unlucky and typical of Lincoln but somehow his proximity to such an important historical discovery made his death appear strangely significant to Helene, as if a new epitaph now competed with his leaping from a bridge.

From the dig, Helene moved three miles inland, retracing her brother's footsteps to the place where he'd made the final recording and where the first leg of her hike would conclude.

The GPS on her phone bade her follow soil paths worn the colour of drying blood: tracks scarring hillsides increasingly used by farm animals, judging by the copious black droppings scattered around her boots.

At some point in the nineteenth century there had been quarrying here. According to her guidebook, a stone was mined and a pigment extracted from it for the manufacture of dye and paint. And it must have been inside one of those disused quarries that Lincoln had recorded the bestial shrieks.

The hound leaped, again and again in an effortless propulsion from all four legs, its reddish eyes drawing level with her own.

Elbows out, hands raised to protect her throat, Helene gave pitiful cries that only excited the barking dog, a big rangy creature with a liverish colouring that suggested a Dobermann, though she'd never seen one as big as this. As it menaced and herded her deeper into the hedge, even with all four paws on the ground its head was still higher than her waist.

She twisted to conceal her exposed skin from the foamy teeth and the dog immediately appeared on her other side, to leap before her face once again, untiring, insistent.

Through her panic-blurred vision, she noticed a blue figure run from the driveway she'd just walked past. There had been a white van, its bonnet open, parked before a dilapidated house.

'Kent! Kent!' It took Helene a moment to realise the man wasn't shouting the name of an English county, but calling the name of the hound barking into her eyes.

The dog ignored the call, continuing to spring up and down, up and down, higher and higher to match its uncontainable excitement.

With her shoulder blades flattened against a stone wall, Helene's head completely disappeared inside overhanging wisteria.

Through the screen of verdure, a man came into sharper focus, dressed in a dirty overall, unzipped at the front, with a ragged red jumper hanging loose beneath. A bearded face loomed. There was something odd going on with his eyes, but she didn't see much more because the dog snapped its jaws through the vines, an inch from her nose. She dropped into a crouch, hands over her skull.

Yelping, the dog was pulled away, the owner's grimy boots sloshing through scarlet puddles where the tarmac was worn to mud. A chain was clipped to the dog's collar.

Up on its hind legs, straining, the hound still matched its owner's full height and like a horseman he applied all of his strength to hold the lead while the dog tottered like a kangaroo, both choking and barking.

Helene shrieked when two more dogs of the same breed turned from the driveway and ran at a low, fast trajectory at her legs. They stopped just short of her body and appeared to smile at her distress. Their tails, mercifully, were wagging.

A thin woman followed them, her body also covered in an overall, shiny with oil stains to the knee. At first glance she was a waif with unkempt blonde hair but she grew older as she drew closer, until her skin was riven with deep clefts about her eyes and nose and heavily freckled. *Too much sun.* Even with the elfin bones of her worn face keeping her handsome, she must have been in her fifties.

'Kent!' the man shouted again, then, 'Private road!' at Helene.

Two of the sinewy dogs retreated to the woman. Like a current they swilled around her booted feet. She came to stand beside Helene, her position obscuring the road ahead.

The bearded man moved beside the woman, crowding

into her, his dog restrained on a shortened chain. The positioning of the people, so uncomfortably close to her, was as discomforting as the presence of the enormous dogs.

Now she could see him clearly, the man might have been blind in one eye. One of his eyeballs was bisected by an oyster-coloured scar, the surrounding sclera grey. A pale-blue iris existed as a residue of his former sight and the eye peered down as if in shame. Around and under his beard his skin was red, his facial hair speckled with flakes of dead skin. A wispy ponytail collected his hair at the back, thinned to several bootlaces on top of his scalp, scraped across the narrow red skull. It looked like psoriasis, his rage further inflaming the skin condition.

'Private road! Private road! Private road!' he roared at Helene. Tiny balls of salivary foam speckled her eyes and made her blink. He was worse than his dog. 'How the fuck did you get in?'

The woman softened her expression of fearful concern to pity. When she touched the man's arm he quietened and stepped back.

'What do you want?' she asked softly, in what might have been sympathy but her eyes remained cold. Their accents were also immediately incongruous: even with voices raised they suggested the upper middle class. In stark contrast to their tatty, dirty appearance and the wretched state of the farm buildings that Helene had assumed were deserted, these people were posh.

'Can't you read?' The man pointed the way she'd just walked, a distance of no more than fifty metres.

The thin woman caught his eye. 'The gate must have been left open. She wouldn't have seen the sign.'

'Richey! Fucking retard!' the man spat at the woman at his side. 'How many times has he been told to close that bloody gate?'

Helene hadn't noticed a gate, let alone a sign. So overgrown was the hedgerow she'd not looked at the sides of the lane. Relieved to see a road after passing up through woods to reach the crossroads, she'd merely walked south to where she guessed the quarry would be. She'd assumed she was on a public road.

The bearded man turned down the volume but his anger maintained itself as an ugly sneer. 'Who the bloody hell are you? What are you doing here?'

Helene straightened and stepped out of the overhanging wisteria. 'Walking. I was just walking.' She took the guidebook from the pocket of her coat. 'I didn't know. . . I thought the road might go to the quarry.'

Her interrogators looked at each other, then at her book. The woman snatched it from her hand without asking. She looked at the page Helene had marked with a post-it, then showed the man, who stared at Helene as if he'd just caught her stealing.

'I just wanted to see the old quarry.'

'Well, you can't! This land is private!'

It may have been thin and forced but at least the woman managed to smile. As if weary of his ranting, she touched the man's elbow again.

'There's nothing left,' she said. 'A half-demolished kiln. All overgrown. Some big scars on the earth. They're only visible from the air and they are not open to the public.'

'I'm sorry. I didn't know. I was just walking. I didn't know. I'm sorry. It doesn't look like a private road.'

'Where did you come from?' the woman asked, her stare unwavering.

Helene had to think. In her agitated state she thought she'd been asked where she was from. 'Walsall' slipped out. Then she corrected herself. 'The coast path. I'm staying in Divilmouth. I just wanted to see the quarry before I walked back.'

The couple seemed to relax at that, as if realising they'd only confronted a harmless idiot, but the smirk within the man's scratchy beard boiled Helene's relief into anger.

'Was all of this necessary? Do I look like a bloody thief? Jesus Christ! It's an easy mistake to make. The path from

Whaleham Point leads here. My book says there's a quarry. Redstone Cross.'

It must happen all the time, she wanted to say, and then realised that the violence of their greeting was sufficient indication that it probably did.

The man released his dog.

Helene gasped, flinched.

The hound ran off to find the other two, but its owner clearly enjoyed the sharp and visible ascent of her fear. Trying not to betray her amusement, the woman dipped her face to read Helene's map.

'The track for walkers you used from Whaleham is the original lane. An old green track. But this road is private and always has been. That gate should not have been left open.'

The man jerked his thin ferrety head behind him. 'There's nothing down there. Nothing.'

Two other men wearing raincoats and Wellington boots appeared outside one of the dilapidated wooden buildings, farther down the lane. They came to a standstill, content to watch at a distance.

The woman touched Helene's forearm to reclaim her attention. 'There are two public lanes. One goes north to Brickburgh. They use it for the dig. The other one heads west but there's nothing that way until Divilmouth. See, *here*. If you'd carried on down this road you'd have an awful long way back to Divilmouth in the dark. We've done you a favour.'

'A bloody big favour,' the man said, then seemed to think better about embellishing the admonishment and looked to his dogs instead.

'I see,' Helene said. Shock wilting, she now felt chastened and out of her depth: an unwelcome outsider that worried sheep and left gates open. A trespasser. She wasn't sure she'd ever trespassed before but Lincoln must have done to make his final recording. He'd either walked further down this private road or approached the quarry through the beard of woodland beneath the farm that her path had partly circumscribed. At the meagre crossroads, she could now see how walkers were supposed to walk straight on or turn right and not left as she'd done.

Helene thought of mentioning her brother. But explaining that he'd been here the week before taking his own life was a story she didn't want to share with hostile strangers whose private road she'd traipsed across.

She peered over their shoulders at the few miserable buildings in the distance: dark wood and grey stones at a slouch. A door sagged, green with mildew. From beneath an awning, the black face of a ram peered back at her.

The woman caught her interest. 'You better get going. I'd advise heading back the way you came. Or walk to Brickburgh and catch the bus.'

Helene nodded, tersely thanked the woman for her help and hurried away. Retracing her footsteps, she glanced at the house she'd passed on the way in. A building that seemed to have been transplanted from the Deep South of America, intact with peeling porch, shuttered windows and neglected laundry haggard from days and nights left on the wire. A myriad engine parts were strewn across overgrown lawns. When she'd come up she'd thought the house eerie but strangely enchanting.

Going out she noticed part of a gate and the back of a white sign riveted to a metal rung. Both had been pushed deep inside the overgrowth so that a vehicle could drive through.

Her hands were trembling. Helene tucked them inside her pockets, her urge to return to the coast path desperate. She might even run down the valley. The encounter had come close to spoiling the entire day, the wild land she'd walked since dawn acquiring a sudden, unwelcome association with the awful sounds on Lincoln's recordings.

But her new respect for her brother and his daring deepened: he'd camped out here for weeks, in the wild, where horrible pricks lived, which also made her wonder if he'd crossed paths with the posh nutters and their terrifying dogs. Maybe those very dogs had sniffed out his equipment.

Could a dog have made those sounds?

The Reddening

Before she picked up the green path to Whaleham, Helene looked back. The vicious man and the dogs had gone but the thin woman had remained in the lane to watch her leave.

7

The occupant's lengthy unlatching of the front door was Kat's first indication of trouble. When the barrier eventually opened, a haggard face appeared in the gap. A pair of faded blue eyes studied the street.

In a prickly seizure of mortification, Kat believed she'd knocked on the wrong door in the row of identical former miners' cottages. The quartet of doors, in the lane adjacent to the main thoroughfare of Redhill, were all painted brown and studded into uniformly grey stone facades.

She rechecked the number on the door – 4. Right house, so maybe this was one of Matt Hull's elderly relatives standing on the threshold.

When the door widened and became an invitation to enter, the frail figure spoke softly. 'Hey, Katrine. Good to see you.' Only then did she recognise the paraglider.

She'd interviewed him two years earlier at the first Brickburgh cave exhibition, when the cave's discovery wrote international headlines. Two years prior to the first exhibition, it was Matt Hull who'd directed the light from his phone inside a cliff fissure and revealed a cave filled with prehistoric artefacts. When the broad, sparsely populated spur on the Devonshire coast had drawn the eyes of the world, they'd lingered on this man for a few weeks. He'd become a celebrity overnight.

Two years after their interview, she found herself startled by Matt Hull's appearance. Maybe a serious illness had subsequently harrowed the diminutive figure on the doorstep to this form: redrawn as worn and sticklike, the facial skin craggy. She remembered him being small, slim and muscular, but the sleeves of his shirt now sagged from a pair of wasted arms. Above his belt his shirt billowed over empty space.

What she recalled was a working-class man with a warm smile. A local character, case-hardened by manual work and misfortune, divorced and shaken by the trauma of his family breaking apart, yet gentle. She'd been impressed by his resilience and the quiet wisdom he'd evinced: a father devoted to his boy, who'd accepted the breakup of his marriage in order to stem his own bitterness, to catch it in time.

A painter and decorator, too, who crafted exquisite furniture as a sideline from materials foraged in local woodland. Addicted to another hobby, paragliding, in his thirties, he'd originally described himself to her as a man happier in the sky than upon the earth. That kindly impression had lingered and she'd looked forward to his company today.

A very different impression was forming now. The village he called home had altered just as much, albeit in another way entirely.

Redhill was the nearest settlement to the Brickburgh dig and though she'd not been back to the village since their first interview, its regeneration surprised her.

Composed of six streets, five curling about the main road and petering out into tributaries blunted by farmland, Redhill had since laid claim to a grocery store and a pub. Three houses had been converted into hotels. A nearby field was now a large campsite for motor homes, tents and glamping huts. Messy lines of performance vehicles choked the narrow lanes. Several building sites dotting the village's outskirts revealed the bones of large detached houses undergoing assembly upon the bare red earth. Swimming pools were being dug in expansive gardens. If Matt Hull's discovery of the caves had led to this level of prosperity in a decaying village, the crumpled figure on the doorstep appeared to be the only thing remaining in Redhill moving in the opposite direction.

Feeling as delicate as if she were visiting someone in hospital, Kat lowered herself carefully into an easy chair in the small front room that opened onto the road. To put them both at ease she accepted Matt's offer of a hot drink, though when she inspected the contents of the mug that arrived after some delay, there was no milk in the instant coffee. She also detected the presence of several spoonfuls of sugar. She'd asked for tea, milk, no sugar.

Through a connecting doorway she'd watched her host's slow preparation of the drinks, his rough, shaky hands scattering the unasked-for sugar. Perhaps the soul within the tired shell had been subjected to some whittling from painful preoccupations. As a sufferer from anxiety and depression herself, she allowed herself to presume as much, knowing too well what fatigue and exhaustion looked like and how simple movements became painful exertions.

Dull, tired and too heavy for their sockets were the eyes that soon confronted her, their light reduced, snuffed by what throttled the mind behind. His attention was either projected beyond the room or back inside his skull, giving his worn face the appearance of vacancy. And when he was seated, his knees jumped and hands trembled without cease. That looked like Parkinson's. His fingers only calmed to roll a cigarette.

'You still fly?' Kat asked.

'Stopped all that.' His words accompanied by a wince that nearly shut an eye. 'Been put off . . .'

Katrine maintained a cheery tone. 'Tell me you still make that beautiful furniture. I still think about the table you'd made from mountain ash. If I'd had the space at home I'd have bitten your hand off.'

The smile Matt attempted required too much effort, which made Kat unsure whether to ask after his boy. The man's domestic situation might be the cause of his current plight. During their first interview most of what Matt Hull had confided was about his son. When she couldn't think of anything else to say, her nerves prompted, 'Your son doing okay?'

He calmed a fraction at the mention of his child. 'Colin's doing well, yeah. Cracking little rugby player. He'll play for the county at Colts. Sailing too. Really taken to that.'

'Great. How exciting for both of you.'

The twitching resumed. 'I'm only here because of my boy. He's with his mum in Brickburgh. I don't want to be any further away.'

Kat fidgeted to stir her own mind into less of the blank it was intent on becoming, which prompted him to add, 'I can't talk about *it* any more. Not in the way we did.' His doleful gaze rose from the end of his cigarette. 'The caves. It's something I try not to think about. Without much success, it must be said. Gotta move on, though. At least try. Been over four years. Colin's my priority.'

'Of course.'

But if talking about the dig was off the table, Kat couldn't fathom why he'd accepted her request for a follow-up interview. The magazine had space for a few comments to augment her feature on the second exhibition, a showcase of finds from the excavation's second phase, housed in Exeter Museum. Most of the article would be pictorial. A chat over the phone with the man who discovered the cave would have sufficed. At best, Matt Hull was a footnote in the cave's history, his name rarely mentioned now. But when she'd called him, he'd insisted they meet at his home.

'I will say I wish I'd never found it.'

Tense, her awkwardness increasing with the cooling of the terrible coffee in her hand, Kat struggled to respond. 'I'm surprised to hear you say that, Matt. I really am.' She braced herself for a story of how finding the cave had brought him nothing but misery.

'A few years back, I never thought I'd hear myself say it either.'

'I'm curious about what's changed for you.'

'This off the record?'

'If you like. I was only looking for a follow-up comment. A then-and-now quote because of what the site has clearly done for the area and economy. I have to say, I'm a bit taken aback at just how rapidly the village has changed. It's almost unrecognisable from two years ago.'

Matt nodded, smiling a wry acknowledgement as if she'd hit upon the very thing, though she had no idea what that might be.

'The article will only be about the new finds,' she offered. 'I take it you've heard the hints about what they found in the new caves? So I thought you might want to contribute something. A few words. None of the new developments would have been possible if you'd not been flying over there.'

Matt returned his attention to the end of his cigarette and his smile vanished in the trail of smoke, his face turning an even unhealthier grey.

'Matt, are you all right? You seem . . . very tense.'

His lips moved for a while but he didn't speak out loud.

'Would another time be better?'

He pulled on his cigarette in an attempt at composure, though one betrayed by a shaky hand. 'For the first exhibition I was interviewed in all the local press. TV, radio, the works. I was on the BBC too. Sky, everything. In America too. All over. I was at all the UK openings.'

'I know.'

'But back then, you were the only person I spoke to who was different.'

'I'm not sure what you mean.'

'In all the excitement you saw things a bit differently. About the cave. That was my impression.'

Katrine scoured her memory to identify what signals she might have transmitted to him during the first interview.

'I'm good at reading people and you had a bad feeling about what they found. And I remember you telling me that you came down here for a new start, away from the city. London, was it?'

Kat nodded.

'You'd had it hard there. That's what I felt. I think a person who's had a bad time of it makes a particular kind of impression. Like I did after the breakup with my wife. Makes you tuned-in to others too. Their distress, you know? You said you'd been through something similar to me. Bad relationship. Even if you'd said nothing specific, I'd seen it in your eyes. It made you sensitive . . . to people, situations that could cause you more trouble. Instinct sharpens. Sixth sense, yeah. Same with flying. I just knew when to call it a day if things didn't feel right on the cliffs. I *knew.*

'And no matter how much time passed between when the caves was in use and me finding that hole, you suspected something was off about the place. Because of all the terrible things that happened there, even such a long time ago, you still knew what they found wasn't for gawping at or raking over. The caves still had a kind of . . . I don't know, power. Like they wasn't dead.'

Kat shifted her position and couldn't prevent a noisy swallow.

'Down there by the sea, that place was special, you know, like . . . Stonehenge or something, to people in the past. And when I got over the adrenalin of finding the skull and that little carving, it hit me too, in a weird way. That all took a while to sink in. Maybe even a year. But things changed for me. Lots of things. They never stopped changing.' His rapidly blinking eyes paused to watch her with so keen a scrutiny that Kat coughed to create a distraction.

Matt was unstable. What he said next confirmed her diagnosis.

'*Morbid.* From that time onwards, my thoughts were very morbid. That's when it started. And I'd never thought about things in that way before. I can assure you of that. Strange, I felt strange, *here.* Here was different afterwards. And I got a sense that you felt something similar. You didn't even like thinking about what they'd dug up. I remember that as clear as day. What was done in there, in that dark, horrible place, should have stayed buried. And no good will come of them digging up any more of what's down there.

'You remember, we ended up talking over our problems?

Me mostly, about my boy. But your ex came up. It was like we were always avoiding the real subject of the interview, which was the cave.'

An unusual observation but Matt was right. After the press conference in Plymouth Kat hadn't wanted to cover the first exhibition two years later. She'd have been happy to skip the new revelations, the latest cycle of prehistorical horror.

Initial reports and rumours suggested that what had been uncovered in the Brickburgh cavern during the previous two years was even more barbaric and gruesome than what had been excavated at the first level. But she needed the money. Steve needed work for his portfolio too. And as affable as Sheila, her editor, was, she was not to be defied. The assignment was always going to be Kat's.

Matt pulled on his cigarette. 'It's different for me. I'm local. I live on the same land as the caves. That place is only a few miles from where I sleep. But you ain't that far away either. And there's miles of tunnels down there. They reach out, like.'

'Miles?' Not to Kat's knowledge. And though a larger chamber had been found and several annexes attached to the first cave, she was curious as to what brought Matt to this conclusion.

'We're separated from what happened by thousands of years, Matt.'

'You tell that to my dreams.'

'Dreams?'

'Dreams. What got inside me. My moods too.'

'I don't understand.'

'Or you don't want to. But I wanted to tell you a few things that you can't print. This, today, is not for that, for the news and all that. The magazine. You wouldn't get it in there anyway. Your readers would think I'm mad. Maybe I'm going that way but this is something I wanted to tell you. Only you, because I think you might get it. And today is also for insurance.'

The Brickburgh Curse. She wondered if his imagination had dialled itself into that story. Did he believe that his mind had been influenced by his proximity to the cave? These would have been her questions on a professional basis. His answers might even add an interesting local angle to the better-known stories circulating about the fate of several members of the archaeological team, who'd spent so much time underground in the early period of the excavation. But that would be unsuitable for *Devon Life and Style.* Sheila had little time for the conspiracies. That was the preserve of the internet and the tabloids. *Life and Style*, or *L&S*, filled its glossy pages with coastal vistas, restaurant reviews, local conservation. Not features on curses, unless it was a cosy ghost story, something cheesy about a lady in white in a castle tower. Over the years, her editor had even managed to erase any mention of the cannibalism in any story related to the caves. That didn't fit with editorial direction or the publication's tone. *L&S*'s sole focus had been on the carved artefacts, the bone flutes and the idea of primitive music, the opportunities for upscale tourists. This time around, the feature would be dedicated to the incredible cave paintings. Some details of those had already surfaced. 'Insurance?' she ventured.

Matt nodded. 'There's no one else I can say this to. Not round here.'

'No neighbours, a friend?' She stopped short of suggesting a GP.

He cleared his throat to speak, circling a trembling hand around his head. 'It's hard to explain.'

Kat pondered making an excuse and leaving but there was a conviction in what Matt was trying to impart: *to her*, only to her.

'It's more surface with some folks. An attitude that covers something deeper. Only I don't know what. I can identify the signs though. Maybe you think I'm paranoid or something but I don't think it'd be in my best interests to mention any of this out loud, not round here.'

'You think you're in danger?'

Matt chuckled humourlessly, then whispered, 'I'm a bit past figuring that out.'

'Because of the caves?'

'There's a connection. But I think this vibe has been round here for a while. In other things. Other business. Hints of *it*. An atmosphere is what I'm talking about. Like an influence. And it's got this kind of momentum now. Even if *it* was mostly buried in those cliffs, maybe it was the cause of the change. As well as the other stuff that's been happening. *Here.*'

Kat frowned. He'd lost her.

'It's like something was restless, you know, in them rocks. In the spaces between them. How deep they go and keep on going . . . all that's buried, you know, could still come out a bit. That's what I reckon. Been that way before I found the cave. There's lots of local stuff you don't know about.'

Kat's disappointment and pity came close to a physical manifestation, a sensation akin to indigestion. Matt Hull wouldn't be included in the article at all: that was clear to her. She also worried that if he didn't get it together as a parent, he'd be facing problems with access to the most important person in his life, his son. She found that idea unbearable; it would destroy what was left of the twitching man on the worn leather couch.

'You see, Kat, I've had a privileged perspective. If privilege is the right word. Up there, in the sky, I've seen things. Seen a lot of things. *They* know it. My gear is bright orange. It was always hard to miss me when I was airborne and I've been all over, all round here, twenty miles in every direction. I've noticed stuff.'

Kat's discomfort merged with bewilderment. Curiosity was the only thing keeping her in the room.

'There are things I've seen that I won't mention to you. Things that'd bring some real trouble down on me and on the people who are important to me. Stuff that goes on round here. *Things* that make people desperate to protect their interests, if you follow. Ruthless. And they have been ruthless, at times. I know they have been. But that's got nothing to do with me or my boy. So I always looked the other way. Always kept my head down. Told them that too when they've confronted me about flying round here.'

'I'm not following, Matt.'

'That's . . . just background. You probably know how some folks make their money round here. That's not what this is about, not what I wanted to talk to you about. Forget it. That's something else.'

Now she got it: illegal activity. Unlicensed alcohol: she'd heard the rumours. And the talk about cannabis farms. That's what Matt was alluding to, the drug farms. She'd never believed there was much validity to the rumours but assumed a kernel of truth existed at the root of the tales. Not everyone was content with fruit picking, serving in a café, emptying bedpans in care homes or selling ice cream on the beach for £3 an hour. Hydroponics in a loft was, allegedly, a traditional income stream north of Divilmouth.

'There's a connection, yeah. One thing getting into another. The caves have already seen to that. That's what I am saying. And then bad places and hard people get worse. More lines get crossed, until what's done on the other side of the lines becomes normal. Part and parcel. Perfect environment was in place here. This is what I am telling you. You'd not notice if you were only passing through, like a holidaymaker. But if this was your home, you'd get it. And you get noticed by it too, because it spreads.'

No matter how subtle she'd tried to be, Matt caught her inspecting her watch.

'This is hard for me to say, Kat.'

'Can you tell me something more specific about what is upsetting you so much?'

Before he spoke again, Matt looked at the floor for the best part of a minute before sighing resignedly. 'Not long after I found that cave, I was told that the sky, the actual air, yeah, above Brickburgh, was out of bounds to me. All of it.'

'By who?'

'I'm not getting into that. For your sake, not mine. Trust

me, girl, you don't want to go there. But why did *they* want to ground me not long after I found that cave? I already knew what they were doing round here, on some of the farms. I'd seen parts of their operations, yeah. They let that slide. I'm talking about other things . . . things that have happened that they never wanted anyone to see. The bigger *changes* is what I am talking about. The *change* is common knowledge here.'

Kat's skin chilled. She didn't want to hear any more. A horrible suspicion of becoming implicated in an unpleasant racket or local feud seemed to alter the air pressure around her head. She was a lifestyle journalist, her specialty being fashion, luxury properties, holidays, not organised crime. 'I'd rather not . . . I'm not sure I want to . . . not sure this is in my brief –'

'They don't want me flying in case I see something as bad as I have already. And they aren't the kind of people you can disagree with. A heavy presence. Their spies here, they have this air about them too. Call it a tone. Just looks and things, you know? But people have been getting hurt, Kat. Here. Since I found that cave. Before that too, I reckon. That crack in the cliff wasn't the only opening, yeah, to what's down there.'

Katrine's body tensed. 'The police? I don't know what it is you're trying to tell me, Matt. But maybe you should go to the police.'

'As I said, things have changed. You can't be sure who already knows *stuff.* Who's on which side now. This goes deep. It's spread wide.'

A confused conspiracy, that's all it was, whipped to critical mass by a shut-in's paranoia. But something Matt said earlier continued to work at her mind as a source of discomfort, like a stone in a cerebral shoe. 'Dreams. Matt, you mentioned your dreams?'

Though she was keen to change the subject from the topic of criminal activity, her own unpleasant imaginings had lasted for months following the first press conference. Her nightmares had also been reignited by the first exhibition of the earliest artefacts. They'd never really gone away.

Matt grinned. 'I guessed as much.'

'What?'

'You know what I'm talking about. You had them too.'

'I had a natural reaction to some very upsetting revelations and to the physical evidence found in those caves. I'd say that was a healthy response.'

'Or for someone on the edge emotionally and up here.' Matt tapped his head. 'Even if you only brushed against what had been in that ground for so long.'

'And you're saying that because you found the cave it's been worse for you?'

'Not just found it but reached inside and took a few things out. I admit it, I kept a few things here, for a while.'

'More than enough has been discovered in that cave. No one will worry about you taking a few souvenirs.'

'It's not them I worry about, the museums and universities, or the Land Trust. It's others . . . who've been touched by that place more than most.'

'Who?'

Matt smiled grimly and shook his head. 'Let me put it another way. Don't you think it's strange that two of the archaeologists topped themselves? They'd been inside those cliffs for over a year. No past history to account for suicide. They went downhill inside that place, in the caves. The head of the project even quit. They say he's a mental case, a wreck.'

'There were other contributing factors. Stress, his relationship fell apart –'

'Sure, I've heard the official line too. They always stay on message. But he wasn't the only one who lost the plot down there. None of those working at the start are there any more.'

Katrine shrugged. 'I'm not privy to the staffing arrangements. But I assume that lots of universities are involved and a great many people are queuing up to work there.'

'I wonder how long they'll stick around. Not long, so I've heard. Think about it.'

'People might come and go for all kinds of reasons.'

'True, but I know it's because of their dreams. And let's

call it the atmosphere that they've *breathed in*. Sounds raving mad, doesn't it?'

It did, though within Katrine's mind the heavy curvature of the clay Venus figure rotated again through a dim background of darkness and blood; a mere memory, a fragment from her own unhealthy thoughts.

'It's not just the archaeologists and me. I've got a mate who works in two old people's homes round here. Dementia, end of life care, that sort of thing. And he says he's never seen anything like it. The way they're all behaving in there, yeah. Elderly people who can't look after themselves. He's no liar. But it's in their heads now too. It's why I got rid, took it all back. The pieces I had. The statue, the skull-cup, the little pipe, all of it. Chucked it all away, into the sea. I know what you're thinking but I'm not superstitious, not religious. What I experienced was unnatural. And what I saw from the sky, two weeks after I found that cave, wasn't right either. But it was all part of the same thing.'

'Same thing?'

'As what's in my dreams. It's connected.'

Half of her didn't want to hear any more. The other half, the half she had no control over, asked, 'What did you see from the air?'

8

'Sorry, what did you say?' Kat hadn't caught Steve's request.

He reappeared in the mouth of her tiny kitchen, the jazz on the kitchen stereo muffling behind his bulk. 'Baked, mashed or chips?'

'Oh, anything.'

He rolled his eyes.

'Er, baked.'

Steve returned to the stove. A percussion of rattling utensil drawers followed.

The troubled and wizened figure of Matt Hull had lingered vividly in Kat's thoughts. Steve's arrival hadn't banished the spectre of that frail figure with unkempt hair, standing in the doorway of his small grey home, anxiously peering about the street. In the rear-view mirror she'd watched his front door close, sealing him off from the village once more: where he'd lived all of his life but now resided as if hunted. A grown man made unstable by acute fear.

Often hard to follow, most of what he'd confided of his ideas, dreams or whatever inspired his jumbled mixture of fantasy, conspiracy and paranoia had been disturbing. Before Kat left she'd advised him to see a doctor but known he wouldn't.

His sincerity regarding the threats made against him she didn't doubt. Genuine terror was hard to fake and that's what she'd seen in his eyes. He'd refrained from disclosing a single identity too, yet from what she could gather he was claiming he'd been victimised by a group of local people for years. He'd complied with their requests, eschewed paragliding and kept his feet on the ground.

The idea of him being bullied upset her more than what he'd recounted about the effect of the caves. At least until Matt Hull intimated he'd witnessed a double murder.

That she still balked at: the rambling about bad dreams, an *influence* seeping from the caves she could weather, but murder? A fantasy, surely.

Of what lay between Divilmouth and Brickburgh she knew little. Excluding the excavation of the cave, the area had produced nothing newsworthy during her time in Devon. She couldn't even recall a minor crime, let alone what Matt Hull wanted her to believe. Her professional assignments involved the higher-profile tourist destinations of South Hams, Dartmoor and parts of North Devon: the affluent, picturesque bits. Which is why she'd come home after the interview surprised that Sheila had never commissioned a feature on Redhill's astounding regeneration.

They were never here before they opened the cave. The red people.

Another new addition to Brickburgh and Redhill and news to her, what Matt Hull had called 'the red people'. They'd formed the ultimate focus of his chaotic narrative.

His first sighting of these strange characters was the most bizarre story that Kat had yet heard in her career as a journalist. A story that had stuttered from the mouth of the same man who'd also admitted to being consumed with psychotic thoughts directed towards anyone he perceived as a threat. Not something he'd ever experienced before, or so he'd claimed. 'I see red too. I do. For hours some days. I've broken two teeth from grinding.' At that point Kat had nearly grabbed her coat and run from his home.

Rage was a natural response to victimisation. It was also a symptom of depression, though she'd been truly baffled by his story about 'red people' attacking a campsite. She hadn't asked if she could record the interview but had surreptitiously set her phone to record when his story took an especially sinister turn.

The second bedroom of the cottage she used as an office and just before dinner she replayed the recording in there.

'This swarm of them red people came down the hill at Slagcombe. Taking their time. They just walked towards each other and surrounded this couple at the bottom. And that valley became a pit with two animals trapped inside it.

'I stayed in the air, because I didn't like the look of how things were going on the ground.

'One of the campers was by the tent, the woman. The other was on the beach, her fella, I think. She was running this way and that but gave up and went back to the tent. I don't know why. I was shouting, *get in the water, get in the water*, but she'd never have heard me. And this whole time, her fella was running up from the shore to get back to her. But it was too late. They were surrounded.

'The red ones came into the valley naked but painted like they were from another place. Like they were from the past. I remember looking for cameras and thinking, Is this a film? But there was none of that, no cameras or the lights they use. This was real. It was happening. And these two people, the campers, didn't know what to do . . . The ring of red people just got tighter.

'In the end, the woman gave up. Was resigned, like. I'll never forget it. I heard her voice before that. Faint. She was shouting something. I don't know what.

'But the bloke was done first. He stopped running and they got round him. He went into the reeds. I saw his arms in the air as they got close, crowding him. That's when I realised they had something in their hands. Small black things, these objects. Like rocks.

'And it kicked off. He tried to break through them and they were hanging on to him, like a pack of animals. But when they got hold of that woman I'd seen enough. I flew north. Back to where me gear was, near Whaleham where I launched. My phone was there and I was going to call the law. But those red bastards were already waiting, you see, waiting for me. Three of them had got there first and were staring into the sky, right at me. Just all standing beside my gear. A woman, two men. They'd have done me too, like the campers.

'So I carried on, further up the coast, and I came down hard on Saviour Bay. Nearly came a cropper too and took a dip in the water because I was so rattled by what I'd seen. But I got untangled and put everything away and hiked back home.

'And that's when I had the first visit. You see, they were waiting for me to get here. They already knew who I was. But these others, inside here, weren't red. They . . .'

He'd broken off then so as not to reveal the identities of who had been waiting for him at his home.

'They were sitting in my chairs. They'd broken in. And I was told, in no uncertain terms, that I was not to fly again and that the air belonged to them from now on. They knew all about my boy too and I lost it when they said his name. But what they did to me . . . what they showed me left me with no choice. I hadn't a chance against them. There was no fighting back and there was no leaving here. They made that clear. They told me I couldn't go. They wanted me where they could keep an eye on me. And so I could do a few favours for them.'

Kat remembered Matt Hull pausing again at that point to rub his face. He'd wiped tears from his eye sockets. 'The red ones came that night too. To make sure I knew how much shit I was in because of what I'd seen in that valley with the campers. The first one I saw was in the garden. She was just standing there staring at the windows. I went out with the torch to see who'd set the neighbour's dog off and there she was. Naked, all red and shining like her skin was peeled off. All her hair was pulled out too, from her head. And twisted round this horrible old face.

'I went back inside double-quick. But there were more of them and all looking through the front windows, showing me their red faces . . . their teeth. The white eyes. Never been able to put that out of my mind. They weren't right, their eyes.

'I've never been so freaked out. I shut myself in the bloody bathroom upstairs. But they left something. The backdoor had handprints on it, red handprints. A sign. All of this was a warning, like I was marked. That night was a demonstration of their reach. They could show up anytime unless I did exactly what they wanted.

'Couple of days later, my ex-wife mentioned that someone had painted a red hand on her back door. My lad and his mates swore they weren't responsible and she believed them. I did too because I knew who'd done it.

'I've been on the ground and mostly in here ever since, losing my mind. Work's gone to shit. I'm unreliable. I know I am. They took my gear with them. All of it. *Clipping my wings*, that's what they said they were doing. But they'd bring me gear back when they wanted favours doing. They left this too. It was just sat on my doorstep the next morning.'

Matt had shown her the effigy he'd found on his doorstep: a marker set in place by the strangers who'd apparently peered through his windows and stood in his garden, naked and painted red. She'd seen a similar design before: a crude figure of a woman, about the size of a Barbie doll, carven from bone, with the head of a snouty dog. Its small skull was made unnervingly alert and eager, the pair of small ears pricked upright. A thing with origins in the Brickburgh caverns.

'You might be content, and for the rest of your life, covering the fun runs, the new musicals down the coast, the Michelin stars, the guide dogs, ponies, the new llama at the zoo, or whatever the fuck it is that we're always doing here, but I can't take another year of it, Kat.'

The argument with Steve began after dinner within minutes of her playing her recording of Matt Hull to him, and he'd been quick to make his accusations too, leaving Kat desperately wishing that she'd never shared the information with her boyfriend.

But keeping it to herself would have made her unbearably tense and anxious. She'd only wanted to lighten her load, to get a second opinion from someone who cared about her, who'd tell her that Matt was unstable, exaggerating, that everything would be all right and that she'd not need to break his confidence any further by going to the police, or getting involved in any inquiries into a local drug gang. Her compulsion to confess to Steve now made her feel pathetic.

As much as she tried not to dwell on the issue, Steve was much younger than her and less experienced in just about any way that she could imagine, save windsurfing and partying. But since they'd met, she'd been the catalyst for Steve to grow more ambitious professionally than she would ever be again. And within seconds of sharing Matt's story they'd been competing, *again*. A situation that always made her feel ill.

During a playback of the interview, Steve had been enraptured. Only after she'd admitted she intended to do nothing about Matt Hull's claims, had his response been harsh, the scold burning hours later.

Admittedly, Steve had been tipsy, having moved from beer to wine from the afternoon to the evening and although he rarely spoke to her in that tone, his dissatisfaction with what he was doing with his life had clearly been festering more toxically than she'd hitherto intuited.

She'd secured all of Steve's freelance work at *Life and Style*, as well as work for several digital marketing companies. But of late, he'd increasingly had the gall to make her feel like an impediment holding him back professionally.

Kat had long taken therapeutic measures to prohibit her own history's intrusion into the present. But they didn't always work. The past was a greater part of the present than the present itself seemed to be. And that evening her head had filled with the pretty face of a girl called Clarabelle.

At a magazine Kat had worked for in London, she'd employed Clarabelle as an intern: a young woman from a privileged background who'd wasted no time in undermining Kat in editorial meetings. And she'd been surreptitiously encouraged to do so by Kat's rivals. Kat had lost the job eighteen months later when another round of cuts had kicked in: it was, in fact, her final staff position in magazine editorial. The redundancy had occurred at the same time as Kat's twelve-year relationship with her fiancé, Graham, fell apart.

The fallout from Graham she was still dealing with and Steve had unpicked the stitches. That evening in her cottage he'd exuded Clarabelle's sense of entitlement to the best professional work and an assumption of all that came with it.

Steve came from money and like the intern it was as if he found it preposterous that someone from the lower social orders, like Kat, should hold a position senior to them. *There must have been some mistake. You're not one of us.*

That's how Kat read both situations and her personal experience wouldn't allow an alternative interpretation.

She and Steve had been together, on and off with non-committed periods, for over three years. But what was the relationship built on? That was the question she asked herself again. *What you can do for him. That's what this is about.*

Within moments of Steve's outburst, their age differences and the disapproval Kat harboured about his co-dependency upon his parents also reared scaly heads. His criticism of her an inevitable tripwire.

She'd always found Steve's terror of his mother hard to respect, though she managed to suppress judgement. He was thirty-two but Mum and Dad were still bankrolling him. They owned the flat he lived in rent-free. They wanted grandchildren too. A desire for multiple heirs, the enhanced social standing: it still concerned the affluent as much as it had ever done. And she was unable to give Steve children. *So how was this going to work?*

Her internal cacophony had included her certainty that Steve's mother disapproved of her being ten years his senior. His parents were present in all of their arguments, at least in spirit: an unfailingly polite couple who'd never really warmed to Kat, who were potentially of the unspoken but implied opinion that she wasn't good enough for their son. And once the disapproving spectres of Delia and Reg appeared in her mind, her repressed anger unsuppressed itself. The argument with Steve had escalated fast.

When Steve had said, 'I'll go to Sheila myself,' Kat had genuinely loathed him for several minutes that had made her skin go cold.

'She doesn't want to know, Steve! I nearly had to revive her with smelling salts when she saw a picture of a gnawed bone that was twelve thousand years old!'

'*The Gazette* in Torbay. Plenty will be interested in this.'

'It's privileged information from my source, not yours. I only told you because it upset me and because I needed to share it with someone. I wanted your support. Support from someone who keeps telling me that he's in love with me. Makes me wonder what the fuck this is all about. Am I useful to you, is that it? A stepping stone?'

'That's low!'

'This is not material for you! You're not even a journalist!'

When Steve had hit thirty he'd become tired of 'bumming around' and 'doing his own thing', as he'd initially pitched it to her. Nigh on a decade of windsurfing, raving and the creation of a Dad-funded app that never worked had given him a premature midlife crisis. Meeting Kat had incrementally worsened his frustration.

Despite her world-weary air – and her consistent efforts to detox her former lifestyle from her system with diets, yoga, meditation and anything that helped her cope with the post-traumatic stress disorder that she'd been diagnosed with seven years before – by the time she was Steve's age she'd already been working in the capital's top-flight media for nine years. Her CV bothered Steve. His resentment had acidified.

'It's just not right to keep this quiet,' he'd insisted that evening. Preposterous too, his lecturing her like that. It had been worse than his pretence that he gave a damn about Matt Hull.

She'd exploded. 'You're going to lecture me about press ethics? From your considerable experience as a press photographer? Not even one year's freelance work under your belt. Work that I bloody secured for you! You do realise that Sheila has far better people available?'

'My pictures are good!'

'For a fish restaurant in Plymouth, so don't get ahead of yourself. I am not an investigative reporter. I never wanted to be.'

'So you're just going to let them get away with it? With what they did to that poor bloke?'

'He's unstable. Probably delusional. If I had a name or a shred of evidence besides some crazy stories about red people attacking a campsite that he saw from a thousand feet up, I'd contact the police. But all I have is a garbled story of the Brickburgh curse from a man who needs psychiatric help.'

At that, Steve had smirked triumphantly and she'd really wanted to slap his face. 'Oh, he's not alone,' he'd carped. 'There are others. I've heard all kinds of things about that area. It's notorious. You wouldn't know that. You're not from here.'

At that attempt to exclude her, he'd quickly looked sheepish, embarrassed and out of his depth.

He'd left soon after, unable to withstand the cast of Kat's trembling face.

Unable to sleep after the row, Kat dug around online.

She vowed that whatever she found would not be shared with Steve. His enthusiasm for 'checking it all out' needed little encouragement and she wouldn't risk his appropriation of the story because he was bored and desperate.

A competing guilty suspicion that her courage had failed, that Steve was morally right and that she should help Matt Hull by going to the police was exacerbated by the results of her online search into missing persons, in or near Brickburgh and Divilmouth.

On the *Torbay Gazette's* website she quickly located two stories relevant to her search as well as old appeals for information. The same information was repeated at two further newspaper websites in Plymouth and another in Exeter.

The incidents were five years old and must have occurred around the time Matt Hull discovered the cliff fissure. Matt had said the camping incident had occurred at the beginning of spring. While aloft that final time he'd seen wheatears, a red kite and meadow pipits over the coastline. A flock of Brent geese had been flying in the opposite direction on their long journey to Siberia.

At the same time, a pair of campers who were believed to have been camping near Brickburgh had instead performed a curious double suicide in North Cornwall, not long after being reported missing. Shortly before their demise, a walker had vanished from the coast path near Brickburgh.

Curiously, articles of the missing couple's clothing had been found in a remote Cornish cove, folded into two piles and left together besides other personal effects. Though alerts had been posted as far away as Dorset due to the sea's currents, their bodies were never recovered.

Their yellow Volkswagen Transporter had also been found near their clothes, their camping equipment packed inside, some twenty miles from where they'd been staying in Divilmouth. There was no motive for the double suicide or why Cornwall had been chosen. The case had mystified their families.

But they'd last been seen in Divilmouth. They'd even told a guest at the hotel where they were staying that they'd intended to hike and camp near Brickburgh. Cornwall had never been mentioned by either of them. But as their vehicle and effects were found in Cornwall, the search had moved twenty miles down the coast and the official focus, while it lasted, appeared to have remained there.

Had she not heard Matt Hull's story that afternoon nothing about the incident would have inspired her curiosity.

But two campers going missing at the same time he flew over Brickburgh who'd never been found? She thought that odd.

By the time Kat was scrolling through page seven of a Google search she found the second missing person case from the same area. Earlier in the year the campers vanished, a walker called Andy Little had also been reported missing near Brickburgh.

It was believed that he'd been overcome by darkness and fallen from the cliffs, misjudging a walk on difficult terrain. His body had never been found either. No suspicious circumstances were reported and his rucksack had washed up in the next county on Chesil Beach.

An accident by all accounts. They often happened near the sea and cliffs. But when the Andy Little incident was considered in relation to the missing campers, whose intentions had been to hike to the same place as the walker and around the very time that Matt Hull claimed to have witnessed 'red people' attacking a campsite, Kat did wonder.

Old news, five years distant, and it wasn't impossible to assume that Matt Hull had read about the campers' disappearance and concocted a story. But when she recalled the torment in his eyes and his twitching limbs, her instincts insinuated that he *might* have seen *something* on that beach, not far from where he lived in Redhill.

The following morning, before she left home to gather material for an *L&S* feature on a sculptor in Dartington, Kat called a contact stationed with the police at Brickburgh.

Rick worked in community liaison. He was the press officer for the emergency services covering the area and might ask around for her. She knew him via the news desk of the magazine: in effect, a communal phone in the magazine's tiny office.

Kat lied to Rick and claimed she was undertaking consultancy work for a property developer and prospecting a potential cottage renovation near Redhill. She asked him about illegal activity near the village, adding an emphasis on the drug rumours she was picking up. She said she was being lazy on due diligence and would rather talk to the law than wade through the council archives.

Rick happily told her that three years before she'd arrived in Devon, a large cannabis factory had been found and closed down at a Brickburgh farm, about seven miles from the cave, resulting in four arrests.

Rick also admitted that 'everyone' knew the crop was still being grown surreptitiously in pockets, here and there, but little was sold locally. Unless anyone was hurt or tougher criminal elements were drawn to the area, they had little chance of finding the operations.

'That area is massive,' he'd said. 'Better the devil you know, between us, when there's no violence and us being so short-handed from the cuts.'

Matt Hull had alluded to organised criminal behaviour, though not specified a line of business. But he'd said the perpetrators were 'ruthless'. Didn't drugs inspire ruthless behaviour throughout their supply chains?

Besides a plethora of minor drug busts in Torbay, Plymouth and Exeter – local operations selling narcotics received through the harbours and rumbled through occasional police operations – the only other headline-grabbing drug-related incident that Kat uncovered online occurred in the early Eighties. This story appeared at the end of her search, some twenty pages deep. A story that interested Kat for a reason unconnected to Matt Hull.

Oddly, the story was not carried by any local press sites, probably because it predated the internet. Instead it was posted on Wikipedia, as well as several other websites concerned with folk and folk rock music.

'Brickburgh', 'Redhill' and 'drugs' had been the keywords

that had dredged the information from the depths of the online cosmos.

Although she'd lived in South Devon for seven years she'd not known that a folk rock singer, Tony Willows, owned a farm at Redstone Cross, near the Brickburgh dig. His band, Witchfinder Apprentice, had been a cult band in the Seventies. She'd heard of them and remained vaguely aware of one eerie song, 'Old Black Mag', that her ex, Graham, had often played in their flat in Westbourne Grove. She'd never taken much interest in Graham's music collection but recalled him regarding Witchfinder Apprentice as the Black Sabbath of British folk rock.

A quick check of their Wikipedia page confirmed they'd charted at number two with a song, 'All Around My Throne', at Christmas in 1974. Another tune that Graham had often played at weekends.

At the edge of Tony Willows's farm in 1979, the dead body of a young woman had been discovered the day after the solstice, her system full of cocaine, LSD and alcohol. Apparently, the girl had been a guest at one of the raucous, seasonal private parties that Willows had thrown for his old entourage. The woman had also suffered head trauma from a fall. Willows briefly went to prison for manslaughter and possession. After his release he was never seen in public again.

The excess of the singer's lifestyle was also documented at length on the band's Wikipedia page. Kat skim-read it, learning that he'd suffered a massive breakdown in 1977, either brought on, or worsened, by long-term LSD and tranquilliser use. He'd left the band and released one eclectic solo album of folk music on his own label. The record had surfaced in 1986 but he never appeared on a stage after 1977.

Elsewhere online, his biography petered out with his current status as a breeder of rare ponies and Black Welsh Mountain sheep at Redstone Cross Farm.

When Kat searched for the farm, Google maps placed it three miles above the Brickburgh caves.

She quelled her own instinct for conspiracy and random but easily made connections. Famous entertainers hiding in South Hams and Cornwall were not uncommon. She knew of at least three from the same period as Willows's heyday in British rock music.

As so often happened with an online search, she found herself being dragged into an annexe unrelated to what she'd first attempted to research. But what surprised her most about the Willows information was that no one at the magazine had ever mentioned him, which was odd considering *Life and Style*'s obsession with local success, affluence and celebrity. Kat made a note to ask Sheila about Tony Willows the next time she called the *L&S* office.

By the evening, her interest had drifted away from missing campers and Matt Hull; her priority became a persistent desire to mend the recent fracture with Steve. They needed to produce a feature article together on the new Brickburgh dig exhibition in Exeter and the last thing she wanted was an atmosphere, with him sullen and monosyllabic, as she directed him around the displays, telling him what to photograph.

Before she lay down, Kat sent him a text: *We need to talk about Exeter. Tomorrow. K x*

9

The great expanse of time elapsing between the exhibition and the distant inhabitation of the caves was not as apparent as Helene thought it should be. The condition of the recently recovered artefacts was remarkable. What she saw was also unpleasant.

The Home of a Lost People: 60,000 Years BC. The relics on display had been recovered from the deepest level of the Brickburgh caves so far, the most important Neanderthal site ever found in Britain. An extinct people occupying the Brickburgh caves, periodically, across another fifteen thousand years.

Helene paused to glance at maps, illustrations, read some information boards. She'd liked to have watched the films but there was always one child or another drawn to the glowing screens and pushing buttons.

The *bout coupé* hand-axe had been the first artefact identifying the remains in the cave as Neanderthal. U-shaped in silhouette, the tool had a convex blade, a surface curved like a sphere, its bluish-black flint glinting under electric light.

A sign explained its purpose: 'Butchery: decapitation, dismemberment, defleshing carcasses.' A stone knapped and flaked to hack and carve flesh. Merely by looking at the blades Helene could effortlessly imagine the damage the tools could inflict. And beneath the forbidding and starkly beautiful landscape that had swallowed and rejected her while she'd looked for vestiges of her brother's final path, these very tools had once been slippery with a great volume of blood.

The foaming mouths of the dogs at Redstone Cross, her being so tired on the windswept hills, the bestial noises her brother had recorded, must also have conspired to form the unpleasant collusions inside her sleeping mind the night before. She'd first woken at four with a start, suffering the terror of finding herself inside an unfamiliar room, separated from her daughter.

Unable to recall specific details of her dream – most of it obscured by a dark-red smear suggesting a frenzy of activity – she'd woken unrested that morning, suffering something akin to a hangover. But the exhibition both revived and worsened the lingering sense of having witnessed something terrible in her sleep.

Detailed copies of the cave paintings were reproduced on large photographic boards, installed in connecting stairwells. Helene suspected it was these images she'd dreamed of, though in sleep the figures on the red walls had been moving. A constant, hypnotic sound of wind, piped through the claustrophobic confines of a wet tunnel, had formed a soundtrack.

A 3D graphic beside the axes caught her eye. The illustration depicted a group of thickset figures, hoary of face and made bulky by their animal-skin coverings. In the long grass where a vast creature had fallen, exhausted from many wounds, the men stripped the elephantine beast of its flesh, exposing the sturdy scaffolding of its bones. A thicket of black spear shafts and the animal's tusks thrust through misty air. Vultures circled and alighted to feast. A wounded hunter lay on his side, clutching ribs and a limp arm, his face grey. Hard times.

A thousand tons of sediment had been mined and sifted from atop the exhibited remains. A great layer of earth installed by natural soil movements, floodwater and glacial activity, separating this group of early humans from those that came after them, fifteen thousand years later at around 45,000 BC. The latter remains were found in another section of the cave system and were displayed on level 1. She'd get to them next.

But while the Neanderthals resided in the Brickburgh Caves, it appeared that *other things* had occurred in those black recesses of the earth: terrible things, happening for reasons unclear to the experts.

Hunger in the extreme weather had probably played its part: the perpetual drops in temperature, the stalling of the Gulf Stream, the frozen tundras pushed forward by the Northern ice sheets. And with some help from the illustrations, Helene had no difficulty imagining hunters returning home, gaunt and empty-handed, the vulnerable drawing deeper inside the cave and about the fire as the hungry dogs of an eternal winter howled outside and inside a cold labyrinth of moist burrows.

The final chapter in the Neanderthal display, the one that had drawn so many excited schoolchildren to itself, shaded Helene's thoughts even darker than they'd been at first light. These were artefacts to make any mother want to hold her child tight.

Fragments of a human skull obliterated by a large stone littered the *faux* rock floor of the display case. The scattering of shards resembled stone chippings but the pieces had once formed a child's head. A boy's skull reduced to a vase dropped upon a hard floor.

Beneath the incomplete skull a collapsed human skeleton was splayed. Like splinters of ancient pottery each component of the skeletal structure was set in a ruddy coloured stone: a rectangular plinth cut from a section of the cave floor and removed in its entirety. The final resting place of a young Neanderthal male, malnourished at the time of death.

Stanzas of unintended horror poetry on white display cards indicated that seven children and three young adults had been found upon a slope inside the Neanderthal cave, their pitiful forms concealed by debris. Now installed inside a cabinet, three tiny infant skulls grimaced their little faces at the light of the future, where their unspeakable story was interpreted. Large eye sockets and small jaws offered determined expressions. Initially, archaeologists assumed the group of youngsters had been crushed by a cave-in. A forensic examination of the bones revealed a different fate: each of the individuals had been manually disarticulated. Many of their bones were then smashed apart and gnawed by other Neanderthal teeth, perhaps by their fellows, even family members.

Their demise had been established through the indicative Neanderthal dental condition, 'taurodontism', that produced stronger teeth, more exposed from the gums. On receipt of that information, Helene had shut her eyes to dispel an image of yellow teeth clamped on a small bone . . . *apelike mouths sucking.*

Origins. How it began.

Helene moved away, before her imagination coated the little skulls with other features and expressions. She stopped by photographs of rock piles. Only they weren't stones but pictures of hyena droppings. Petrified mounds rich in both animal and human bone deposits. A hyena den had existed close to the Neanderthals, a pit inside an adjoining branch of the cave system. A section filled by the earth's movements but a chamber once accessed through a crevice on the surface.

The card accompanying the photographs postulated that prey was 'dragged through the fissure and devoured below'. Teeth marks on the pelvis and skull of a mammoth suggested a new species of hyena had existed, as large as those previously thought extinct.

Neanderthal teeth and bones discarded as indigestible were also discovered inside the petrified droppings of the jackals occupying the pit. Following herds of mammoth, Neanderthal hunters, wolves and hyenas had loped from the plains of northwestern Europe, crossing Doggerland.

Some distance from the bone larders of the children, devoured by their own, another six Neanderthal bodies had been found. These were buried in a different manner, side by side.

At the time of their death, these people had been old. Their skulls were intact and each revealed the characteristic Neanderthal bulge at the rear, the 'occipital bun'. Palaeoanthropologist artists had fashioned a resemblance of one of the inhabitants on a mounted bust.

Level with Helene's eyes, the face leered directly out of prehistory, its wrinkled flesh the colour of tea and as riven by deep lines as an eighty-year-old woman of Helene's time, one who had spent a life working outdoors without sun-cream.

Tufty white hair sprouted from the elongated head. The murky brown eyes displayed a clear, hard, human intelligence. A bulbous nose flared into black nostril pits and Helene recalled the weathered vagrant she'd once seen in London's Soho, who'd worn a Union Jack flag like an emperor's cape.

Unlike the children's remains, the mature individuals had been interned with reverence and care: 'Elders' prized after they'd died in their fourth decade. Perhaps they'd been laid to rest when food had not been so scarce. No animals had worried their remains and they'd stayed undisturbed in the very places in which they'd first been laid out in the caves, some time between 55,000 and 50,000 BC.

Conditions in the sealed limestone cave had preserved their bones: even signs of arthritis and tooth decay had been revealed in analysis. That they'd been cared for in their dotage, even loved, offered some much-needed evidence of humanity within such an abattoir..

Inside the shallow trenches of their graves, a ruddy stain, an iron oxide dye, had also been detected by chemists. Across generations of Neanderthal occupation, the remains of the 'special dead' had been painted before interment. And each rust-stained figure had ventured into eternity with a cruel black hand-axe within reach of its skeletal hand.

10

I's *the faces I keep seeing. Red faces. Every time I fall asleep. They come in and out of a dark place. There's smoke. Red light on the walls. The wind too, always the wind.*

But they're not all the same, the things in that black place. There's something much bigger than the red people. It has a dark face... And there's these white things, like big rats... They all walk like them little dogs you see in a circus, on their back legs, but they're bigger than bears. Devils. It's like I'm dreaming of devils.

It's the noise of the young ones I can't stand, the babies, the kids. And when the dogs, these devils, start whining and the babies start screaming, I wake up. I wake up and I'm crying.

On seeing the reproduced cave paintings at the exhibition, the dreams that Matt Hull had narrated to Kat found further synchronicity with her position on mankind's perpetually harsh, savage and troubled past. To her, history itself was an epitome of darkness and it seemed humanity's very origins had been made epochal by their ghastliness.

Even simple articles of clothing stored behind glass in museums suggested the grotesque and death to her. From end to end, history was collected horror, preserved for the fascination of a bestial species. Her experience of museums had never been sufficiently different from her experience of funerals. And the most recent fragments exhumed from Brickburgh's famous caves, curiously sharpened a sense of her

104

own time, while reducing her sense of security within it.

The artefacts were stored behind glass so highly polished that Kat felt she might step inside the larger exhibits. *Then* and *now* seemed uncannily closer. Too close.

Clean bathrooms and a chic café awaited downstairs. Traffic rumbled and swished past the museum's red bricks. Here were ordinary people wearing contemporary clothes. A boisterous school party wandered past her before dispersing to mill elsewhere. And yet, despite the modern screens, a sense of the cave's raw primitive presence, this brutal time on exhibition, had truly been evoked as a morbid and most vivid spectacle, its atmosphere intensifying within the artificial space.

Kat found herself looking at the ceiling and windows to break a trancelike fatigue as if she'd been forced to look at the evidence of war crimes. The presence of other people and Steve with his camera offered some comfort. She wouldn't have walked here alone.

Conscious of their solemn, hesitant progress, Steve said, 'Like a crypt, isn't it?' At least their heads, for once, were inhabiting the same space.

By design, the first level of the gallery space resembled the largest cavern discovered in the Brickburgh cave system: the 'Grand Chamber'. Between the installations, the walls and ceilings were decorated with the same ochre and charcoal colours of the caves. Dark-blooded and womblike was the atmosphere and made doubly oppressive with shadow to replicate the enclosed stone environment.

The slit Matt Hull had reached through to grab a few souvenirs years before had subsequently revealed itself to be the equivalent of a small rear window, opening onto a large subterranean burrow divided into separate chambers. All of the caves had been used intermittently by various subspecies of humans across tens of thousands of years.

And this was a big deal. The cultural significance alone of what had been displayed, the manufactured relics left behind by ancient societies, had shattered much of what was known of early man. Existing knowledge about the first colonisations of Britain was currently under root-and-branch review. Kat had been given the opportunity to write the *L&S* feature, an assignment coveted by the magazine's freelancers. Kat told herself she was lucky.

About her head, a herd of horses fled across the walls, their swift passage defined by long, sensual curves, shaped from thick sweeps of charcoal. These were the first things her eyes had been drawn to: reproductions of the cave's art. Discreet speakers even transmitted a reproduction of animal shrieks and of a galloping rout across the ancient turf of Devon.

Expressions of terror were still frozen upon the horses' red muzzles because of the great dogs that bounded behind them.

The hunched, black-muzzled creature that led the pack's hunt was of an unnatural size, the centrepiece. Unto it the ancient artist had drawn the eyes of his audience. Seemingly, the dog-thing had risen upon its hind legs, or had been depicted leaping for the last horse. It was hard to tell.

The eyes above the creature's wrinkled muzzle were crazed, maliciously eager, idiotically sadistic. The face had been chipped into the rock and impacted with red dye, over and over for millennia, and with so much care by successive generations of occupant. The 'therianthrope', as it had been called, had confounded the dig's archaeologists.

Bizarre chimeras. Three of the savage amalgamations of human and animal had been found depicted on the walls. Much patient digging and sifting across four years had led to a revelation of their ghastly forms.

Inside this dark place, within the humid air, so fraught with the sounds of animal distress, Kat was unwilling to look at them for long. To her, the jackal-headed *things* functioned as a sudden, startling distillation of the natural order's horror: the eternal repetition of bloodshed occurring the world over.

Those curating the exhibition proposed that the three hound-headed human figures – one was large and jet-black, the other two smaller and sickeningly pale – might have been gods or some curious supernormal forms into which shamans believed they could transform themselves. Only vestiges of Stone Age and Aboriginal belief systems offered any clues as to what these curious figures represented.

Kat cribbed notes: *Were these people suggesting they could access a spiritual world? Was this a religion that far pre-dated the Bible?*

As she scribbled, her focus was broken by images of Matt Hull's haggard face and of what he'd so recently recounted to her.

The people's faces are red. Always. But the red faces are filled with fear. Lined, scarred, dirty, painted faces, terrified. And they're beating things, rocks with sticks, all of them together. They're talking or singing something. It's all high-pitched and weird in this wind. A wind that's in the darkness with them. The wind comes out of the earth with the dogs, the devils. I can always hear them. The devils. Coming up.

Kat refocused on her notes and on directing Steve's photographs. She needed the information boards captured for reference. Steve didn't notice her preoccupation, nor did he seem aware of her distress. He only saw what was before his camera lens.

When they reached the 3D model of an elder's head, he whispered, 'Ugly bastard,' from the side of his mouth. 'I get a bit of Shrek. What do you think?'

Kat found the crinkled face profoundly unappealing. Several of its brown teeth were missing from the dark gums. Set amidst wild white hair, its bloodshot eyes leered from out of a face powdered the red of paprika. The flesh might have been flecked with dried blood and was far worse than the Neanderthal head upstairs. This one's features were flatter and broader.

Red people.

Matt's rambling narrative remained prescient. Kat wondered if the man's sinister fantasies had only worsened after persecution at the hands of local criminals, who'd suspected he'd witnessed their drug operations from the air. Maybe the intimidation he'd suffered had mixed itself up with these artefacts. He lived near the site. Due to the size and expense of the operation, local volunteers had been involved from the start, to delicately remove thousands of tons of earth from the cave. They'd have seen the cave paintings and buried elders and been told that they were once painted red. Redhill's small population must have chattered about what had been dug up. Matt would have heard things. *Suggestion.*

Kat rediscovered the thread of her notes.

The original entrance of the hyenas' 'dog chamber' had been reopened as part of the ongoing excavation of the Grand Chamber. It had led the dig team to the lower Neanderthal level. Impossible to imagine, but the later human species and the Neanderthals before them had shared the caves with hyenas. In each era of human occupation this natural abattoir had been filled with large hyenas. They had been the size of African lions and should have been long extinct.

Inside the 'dog pit', as well as the bones of horse, woolly rhino, bison and Irish Elk (prey hunted down and dragged through a crack in the earth), and much like the older Neanderthal remains, the chewed bones of later human occupants had been discovered. In abundance.

Tests proved that many of the human remains had been broken and gnawed by hyena teeth in the terrible darkness of the earth. Bodies torn apart before their bones were cracked open for their rich marrow.

Nor was this the last of the macabre connections between the Neanderthals and what was found at the first level, dated at 12,000 BC: at the press conference in Plymouth, and in the first exhibition, it was revealed that the humans had also eaten each other in the same way that their canine superiors had eaten them. In these caves, in all three periods of occupation, it was as if people had been tutored by the greater predator.

And I can hear wind. The people are in that cave, close to a fire. It's all red and black with shadows spiking across the ceiling . . . their faces are red and creased and their eyes are white . . . and mad, all rolled up . . .

That's when I hear them. Coming through the dark. The devils.

Am I seeing hell? That's what I ask myself when I wake up. Is this hell in my head?

And the devils always come for that woman who's crouching in front of her kids. They've come for those dirty kids in the corner who are grabbing at their mother. She keeps looking for a way out . . . That woman and kids have been given to the devils by the red people.

They're like shadows. The devils. Their shadows dim the firelight. It shrinks. But I can still see them. These things with the long bodies that get up on two legs. Everywhere, there's the sounds of devils in the smoke. The rocks are wet, red and wet.

They laugh like men but growl like dogs. Deep. Horrible. Whining and whistling and laughing in the wind . . .

They . . . them kids . . . shaking them in its mouth . . .

This is hell. This is hell I keep seeing.

When Matt had told Kat of his nightmares she'd been able to picture them vividly. She'd had them too. The half-remembered dreams, the ruddy black smears of places filled with frantic movements and screams. She and Matt Hull had shared the same dreams.

Children. The cries of children. Matt Hull had only ever been describing what she'd also experienced; his narrative had only given clarity to what she'd been suppressing in her own disturbed sleep since the press conference in Plymouth.

Kat looked for somewhere to sit down. She needed water.

Steve was quick to express his own fatigue with a nearby sixth-form lecturer, who was holding forth to his blazered students. 'That teacher could use a hand-axe in the mouth.'

'Ssh. Let's get a drink.'

11

'*Y*ou all right?' A voice beside her.

Helene dabbed her nose and blotted tears with the napkin that had come with her coffee. Tired legs, a poor night's sleep, missing her daughter, none of it was helping. Mostly, she'd just been unsettled by the exhibition and in a way that she'd never anticipated.

When she'd reached the final section, her thoughts had returned to the bearded face and scarred eye of the hostile man at the farm the day before. Him shouting at her, the thin woman watching her retreat, the dog leaping, its wet teeth, the mad brown eyes streaked red: images impressed into her memory by fear. The only confrontations she was accustomed to were with a recalcitrant six-year-old.

Lincoln and his desperate, inexplicable end. The reason she'd come here: to better understand and to say farewell. He'd killed himself mere weeks after recording those horrid sounds from a quarry neighbouring the subject of this very exhibition. *A crying child. A relentless trickling of water. An agitated animal in a lightless space.* Her instincts and imagination made connections she couldn't rationalise. The displays had also opened a path into the previous night's dream, equally ineffable. She couldn't remember when she'd felt as mixed-up.

Sipping at her water bottle to create a barrier, she returned her attention to the concerned face of the young man sat at the next table who'd spoken to her. A camera hung from his neck on a red and black strap. A plastic badge on a lanyard read PRESS PASS.

A dark-haired woman with a plump, handsome face sat across the table from the photographer and eyed Helene with what looked like disapproval twinned with wariness. Perhaps she was only preoccupied with the book and papers spread on the table top before her; a woman engaged in a professional task, no time for distractions, her stiff courtesy a first defence. Helene had seen the couple inside the Grand Chamber and again on the stairs between the floors of the exhibition.

The man's face was slim and attractive, his beard producing the effect of noble and hipster. He was much younger than the woman, so she doubted they were together romantically. And yet the woman's cool demeanour might yet be born of a perceived threat, an intrusion into her space and onto her ground. Helene loathed that kind of tension between herself and other women; she'd made a few jealous in her time.

'Get to you, did it?' the man said, his smile kind. 'It's why we came down here. Those children's skulls were the final straw.' He winced. 'Awful.'

Some men could effortlessly offer companionable support, without seeming intrusive. Helene found him attractive too but made sure not to show it. She nodded her agreement. 'I'm a mum,' she added to placate the woman, in case they were an item.

'Must make it worse,' the man said. 'Even though it happened tens of thousands of years ago, it must still get to you.'

'You're not wrong.' But to change a subject she didn't want to dwell on, Helene asked the couple what they were doing at the exhibition.

The man answered, 'She's words, I'm pictures.' He then introduced himself as Steve and said other things about an assignment for a magazine. The name of the publication didn't register. Helene asked if they were local and they said they were.

'Mind if we join you?' Steve asked and Helene raised no objection. But the woman, who had been introduced as Kat, cast a black look at Steve that only reached the back of his head.

Once they'd shifted to her table, Helene shared a few tentative details about Valda. She felt obliged to account for her tears, how the exhibition had made her needy.

The journalist, Kat, finally softened when Helene offered a few photographs of Valda she kept in her phone: a jam-smeared face, a small figure dressed as a fairy with wings, a face split with crazed laughter during some antic that Helene couldn't recall.

Steve said he loved kids, and Kat appeared to stiffen for a second at this admission.

When Helene tactfully moved the conversation away from herself and asked about their work, she found herself immediately impressed with Kat and wanted the woman's resistance to disappear. She wanted to be liked by her. Not once did the journalist brag about her career; she only mentioned her work in vague terms. It was Steve who recited Kat's CV to Helene. Three of the magazines Kat had worked on in London Helene still read. She must have read Kat's work in the past. The journalist offered a thin smile when Helene stated as much and quickly quelled Helene's admiration by suggesting that her career had been 'of no consequence'.

The couple's attitude only shifted from polite friendliness when Steve asked what brought Helene to Devon.

'He was here? And then he went missing?' Steve asked Helene, after she'd nutshelled Lincoln's story. He and Kat had exchanged glances. Perhaps the mention of a suicide accounted for their reaction.

'Two weeks before he passed.'

'Sorry, I don't mean to pry,' Steve said.

'Then why are you?' Kat asked him.

Steve looked chastened but was clearly irritated by Kat's terse remark.

'It's all right,' Helene said. 'It happened a long time ago.

But it's weird, I think I'm only coming to terms with it now. It's another reason why I was upset.'

'Grief affects people in different ways,' Steve offered and Kat looked at him again as if to question the experience behind such an observation.

As if he were present, a startling sense of Lincoln warmed through Helene. It had happened the day before. 'My brother was quite a character. It was typical of him to spend a whole summer here, camping and recording underground noises for an obscure website.'

At further prompting from Steve, she described the recordings and confessed how uncanny she found their connection to the sound effects piped into the exhibition. She'd never see Kat and Steve again so it didn't matter if they thought her a weirdo.

'The soundtrack here was probably recorded in a zoo, or taken from a music library with a safari section,' Steve offered. But he appeared unable to contain his excitement when Helene mentioned where Lincoln had camped, though she wasn't sure why.

She also feared she was out of touch with what was interesting to people like Steve and Kat. This made her wonder how switched on her brother had been and how clueless she was about what was 'cool': she'd always believed the opposite to be true.

Kat only frowned as Helene narrated her story and she sensed discontent in the journalist, even a store of unhappiness. She thought Kat was glamorous but careless with her appearance, offering an impression of not really caring about what she'd thrown on. Helene found that odd when someone could afford such nice clothes.

On discovering that the journalist and Steve were in a relationship she had to suppress her surprise, as well as a tinge of disappointment.

Gradually, Kat overcame her irritation with Steve's wooing of the single mum in the museum café. He was definitely flirting and that made her dwell on how often he flirted, or worse, with other women. A familiar preoccupation.

For far too long she'd liked the fact that she wasn't in love with Steve. The mutual lack of expectation suited her. But recently it had dawned upon her that she'd fallen for him.

Steve was out all the time and Kat only saw him twice a week, at most, which suited her more than him. She never kept tabs. Maybe he'd made the most of that arrangement. And there had been an assurance, an easy confidence with no inhibition, when he'd identified a damsel in distress in the café and attended to her. An approach much practised? He'd picked out a hot one too. Helene was leaner than her, taller. Her short haircut suggested Paris more than Walsall and boyishly framed the strong bones of her even features.

Steve had always paid a lot of attention to Kat's legs but this woman's were longer, more slender, stronger, with a second skin of skinny-fit denim emphasising powerful calf and thigh muscles. She was athletic and probably worked out to remain so rangy yet feminine. In time she might go stringy.

Helene also seemed moody, though it only contributed to her air of being effortlessly sexy. Single, with a lovely daughter – and Steve was becoming increasingly interested in having kids. Kat's penchant for paranoia enabled her to imagine Steve with the woman and her ready-made family. His boyish antics would delight the six-year-old.

When she felt sick Kat stopped the punishing fantasy. A dark presence, a cold pall more than a cloud, pushed again at the edges of her memory: Graham and his horrible rejection.

They'd had twelve years together in London. Eight years gone but the coals of that relationship were prone to being raked over if she didn't remain disciplined.

Her separation from the only man she'd ever wholly loved had been excruciating. Graham had left her to start a family with someone else: a family already under construction, in another flat in West London, while she and Graham were still together. His deception had been monumental.

Jane had been a mutual friend. Graham had made her pregnant during the five-month affair that Kat had missed while consumed by the unravelling of her career and her war with the intern, Clarabelle.

Jane's pregnancy had finally turned Graham's sullen dissatisfaction into a conclusive rejection of what he'd had with Kat. He'd been so relieved once he'd finished with her. She could still hear the sentence that tore her apart: 'I can't do this any more.'

She'd sat still, bloated yet weightless with trauma in their flat in Westbourne Grove. A linen curtain had wafted across her face like a shroud. In that moment, the world had been lifted from Atlas's shoulders and dropped onto her face.

Graham had already made Kat infertile. Chlamydia. She'd not known he'd passed it on when they'd first met. By the time she found out and they were treated it was too late for her. But not for Graham.

In the café, Kat had to close her eyes for a few seconds before she lost control of her jaw. She then scraped herself back into the present.

She shouldn't dislike Helene. *Jesus Christ, she lost her brother.* A suicide too. Kat thought of a long drop from a bridge into cold water and shuddered. She knew unhappiness, she knew desperation, but she'd known nothing like that. And Helene was here for closure. On that matter, Kat was tempted to inform her that closure never happened, not really. In time, the past was partially covered and your memory moved on to fill itself with other things. But the damage to your hardware remained permanent.

'You hear this, Kat?' Steve asked. 'Her brother ended . . . this happened near Bristol, not here. But the last anyone knew he was *here.*' Steve emphasised his point by pressing an index finger upon the table. 'Mmm? The couple in Cornwall? The walker?'

Helene was frowning. 'Sorry, I don't follow.'

Steve turned to her. 'Oh, just something we're looking into –'

'Hardly,' Kat said quickly to curb Steve's conspiracy theorising: it was getting out of hand again. He'd started first thing that morning when she'd allowed the discussion about Matt Hull to resume. She'd also broken her vow to herself and shared with Steve what she'd found online – though it would only have been a matter of time until he discovered it himself and went mad at her for keeping her findings to herself.

She'd also told Steve that she would consider looking into the information further before sharing it with her contact on the force, because she needed more information. Under the table she tapped Steve's thigh with her knuckles.

Steve turned to Kat. 'We'd love to listen to the recordings, though. Wouldn't we?'

'They're her recordings. And important to Helene.'

'It wouldn't be a problem,' Helene said, looking from Kat to Steve with her alert blue eyes: long eyelashes, jet-black and velvety. *So pretty.* 'Lincoln wanted to share them. He'd been really excited about having his own album of noise but it never happened.' She dabbed at the wet weight of another tear that had formed in the corner of an eye.

Kat's heart cracked. She clenched inside with self-loathing for perceiving this grieving woman as a rival.

Helene blinked her eyes dry and cleared her throat. 'They are really weird though. I have no idea what's making the noises. But they'd be a better soundtrack than the one they've got here. Everything Lincoln recorded actually came from underground too. Some of it was recorded close to the caves.'

'Fantastic,' Steve said. He clapped his hands. 'Then we can eat.'

12

'Steve, no. Absolutely not. What would you achieve?'

'But it's what you should be doing. You said you would look into this more. Well, this is one way of doing that. Just hear me out. This is a story. Your story, I get that, if it's anybody's, but I can help.'

Steve smoothed his hands over the great paper blanket created by the Ordnance Survey map that he'd brought to her cottage and spread across her living room floor. The corners were weighted with used Witchfinder Apprentice CDs he'd mail-ordered.

'Kat,' he added with an exasperated finality. 'Just join the bloody dots. That paraglider wasn't lying. Matt. He was clearly warned off from flying here. People got hurt because one of these farms is growing dope, and big time.'

'Matt could be suffering from paranoid delusions, Steve. He had a bad breakup with his wife. He was also a local hero for finding that cave, but the cameras moved off him years ago. He's been left high and dry. I'm not so sure he handled his fleeting moment of fame all that well, never mind the fact that it's now over.'

'The copper you know in Brickburgh also said there's past history. A drug farm bust went down –'

'Long time ago. Nothing since. Ancient history.'

Steve pointed at the iPod speakers. 'Then there's this guy's parties that got out of hand.' A download of Tony Willows solo album, *Hark! Hear the Red Folk Sing* played quietly.

'In the Seventies! Old, old news, mate.'

What drifted through the air of her living room was morbidly haunting; even the jaunty passages darkened by bleak lyrics. The voice she remembered distinctly from when Graham had played his Witchfinder albums. It was thinner on the solo album but still high, melodic, almost feminine for a man and quavering with more anguish than she remembered. The pipes accompanying the acoustic guitars were unusual too. Other than that, it was folk music plain and simple, conjuring a sense of the past or mediaeval balladry.

'But a woman even died. At his farm.'

'People die of overdoses all the time, Steve. In the towns, in the cities round here now. It's not uncommon, despite appearances in the tourist brochures and our rag. You're trying to rake over a minuscule, out of date scandal.'

'Those might not have been parties on Willows's land. They were more like . . . like festivals. Rites. Unofficial. All very secretive. Need to know. Private. Invite only. Crashers were dealt with. That's what I've been told. It's weird, but someone – this old guy, Mac, in the pub – said that Willows wasn't even present. He was in prison when this stuff really took off. They were held at certain times each year, for a long time. That's what Mac said. Some were an annual thing connected to the moon or something.'

'Or something? Mac said? Mac? Jesus, Steve! A party once got out of hand and Willows got in trouble. He's not interested in any kind of public life. He's retired and reclusive. He burned out in the Seventies. Went a bit Syd Barrett from what I've read. It's safe to assume he'd had enough of drugs and all that they bring a long time ago.

'And I asked Sheila about him yesterday. She said they tried, over and over again, to get him involved with the Divilmouth folk festival and the big one in Sidmouth. He always regretfully declined. He gave up touring in the Seventies and he's just an old hippy that breeds sheep now. No one's seen him in public for years. A few old crusties kept his music alive until the new folk bands revived his back catalogue. That's the only reason anyone even mentions him now.'

Steve rolled his eyes. 'Helene's brother? He was up there. Redstone Cross. Where he made those recordings was in the heart of the quarries that supplied the old paint factories. Redstone. Some of those quarries are on Willows's land. Her brother was recording those noises we heard a fortnight before he died, at Redstone Cross. In a frickin' quarry, Kat. Come on. And the couple who said they were going to camp out there? Why did they top themselves? Did they really? There's that walker they never found. People get lost, they climb over the wrong fences, but who knows what he might have seen out that way? Matt was threatened, victimised, just for paragliding.'

'Steve. Down a notch, please. We don't know anything about Helene's brother. Not really, besides him being into drugs. His sister said as much. He had a weird lifestyle, blah, blah. There could be any number of contributing factors to his suicide, which, by the way, was near *Bristol*. Bristol, Steve. Not Brickburgh. The campers had some kind of suicide pact in *Cornwall*. They were nowhere near here when they topped themselves. The links are tenuous. We have no idea what was going on in their minds either.'

I mean, you've very little idea of what goes on inside mine.

Steve looked at his map in silence. He seemed so young then, a thwarted boy who desperately wanted an adventure. When he spoke again his voice had lost its power. 'What about Google Earth, yeah? What is that?'

He'd shown her the Google Earth satellite photographs of the Redstone Cross area and Tony Willows's farm: a few buildings with dark roofs, strewn down a lane surrounded by unbroken woodland on all sides. Beyond the trees were miles of pasture, copses of woodland, a series of steep valleys cut by streams that drained water from the hills: great clefts separating his land from two neighbouring farms. All remote.

Further along the private lane where Helene said she'd unwittingly trespassed was another, bigger structure with a newer roof.

What did surprise Kat was how much land Willows owned. She guessed he must have sold a lot of records and invested his money wisely, or maybe got a good deal on the land in an economic downturn. The Seventies were a time of heavy recession. Perhaps the sheep farming had done well, though that was not something she often heard about the local farming industry. But what did she and Steve know about farming? Nothing.

West of the buildings was a great flat expanse of ground, bordered by a thick perimeter of trees. It was this area that Steve had become excited about. The grass between the woods was marked by what appeared to be a paler strip of land, resembling a giant cricket pitch. 'Airstrip,' Steve had ventured confidently, tapping it with a finger. 'Why would a retired folk singer and breeder of odd-looking sheep need an airstrip? Think about it.'

Only when Steve mentioned an airstrip did Kat see the similarity. But it might just as easily have been the patterning of crops. How would they know?

'Steve, there's a Land Trust country house right in the middle of all that farmland, Redacre House. Part of a national organisation and about three miles from that farm. No one would erect a drug operation anywhere near one of those places. You've got the Saga crowd trekking in and out all summer to see the award-winning gardens. And don't say "hidden in plain sight" or anything like that, because if you start down that road then you might as well introduce UFOs into your theory. Maybe aliens use the airstrip and harvest DNA from his sheep?'

Steve took another long swig from his beer bottle. 'All I am saying is there's no harm in just nosing around a bit, on foot. See what gives. Land Trust put some walkers' paths through here. It's not all private land. You can go on some of it. Public right to roam. The coastal path is open too. They've widened another old green track for the dig traffic. It's an accessible area. We'd not be trespassing, just taking a look around.'

'Big area, Steve. Over twelve miles wide. You might have the leisure to stroll around it but I haven't. I need to earn a living from paying assignments in line with editorial direction.'

'Not the bit I'm looking at between the cave and Redstone Cross. That's no more than three miles as the crow flies.'

'And what happened to Helene when she wandered up there? Someone set their dogs on her. She said herself that her brother must have been trespassing. The quarry, or whatever is left of it, is on private land. And there are kilns and quarries all over that area. If they weren't preserved they'll be overgrown. All you can see are big gouges in the earth and a few bricks. I know, I covered the Industrial Revolution Season in South Devon that was run from Torbay. You could walk straight past an old quarry and not know it. These aren't filled with water. They're just overgrown earthworks. You'll never find where Helene's brother stuck his microphone in the ground.'

'How do you explain those noises on the discs then? Shit, they were freaky.'

They had been: disembodied, ghostly sounds, varying from faint and enigmatic to outlandish and horrid as they'd filled Helene's tiny car. Kat couldn't think why Helene or her brother would fake the sounds. Nor had she shared the discs with anyone else in six years.

'I can't explain them, Steve. But there is an explanation. Some kind of wildlife. Little creatures can make huge sounds, especially in enclosed spaces. The earth moves, you know. It never stays still. The wind can produce all kinds of noises, even like voices underground. So can water.'

'You're reaching.'

'Not as much as you. You were just talking about some mammoth drug operation with an airstrip and now you're basing your story on weird underground noises. Narcotics and the paranormal. Not my bag, mate.'

Steve took another draught of beer and returned his attention to the map. 'It could be . . . I dunno. It's weird.'

'Can I turn this off now?' Kat pointed at the iPod.

'Nah. I like it.'

Steve didn't stay over. Kat had assumed he would. He'd sloped off in another sulk, taking his map and music with him.

She didn't like discouraging him but her boyfriend hatched ideas for new projects on a monthly basis. When in that mood she found him exhausting. He was a stick-at-nought, a flitter, possessing a restless soul, one somehow both idle and sporadically bursting with energy.

But something sinister had happened to the paraglider Matt Hull. Kat believed that much, though whoever Matt had tangled with was never going to be anyone she planned on doorstepping. People growing cannabis were none of her business. Though thoughts of the campers, the hiker, the curious sounds and the recurring idea of red people in the area confounded her. As did the coincidence she'd happened upon the day before, when she'd spoken to members of the archaeological team who'd taken part in recent digs inside the caves: information she'd decided not to share with Steve.

For her feature about the new exhibition she'd requested an interview with the dig's site staff. She'd only been seeking a couple of quotes about the second phase of the dig but had received far more. At the end of the interview, she'd dropped a few hints about the weirder aspects of the caves, suggested by Matt Hull's sinister tales and Helene's recordings, and been astonished by her interviewees' response.

Helene couldn't have known that similar noises, effectively the sounds of life that Helene's brother had accidentally recorded, were reported by staff working on the dig's second phase: disturbances transmitted through solid rock from the direction of a sediment-packed enclave of the cave system.

From a senior geophysicist, Roger Price, Kat had learned that a number of on-site staff also claimed to have heard sounds of distress underground: those of animals and even children trapped on the other side of walls. The reports had encouraged the archaeological team to explore further south.

What the geophysicist had told her had never gone public. According to him, a world-famous sedimentologist, a palaeontologist, a palynologist who'd been examining the soils, two geophysicists who'd mapped below the surface to detect new artefacts, and a cultural archaeologist who'd been identifying and interpreting the manmade tools they'd found in the Grand Chamber, had each encountered the ghostly sounds at some point in their work. Roger knew them all well. They were scientists and academics and not prone to spreading stories about unexplained phenomena.

And if Helene's recordings could be trusted, the caves of Brickburgh had been issuing strange sounds long before Matt Hull discovered the original fissure.

Eventually, surely, there would be a theory citing natural causes for the disturbances. There always was. But there was a story here that could be printed. She wasn't going to allude to drug farms or red people or anything Steve was pawing at her to chase up. But a piece on the eerie sounds from ancient graves might just bring in another billable assignment.

Over the phone, she'd discussed Roger's story with Sheila and her editor had been intrigued by the idea of 'ghosts' within the caves. Sheila had suggested Kat research a supplementary story to the main feature: a nod to Tutankhamen's curse in the Valley of the Kings.

By a pure-chance meeting, Helene had put her within reach of a soundtrack; they could play the soundfiles on the magazine's website with a link to the story and credit her brother. Helene might like that.

Kat had sent Helene a message: *Was lovely to have met you. Next time you are down this way do get in touch.* She also reminded Helene to let her have copies of her brother's recordings from an FTP site.

Helene had readily agreed. And once the article about the cave's 'ghosts' was done, Kat would consign the cave and all of its strange sounds and curious tragedies to the past.

As for Matt Hull's situation, she'd unobtrusively keep an eye on that front but do nothing rash. Steve, she'd keep on a leash.

Kat turned in early. But when her alarm sounded the following morning it quickly became apparent that her involvement with Redstone Cross and with all that was piped, whispered and shrieked beneath that hilly earth, was unwilling to remain at the safe remove she wished for.

Kat. They're back. They paid me another visit. I'm sick of this shit. Just sick of it. So I'm getting out, yeah? It's gone too far.

I'm being watched, yeah. All the time now. There's a car . . . I know it's them. It's getting worse.

The message had been left on her phone in the early hours, and Kat picked it up later that morning. Matt Hull had also sent photographs.

I swore . . . I swore that next time they tried this shit, I'd be ready. I'd get a picture. And I did. I got one of them looking through the kitchen window.

I tore out into the garden and I caught one of them running away.

This is sick. So I'm taking off. Clearing out. I'm going to my brother's in Somerset for a bit. I won't be far from my boy. I swear, anything happens to any of us then you know who's behind this.

It's them at Redstone. At the farm. Yeah, I've said it. Something's up with them again. I don't know if it's because I spoke to you. I don't know. I don't know. How would they know who you are? Unless they saw . . . when you came over. But why now? Nothing for over a year and now I've got red handprints on my door again.

Don't bother with the police. I've called the law. This time I did. And one of them came round and saw what I've sent you. He said he'd look into it. I've heard nothing since.

While he was here, he said it was a prank. Prank? What kind of prank, I said to him? Painting yourself red, yeah, and looking in a window. What's that? That's sick. It's threatening behaviour because of what I know.

Has anything been stolen, any damage to your property? That's what he asked me. I mean, what's that? It's not about that. And there are prints on the window and door. Get the prints, I told him. Get those prints. He never did. No one's been since. I've heard nothing.

I'm sorry. Sorry for bothering you with this. It's my problem, not yours. Because of what I've seen, you know, from the air. And what I did for them. They know that I know, yeah. They won't leave it alone, not ever. They were never going to. I've been kidding myself. But everyone's got a limit. I've reached mine. I'm sick of it. Sick of this shit. I'm in serious —

The message reached the end of its permitted duration and cut off.

Matt Hull had made the call at 2 a.m. He'd been agitated, breathless and frightened but trying to mask his fear with the bravado that follows confrontation.

Kat was glad her phone had been recharging in the kitchen: it wasn't a call she'd have wanted to entertain alone, half-asleep, after midnight.

At 10 a.m. she called him. He didn't pick up. She left a brief message on his voicemail then transferred his picture attachments to her laptop and enlarged them.

The first picture was of a small window, set deeply inside white walls, above an untidy kitchen sink. But beyond the glass appeared the murky suggestion of a human face. A woman's face, Kat thought.

Definitely a head with the skin and features thickly coated in a red daub: a cosmetic lined by the worn skin beneath and smeared about a pair of wide, horridly white eyes. A hand with thin fingers had pressed itself against the window pane, the palm lighter in colour, the nails unpleasantly extending from three fingers.

The second picture was blurred. Taken as the subject turned from the glass, perhaps after seeing the flash of Matt's camera inside the kitchen. But he'd raced outside his cottage to confront the intruder, touching the screen as he moved; he'd also uploaded a blurred picture of his own scrawny legs, another of a foot splayed on the wood-effect lino of his kitchen floor. But outside, in the rear garden, against a background of night and amidst evidence of a peeling shed, three large planters on patio stones and the glimmer of a washing line, ran a single human figure.

The picture had been taken from behind the intruder as she'd retreated, providing a glimpse of a body darkened by paint: the ankles, knees, hips and elbows all defined, if not pronounced. Between the spiky joints the corresponding limbs were narrow, the buttocks pinched and creased above the top of the thighs. A rack of ribs was discernible below prominent scapulae and the arms were cast out for balance.

The figure seemed aged, or suffering from an eating disorder, perhaps an addiction. But an impression of a certain daintiness to its flit across the small lawn was unpleasantly at odds with the fearsome sight of bemired skin and emaciation.

What Kat found most unnerving was the wild hair, stretched out into lengths and oiled into a series of haphazard spikes and tufts. Above such narrow shoulders it made the head grotesquely large.

The visitor to Matt's home was horrible. Surely the police would investigate such a reprehensible intrusion, one solely intended to frighten a resident. What other reason could account for such behaviour? The woman, if it was a woman, was surely mentally ill.

At the very least she should call Rick, her contact in police community liaison. And yet she found herself hesitating and sufficiently nervous to feel sick. The 'red people' existed.

At least Matt was leaving Redhill and not before time. He would be in less danger in Somerset with his brother. She refused to accept that his son was in jeopardy at his mum's in the harbour town. And maybe Matt was right and it wasn't her problem.

It did resemble a prank, a horrible one, but a prank all the same. It wasn't as if Matt was a vulnerable woman stalked at home: he was a grown man being menaced by a horrible clown-thing covered in red paint. He was paranoid and frightened and that was contagious. *But who wouldn't be in that situation?*

Eventually, Kat found herself not wanting to think about it at all, particularly not his allusions to her being observed at his home by the same people who'd appeared in his yard and left red handprints on his door.

But by the afternoon, staying silent about Matt's plight had felt irresponsible, it nagged and twisted her. Should she have already reported what he had seen from the air to the police or to Sheila? The two people ambushed beside their tent: had that really happened?

Because Matt saw her as insurance, he'd talked about her contacting the police if something happened to him, but not otherwise. She didn't want to be insurance but why wasn't he answering his phone? Feeling sick and drained, she soon half-convinced herself that she was now implicated in whatever he was mixed up in. But what was that?

Kat called Steve at home. He didn't pick up so she tried his mobile. He didn't answer straightaway but while she was leaving a message he called her.

His breathless, excited voice burst through her phone's speaker. 'Babe, hiya. Don't ask where I am, yeah? Just don't ask.'

He was outside, she knew that much. Wind buffeted the phone's microphone, suggesting open sky. Gortex rustled near his mouthpiece.

'You're outside.' She didn't say any more but her body tensed.

'Just passed the dig and on my way to Redstone Cross.'

'No.'

'What?'

'No. I don't want you to be . . . don't want you to go up there.'

'Don't fuss. It's cool. I'm not going to do anything.'

13

One by one, the black sheep stopped walking when Steve did and stared at him. The posture of their bulbous forms suggested expectation. Their thin legs were set apart and braced for his next move. He imagined they were waiting for him to speak and was reminded of the sudden interaction with strange children: patient, insistent kids, instinctively following an adult. Their presence made him tense.

Ninety minutes of breathless weaving had elapsed before he reached this impenetrable tangle of brushwood and blackberry vines, untamed between the boughs of the unappealing wood. Up across the valley floor he'd crossed spongy turf, turning marshy at the very foot of the valley; following a stream that often disappeared underground, its hypnotic trickling on his left side.

Most of the animals were rams, their expressions impassive, though almost noble in a peculiar way, with long muzzles like the faces in Phoenician bas reliefs, and powerful grey horns curled into crowns.

He was an interloper here, an intruder, and he imagined that other eyes might be upon him too. Maybe the landscape itself was aware of his passage. The suspicion was hard to suppress and contributed to his unease. A drop in temperature and the dimming light further eroded his resolve to continue.

The sun's descent had been swallowed by a sagging ceiling of dark cloud, an underbelly compressing earthbound shadows into swathes of gloom. Along the horizon, where the sun remained visible, the light was intense: white, yet smoky and brushed with sulfur, a nuclear explosion casting out fiery skirts from end to end of the visible horizon.

And from the darkening cliffs these horned creatures had tottered out to him, their bellies swinging, black muzzled, Satan-horned. Nine pairs of beautiful feminine eyes had immediately fixed upon him.

They'd been positioned like sentries on the buttresses of rock at Whaleham Point, near the Brickburgh Caves. Black shapes standing on their spindly, ebony limbs above rock faces. The distance between them and him had been hard to judge, but they'd appeared effortlessly poised upon narrow grooves in the cliffs, as wide as a human foot, worn by generations of hooves.

He'd taken photographs of the sheep before the celestial backdrop, their horned silhouettes in the foreground. Eerie pictures that could have served for a cover of an old Witchfinder Apprentice album: a landscape at dusk, the very tones of the artist's mind. Perhaps the very atmosphere accounted for why Willows settled here.

The soles of his boots were now claggy with dung. Every square foot of land seemed beset by leathery plums that squashed and adhered to his feet. The inside of each calf was shit-smeared. Hasty, he'd been hasty. Not entirely prepped for this one-man mission either, if he were honest with himself; he'd left his flat late. That grated.

Kat hadn't wanted him to come here, but she'd laugh at him if he bailed now. He'd bailed on a lot of stuff since meeting her. She inspired him but just as quickly identified the flaws in his designs. He hated that and was now ignoring her repeated calls. He planned to BS her about there being no signal on his phone.

Steve looked down the valley and was struck again by the fact that although he lived not far from this area, and had done for most of his life, he was unfamiliar with this part of the coast. He hailed from the other side of Divilmouth, twelve miles south, and had never walked here. It made him question his desire to escape a place more unfamiliar to him than he'd ever imagined. He didn't know anyone who'd walked the coast from Divilmouth to Brickburgh. This place was truly overlooked. Had it not been for the cave, no one would ever have come here at all.

Odd, he'd always thought the countryside odd too. No one about. No one visibly working. British flags on bags of carrots and the odd tractor holding up traffic were the only evidence of activity in the countryside. And here was this epic silence about land so open and exposed and inactive but fenced off, in which these four-legged creatures ambled freely and chewed and shat. What was the point of it?

Respect to Helene: she'd been fit in more ways than one. Her lungs must have been bellows to get her lean body up the valley slope. She'd walked all the way here from the north banks of Divilmouth. He'd not covered half that ground and was spent. She'd then walked all the way back to her car once she'd been caught trespassing.

A brief consideration of the young woman's legs and slender hips consumed him.

A swimmer's body.

Stop it.

Kat was too clever not to have noticed his amorous fascination with Helene. He'd deliberately sat near her in the café. And though hating himself for the thought, he'd pretty much seen Kat as a hindrance from then on.

Some women just hung around in his head; Helene was one of them. Before he'd uploaded his exhibition pictures to the FTP site for Kat, he'd also made sure to extract the incriminating images. Photos he'd surreptitiously taken of Helene at the exhibition that were now hidden on his hard drive. There was an absolute gem featuring her bent over, her skinny-fit jeans taut as she read a sign before a case of bones.

But this was no good. The sheep had to fuck off now. He needed to press through the woods beneath the buildings at Redstone Cross Farm. Willows's homestead was somewhere on the far side of these trees. The ground was steep inside the woods and he was at a loss as to how to get through. But his current upward trajectory should put him near the middle of the longest buildings as indicated on the satellite map. This next part of the operation called for stealth, not an entrance heralded by a herd of livestock. The situation was not without humour and he couldn't wait to tell Kat later, though she'd probably blow her stack.

As if arriving with a solution, a ram clopped nearer. Ashamed of his fear, Steve stiffened. He tried to remember if rams charged and butted with their horns. *Or was that goats?*

The creature's muzzle was stringed with snot. Three of its fellows followed the leader and ambled over too. The lead sheep bleated at Steve before disappearing into the trees. They knew the way through. It was as if they were guiding him now.

Ponies. They were staring at him. Black ponies with stocky legs and small muscular bodies, short heads, broad, bushy tails. Four of them, standing a few feet from the open door of a barn. Save one strip of light in the roof where the tiles were long gone, the interior of the building was pitch. The whole area stank of dung, compost and urine.

Once out of the woods this was the first building he'd found: a shack tilting in the corner of a muddy paddock. Constructed from vertical planks of wood, the exterior faded, buckling near the earth. The ground was churned red mud and black loaves of dung. Not a blade of grass had survived.

This was not what he expected to find: he'd thought a rock star's farm would be smarter.

Farther along the lane, between the barn and another three scruffy buildings, the verge was overgrown and tangled with thorny vines. Dandelion stalks protruded *en masse*.

When he looked in the opposite direction towards

Redstone Crossroads, another roof and part of the upper storey of a dirty house were partially visible between unmanaged trees and an unruly hedgerow.

An ancient stone wall before the building occasionally showed between cascades of ivy and wisteria. A metal gate closed off the road a short distance from the house: the barrier must have been open when Helene visited. And she'd just wandered in.

While the ponies watched him in silence, Steve knelt down and took pictures. Hugging the side of the road, his ears straining, he then moved towards the trio of grey buildings ahead. The sheep were headed in that direction too; he was following them again, or being led.

Green vegetation, grey slate, rusticated wood and tarmac, dark-red soil; the colours of the world had been reduced here. And no one cleared the animal dung. Wheels had visibly compressed it into huge discs on the tarmac. Tyre treads offered the only sign of recent human occupation. Take away the farm animals and the place was derelict.

Steve crossed the lane to the other side, his head down. He found a gap in the long hedgerow to peer at an apple orchard.

From that side of the road he continued to a clutch of structures with tiled roofs, the largest being the oldest and the second wooden barn he'd seen since emerging from the trees. The walls were suffocated by untamed ivy. Wisterias contorted like pythons to the guttering. No vehicles.

The two small stone buildings next to the wooden barn were single-storey, with greening wooden doors, their padlocks rusted. A single window at the top of each gable was thick with dust and green algae on the outside. The panes of glass dimly reflected branches from the unruly trees. Even if he could reach that high he'd never see anything inside without an interior light.

A concrete extension jutted from one end of the barn at a right angle, its white stucco milky-green with sap. A window at head height was so dirty it only revealed metal bars, painted white and cemented into the sill. An ancient ceramic sign on the door read: DANGEROUS FLOOR: DO NOT ENTER. Steve took pictures.

Where the trees of the orchard thinned on the other side of the road, he found a third barn, also slouching. There were no doors. A black opening gaped at the front and the black sheep had gathered outside the miserable structure. A metal gate, once barring the paddock, lay on its side beside an overgrown drainage ditch. There was nothing else to see unless he broke a padlock. The place was impoverished.

Beyond where the sheep congregated the air lightened, suggesting an open expanse. That must be his 'airstrip'. Steve called himself a twat.

The lane continued further past the peeling, ivy-smothered buildings then turned. Untidy hedges curved with it. According to Google, fields and a continuation of the boundary wood moved eastwards towards a final building: the one with the newer roof he'd seen on Google Earth.

He wondered if he should check the 'airstrip' but if he left the hedgerow and ventured into open space he'd be more visible. *But to whom?* Helene had met two 'rough-looking posh people' with dogs. Maybe the couple lived here with old Tony Willows and that was that. End of story.

No quarry had been marked on the online maps or the most recent Ordnance Survey map he'd purchased. Steve assumed that whatever Helene's brother had mic'd up must be somewhere further down and beyond this knackered, potholed road.

Feeling more confident, he walked back on himself, towards what must be the farmhouse. Using the last of the afternoon light, he'd get a few pictures and take off via the sheep track in the woods. Case closed.

Dogs, massive dogs, were still barking and leaping in the road outside the scruffy house. If he moved they'd see him and come scampering. He'd never outrun hounds that rangy, that eager for chase.

He'd been stuck behind a wall for thirty minutes and counting. His pulse hadn't stopped thumping in his ears and surely his heartbeat had been audible outside his body. Jerky, panicky compulsions had periodically urged him to burst from where he'd hidden, to try for the dismal pony paddock. But he'd stayed put.

One, two, three, four, five . . . no, six vehicles had since entered the farm and parked beside the farmhouse. Tony Willows had guests: people who weren't saying much to each other besides a few muffled greetings.

From as close as he thought safe, Steve had quickly inspected the farmhouse before needing to hide fast. Tucked away from the lane and smothered by tree limbs growing over its roof, the building was the kind of place a person might happen across in an American swamp.

White paint peeled from wood panelling, leaving patches of the building entirely green with sap from the encroaching plants. Grass sprouted over the porch like a green wave upon a jetty. Furniture lay discarded, spongy and mottled upon the wild lawn, the grass broken by numerous lumps of discarded machinery: car parts or farm equipment, he hadn't been able to tell. Stiff, weathered articles of clothing had hung for long enough on that washing line to be unrecognisable. And yet so many people had come here in big expensive cars.

Such a state of disrepair was inexplicable unless the musician had fallen on hard times. And why the enduring seclusion? Willows was largely forgotten now but had the world been such a terrible place for him that this was preferable? A mystery Steve was unlikely to unravel, but while he'd been hidden his drug theory had petered into rags of smoke. This was hardly the palace of a drug lord.

The last time Steve had been poised to beat a rapid retreat out the same way he'd come in, a man with a thin ponytail had bounded from the scruffy house and turned towards the metal gate. So taken aback by the man's sudden appearance, Steve had almost spoken out loud and recited his apologetic excuses for trespassing. But he'd not been spotted. The man in the oily overalls had not been looking for an intruder and was only intent on opening the gate to let the vehicles in.

Steve had backed further away from the house, his spine scraping through verdure spilling over a wall. Once he'd reached a collapsed section of masonry, he'd slipped over the weed-smothered rubble and crouched in thick grass. A cascade of ivy now concealed him.

Rumbling and purring cars had filled the lane. And from the old house had come the excitable dogs. Out of sight, a slamming of doors and a scuffling of feet and claws on the road surface had ensued. A film of fear-sweat had frozen over Steve's body and not yet thawed.

When the large Volvo 4x4 had parked level with his position, he'd withdrawn deeper into the foliage, climbing into the broken house's unkempt garden, encircled by a slate wall, where he'd remained trapped.

The three dogs had kept up their running back and forth on the tarmac and the man with the ponytail had remained by the gate, smoking a cigarette.

Due to the length of the grass, he'd only seen the occupants of the cars from above the waist but they'd seemed ordinary enough: of mixed gender, mostly middle-aged and elderly and smartly dressed as if arriving for a celebration. Slowly and quietly they'd filed through a door above the sagging porch, like people entering a church.

A few minutes later, everything at the farm changed, the activity, the very atmosphere and Steve forgot the cold, the damp and the cramp in his legs.

His first reaction to the sound was sheer confusion. Because what kind of gathering would make such a noise and to what end? It wasn't exactly singing but suggested a communal vocal endeavour.

From inside the house came a sustained, high-pitched tone, formed of many voices raised in unison, rising and falling as the participants caught their breath before resuming the odd chant.

Had he not been trespassing and crouching behind a broken wall he might have found the ululation amusing. And though he was unable to decipher a word, one voice soon raised itself inside the building and dominated the others. A man's voice. An elderly voice. Outside in the lane, the dogs bayed an accompaniment.

The thump of feet upon the lane that followed seemed to stop all movement inside Steve's body: footsteps accompanied by the timpani of dog claws on tarmac, closing on his position in the weeds.

The thin, bearded man with the ponytail reappeared, crowded by the excited dogs, all hurrying down the lane as if towards the nearest agricultural building. The man entered the pony paddock. From there he was soon leading the smallest animal into the road. The other three ponies followed, their heads nodding disconsolately before stopping at the verge.

Cantering sideways the pony in the lane shied away from the leaping dogs. The man holding the bridle struggled. What Steve could see of his face was pale, perhaps taut with nervous excitement.

A sound of feet scuffed the wooden boards of the sloping porch and Steve turned to peer at the house. His view was part-obscured by the vines of the boundary wall, though not enough to prevent him from seeing what came out of the back door. A single file, a solemn parade, of naked people. Not a soul wore a stitch of clothing.

These people were much changed in another way too and for some time Steve neither blinked nor inhaled, because each person was coloured red from head to foot.

The red people entered the lane and walked unhurriedly in his direction, their progress accelerating a collision of possible connections that made him grow cold.

Tony Willows's last album, Hark! Hear the Red Folk Sing. *Red Folk.*

Iron oxide had coated the human remains found in the Brickburgh cave, on and off, for sixty thousand years.

All too much to be a coincidence with the Grand Chamber no more than three miles east of where he crouched on Willows's knackered old farm.

A hippy, folksy thing then? Must be. Pagan folk music thing... a tradition.

Forget the drug farm, this was a weird backwoods Devon thing: an old man with some influence enacting old practices.

His festivals from the past. A relic of those. Must be. But harmless. Don't freak out.

Willows had fried his brains with LSD in the Seventies. Maybe there was no coming back for Tony. Sure didn't look like it.

But the campers Matt Hull had seen from the air?

A sudden imagined scenario of himself surrounded by the grotesque red figures made Steve deeply uneasy.

Along the potholed tarmac the red folk walked barefoot. Sagging bellies, shrivelled genitalia, wasted breasts: most of the people were getting on. Pale bluish tattoos, not completely covered by the dye, were visible on some arms and legs. But only when the last few figures reached his position did he spot the objects they clutched in their scarlet hands.

All but two of the figures held a dark rock. Two bald, overweight men trailed spears with stone heads. *Weapons.* Not something Steve wanted to see in this context. Those that had hair had teased and lathered it outwards, stiff with the red stain. They all looked a sight, they looked a fright.

A tiny impulse bade him take a picture, but he dared not even twitch. If anyone in that ghastly procession peered to the side of the road they'd see him. Steve pretended he was made of stone.

As they ambled to the pony in the lane, the scratchily bearded face of the man who held the animal became solemn. His dogs leaped joyously about the red people. The naked figures stroked the pony, caressing the shivering beast with their hands while uttering the curious fluting sounds. Red dye was wiped upon its flanks, ribs and thick neck.

Skittish, the pony's visible eye went big, white and wild. Steve knew how it felt.

And on to the far buildings the strange red procession continued, in single file, led by the man with the paint-smeared pony.

From a distance Steve finally managed to take pictures with the flash disabled. There was still enough light to catch something. Using the zoom he enlarged his view of the gathering, watched them enter the open doors of the largest barn. Inside they went, heads bowed and arms rising as if in greeting.

This was no longer about what he could find out about missing people or drugs: the day was now all about Steve's unrestrained curiosity. His fear on the wane, he shivered with excitement. One half of his mind, driven by instinct, still shrieked and begged him to run away fast. Another part, the one that drove him to surf in high winds and angry breakers, or to dive from cliffs into the sea, bade him tarry a while longer. This place was too damn weird to abandon now.

A reckless impetus drove him through the long grass of the garden, past a sodden sofa, across the moving planks of the porch and right up to the doorway of the old house.

Little had changed inside for some time. Steve doubted it had been cleaned in a while either.

Just inside the door was a large kitchen area connected to a dim dining room crowded with furniture, unclean kitchenware, piles of boxes and building materials. A room reeking of animals and stale grease. Dog biscuits spilled from steel bowls laid on newspaper, pellets that stuck to the shit on his shoes.

Beyond the dining room, the hallway was cluttered with buckets, tools, garden implements, more newspapers. A single lightbulb was lit behind the front door, the top third of the door crowned by a fantail of stained glass.

Piles of coats and clothes sloped across the table in the dining area.

All of those people had come inside this shitty kitchen and taken their clothes off, before painting themselves red.

Steve took pictures.

The dye they'd used for their bodies was stored in four plastic buckets, the kind that DIY stores sold, filled with wood stain.

Confronted by the haphazard domestic arrangements and the electrifying comprehension of being inside someone's house without permission, Steve returned to his senses. He'd seen enough and he turned to head out. Maybe a quick recce of the barn down the lane and then home-time while the light was still good. He had a torch if needed.

But Steve failed to take a single step in the direction of the back door.

There had been many times in his life when regret nearly disabled him; when a terrible disbelief in his own impetuous actions cleared his mind of all thoughts save a realisation that there had always been other choices, other ways of doing things. He just rarely chose the more considered alternatives. These days he experienced the epiphany less, because he was getting older and took fewer risks, but he felt it again now and powerfully too: that mixture of defeat, near haplessness and self-loathing, tinged with nausea.

When he heard the dogs' claws and the scuffle of boots on the path before the porch, this deep sense of regret peppered his forehead with sweat. Only way out for him now was further *inside*.

Before he could think it through, Steve ran across the

kitchen, wheeling around the impediments upon the floor. Inside the adjoining hallway, he ducked through the nearest doorway at his left. And entered a parlour.

Within the moment he had to establish what he'd fled into, he thought the light fitting too ornate for the chaotic space: a bulky shade of red-stained glass, unlit, hanging over a room cramped with heavy furniture.

Dark antique chairs and a settee piled high with clothes and papers choked the floor. Save the big curtained bay window, the entire wall-space was festooned with framed photographs that reflected the thin light escaping the hall.

A dresser was filled with broken stones. A vast fireplace gaped and seemed to exude, like some horrid mouth, a reek of dog, engine oil and a vinegary, sebaceous human odour. But only at the conclusion of his hurried appraisal did Steve catch sight of the wizened form sunk inside the easy chair before the windows. A hunched thing, a wheelchair collapsed against the armrest. So dark had the dye made her shrunken flesh that he'd not seen the occupant when he came in. Now he gaped.

A patterned tray of mostly uneaten food lay beside the figure's lumpy red feet. Asleep, or worse, its eyes were closed. It was a woman. Breasts shrivelled like large raisins gave the gender away. The head was mostly hairless.

Behind the wall, the kitchen filled with dog claws on lino, canine whines, barks and the muted thump of booted feet.

Steve performed a quick one-eighty and dropped behind the open door. Then pulled it towards himself until the door's edge met the armrest of the long sofa. A rustle and a thump sounded as his tailbone struck the skirting board, but there he squatted, squeezing his jaws closed.

All of his concentration and will were required to calm his breathing, the air whistling through his nostrils forming tiny screams. He dearly wished that he was a smaller man so the top of his head would not be visible.

Directly outside the room, a man shouted 'Stay!' To Steve it sounded as if the dogs were jumping up the walls of the hall.

Steve's last act was to slide a musty towel from the back of the sofa to cover his head, which he pressed into the sofa's bristly rear panel. His body behind the door, his towelled head jammed behind the sofa looking down at a scruffy carpet rimed with grey dust, he didn't know how visible he'd be to whoever entered the parlour.

The very presence of the man in the room ignited the inside of Steve's skull into a storm of white terror. He even wondered, stupidly, if he should stand up and apologise for being inside the house.

How he stayed still, he wasn't sure.

He was unable to see what was happening inside the room, only hearing the man's feet on the floor and seemingly too near his head. Mercifully, the dogs had done the man's bidding and waited outside where they whined. They'd have sniffed him out for sure. But as each long second dragged itself through an awful stasis, with his consciousness taut as a snare drum's skin, Steve anticipated the fall of a hand upon his shoulder, a barked challenge or the sudden yanking away of the towel and a horrible exposure.

Instead, he heard the crack of knee joints. Then the man muttered softly on the far side of the room. Steve presumed he was speaking to the old thing in the armchair. 'Now. Time, mother. They're here. The children are waiting. Come now. That's it. That's it.'

There followed a snapping metallic sound and the noise of a spring extending, which Steve understood to be the unfolding of the wheelchair.

A startled cry came next and a sound resembling a child's sob when the woman's rest was disturbed. Then she took to whimpering as if roused from an awful dream.

The man quieted her with cooing sounds from the roof of his mouth. A strange interaction muffled by the density of the ancient upholstery Steve hid behind, but his shock still mingled with a heightened sense of the absurd.

'She's come close,' an elderly voice announced. 'The den is full. She's not alone.'

'Yes, yes. It's time.'

'Up so far. So far again. We must respond.' The voice was cracking and frail but the woman was well spoken, her tone deeper than Steve expected from a person of such advanced years.

'Yes, mother.'

'Their bellies yawn. Are we safe?'

'Of course. Everything's okay.'

'You know what they bay for. What they want. And there's outside getting inside again.'

'No. Everything's fine. Just the red here. I'm going to lift you now. We can't wait any longer or they'll be through . . . with us. We don't want that.'

'It's in the air. The outside. You wouldn't know it.'

'There. That's it, sit.'

Steve heard the sound of springs compressing, the air squeezed from a cushion.

The old woman sounded frightened. 'Around . . . here. They've come in. I can tell.'

'Yes, it's all open. The air is alive. We're only waiting for you. We'd never start without you.'

'But we're safe? The gate?'

'Yes, mother. Just friends here. Only the red.'

'No one else?'

'No one else.'

'Then I must have a face to greet the red.'

'I have it right here.'

The sound of the chair's wheels and the crowding pack of excited dogs moved away from the odoriferous pall in which Steve crouched. Beyond the interior wall he heard the man and his mother navigate the porch.

Slowly, Steve raised his head and peered around himself, half-expecting a trap, their leaving the house mere pretence.

When he finally straightened his spine a picture frame rattled behind his shoulders. He turned his head, afraid he might knock something from the wall, and peered into a dust-filmed photograph of Witchfinder Apprentice.

Sideburns, long hair, two bearded musicians in a folk rock ensemble of eight, posed like kings around a mediaeval banquet. A table heaped with platters of fowl, fruits and bread, mimicking a classical still-life painting.

Already balding, a young Tony Willows was visible at the head of the table, glaring as if with disapproval at the frolics the record company had imposed upon his band for a gatefold sleeve. The picture was taken from the cover artwork of *Below the Green*. Steve had bought a second-hand copy from Amazon.

As he came out from behind the sofa, he listened intently for any sign of movement within the house.

Nothing.

He turned and took photographs of the wall. Lots of strange figures were up there wearing suede jackets with wide lapels and bell-bottom trousers. Arms circled shoulders in pictures so brown with age the subjects seemed to have origins in the American Wild West.

The band had also favoured rural settings for press shots and often stood at gates or sat on fences, or posed before rock formations. Some of the latter might have been the Tors on Dartmoor. There were other pictures of the band playing live in monks' vestments and again in masks with long noses. *Hippy Slipknot*, Steve thought and nearly smiled.

Most of the photographs covering that wall of the dreadful parlour were of the band playing live, standing before mic stands, their fiddles and guitars held high. A wall of folk. The band had been huge for a couple of years. He could see that from the crowd sizes at the festivals: Knebworth, The Isle of Man. And before the stages swayed oceans of handlebar moustaches and girls with dead-straight hair. Cheesecloth, denim and prairie dresses: young people who'd adored the thin musicians in their pointy hats standing on stages strewn with black wires.

Dozens more pictures above the fireplace were similarly faded and dust-filmed: lineup changes, female backing singers that were dead spits for Karen Carpenter, Tony standing beside a Jag, all the guys dressed as Morris dancers. Later in their career there was evidence of berets and trilby hats, white waistcoats and matching flared trousers, sunglasses, when it all went a bit Toto.

Steve listened again for sounds within the house. He held his breath. *Nothing.*

He took in the wall beside the vast wooden dresser. There was a gold disc for *Before the King of Bedlam*. The glass was cracked and the frame strewn with cobwebs. Another gold disc for *Gallow Ballads*, a silver for *Thin Len and Choker Lottie*. A poster for the *Run with Hounds* tour, supported by The Incredible String Band, 1972. Steve took more pictures.

He daren't dither but a quick inspection of the dresser confirmed that the shelves were crowded with stones and bones: artefacts. Reasonable to presume their origin was the Brickburgh caves. Flint hand-axes, tooled bones and spearheads; he'd seen the same at the exhibition. Two Venus figures took pride of place on the top shelf, naked, bulbous and beast-headed. Dull clay bodies absorbing the weak light seeping from the hall's solitary bulb.

He left the parlour. Glancing at the wood-panelled wall that rose with the stairs into the darkness of the first floor, his eyes alighted upon a framed photograph.

A black and white picture featuring a line of men and women in a field, the sun shining on a wide sea behind them. They were naked save for the crude masks. Headdresses crafted to resemble lions or dogs or something like that. Steve wasn't sure.

A second picture outside the kitchen gave further evidence of outdoor shenanigans from mad crusties back in the day. He squinted to better see these women with flowers in their hair, their bared bodies painted dark. All were laughing and tiptoeing around a big dog-thing made from straw, erected in a field. One of the girls held a champagne bottle that looked heavy at the end of her slim wrist.

The ceremonies on his land. The rumours in Divilmouth pubs not so far-fetched after all. *Fuck you, Kat.* Excuses for getting pissed and screwing groupies by the look of it. Posho rock stars living it up through a decade of strikes, IRA bombs and factory closures.

The pictures were a bit sinister too, the age of the images not solely accounting for the unpleasant impression given by these rural antics. Steve really disliked the headgear. All of the people in the fields had their faces concealed by grotesque masks. Wispy hair drifted beneath the snouty and horned concealments.

And what on earth were they enacting while naked and daubed in scarlet body paint in the colour picture? That was set at a tilt before the kitchen doorway. In that scene a dozen people wearing doggish masks surrounded a ram, its horns garlanded with wild flowers. Big wobbly canine heads atop pale English shoulders, red faces peering through the mouthpieces: ten women, two men.

Tony had liked naked girls around him: that was obvious. Girls painted like savages seemed to be the norm. He still favoured the practice too. There was continuity with the present, albeit with adjustments to the age range if the shrivelled woman in the chair served as evidence.

Fuck's sake.

A firelit procession somewhere underground came next on the wall of past shames. A cave maybe. Animal faces and naked cocks, exposed nubile breasts, beer bellies and black body hair slathered in red paint: people walking past a rock wall painted in the style of the Grand Chamber of Brickburgh. *Where was that taken, and when?*

Steve took his own pictures.

At the threshold of the hall, he paused and made sure the coast was clear out back. He heard the wind in the treetops and a distant rhythmic squeak of the wheelchair's rotating wheels, growing quieter.

He stepped out.

No dogs.

But what was that? A tremor? An earth tremor? A grumble beneath his feet, the house, the earth.

It passed away.

With his head down he made it to the garden path. Peered down the lane.

No way. Steve raised his camera and zoomed in on the spectacle in the middle of the private road. At an angle, he could still see the bearded man from behind. His body was also now stained red from his thin neck to his bony feet. His progress was slow and made with measured pomp, displaying a regal absurdity in the manner in which he pushed the elderly woman in the wheelchair.

Though it was obscured by one of the man's arms and his back, Steve was still able to determine that the old woman's head was covered by a bulky and hairy headdress. When she turned her head to one side, almost as if she were trying to look behind her chair and at Steve, through his zoom he glimpsed a horrid black muzzle, detailed with yellowing teeth. *A wolf from a pantomime too scary for kids.*

"Then I must have a face to greet the red". That's what she'd said when Steve had been hiding.

Meet who? The red sickos in the barn? The "children"?

Steve pulled back. Beneath his feet the earth growled again as if a restless giant had just stirred in some cold barrow.

He pushed his head out. The odd couple continued towards their destination: the barn. They seemed unconcerned by the possibility of what appeared to be a freak earthquake.

Like the inside of a furnace seen from a distance, the mouth of the agricultural building now glowed red. And across the darkening, overgrown farm, the couple walked as if to an open mouth, one as fiery as their own bodies.

Fuck's sake.

Steve knelt down and took a picture, catching the watery

grey dusk and fire-flickering gloom. He could blow it up later. And with the doorway so ruddy with light now, he'd chance a couple more shots of the barn. He'd go a bit closer and then split. He'd not be far from the pony paddock and he could slip through there easy. Luck was on his side tonight. So preoccupied were these people with their twisted red shit, it was like he'd been invisible to them.

This decision to linger became irrevocable when his nose detected a familiar scent: cannabis. On the southerly breeze, dope fumes were being blown back toward the house. Hashish. Marijuana. A citrusy, sausage-meat blend of something potent and intensely pungent billowed across the farm. A lot of dope was getting smoked too. If he could smell it from this far away, the fragrance must be literally belching out of that building. It was like those red people were hot-boxing an old barn. Drug farm scenario was back on the table.

Tony, you pervy old fiend.

The man and the elderly woman in the wheelchair disappeared inside the barn. As if to herald their crossing of the threshold, the earth surged again, its vibrations registering through the soles of Steve's boots.

Bent over like a war photographer in a combat zone, he jogged down the lane and paused beside the pony paddock. Crouched, he got off a couple more shots of the doorway in zoom. No one was visible inside the bloodied light of the barn, but sticklike shadows were being cast up the interior walls as if the occupants were prancing about inside.

Steve switched camera mode to film and crept closer. And that's when he became aware of another development: the introduction of a new soundtrack to this surreal evening.

At first he'd thought it was the wind but the fragrant air around him was being moved by little besides a faint breeze. No, it wasn't wind, this was music that he was hearing. Or rather a series of piped notes was now drifting from the direction of the barn.

A new musical direction, Tony?

Steve immediately thought of Helene's recordings, those her brother had made years before: it was definitely the same sound. But louder, bigger, a replication of those subterranean sounds that begged the question: had Helene's brother recorded one of these rituals or whatever *this* was?

The piping's volume increased. Soft and woody but insistent and building to strident as if an orchestra was warming up the recorders to hit the right notes. It would all look eerie on film with the tendrils of smoke drifting from the flashing red interior of the barn.

Steve recorded from the side of the lane until he flinched so hard he nearly fell.

Had he ever heard the sound of a terrified horse before? Maybe, in a film or something, but not one so frightened. The pony's screams of distress projected horribly from the reddish doorway and funnelled up the enclosed lane: cries accompanied by a distant stamp of hooves on stone.

Raised human voices broke into fresh high-pitched whines, in turn transforming into savage shrieks, competing with the pony's. The cacophony was so horrid that Steve hardly noticed the next earth tremor. And he was clueless about what issued the next series of cries. But again, he'd encountered similar on Helene's recordings.

The long howl suggested the wolf. A comparison Steve dropped when the ululating cry descended into a semi-human whine. And then a pair of big cats might have been fighting inside the barn, until the wet growls erupted into apelike screams that twisted again into a sadistic mockery of a human voice. The hideous medley chattered out of the old building and left Steve rigid with a terror he'd not encountered since childhood.

Red light flickered and beat the barn's interior walls. The pony's piteous bellows shot up an octave then abruptly ceased.

Shocked, fearful human sighs rose in group effort.

Wet sounds followed, amidst those of cracking timber, or joints, as something large was torn apart inside that wretched shack.

The rapid jabbering of the aggressor continued, partially impeded by gargles as a wide throat filled with liquid. This final noise muted, then sank as if the animal had returned beneath the ground.

There followed a hushed sound of awe from those gathered inside the building.

The tremors beneath the ground ceased.

On weak legs, Steve turned to leave at precisely the same moment that three dogs bounded from out of the barn. They came at him fast and low, snarling like hounds pouring from the mouth of hell.

Steve had made it as far as the treeline behind the pony paddock when the first dog leaped upon his back.

His face clouded with meat-breath canker and enraged snarls. His mind offered a mental image of a lioness gripping the haunches of a gazelle, and down to his knees he crashed, wet leaves and greasy red soil embracing his tumble. The dog he flung clear.

A second dog seized his forearm with jaws capable of snapping bone like tomato cane. Teeth tore through his coat, his skin stretched taut around the canines before giving way like pastry beneath fork prongs.

Trees, dark sky, nettles and blackberry vines, all of it whirled through his eyes and the inky, dusky air dispersed his hyperventilating breath. Much louder still were the barks and snarls and growls of the dogs, even louder than the foaming of blood between his ears. Here was an urgent desire to destroy him, the only purpose of these hot moments in a realm of soil and yellow teeth.

He clouted a dog's muzzle with his camera. Foamy jaws released his arm. Black gums flashed. A purple tongue curled like a mollusc. In the undergrowth the dog shook its head and tried to sneeze.

Black blood dripped from the cuff of that sleeve. Steve saw the drip-dripping of his own life and sucked in a huge breath. He thought he might cry real tears. He was bitten through. He'd never been bitten by a dog before.

He staggered onwards, going down twice, yet rising to his feet and falling into tree trunks. Careening through scrub he ripped his trousers into sideways mouths. Cold air embraced his balls.

A dog seized his leg, behind the knee. He felt the teeth go right inside his body, slicing fat and piercing muscle. That whole leg bruised to the thigh in a heartbeat. The hound tried to dig its hind legs into the soil to put the brakes on his rout. He dragged it across the ground when its jaws refused to release his leg. Ruffled snout and beady eyes, ears back, it partnered him down the slope between the trees, all four paws skidding.

Another of the hounds took up the wretched colours of his tattered, bleeding forearm. The arm-bone was the lowered shaft of a regimental lance in a massacre. While gripping the exposed pole of his forearm the dog bunched its considerable neck muscles to try and twist him down and onto his face.

Throat. It wants...

He had no speech, no cries save whimpers. Odd words failed to become sentences in his mind. All was darkness and teeth in black mouths that shook meat on the bone. A smell of wet leaves. Mulch and cold air about the thin body of a weary, frightened boy in trouble.

But onwards he dropped, using the slope of the earth and gravity to propel him through the gloaming wood towards the lighter air above the fields below.

I... the pony...

He fell from the treeline and into the dung-bumpy grass. He landed on all fours. Turf sodden with moisture registered through the skin on his knees. His attempts to remove himself from the terrible wet sounds of the hounds' long mouths that gripped his flesh were faltering. His head filled with a light bright and white. He bellowed, pushed on.

This fresh surge of strength raised two dogs completely from the earth. They hung on with their teeth like big leeches. Three were fastened to him now. He could feel another set of teeth grinding against an ankle bone. The backs of his legs were wet. The arse of his trousers was entirely ripped away.

He hurt and kept on hurting but adrenalin pushed him another ten steps out from the treeline where he screamed for help. All three dogs held fast. The pack was wearing him down.

Trained.

Somehow, he still held onto his camera and had it raised above his head like he was wading through water. He brought it down hard on the skull of the dog chewing up his arm. It yelped, closed one eye and staggered sideways.

A human voice bellowed. 'Cunt! Don't you touch my dog!'

Steve looked behind himself, turning his heavy body with a skirt of canine flesh swinging from his limbs. When he saw the line of red people most of his remaining strength leaked out of his legs like warm water.

'Oh, fuck. Oh, fuck,' he said to the sky.

They fanned out, at least a dozen people. Wild, greased hair and intense red faces slowly moved about him, patiently accompanying his insufficient progress into the valley. Like the sheep that had followed him up the slope earlier, the red folk traipsed in silence. And like indifferent animals, the aboriginal horrors were content to survey his terrible sufferings without making any attempt to alleviate them. From the great white orbs of their eyes, he thought he detected excitement at his plight.

Terrible pain washed hotly through his legs, verging on the agony that drains a body white and limp. One foot squelched and he dared not look down. He was slowing, his adrenalin spent. Steve called out for his mother and his voice broke.

The man with the beard stepped forward, came in close. He held a black rock. His ratty face snarled, baring snaggled teeth, a mouth like one of his dogs. An eye was scarred with a milky slash. A sinewy arm punched the black stone into Steve's face.

Crunch.

A tremor jarred Steve's entire head. His sight went out, was all white dots in darkness until half of his vision returned. He saw spit loop from his own mouth. *That scent.* Was he smelling his own brains?

Dogs tugged and tore. A tooth severed some big nerves in a leg, there were pins and needles like he'd never known before and the corresponding foot turned cold, then numb. His balance slid sideways.

Sky, dogs . . . all the red ones watching . . .

Trapped in a delirium of exhaustion, a frantic swirl of thought and memory filled his skull: his mind was objecting to what was happening right now, but refusing to process what *now* meant, or to acknowledge where it was leading. He had odd thoughts that wanted to take him out of himself. He and his cousin wearing matching swimming trunks, running across the sand. They were children, laughing boys. 'Gary, help us out,' he whispered.

There, the sea in the distance . . .

His mother, wearing a brown jumper that he'd not seen in thirty years. A polished wooden brooch of an owl was pinned to the wool. She wiped tears from his freckled cheeks with her thumbs.

I'm down. Mum . . .

Then darkness.

14

andsome and as immaculately presented as ever, Kat's editor clumsily picked around the cabinets of her chic office to locate an additional salve: a bottle of water. Kat never came into her boss's office to cry, but in moments found herself dabbing her eyes with a tissue Sheila provided.

Sheila's glasses blazed in the sunlight lighting up her windows. Only when her eyes were momentarily visible did Kat note her editor's discomfort and assumed, not without prior evidence, that catering for an employee in distress was an unfamiliar activity.

Sheila preferred the 'quiet life'. That was the prevailing opinion at the magazine when Kat began freelancing for *L&S*, seven years earlier. Married to a wealthy man called Adrian, who owned the magazine and kept *L&S* going as a project for his wife, Sheila wasn't difficult as far as bosses went. In fact, she was unfailingly courteous and rarely succumbed to anger. Prone to favouritism maybe, but that tendency had only ever benefited Kat. Sheila had always been deeply impressed with her CV.

Mistaken from the very start, Sheila had assumed that Kat was cut from the same silk as her peer group: an older posho It Girl, who'd led a glamorous life in London before semi-retiring in Devon. A journalist who only continued to keep her hand in as a hobby.

Like so many of the affluent, and Kat had met some seriously wealthy people in her line of work, Sheila's idea of *elsewhere* was lacking. Innumerable and discreet partitions separated her from the ordinary world and the multitude that struggled *out there*. Her name even graced the side of her husband's sixty-foot yacht in Divilmouth. And once Kat had identified Sheila as a conflict-averse socialite and passive control freak, so much about the woman and the periodical made more sense: anyone who threatened Sheila's bubble was anathema. She either pretended they didn't exist, or reached into her extensive social network to outsource the difficulty.

In their professional relationship, Kat had only ever been required to agree with everything that Sheila thought and said. She only ever pitched her ideas to her boss casually, in one-to-one meetings, and only those topics that reinforced Sheila's notions of what was of interest to her world. That was how Kat had prospered at *L&S*.

The discourse the editor maintained in print was directed at those with plenty of disposable income: folks interested in luxury and the leisure opportunities their affluence afforded them. Most of the readership was retired or only resided in the area when using a second home. *L&S* was no place for real news. Nothing could be found in its pages about the multiple local crises in the NHS and Devon's care homes, or the falling wages and paucity of school places, or the lack of infrastructure investment and affordable housing. Those concerns didn't touch the readership.

Subscribers received the publication sealed inside a polythene bag. The magazine's lifespan expired after a few months of idling upon elegant tables in spas, hotels, private dentists and conservatories blessed with panoramic sea views.

Over half of each monthly edition was paid for as advertorial for chi-chi businesses in the Southwest: vast hotels, retirement villages, Michelin-starred restaurants, farm shops, private boarding schools, cruises, wine importers. Kat wrote many of these advertorials: commercial copy dressed up as feature articles. Local interest pieces about notables, cosy histories, wildlife initiatives, charity balls and society news filled what remained of each edition.

Professional survival was about consensus, not creativity, or blue-sky thinking, or rocking the boat, or originality. In Kat's experience, an employee's longevity depended on identifying the key figures in a business who struck the drum, before dancing deferentially to their rhythm.

In light of what Matt Hull dropped on her the night before, before failing to return her calls, and combined with Steve's failure to return her calls or reappear at his flat, when Sheila summoned her to discuss the supplement, Kat's front had slipped for the first time in seven years. But here was also a chance to acquire a second opinion from someone who would know someone, who would know something about Redstone Cross. *Sheila*.

'Well, I really don't know what to make of this, Kat. So much to take in all at once,' Sheila said, peering at one of Matt's pictures on Kat's tablet. Her expression suggested she'd seen half of a worm wriggling in the apple she'd just bitten through.

She looked away from the tablet screen and her concern eventually overrode her distaste. 'Steve first. Where do you think he could be?'

Kat shook her head. 'He always calls back, eventually.'

'He was off on a walk, you say?'

'Not really.' Kat sighed.

Here goes. She then took Sheila through Steve's theory and motivation for taking a 'look around' Tony Willows's farm.

'My word, he is intrepid. I had no idea.' Sheila looked out of the window while she considered the preposterous information she'd just received.

Kat embellished her story with the catalogue of Matt Hull's revelations and grievances about his persecution at the hands of the 'red people'. Finally, she passed her phone to Sheila so that her editor could listen to Matt's recorded message.

'I feel sick with worry, Sheila, for both of them.'

'I can imagine,' the editor said in a neutral tone, though one clearly fringed with the dismay of having to concern herself with the situation.

As a footnote, Kat mentioned the girl she and Steve had met at the exhibition, Helene Brown. Only when she'd described the girl's recordings, adding that her brother went missing, presumably killing himself within two weeks of making his final recordings at Redstone Cross, did Sheila's tone change.

'How simply awful,' she said, though little else and when she spoke again her voice had thinned. 'I can see how a wild imagination might . . .' Her attempt at a reassuring smile was so awkward that the gesture was quickly abandoned. She closed the conversation.

'I have a meeting in five minutes, dear. I'm not even remotely prepared. Can this wait until I've made some calls? If you come back at . . . let's say four thirty, we'll try and get to the bottom of this. I'd also like to show these pictures to someone.'

'Of course.'

'You'll see Steve again. So I don't think you should worry,' Sheila said, swinging her chair left and right to collect papers and to operate her desk mouse: ever Kat's cue to leave. 'The thing is to not get yourself too worked up, dear. Not to let your imagination run riot like our Steve did. I know someone on the force who'll look into this.'

'Thank you, Sheila. I really appreciate it. I'm sorry for bothering you with it.'

'Oh, nonsense. Makes the job a bit more exciting. But keep trying his phone. The cliffs out that way can be . . . a bit tricky.'

15

ony Willows's thematic preoccupations were pre-dominantly derived from M. H. Mason's Ancient English Poems and Ballads, *published in 1908. Some of Mason's verses were, in turn, newer versions of compositions in Francis James Child's* The English and Scottish Popular Ballads *and Thomas Percy's* Reliques of Ancient English Poetry. *Yet almost all of Tony Willows's lyrical output was inspired by the most gruesome and grotesque interpretations in Mason's ballads.*
Wikipedia

Kat unlocked her front door at eight. She'd taken the second meeting with Sheila, at which her 'friend on the force', a detective called Lewis, had been present. Following the editor's summons, the officer had arrived swiftly. That hadn't surprised Kat as her boss's local reach seemed infinite.

After the meeting, Kat had driven to Steve's flat. He'd still not returned so she'd put in an unannounced visit at his parents' vast house in Divilmouth.

As Reg and Delia had been denied contact with their cherished son since the previous evening (apparently he checked in every morning), his mother was already walking the foothills of frantic when Kat rang the doorbell. This served to ease Kat's passage into the six-bedroom mothership.

Reg and Delia had claimed they'd wanted to call Kat but didn't have her number. Although she had been involved with their son for over three years, his parents still had no means of contacting her in an emergency. In a more benign situation, Kat would have spent time analysing the subtext of this communication failure. Instead, she'd extracted their promise to ring round his friends and left.

Kat had written down the names of everyone in the group of men Steve spent so much time with. She didn't have contact details but Reg and Delia knew most of their parents.

Kat's anxious wait beside the phone continued through the evening. By nine, she'd still heard nothing from Detective Lewis, though he'd promised to keep her updated. Earlier he'd patiently, though not without a hint of inappropriate amusement, sat through Kat's retelling of Steve's hunches, Helene's recordings, Mat Hull's stories, his pictures and the recorded message. The pictures Kat had also forwarded to Lewis at his request. He'd told her not to erase Matt Hull's phone message just in case it was 'pertinent'.

The detective had then disappeared to 'ask around' about Steve, as he'd put it. Interestingly, before he left, Lewis claimed to know Willows. He'd been out to his farm several times following a series of break-ins and the theft of some farming equipment. The gang from Plymouth who'd been raiding rural properties in that area had eventually been caught. But Lewis had scoffed at the idea of Tony Willows producing or supplying drugs.

'He's just an old man. Bit grumpy but harmless. I was up there about a year ago. Someone had drained one of his diesel tanks. His health wasn't so good and his place is falling to bits. Has been for years. I don't get the impression he's all that flush these days. Hasn't played gigs in a while and doesn't get the royalties he used to.'

According to Lewis, Steve's 'airstrip' was a field given over to Tony's son for racing his motorbikes.

So where was Steve?

Perhaps Steve and old Tony had become fast friends and were sharing a joint right now as an old Witchfinder Apprentice album played on the stereo. The idea briefly took hold in Kat's imagination only to disperse when she recalled Helene's story about the dogs and the hostile couple who'd confronted her. Trespassers were clearly not welcome at that farm.

In her home office, Kat attempted to distract herself, as much as she was able, by delving deeper online into Tony Willows and Redstone Cross. She'd glanced at Willows's Wikipedia page after Matt Hull had reappeared on her radar and briefly perused it when Steve made it glow brighter with his theories, but she'd never identified anything worth pursuing in depth. Now that Steve had travelled to snoop on Willows's land and not been seen since, she found herself revisiting her internet tracks more thoroughly.

Once her eyes and thoughts had stopped jumping about her laptop screen, she learned a little more about how haematite and limestone had been mined in parts of Brickburgh from the 1800s until the 1950s. The biggest quarry was near Redstone Cross but she could find nothing else about the site online.

She moved on to the scores of articles available about Tony Willows and Witchfinder Apprentice at fan sites.

An online encyclopaedia of folk music seemed to be the most popular site, one recognised and endorsed by many musos and critics. Kat skim-read the biographical entry for Witchfinder Apprentice:

The darker musical tones that accompany their songs distinguished the band from most of their folk rock contemporaries. From the group's founding in Warwickshire in 1966, the musical direction was driven by Willows, who hailed from Leamington Spa . . .

The band's electric sound grew to be harder than any other folk band of 1969. Increasingly, the recorded music was underwritten with big rock arena drumming. Full harmony choruses tempered the sad and tragic tales with lingering melodies . . .

By 1973 Witchfinder Apprentice's ominous down-tuned electric guitar sound was higher in the mix, though still blended with the traditional styles of English folk music . . .

A refusal to lighten the tone hampered more than the fleeting commercial success the band had enjoyed between 1970 and 1973; this heavier direction also disaffected many of the band's musicians.

'I was fed up with Tony the grim and moody. After a while the songs were giving me nightmares. They were a bad trip all by themselves when you were playing them, over and over again, six days a week,' ex bass player Rob Pryor said in a BBC interview in 1973 ...

Most critics believed that Willows's musical obsessions with madness, bloody revenge, demoniac possession, black magic, witchcraft and human transformation by means of the supernatural were solely responsible for enshrining the band's enduring cult status among so many progressive and black metal musicians for subsequent decades. The band's antecedents can be found in heavy metal more than the folk music that followed Witchfinder Apprentice.

The list of song titles for their last album, *Friends of the Dark*, caught Kat's eye. The record had been recorded when all had been going south for the band and released after their acrimonious split in 1978.

'Old Black Mag'
'Call the Hungry Worm with This Horn'
'A Gest of Woe'
'The Death of Proud Lamkin'
'The Slaughter of Bonny Lizie'
'Saw You My Body?'
'The New-Slain Knight'
'Bar the Door to Old Friends'
'The Lord in the Well'
'The Friar Wrapt in Blanchfour's Skin'
'Crust Beggar'
'Young Quin Buried a Fair Lad'
'The Daemon's Rantin Daughter'

Kat got the gist of the subject matter without analysing the lyrics.

There had been seven Witchfinder Apprentice studio albums; their chart positions were given between 1968 and 1978.

Their ascendance was as well documented online as their fall. The latter was attributed to three changes of management, three record labels applying pressure for hit singles and the endless lineup changes caused by Willows's unpredictable, controlling and caustic temperament. No fewer than ten musicians passed through the band in twelve years.

Kat read a dozen pages of text, printed in a small font, to get some idea of what a handful, or serious narcissist, Tony Willows had been. More enlightened critical hindsight suggested that a personality disorder, or mental illness, had reflected the dark side of his musical genius.

The biography also detailed the committal of an oboe player during a tour of Germany in 1974 and the tragic death by electrocution of the beautiful fiddler, and Willows's lover at that time, Agnes Crown, also in 1974.

Heavy and continual use of psychedelic drugs, violent mood swings and hallucinations, even on stage, plagued Tony's life from 1972 to 1978. His unpredictability and antics onstage forged part of the band's appeal to their fans.

Mandrax had been the drug of choice from 1972 . . . During a final Witchfinder Apprentice tour in 1978, cancelled after five dates, Willows was taken into psychiatric care. He discharged himself and fled to the farmhouse he'd purchased the same year in a remote area of South Devon . . .

A female member of the band's entourage, Jessica Usher, accompanied Willows to Redstone. Since her appearance in Tony's life in 1974, they'd become inseparable. This member of the Witchfinder Apprentice entourage, or 'groupie', had long been cited by band members as a divisive influence within the outfit . . . Her status as a Clear in Scientology, was cited as part of Usher's influence over Tony. They never married but had twins after the band broke up . . .

One low profile solo album was later released by Willows on an indie label, recorded in 1986 at his home studio at Redstone Farm. But the rock stylings of Witchfinder Apprentice records were erased from the solo effort. The album marked a complete return to traditional acoustic instruments and an emphasis on woodwind.

There was no mention of festivals on his land but there was a link to the news story of the death of a young woman, Maddy Gross, in 1979. Kat had already read that story: Gross had been a guest at Tony's home and there was no official resolution to the mysterious circumstances that surrounded the discovery of her body on the edge of his land, though toxicology tests had detected high levels of illegal substances in her system. She'd died of heart failure. Tony was convicted of drug possession and manslaughter and served four years of a ten-year sentence. He was released in late 1984.

Maybe the girl's death was an indication that Tony's old habits had died hard. Maybe the incident had even called time on his rock-and-roll lifestyle and career. He'd never toured after 1978 and, following the release of the solo album, completely abandoned professional music in favour of horticulture, agriculture and animal husbandry. That much Kat already knew, but better understood why Steve had been fascinated with the man and thrilled by his close proximity to where they lived.

Beyond cover versions and remastered releases of Witchfinder Apprentice records in a box-set there was little recent news concerning Willows. A site dedicated to the music of Witchfinder Apprentice's longest serving musician, the mandolin player Ade 'Rhymer' Lankin, did mention how Willows was hounded by fans of their early albums for years after they'd broken up. People often made the long trip to Willows's farm to catch sight of the musician or to get their albums signed. Apparently they were given short shrift by his family. The last time Ade Lankin and Tony Willows had any contact was in 1986. Lankin had played mandolin and contributed vocals to Willows's only solo album.

Anxiety overran Kat's mind at 9.30 p.m.

She called Sheila at home, something she'd never done before. As soon as Sheila picked up, Kat became conscious of how thin and breathless her own voice sounded.

'Still not shown up?' Sheila asked, while trying to mask her uninterest, or was it annoyance now? 'Well, I'm not surprised you're worried. Afraid I've not heard a thing, dear. Let me chase Lewis and I'll get back to you.'

After that, Kat was left to the four walls of her cottage for another hour. Fear gnawing at her raw nerves in a suffocating silence, she remained on the sofa, nursing a lukewarm cup of coffee, watching her screens.

Breathless with panic, Steve's mother finally called at 10.30, which did nothing for Kat's nerves either. When Kat claimed she still hadn't heard from Steve, Delia hung up without another word. The role of Steve's girlfriend seemed inconsequential to his mother.

Kat's second attempt to contact Sheila soon after that was met with a recorded voicemail message.

While trying to distract herself with the BBC news and recurring thoughts of cold white wine, the first red face appeared at the window closest to where Kat sat.

16

*T*apping on the glass. That came first. And for reasons Kat later attributed to wishful thinking, she imagined that Steve was outside her home knocking on a window. By then he was all she could think about.

This desire for an external sign to end the terrible wait for her boyfriend compelled her to draw the curtain back from the window.

Before she had an opportunity to regret her haste, she was staring into the primitive face of an adult man. The first feature to claim her attention was the intruder's eyes. They were mean: the sclera yoke-yellow, traversed by blood vessels. From under the crusting thickets of the brows his glare bulged: as clear an expression of instability and rage as she'd ever seen. Pugnacious, leering, a brutish face from times long past. Her sole reaction a sharp intake of breath.

The smeared figure had pressed itself against the window. When he removed the stained palms of each hand from the pane of glass, she saw him more clearly: pot-bellied, flabby-chested, bearded, balding, entirely naked, a stub of purplish genital evident in a scarlet scrub of pubic hair.

The figure stepped backwards into total darkness leaving Kat with a reflection of her own slack face and horrified eyes.

She fell from the sofa where she'd been kneeling, scrabbled to her feet, barking her shin on the side table and sending a coffee mug and three remote controls clattering across the floorboards.

Through tear-blurred eyes she could just make out the phone. Picked it up in hands that shook and struggled to grip the sides of the smooth device. Tried to unlock the screen. *Password Incorrect.*

Get out! Car! Do it outside! Without hesitation, she scraped the catch from the rear of the front entrance, unlocked it by Yale key, twisted the mortise lock and yanked the door open.

Similar in position and posture to an eager cat on her doormat, the effigy of an entirely different beast awaited upon the threshold. Crude head erect and demanding her full attention, the muzzled and spiky-eared statuette cast its fierce gaze upwards.

A mere glance at the thing illumined under the porch light was sufficient to identify the onyx curves about its full breasts, the splay of rounded hips, the glimmer of glazed clay. Unlike the Venus figures she'd seen at the museum exhibition this one retained arms and a head: shaggy, sticklike appendages resembling a dog's forelegs. A spear spiked from the culmination of one limb.

Standing in socks, without a coat, Kat felt the cold night air pass through her skin to shiver her marrow. But brutal naked red things, with their wretched stone idols, could withstand temperatures and commit acts that she'd only wither before: instinct wasted no time informing her of this. She couldn't recall the last time she'd felt as vulnerable and unprotected.

Pitch darkness in the village lane. No streetlights this far out. The only light was spot-cast from the five cottages in Kiln Lane: yellow shards peeking between chinks of drapes and the two dim orbs of exterior lamps. After London, the silence and darkness out here had taken some getting used to. Kat no longer thought about it much but was now reminded of the void that surrounded her home at night. She was also forced to consider what ran through it in the manner of wild dogs.

In a heartbeat she acknowledged another disadvantage of rural living: how darkness could cloak a figure standing mere feet from you.

Three forms rose from the ground and made haste for her front door. One wheeled from behind the front hedge. It skittered on bandy legs, its feet sandalled: a woman with tatty hair clawed into short, wet-looking sprouts. Her face was a vision from Bedlam.

A short, stocky man appeared beside the porch post, his teeth flashing white, the grin malevolent. His knees made a sound similar to snapping celery.

The third visitor ran at speed from across the lane, straight at her door. When he came within reach of the porch light, he revealed a wispy beard trailing over shoulders with the lustre of sunburned skin. An object made from bone hung from his neck.

All were daubed red from head to foot. They wouldn't have looked amiss in the Brickburgh Caves, scrabbling through the damp darkness forty thousand years gone. Each clutched a pointed black stone. Hand-axes.

Kat closed the door and secured the mortise lock again at the same moment as a fist thudded against wood and shook the cottage. Pressing her back into the door she tried to control her jerking arms and hands. Investing what concentration she still had, she pressed a fingertip to the phone's screen and inputted two of the required four digits, this time in the right sequence.

Whenever she was downstairs and Steve used the tiny bathroom upstairs, the floorboards always cracked and ground together. Sitting below was not unlike being inside the hold of a sailing ship. Above her head, the floor upstairs now groaned in this familiar manner to indicate the presence of the uninvited within her home.

They were inside. *They were here the whole time.*

Across the tiny upstairs landing someone strode eagerly. Up there, signs of the desire to get downstairs *with her* became even more pronounced when a red hand gripped the upper newel post and made it creak.

How did they get in? No windows were broken, no doors. No one had a key . . . *except Steve.*

167

Panic enabled Kat to flee into the kitchen. Dizziness made the yellow cupboards swing nauseously through her vision. Her lower back pressed against the cooker. She typed the next two digits of the phone's password.

Password Incorrect.

When a pair of red legs became visible on the staircase, Kat screamed, 'Get out!'

Between the banisters, slender calves and naked feet stepped carefully down from the darkness. A woman. One who paused under the hallway light for an interminable moment and revealed how a pair of pretty blue eyes in a thin face could be deranged by suppressed fury. The loathing projected by those eyes paralysed Kat.

The intruder turned her head and issued a short, high-pitched sound, one that warbled and tailed into a *yip*: a cry more animal than human. She then turned and with one slim arm opened the front door to let the others inside.

17

Helene ended the call and sat in silence. The *Game of Thrones* episode finished without her noticing. On-screen, a group of women in another show were shouting at each other. She turned the TV off and refilled her wine glass.

The contact had been unexpected, as was the information she'd received. According to the call register, Kat, the journalist whom she'd met in Devon, had also called twice earlier when Helene had been reading *The Little Grey Men* to Valda.

Her daughter was still awake and was animating soft toys on her duvet; through the ceiling of the living room Helene heard the muted voices Valda attributed to each character.

If Kat had called three times then what she had to say was important. But what exactly had Kat just relayed to her during the third call that Helene had managed to pick up?

The entire communication remained vague because of the enigma of its contents. But Kat had alluded to the fact that she had come into some information about Helene's brother Lincoln. News pertinent to the time that he'd spent in South Devon during his final summer alive.

Prior to this revelation, Kat had issued a caveat: that she'd been reluctant to call Helene because she didn't want to upset her. Kat had also judged an email to be too 'cold': that's what she'd said. 'It's best that we talk about this.'

Information; Kat had received information about Lincoln. 'Trust me,' Kat had said. 'You really need to come down and see this for yourself.' The journalist claimed that she'd met people whom Helene 'should definitely speak to about Lincoln. People he met while he was here.'

So if she'd correctly understood Kat, then the journalist had somehow located people who'd been with her brother near the end of his life. Only she'd omitted to explain how she found these people, or who they were, or anything about the information they possessed about Lincoln. She'd only mentioned that they were 'local people your brother stayed with'.

This was more than Helene had hoped for when she'd travelled to Divilmouth alone. But it now appeared that her chance encounter with the journalist and photographer in the museum café would lead to something far more meaningful. From these locals she might learn how Lincoln had seemed at the end: she might even solve the mystery of what had troubled her little brother enough for him to take his own life. Helene still had no idea where he'd camped or slept during his last two weeks in Devon.

She was only just coming up for air from an exhaustion of delayed grief that had accompanied her home from the trip to Devon, but if Kat had found people who had known her brother, then another trip was worth the risk of getting upset again.

Only work and the relentless intensity of motherhood, after returning home from Divilmouth, had prevented her from taking to her bed and not getting up for a while. The trip had upset her in ways she couldn't fully define. But she'd been left with a lingering, almost psychic sense that her brother had somehow been engulfed, psychologically, by that unforgiving and hostile landscape, a place crowded with unpleasant echoes from prehistory. At times, when she'd been down there, she'd even felt as if his spirit had been passing through her body.

Kat had also confided that she'd 'sensed how unhappy' Helene had been when they met. Helene was flooded with a clear sense of Kat's experience and maturity and her kind-heartedness. No one had done anything like this for her in her life. Kat had clearly taken a keen interest in her brother's tragedy and had wanted to help a grieving woman find some resolution.

Oddly, Kat had seemed emotional on the phone. There had been a tremor in her voice, a frailty Helene had not heard when they'd met. This tone had prompted her to ask if the news about Lincoln was bad. Kat had said, 'Not at all.'

Helene stared at the phone number of the guesthouse that Kat had told her about: a place where she could stay free of charge. 'My friends own a guesthouse, the Red Barn. They're happy to offer you a place to stay while you're here.' That was just as well as Helene would struggle to find the money to pay for another trip south. She would call the number of the B&B in the morning. Maybe she could even make another trip this coming weekend as Kat had suggested she should. Kat would be covering a local festival on the Saturday in Redhill and had suggested they meet there.

But Valda? How she'd pined for her mother the last time Helene had left home: the only time they'd ever been apart. That had only been for three days. Her mother had cared for Valda while she'd been away but there had been tears and many questions: *Is Mummy coming back? Is that Mummy?* (every time the front doorbell chimed). *I'm starving for Mummy.*

Taking Valda with her was out of the question. It wouldn't be practical: she didn't want Valda to see her upset and the drive was too long. *Forget it.* The journey would also have to be undertaken twice in two days.

Valda wouldn't understand why her mum wanted to go away again: she'd never known her uncle. All the same, Helene needed to go back.

Before she called her mother to ask for childcare cover at the weekend, she dug Lincoln's box of recordings out of the garage. Kat had asked her to bring the discs, almost insisting that she didn't forget them and that they were 'important'. The journalist had also stressed that the recordings would 'make sense now'. An odd thing to say but if the recordings helped her understand anything about Lincoln at the end of his short life, then Helene would take them.

18

*T*he large creature spotted Helene. The very moment she appeared its shaggy black face turned towards her, the muzzle rising as if to inhale her scent. Having selected her from the herd it hobbled at her, moving like an arthritic animal. When the fraying edge of the crowd, at the mouth of the village festival, parted to let the creature lumber through, Helene raised a hand to ward off the attentions of the ungainly, grotesque form. The lumpy body was coated in dirty black wool to its four feet.

Even as it closed on her, the features of the thing's head remained indistinct. Until, up closer, a pair of wooden jaws clacked like clogs below big, white eyes: rolling, rattling, lunatic orbs that bulged from ragged sockets in the creature's mangy head.

The disagreeable mouth momentarily engulfed her head as if the thing intended to decapitate her. An odour of mildewed fabric and old gym equipment in a primary school filled her sinuses. Inside the open mouth, between rows of yellow teeth carven from painted wood, sat an oafish male face, sheened with sweat. The man's breath reeked of cider and tobacco and he was grinning with the delinquent pleasure that pranking a stranger gave him. Helene had difficulty returning his enthusiasm. He was trying to make a fool of her in public.

The creature reared back, releasing her head. After an ungainly manoeuvre on the tarmac of the road that resembled a big hound turning in too small a space, the thing shuffled around her in a circle. But her nose remained filled with the odours of dust and vintage sweat, a miasma that now trailed from the wretched hide and its fetid innards.

She wasn't sure what it was supposed to be: a thing that suggested a bull or cow, horse or dog. She only wished that it would go away.

The shabby four-legged figure might even suggest a grotesque vestige from another, much older era: a mythical beast from the Middle Ages, or even possessing origins in Middle Earth. Grinning people in the street seemed intent on filming it and taking selfies beside its mad, hairy face.

'Don't worry luv, won't bite!' a man shouted from a crowd that both filled the pub's beer garden and spilled out to encircle a low stone wall. A woman issued a hag-laugh, her throat coarsened by cigarettes.

The shambling animal effigy would have made Valda wail. Even though two men were clearly inside the costume, Helene didn't like being near it herself: a threadbare pantomime horse with the face of a devil. Instead of hooves, the creature's feet were two pairs of dirty trainers that clumsily pranced about.

Bedraggled and sinister and parting the crowd, the thing finally stomped away, down the lane. Dodging about like a Chinese dragon, undulating and excitable, it eventually sagged amidst the revellers' heads and vanished.

If this beast-puppet was a local tradition, why revive it? She couldn't imagine children appreciating its presence at all.

The raucous voices from the pub were soon obliterated by a local jazz band's brassy rendition of a Glenn Miller song. Bombarded on every side with noise, colour, motion, raised voices, Helene's entrance to the fête continued to disorient her.

A few hundred people had gathered at Redhill and milled in the main road that forked up and down a hill. The pub, the streetlights, the stage, the church and the community centre were all edged with red, white and blue bunting.

From a cursory inspection of the stalls lining each side of the lane, she learned that the mascot character was called 'Creel'. It was well known locally; there was plenty of merchandise featuring the creature's image, but none of it indicated what kind of an animal Creel was. Where it was depicted as a cartoon, it resembled a dog with a cat's face, a permanently leering hound-thing equipped with mad eyes and a looping tongue. 'Yip yip!' it said on banners, decals and printed shirts. 'I buy my meat local!'

When printed, it regularly sported clothes in the colours of the Devon flag or the Union Jack. The animal was even depicted on some shirts wearing a top hat and monocle. A set of coffee mugs showed an image of Creel wiping its clawed feet, and worse, on the European flag.

A new irritation replaced Helene's last when a barking, amplified voice impacted against her ears, hurting them inside.

Before the Tudor-styled pub, The Red Sky, and the fête's thumping heart, a man stood on a temporary stage and roared into a microphone. The spanking, metallic sounds issuing from his flabby mouth were broadcast through speakers fixed to aluminium posts. The wheezy static of the speaker's inhalations rasped between his words.

The MC was a purple-faced drinker with a ponderous belly who continually wiped sweat from his bilious jowls. But most of the aggressively jolly, burly figure's rant was impossible to discern. Helene only caught snatches:

'Tradition and fam'ly! . . . 'sall about, innit . . . been goin' four hundred years, if you can believe that! . . . She's on her way up from *Dillmuth* right now! . . . Forty-stone boar! . . . All proceeds go to chariteeeee! Ssssso dig deep when the time comes, ladies and gentlemen . . . fink of a few people we'd like to roast 'ere instead, aye!'

A line of bewildered elderly ex-servicemen wearing berets stood before the stage. Their seemingly oversized or nearly empty blazers were festooned with ribbons and medals. They lined up before the ranting face like a Praetorian guard that had not been dismissed in decades. Each man held a plastic charity box.

A squeal of feedback pierced the air and a baby howled. Helene walked on. She'd imagined her Saturday afternoon might have been spent outside a quiet village pub in the company of Kat and the people her brother had known.

She walked the length of the narrow lane and back again, checking the stalls: home-baked cakes, sweets, an ice-cream van, barbecue, handmade toys, cider in clay jugs, a Land Trust Countryside Membership table, dated souvenirs. Her browse lasted five minutes.

All about her, the people were loudly and assertively happy, though Helene sensed a taut wire of defiance in the gathering too. An angry, tipsy energy bustled in places, particularly near the pub. She didn't know where the ire was directed but suspected she'd walked into a community forcing a confirmation of its identity: an idea of itself based on what it knew of the past, or had even lived through but only selectively remembered.

Maybe she was detecting aspects of that familiar, depressing working-class nationalism: like at home, where a community orbited hard times and found itself baited and antagonised by low wages, unemployment, benefit cuts and a drinking culture.

From window sills and wooden poles a dozen Cross of St George flags drooped in the warm air. Limp banners that gave the gathering a strange, perhaps unintended political flavour. In Brickburgh Harbour people seemed keen on flags too.

In the street beyond the pub, pushchairs and elderly people crowded, and after the briefest attention from the drinkers and Creel, the presence of the young and old reassured her, as did the fragrance of candy floss and burgers on grills. Though the sight of so many children created a pang in her stomach and her throat involuntarily thickened. From one of the Nans who'd set out a stall in the pub carpark, Helene bought a bag of fruit jellies for Valda.

She checked her phone. No reply from Kat. She'd texted, 'I'm here' from outside the festival entrance.

Getting away from the street and the ominous return of Creel, Helene stepped into a shadowed passage between the community centre and Methodist chapel. She entered a small park.

Set up on the grass, other attractions sheltered from the hot sun under plastic canopies. The close, moist, beery atmosphere of the main street immediately surrendered to a bigger sky, the heat in the park less oppressive. Breathing became easier and the clamminess between her shoulder blades vanished. The infernal jabber of the man with the microphone dulled to a distant tinny garble, his chesty roars and rasps contained by the old stone houses. The last thing he'd barked, with provocative eagerness, as if proud of his skill to shock, was something about 'roasting a big pig!'

In the park, an elderly magician in a battered suit tugged bright chiffon tissues from a sleeve. At the end of a chain of sheer fabric that appeared incongruous between his withered hands came an explosion of Haribo party bags that showered the kneeling children. They fell to the ground at once and commenced scrabbling as if an aid truck had just made a drop in a refugee camp.

The little ones won't get any sweets. That blonde girl is about to cry. You'll get upset too.

Valda would have stood and watched the scrum, infuriated by any evidence of snatching or unfairness. And as Valda grew older, Helene often wondered if she'd brought her daughter up purely to be torn apart in a world content with a permanent state of unfairness and inequality.

A sharp smell of wood and sawdust soaked by urine stung her nose, distracting her from the magician. Beside the tired playground equipment, a circle of hay bales was arranged about a tier of small cages. Sitting upon the straw cubes, children stroked rabbits and guinea pigs, the animals handed out and passed around by two women in red polo shirts. Valda would have loved that part and Helene sensed a ghost-child swinging on her arm, pulling her towards the little candy-striped tent labelled 'Make Your Own Teddy Bear'. She'd make one later and take it home.

Her phone buzzed, vibrating in the palm of her hand. *Kat.* A text message: *Burrow Street too busy. I'm in park near bonfire.*

Shielding her eyes with one hand, Helene peered about the grass until she located a triangular pyre of wood, set between an area cordoned off for a firework display and a long queue outside two lopsided portable toilets. She saw Kat, sitting on a bench.

A man and woman stood behind her. The man's hands were folded over the back of the bench, close to Kat's shoulders. He was heavily bearded, the woman slight and elderly. She wore sunglasses and her hair was covered by a head scarf as if she were undergoing treatment for cancer. The couple's unsmiling faces were directed at Helene.

As she drew closer, the couple moved away, in the direction of the main street.

Helene couldn't see Steve anywhere. She'd assumed he'd be here to take photographs but she didn't dwell on his absence because of her shock at the unexpected change in Kat's demeanour and appearance. The reserved, confident lifestyle journalist seemed to have been replaced by someone else. Helene recalled the tremor in Kat's voice on the phone.

'Kat. Hi.' Kat's handshake was weaker, her soft hand trembling in Helene's grasp. She was much paler as if ill. Even her bottom lip quivered when Helene asked, 'Steve taking pictures? I never saw him in the street.'

'No. Not today,' Kat replied and so quietly that her words qualified as a whisper. Her eyes, or what Helene could see of them around Kat's Dior sunglasses, moved so slowly that she might have been drugged. Aware of Helene's scrutiny, Kat moved her head to keep her eyes hidden.

How are you? Good journey? How's Valda? Yes, good, I'm pleased to hear that. Have you been keeping well? Work okay? Good. Good. Good. Kat's words came out slowly and were muttered without feeling or enthusiasm as if she were reading from a card.

Helene answered the questions, though Kat began repeating herself without realising she'd done so. She didn't listen to Helene's answers either.

It dawned on her that Kat must be terrified of upsetting her. Maybe she'd learned something terrible about Lincoln that she was afraid to share in case Helene broke down.

'Are you all right, Kat?' Helene eventually ventured when Kat could no longer concentrate on the stilted, failing conversation. She wasn't even looking at Helene: her eyes had drifted to the distance, her thoughts no doubt preceding her gaze.

'Yes. Yes. All good,' Kat replied after an awkward pause.

They then sat together in silence for longer than seemed bearable and Helene felt the first scorch of impatience behind her sternum. 'May I ask where they are?'

Kat turned to her. 'Who?'

'The people you wanted me to meet. Who Lincoln knew down here.' She wondered if they had been the couple behind the bench.

'Working. They're working.'

Then what the fuck am I doing here? I've driven half the day to get here and left my bloody daughter in tears.

'But they'll see you later,' Kat added. She smiled weakly, her half-hidden eyes anxious. And then Kat reached out a hand and placed it upon the back of Helene's. The contact was feeble and the hand was retracted a moment after it was offered.

'Is it serious then?'

'What?' Kat said.

'What they have to tell me? You know, about Lincoln, my brother.' She felt the need to add her brother's name to the sentence because Kat seemed oblivious to the topic of conversation.

Kat's mouth sagged. The expression made her appear much older than she was, as if she'd been forced to remember something terrible. 'Lincoln? No. No.'

'Because if it is, you don't need to feel bad, Kat. I just want to know anything they can tell me about him. You know, from before the end. That's all. I'm a big girl with broad shoulders.'

'From the swimming. All your swimming.'

Kat's distress and preoccupation soon reminded Helene of visits she'd made to an elderly grandmother: the faint voice, distracted expression, an inability to concentrate or connect with whoever sat beside her, the struggle to even smile.

'Shall we get a drink, Kat? Though maybe not in that pub.'

Kat seemed to pale further at the suggestion. 'I'm not allowed,' she said, as if without forethought. 'Working. I'm working here.'

Helene shrugged. 'Soft drink?'

'I'm okay, thank you.'

'Forgive me for saying so, Kat, but I've come a long way and I came straight here from the motorway. I was under the impression that I was going to meet the people who knew something about Lincoln. That's what you said on the phone. It's why I came to the fair. But you seem . . .'

'Oh, don't worry. Soon. That . . . they . . . will be here soon.'

'But it was really important that I came. You said that.'

Kat swallowed again. Her hands knotted white within the lap of her jeans. 'You brought the discs?'

'Yes. But these people? I'd like to establish when I can meet them. It wasn't easy for me to get away at such short notice.'

'Yes. Yes. Of course.' Kat was now looking past Helene again and into the distance. *And God how her mouth was drawn.* There was a long stain on her blouse too. It looked like coffee. Had Kat not noticed that? She hadn't put herself together very well: no makeup, she'd barely touched her hair. Something was wrong. Helene really wished that Steve was here; he wouldn't have been short of something to say.

'So, maybe later,' Helene prompted, 'I was thinking that you, me and Steve could grab a bite to eat. If you're both free?'

A visible shudder passed through Kat as if she'd been pricked by internal pain. Yes, she was actually crying too.

Kat slipped a finger behind her glasses to touch an eye. 'I'm not . . . We're not . . . Steve . . . not seeing each other any more.'

'Oh, God, Kat. I'm sorry. You broke up? I didn't know. I'm sorry.' That would provide something of an explanation for Kat's behaviour and appearance. The woman was shattered, cut up. 'You sure I can't get you a drink? I think we could both use one. Who's ever going to find out?'

'Love to.' Kat swallowed to regain control of her voice. 'But I can't. I'm in recovery.'

'Oh, shit. Sorry. I didn't –'

'Could I have the discs?' Kat said, while looking at her own bloodless hands.

'Sure.' Helene took her bag from her shoulder.

'It's very important,' Kat whispered. 'They . . .'

'I don't know what these recordings have to do with anything, so can you at least tell me how they come into *this*?' Helene wasn't keen on hearing them again.

'The magazine. We'd like to use them.' Kat said in the same vague, non-committal manner she'd displayed since Helene arrived.

'I don't have copies, Kat. I didn't get a chance to make a copy.'

'Good. That's good.'

'What is?'

Kat looked flustered for a moment. 'That you brought them. This will help.'

Helene had given up any hope of getting any sense out of the woman but experienced an unexpected tug of attachment to the discs. They had Lincoln's handwriting upon the shiny surfaces and the titles might have been the last thing he'd ever written. 'I don't want to lose these. They're the last things he ever made.'

One of Kat's trembling hands reached forcefully toward the discs in Helene's hand, making Helene think of an addict reaching for its junk or a beggar snatching at change. She moved her body to put the discs out of Kat's reach. 'So, I'll tell you what I'll do. I'll copy them. I've brought my laptop –'

'No! No need. I can take them now.'

'It's better I copy them. I'll do it at the B&B, which reminds me, I better check in. They said to come by three and it's nearly that now. I'll upload them to a transfer site and you can download them.'

A quiver crossed Kat's mouth and her words tumbled out breathlessly. 'Oh, no, don't copy them. No. No need. I can take them and return them later.'

Kat's grasping and eager, bloodless face was really starting to make her anxious.. Her half-hidden eyes mooned wide behind the tinted lenses as if with fear.

Only a concern that she'd never see the CDs again compelled Helene to further resist the journalist's clutching hands. 'I'd rather make the copies, Kat. If that's all right with you. These have sentimental value.'

Kat's posture stiffened. 'The Red Barn. You'll have them there?'

This meeting was going nowhere. 'Er, I guess so. I better get there now.'

'And you'll wait.'

'Sorry?'

'I'll call you and we can meet.' Kat noisily cleared her throat. 'I'll make the introductions.'

'With the people who knew Lincoln?'

'Of course. You'll definitely be there, won't you, at the hotel?'

Helene couldn't restrain her sarcasm a moment longer. 'Well, I guess so, Kat, as I have nowhere else to be. I'm really sorry to hear about Steve, and this is clearly not a good time for you, but I've moved mountains to get here and my daughter was very upset the last time I left her. I can't just motor up and down between Walsall and Devon at the drop of a hat.'

Kat dipped her head and Helene could see how her hands were gripping the edge of the bench. The woman might have been trying to hold herself upright.

It was time to leave. Breakup or not, she was getting close to losing it with the journalist: the long drive, an hour's holdup at Bristol, with the constantly recurring memory of Valda's tear-streaked face haunting the entire journey, had done nothing to improve her mood. 'I need to get one of those bears made up and then I need to check in, yeah?' Helene stuffed the discs inside her shoulder bag and stood up.

Kat looked bewildered. 'You're going now?'

Kat had to be on something. Probably tranqs. 'That's right, Kat. I just told you . . . Never mind. But I'll hear from you later? I need to take off by ten tomorrow. Maybe you could give me the names and numbers of these people so I can contact them myself. You know, in case you're not feeling up to it later.'

'I'll call. I promise.'

'Okay. Until then.' Helene walked off with more purpose than when she'd entered the fête.

From the distance, the red-faced orator belted out fresh information about the arrival of a dead pig on a truck.

Inside the stifling teddy-bear tent, Helene created a toy for Valda. She chose a rabbit and stuffed the furry skin with foam, then covered the bunny in a pink dress. While doing so, she noticed that a Creel toy was available, but again, neither the empty skins nor the stuffed sample hanging from the roof indicated what the animal was supposed to be. As Helene paid the woman who ran the stall, she asked, 'What is this Creel thing?'

The woman shrugged. 'I'm not from here. I came over from Torbay. But it's something from a story, like a legend, I think. A monster.'

It certainly was one of those.

'They was on the walls of that cave, I think. People is using it on souvenirs now. Been really popular too. I've nearly run out.' The woman dropped her voice to a whisper. 'Not the sort of thing a child would want sitting on its bed, I'd have thought.'

Before she left the little park and re-entered the street,

Helene looked to where she'd left Kat. The journalist remained seated on the bench but the bearded man and the woman in the headscarf had rejoined her. The old woman's face was lowered close to Kat's to whisper into her ear. And if she wasn't mistaken, Kat had covered her face with her hands. Maybe that was Kat's mum, comforting her after splitting up with her boyfriend.

A blurt from the speakers, an amplified roar from the MC twisted her nerves anew. A rattle of applause and the crowd's murmur spiked with excited shrieks.

Helene looked to the main street and saw a large flatbed truck slowly shake and wheeze between the buildings, parting the crowd to bump over the grass.

The vehicle parked beside the dormant bonfire pyre. About the truck's cabin a row of red faces grinned their white teeth and waved at the crowd. The people on the back of the truck were dressed in furry loincloths and bikinis, their exposed skin daubed red. Two figures, arranged on mock thrones like a king and queen, wore what looked like black Creel masks to hide their faces.

In the middle of the flatbed, a pale carcass lay upon a wooden box. Presumably this was the huge pig the MC had been ranting about, soon to be roasted and offered up to the gathering.

Helene made haste for her car.

19

*D*uring the lengthy wait for Kat's call, Helene had phoned her mum and the report was good. 'She actually went to bed at seven thirty?'

'*She did. I think she liked showing me her routines and her pyjamas. But she's still awake. I can hear her talking to that pink fish she's got up there.*'

Helene laughed. 'It's a dolphin. Splashy.'

'*That's the one.*'

'Thanks, Mom, for putting my mind at rest. I better ring off. I'm still waiting for Kat to call. As I've come all this way I don't want to miss it now. But I'm getting a bit fed up.'

'*Well, I can't see why she couldn't have told you what she knows on the phone.*'

Helene had done more than wonder about that too. 'I thought these people might have pictures. Or they'd take me somewhere Lincoln had been. I don't know what I was expecting. But I'll say cheerio, Mom.'

'*Oh, one last thing, luv. I saw you had one of those red cards from the postie so I picked up a parcel from the sorting office today when I was up the shops. I let Valda open it. Hope that's all right?*'

'She usually opens everything. Was it the hair straighteners from Amazon?'

'*No. This parcel was addressed to Valda. But I'm not sure it was meant for her. That's the odd bit and I don't know what to make of the bloody thing. It's not the sort of present that I'd send to a child. I can't say as I could tell you what it is. It's an ornament, I think.*'

A horrible-looking thing with a spear.'

'What?'

'*I can't tell what it's supposed to be and it's a bit primitive-looking, like it's very old. You know, like something they find in those old tombs. It's got a human body and that's a bit suggestive too. I mean it's got these big . . . a bosom.'* Helene's mother laughed. '*But like a dog's head on top.'*

Helene felt a sudden urge to get herself home. The object that had been addressed to her daughter by name sounded very much like what she'd recently seen at the Brickburgh Cave exhibition and subsequently learned was the inspiration for the loathsome Creel character at the festival. Why would a replica, if that was what this thing was, have been sent to her daughter? *And by who? Kat?*

'No sender's address?'

'*Nothing.'*

Helene could only presume that Kat, in her mentally unsound state of mind, had thought the figure was a suitable gift for a child, or some sort of gesture commemorating how they'd met. But it didn't take much thought for either of those explanations to fail to convince her. Kat wasn't clueless. Heartbroken for sure but that wasn't sufficient cause for her to send Valda a dog-headed ornament with big tits.

'*No card inside either,'* her mum said. '*It was in a little box and all covered in bubble-wrap. I didn't know what to do with it. V's been playing with it but I'm not sure how valuable it is, so I took it off her.'*

'Okay. Keep it off her until I get back.'

'*That's what I thought.'*

Helene's phone pinged in her ear. She checked the screen: an incoming call from Kat. Stress creased her mind. 'Mom, that call's just come in. Gotta put you on hold.' Helene picked up the new call. 'Kat?'

Kat's sniff broke the silence. She was crying. Her shaky voice eventually said, '*Sorry.'* One word, spoken softly before she ended the call.

'Hang on.' Helene tried to redial Kat's number. To add to her confusion, the landline phone beside the bed buzzed. Helene dithered. She still had her mum on hold and Kat wasn't picking up.

Sorry. From that one word from Kat, was Helene to deduce that the evening's meeting was cancelled?

Helene picked up the room phone. 'Hello?'

'It's Carol, in reception. They're down here, waiting.'

'Who is?'

Did Carol mean the people that Kat wanted her to meet? So had Kat just called her to say that *she* couldn't make it but the others were available? 'Sorry, Carol, who is waiting?'

Carol ended the call.

'What the . . .?' Helene reopened the call to her mother. 'Mom, gotta fly. Someone's downstairs. I think it's the people I'm supposed to meet.' They hurried their goodbyes.

Once she'd had a moment to consider the two incoming calls Helen guessed that if the visitors were the people that Lincoln had known, then maybe Kat might be with them after all. The solitary 'Sorry' on the phone might have been an apology for being so late.

There'd be no time now to go out and eat. But surely her brother's acquaintances wouldn't just show up at the Red Barn? They didn't know her. At the festival Kat had said they'd been working during the day.

Confused and irritable, Helene left her room. From the staircase she could see the ground-floor hallway. It was empty.

The lounge doubled as a dining room and was also deserted. The front door was open but no one stood in the porch. Damp air drifted into the building carrying a vague scent of manure. Beyond the porch, the blue ink of early night pressed the land and chilled the air.

Helene peered out of the entrance. Only her car was parked on the forecourt. She walked to the reception desk and dinged the bell. 'Hello? Carol?'

Earlier, Carol had been civil with Helene, or courteously uninterested, and had discouraged any conversation beyond stilted small talk. Being in receipt of a stranger's charity had made Helene feel awkward, so when she'd collected the keys she'd mentioned the reason for her visit and thanked Carol for her kindness.

Carol had merely considered her with blank indifference or even irritation. A reaction that had also suggested she didn't know Kat. So perhaps the journalist was owed a favour through the magazine and Carol was a contact as opposed to a friend? Helene didn't know, but ever since she'd arrived, the situation had grown weirder and more frustrating by the hour.

'Hello, Carol?' Helene repeated over the reception counter.

'They're here for you.' That was Carol's voice in the room behind the reception counter, situated to the side of the desk.

Helene leaned over the front desk and peered in the direction of Carol's voice. 'Sorry, who is?'

Through an open door a kitchen became visible. Carol was preparing food with her back to the entrance. Helene recognised the thin shoulders and the small birdlike frame topped by a functional bob of thick grey hair. 'Sorry, Carol, no one seems to be here. Carol?'

When Carol turned around, Helene understood even less about why she'd been called downstairs but she also wished that Carol had remained facing forwards. The sight of her was a shock because the woman had painted her face red, a bright blood-red from lined forehead to grooved chin.

Was she injured? But then, did people in pain grin to reveal oversized teeth amidst the stained scarlet flesh of their mouths? The incongruity of the red skin amidst the hood of grey hair appeared especially fiendish: grotesque in contrast to the woman's ordinary clothing, the brown trousers and floral-patterned blouse.

The woman's throat was also stained red, indicating that her entire body beneath the clothing might be dyed.

As Helene tried to fathom if Carol's appearance had some bizarre connection to the nearby festival and to those characters waving from the flatbed truck, a patter of bare feet announced a new presence inside reception: behind her.

Helene turned. What had come in through the open door of the Red Barn, or had been hiding on the ground floor, immediately reduced her to a motionless gawping. And when one of the red things issued the first shriek and rushed at her, all she managed to do was clap a hand to her chest to steady her heart.

20

*W*hen Kat closed her eyes the darkness spun but nothing came up to dribble into the toilet bowl. After what she'd seen, she hadn't trusted her stomach with more than a few pieces of dry toast and plain biscuits in days.

The woman in the headscarf was waiting for her on the landing, watching through the open door. Either the woman or the bearded man followed her about her tiny home now, everywhere, from room to room. They were occupying her existence, or what remained of it.

The bearded man had just retaken possession of her phone. He'd yanked it from her hand once she'd made the pitiful attempt at phoning Helene.

During the call to the guesthouse, Kat had been unable to follow their script and instructions. Her uninvited visitors had been especially displeased when she'd failed to tell Helene: 'Some people who knew your brother are coming to see you.' Instead, all she'd managed was a solitary word encased by a sob: 'Sorry.' And that might have been the first truthful thing that she'd said to Helene since asking her to return to Devon.

During the brief call, as with all the calls they'd made her make, the bearded man had been gripping her hair in his fist and his horrid breath had slathered her cheeks and left them moist. In his other hand he'd held a flint knife against her throat.

But Kat *was* sorry. So dreadfully sorry. She'd never been as sorry in her life: the apology a caustic blend of guilt, remorse, self-loathing and fear. Pretty much how she'd felt for every waking second of each day and night since they'd come for her. Kat had lured Helene Brown here to die.

Matt Hull must have been the first to go. Then Steve. *Oh, God, Steve. Steve. Steve . . .* Now it was Helene's turn. *A mother to that sweet little girl.*

And then you. Then it's your turn. You're next.

Kat hated the people who'd invaded her home and life more than she'd hated anyone or anything in her entire existence. She hadn't known it was possible to hate someone with a force and fury that burned like an ember swallowed whole. By comparison, her hatred of her ex, Graham, was a petty aversion.

For brief moments she even believed herself capable of attacking her jailers and tearing their faces apart with her fingernails. But in these passing moments of incendiary fury, she would remember the painful clench of the man's rough hands whenever the bearded bastard got hold of her arms and dragged her to and from the cottage to make her run their errands. The sensation of those brutish hands on her, twisting and burning the skin of her wrists, had left a permanent trace.

Her captors had not stood more than a few feet from her since the night they'd tapped at her window.

They said they aren't going to kill you if you do what they ask of you.

Kat hated herself during the moments when she tried to believe her abductors' assurances about her safety. She was a coward: even after all they had done to her and to the man she loved, she still followed their instructions to the letter. Years of avoiding stress and responsibility had set their own insidious precedent.

You have no choice.

She'd seen what they could do and would do again to anyone they decided was a threat to . . . *to what?* To what they were *doing*. Those psychotic and loathsome practices out at that awful farm.

The person she'd been before *the* night they took her to Redstone Farm was gone, over. Now she was a woman far more broken than she'd ever been in London. That time in her life seemed silly now. Those travails with jobs and bullies and her ex were irrelevant; the breakups and redundancies, the drunkenness and tears, all nonsense.

She'd not known what rock-bottom was because she'd never before experienced *things* on this earth that were too awful for most people to even imagine. And she'd done far more than merely imagine these things: while on her knees in the dirt and the stinking darkness of that barn, she'd been forced to bear witness to them. She'd heard every sound that had arisen from the very ground of *that place*.

Kat slipped her head back over the toilet bowl, retched, gasped for breath.

How could anyone defend themselves against *that*? Steve hadn't been able to or Matt Hull. Fit men. What chance did she have? She'd never physically struck another person in her life. And the red folk went further than mere beatings. Much further. There were so many of them too.

So many.

Her turn would come soon. It would have to. She didn't know the names of the two people in her home and had never seen them before they'd invaded her life. But she would recognise their faces anywhere now. She'd seen their colleagues too, their partners in crime: those they'd colluded with to murder in ways this land couldn't have known in millennia. Even though all of their faces had been painted red, she'd recognise them again.

She also knew who was behind what they were doing and what they'd done to Steve and probably to others. Assuredly, Kat knew far too much. And after Helene disappeared and now her brother's discs had changed hands then what use was she to the red folk?

Kat washed her face and left the bathroom. 'I'd like to go to my room now,' she said to the woman in the headscarf, who squinted at her in a manner that was now horribly familiar. A scrunched expression, the eye sockets creasing like wrinkled linen about permanently narrowed eyes: as hard and mean as the shard of flint she carried in an old, veiny hand. Bitter eyes, so alight with suspicion at all times, yet suggesting the feral volatility Kat had observed them all to be capable of.

'Then winders stay shut, or else,' the creature said in a tobacco-roughened voice, blanched of compassion. 'You even fink –'

'I know! I know.'

'Just so's you do know, door still stays open till you can be trusted.'

The woman sat down on the kitchen stool on the landing outside Kat's bedroom. She'd positioned it there three days before so that Kat could be observed in her bedroom even when she slept.

Downstairs, the bearded oaf opened the fridge door to take out her milk. The electric jug bubbled.

How would they *do it* when the time came? That was her enduring concern now. *In here?* She doubted that. *Too messy,* which made her recall their own unique method for the disposal of human remains and her body chilled to nausea once more.

No matter the endless circling of sickening anxiety and terror, her preoccupations always returned to that question: when the time comes, when their use of me has finished, will they butcher me in *that place*? And then her interior, her weight, her sense of permanency in the world, would appear to diffuse into thin air like a gas and she would rush for the toilet.

Short of being caught up in a war, or involved in a catastrophic accident, she would never have believed that it was possible for a person's life to change beyond recognition in so short a time and by the most brutal means.

Oh, Steve.

'God, no.' Pressing her face deep into the pillow to stifle her anguish, Kat acknowledged an urgent desire to run. She'd gladly run across broken glass with bare feet and she wouldn't stop, to avoid what they'd done to Steve.

Kat closed her eyes. And again, her self-tormenting thoughts returned her to *that place*.

When the stinking black hood had been yanked from her head, the vision confronting Kat's blinking eyes might have been one of hell itself. A version of damnation recreated in mud and wood.

Through the enclosure of shadow, long tongues of reflected firelight had leaped across an earthen floor, soil strewn with matted straw, the tall flames glowing upon the wall's stained planks. Where gaps existed between the boards obsidian night had swallowed the outside world.

A stench of manure, blood and farm animals had arisen from the wet ground. A noisome stink only partly tempered by the pungency of a spicy fragrance, reminiscent of citrus fruit. Intoxicating and so strong, her eyes had watered from exposure to the fumes. Overpowering smoke with a fragrance similar to the skunk weed that Steve had occasionally smoked in her presence. Only this smell was one thousand times stronger and almost living: visible as a bluish smog among rafters intermittently revealed by the spiking flames.

The assault on her senses – her sight, sense of smell, her hearing, the taste in her mouth and the instinctive primal sense that screamed danger – had immediately killed the desperate entreaties she'd been making to her abductors.

During the journey in a vehicle she'd never glimpsed while hooded, she'd pleaded, begged for mercy. But inside *that place*, Kat soon stopped whimpering. Slumped beside the fire, she'd been rendered mute in horrified awe.

They'd unmasked her a few feet from the snap and crackle of a fiery conflagration. Sweat, joining tears, mucus and the horrible condensation from inside the sack, had run freely off her chin, secretions both smearing her face and sliding down her throat.

Red sparks had circled upwards through rags of dirty smoke while embers had spat onto the earthen floor where they'd forced her to kneel. Instantly, the heat had cupped and dried her eyeballs.

Her hands had been secured with green twine. Gardeners used the same string on rose stems. Earlier, in her home, she'd been wrestled to the ground like a steer. A bony, naked knee had been forced between her shoulders and she'd been trussed like livestock. Her one attempt at a scream had been silenced by a blow to the side of the head. One ear had seemed to fill with warm water. A thickening lump had grown on her right temple and pulsed like a small heart. Moving her jaw had remained painful.

Kat didn't know which of the four intruders had struck her. But one of the frightful red things that had broken into her home had knocked her near senseless at the first sign of resistance, enabling the gang to gag her mouth with a rag, bind her, hood her and carry her from the cottage into the cold night.

She'd been dropped onto the unforgiving metal floor of a vehicle that had stunk of dogs and engine oil and driven from her home as her mind had swirled with images of beheadings, figures kneeling before trenches and the wretched remains unearthed in woodlands by policemen who held their forearms across their mouths as they dug . . . The whole process of her capture had felt like a one-way street to a morgue and a coroner's report.

Beside the great fire in the barn, the bearded man and the thin woman with the headscarf had held her still. Her appointed handlers' horrid hands had been clenched in her hair. 'See. See!' the woman had shrieked. And Kat had finally seen: the naked body of a man, a few feet from where she'd knelt.

So smeared with dried blood was the figure and with the filth of the dirty floors that he had lain upon, and so great were the black-green bruises blossoming from swollen puncture wounds and wet rents in the flesh of his limbs, that it had taken Kat a few seconds to recognise her lover, Steve.

He truly had been missing. He'd been snatched from out of the world, like her, and brought here too.

It took Steve far longer to recognise her.

'Love . . . Steve. Steve!' Then, 'What did you do?' she'd screamed at her captors.

In response, her head had been yanked to the side. 'Shut it,' the bearded man had commanded.

Frantic, her burning eyes had swivelled, desperate for understanding, for a sympathetic look, for anything that wasn't the fire and dirt and Steve so physically ruined. And it had hurt her eyes to focus when her teary vision had groped the walls. Firelight had only flickered so far but in places it had pawed at the black edge of the building's grubby interior. Against these walls, where the darkness reddened, murky forms had stood upright. A dozen or so people. All unclothed, their flesh made oily with the scarlet stain. Bare legs, sloppy breasts, rotund bellies, thin legs, the moonlike whites of eyes maddened by fear or excitement, perhaps both. Faces showing even more than that: those teeth-bared expressions had appeared awestruck. To keep her feet, a woman had clung to the wall with her stained hands as if suffering a swoon.

Kat's gorge had risen. Exhausted either by unrelenting terror or by what she suspected might be shock, she'd shivered hard enough to lose control of her body. Coherent thoughts barely forming, her paranoia so intense, she'd hyperventilated. Ever averse to the sight of blood, now exposed to it on the body of someone she loved, she'd retched freely into the soil.

From the braziers mounted on iron stands and set against the walls, the suffocating fumes from the burning drug had potent effect upon her mind. The same smoke must have been disordering Steve's, but for longer.

Stricken by the idea that her mind was unravelling and

erasing itself, she'd believed that her brain was shredding its files in some deluded sense of self-protection, shutting down her system to prevent her continued exposure to what was around her. She'd recalled things she hadn't thought of in years.

Her mother and father at her graduation.

Graham sitting on the end of their bed, staring at the blinds.

Waking up beside a bed after a binge, her nose bleeding.

Her flat in London as the sun poured through the windows in summer.

Viewing her cottage in Devon for the first time.

Slipping down the stairs in a nightclub.

Steve in his wetsuit, shaking water from his hair.

A birthday cake she had as a child, a castle made from chocolate fingers . . .

Opening and closing in fast motion, memories had flashed vividly then disappeared, like the film of a flower opening but speeded up. Her heart had beat four times the recommended speed. She'd retched saliva.

Her straining senses had then become dimly aware of a new and equally undesirable stimulus: another fresh exposure to a horror unwilling to pause. Voices had raised themselves near her. Shrill wails joining each other, forming a piercing falsetto and rising into a horrible skirl as much animal as human.

A reedy piping had caught the clamour of caterwauling voices and directed them higher. Some vocal cords had even broken into shrieks seeking the black rafters high above, smoke-stained, web-choked beams. A crude hole had been fashioned in the tiled roof to let out the smoke, but not enough of it.

Kat had imagined that her skin was about to blister. Her hair would surely catch alight. She'd been placed too close to the pyre and was soon only able to taste smoke and her own stomach acid. A terrible thirst had made her cough. When she'd tried again to pull away from the fire she'd been held fast.

The female shrieks in the choir had transformed to wails never heard at Christian funerals. An elderly woman had batted her head with her hands. Kat had glimpsed the face within that small skull, crowned with bemired spikes of hair, being thumped by scarlet hands: a face so wrinkled it might have been made of bark.

A plump, bald man had stepped forward from the wall and raised his hands into the air, his eyes fixed on something that Kat could not see. Other men had roared, full-throated, straining their lungs. And then the woodwind section had quickly fallen silent and the voices had dropped to a dying wail. Someone had sobbed, briefly, in the darkness on the other side of the pyre, then quietened until only the spit and whoosh of the flames had been audible.

A new voice had broken the lull: one elderly and female, its words so carefully enunciated that Kat might have been in the presence of an aristocrat. A voice from another world, educated and imperious. A voice at once absurd amidst the filth, fire, blood, the white eyes and the noise that had pierced Kat's ears and disintegrated her thoughts.

'The past is red. The earth is red. The sky is red.'

She'd turned to the sound of the voice.

Against the dark rectangle of the double door of the agricultural building, she'd seen that a diminutive figure had been wheeled inside. Behind the ancient figure in the wheelchair, and about its tatty head and through the haze of stinging smoke, the silhouettes of trees beyond the doorway had become momentarily visible.

Crippled and sunken but unclothed, the woman had continued to speak in a voice that sweetened to the melodic: a voice that had issued from the black muzzle of an animal's head. 'Behind is red. Forward is red. The Queen is risen and she is red.'

A tongue of fire had flapped in the direction of the speaker, this aboriginal elder in its wheelchair, the sole item in the building to suggest that Kat remained in the twenty-first century.

The crude red figures of the wretched barn had sniffed and wept at the elderly woman's arrival. They'd wiped at their white, glistening eyes.

'All we children are red. Amen.'

'Amen' had been rumbled in unison around the black walls. Above Kat's lowered head, her captors had muttered the word too. Each of them had then spat on the earthen floor and stamped a naked foot upon the saliva. All around the barn the red people had ground their expulsions into the dirt.

'So close to us now,' the elderly woman had cried out, her voice breathless with excitement, her frail body atremble with emotion. 'So close beneath our feet but also our hearts.'

About the perimeter of the fire's light people had embraced each other. They'd all come together in the darkness. The faces she'd glimpsed had been alight with an unmistakable love, an intense devotion. And they'd begun a horrid dance. A movement as grotesque as it was absurd. Backwards they'd all gone, in a circle, in and out of the firelight, as if entranced by the new, solemn notes of the pipes, functioning like a marionette's strings to jerk them about her and poor broken Steve.

The dreadful eyes of the red people had rolled up white and it must have been the effects of the burning drug that suggested that their arms could snap and move in such contortions behind their backs, or when raised into the air in exultation. Kat had never imagined that the aged could contort themselves so.

Confusion mingling with terror, her eyes blurring with smoke, her face filmed with grease, she'd panted like a dog. And for several seconds Kat had believed that she'd been rising into the air; terrified that if she didn't grip the floor, her feet would have ascended to the roof beams. Her trainers might have been filled with helium. Her head, disproportionately, had been as heavy as a bag of wet sand. She'd doubted her neck could support the weight of her skull.

'Kat.' It was Steve. He'd finally become aware of her. He'd been crying.

Kat had opened her mouth but her tongue had been too thick and heavy, a large slug. She'd doubted she had a voice left at all.

A vibration had passed beneath her knees. Through the soil a mighty current of electricity may have thrummed. Deeper still had come the rumble of thunder, or rocks grinding, or the earth moving. A tremor from deep within the soil.

'Give her scent,' the old creature in the chair had intoned. 'Let what is so great fill red. Let the walls and the air be red. Let the earth soak red and the sky be red. Let us be blessed in the red. We are red. This, our reddening.'

'Reddening' was shrieked about the barn.

The wizened figure in the wheel chair had risen swiftly from its seated position, thin arms raised high. And as if young again, the woman had walked, in a wretched parody of provocation, across the dung and soil. Each heel placed perfectly before each set of toes, her withered hips swaying: a demented pastiche of a catwalk model with that shaggy, bestial head grinning through the firelight.

And at the figure's approach, Kat had suddenly cramped with a fear that the attention of whatever peered through the black muzzle would turn upon her.

The congregation had issued fresh cries of awe before the miracle, if that was what it had been: the lame walking, the decrepit renewed. Others had ventured forward from the far side of the fire and out of the darkness. Naked, oiled forms. Devil faces creosoted in dye. In their midst had been a thin, bent figure, leaning upon a stick. A furred wolfish head had dwarfed its frail body, seeming to weigh the torso down at a tilt.

With reverence, a younger woman and a portly man had each held an elbow to lead the tottering figure closer to the fire. They encircled Steve.

What happened next did not remain entirely clear in Kat's memory. One of few mercies she was granted that night. And she'd later wondered how much she'd seen or only imagined. She now even wondered if she'd been dreaming in that barn with her eyes wide open.

Through the skeins of smoke, the barn's timbers had transformed into walls of stone, but without her noticing the transition. Rock walls had appeared on either side of her and above her head. A cave chalked, painted red. Upon the rough rock surfaces the sensual silhouettes of beasts had been shaped from charcoal: herds of animals, glimpsed betwixt rags of smoke. The creatures had been moving too. Their thin legs had flickered back and forth as the beasts had surged. Horses, oxen, reindeer. And yet, impossibly, the animals had remained in place upon the walls, running forever but never progressing.

It was around the time of her hallucinations when she'd realised that Steve had been tethered to an iron ring, cemented into the rough floor: a short chain lying idle beneath his legs, the links connecting his ankle to a circular mooring. He'd been placed upon a patch of firmer ground, a lighter patch of floor, level with the soil. A portion partly cleared of dung and straw to reveal cement and a metal grille. Steve hadn't been lying on the earth.

When the elderly male figure in the mask had begun uttering a series of deep, croaking noises at the back of its throat, Kat had been reminded of a Siberian throat singer she'd once seen in London at a music festival. But this man's performance would never make *Time Out*: this was something the general public were not supposed to see.

Two men had immediately stepped forward from behind the masked elder and seized Steve under his arms.

Kat's lover hadn't resisted. It seemed he'd become accustomed, or broken, to this method of transport.

The fire's light had offered a better view of the shaggy muzzle of the beast man's mask. Flame-red illumination had flickered over black gums and the aged enamel protruding from a permanently open mouth, the mask's jaws and teeth resembling those of a great animal, a preserved panther or lion. The surrounding features might also have been a replication of a canine head: pug-snouted, whiskered, flat-skulled and broad in the forehead. And from within the darkness of the tatty jaws the elderly man had gutturalised and grunted what might have been human words rendered in a savage tongue.

It had been a command.

Hair gripped in a greasy, red fist, Steve's head had promptly been pushed into the noisome floor of the barn. And his arms had been arranged at the side of his body, his legs following: his body shaped into a star, face-down.

Instinctively, Kat had surged toward him but was held fast by the hair and throat. She'd instantly suffered thoughts of broken bones in glass cubicles at Exeter Museum: shattered fragments, rusticated the colour of bleached seashells.

The old man's dog head had grunted out fresh commands in the bestial language and Kat had recalled where she'd heard similar before: the voice on the recordings that Helene's brother had made at Redstone Cross, the brother who'd vanished.

She'd sobbed then, sobbed at her own helplessness. And at that point in the wretched proceedings, Kat might have pleaded too, on Steve's behalf, but hadn't known if she'd been shouting or merely whispering, or only thinking of a protest. Confusion, terror and a sickening dread had swamped her consciousness.

A burly male figure, its beard a tangled mess of red scrub, had then knelt beside Steve's ear. He'd held a dark lump of stone against Steve's face. The rock had flickered with the pyre's reflections before the point of the tool was repositioned above the nape of Steve's neck.

Kat had later queried whether she'd passed out at that point because she remembered being shaken while someone had hissed, 'See!' into her ear. But she'd kept her eyes closed as a human scream had broken into a cough. The cough had then evolved into a moist, glottal rasp, suggesting that a terrible finality had been achieved.

When she'd been slapped alert, what she saw had since existed in haphazard form, in flashes.

Sinewy forearms glistening by firelight. Hands slippery and gloved in bright scarlet. A hand sawing. Another hand tugging at hair and raising a head too far from its shoulders.

The congregation had committed their voices to fresh ululations: exultant, deafening, born from their rejoicing. And in the red barn the fire had leaped higher as four men worked like butchers.

Slick, wet sounds from the carving. Sharp black stones in wet fists, up and down. *Hack hack hack.* Crack of bone, the stretching and splitting of sinew. The black air seething yet squeezing her with its undersea pressures. Smoke billowing about wet straw.

The stone ceiling had seemed to lower to crush Kat's mind. Then the roof had vaulted up and away and she'd wondered if the ceiling of rock had completely gone and the only remaining things were the fire, the stars she saw and the nothingness between them. A void that she could have fallen into at any time.

Her stomach had turned itself inside out. She'd gulped for air but swallowed more of the burning blue smoke. Around her skull thoughts and nonsense had swirled as if it had been stirred from above with a ladle. Her head had been pulled about to watch the slap of a heavy, whitish limb upon the ground before her eyes.

Followed by another.

On the ground there had been a dirty torso with no arms. The neck an oval, white at the centre, a thick snake cut in half.

Forceful sawing between the legs into the V of the groin's meat.

Kat had coughed saliva onto her thighs.

At the edge of her vision had lain an upturned hand, lifeless, the curling fingers dirty.

She'd screamed and screamed.

The red people had shrieked too, they'd brayed like beasts of the field. Their vocal cords had found impossible ranges. Their reedy ululations had made them eunuchs, castrated animals. Each oily face she'd glimpsed had broadened, become more bulbous, scarred and pugnacious. Brute faces, oaf mouths, leather-breasted and bloodied forms shrieking amidst the smoke.

On the walls the animals had continued to lurch, wide-eyed, forever stampeding the ground that had trembled beneath Kat's shivering body.

Wet parts had been raised from the mess on the floor. Heavy meats had been passed out to so many reaching red hands.

Slippery fingers had pulled her forehead upwards so that she could better see a tongue being sawn from out of a human head: one already missing its lower jaw.

'Cuckoos, gabbers and narks all get theirs,' a voice had said.

Dirty knees had bumped her arms. Naked feet had slapped the soil about her fingers. A woman had panted with sexual desire.

She'd looked away, to the side, to the door, as if to draw the colder air into her polluted lungs. But, alas, in such places where hell is made on earth one can never look away from the business of depravity. That had been *his* jawbone that *she* had. That old thing that had risen so youthfully from the wheelchair was unmasked now. And a jawbone had been cracked open and was grasped within its long fingers. Her wrinkled mouth had suckled.

They didn't cook him. They'd consumed his parts raw.

The horror that was behind us in this land is the horror that is now and ahead of us. That has already begun . . . That is come again.

Kat had known it at once, had accepted it. The awareness had dawned with the clarity of a single, finely wrought note, piercing her paddings of disbelief, shock and the nausea of intoxication.

A voice then. From the bearded man who'd held her face upwards, her handler: 'The old ones feed in the old way.' She thought that's what he'd said. And then, 'Watchum your bastard git capped.'

That she hadn't watched. She'd have put her own eyes out with her fingernails when the butcher began his careful chiselling upon the beloved crown of Steve's head. And at that moment she understood that she'd never loved him as much as she had done right then.

Nothing left in her stomach but still it had attempted to empty her body of contaminated air and the brutal sounds of stone on meat and bone and of the sight of those ape-mouths sucking on what grimy fingers had pulled from the feast. And when Kat had dared to hope that her own end would arrive, so that she could be spared what they were making her see, a devil had opened its throat beneath the ground.

Echoing from out of a chamber beneath the barn, or this cave, or whatever this wretched space had become in a fog of smoke, transforming the walls from wood to stone, had come a cackle and yip that Kat had been certain was a human laugh.

A shriek had followed, one distorted by schizophrenia and amplified to ear-splitting volume.

The full-throated baying of a hound.

Followed by the chitter-chatter of an ape.

Nasal whines from a vast muzzle.

Yelps and whinnies. Exotic, zoolike, unearthly.

The ground had shaken from sounds culled from the lowest part of a vocal range, below her knees, *but no longer so far down*. Her mind was squeezed, crushed and flattened by what had vibrated through her ears.

The metal grille, in the centre of the cement that Steve had been tethered to, had been raised from the earth and a noxious wave of air had plumed from the aperture. The stench had made Kat panic as if she'd been exposed to poisonous gas.

Yip yip yip.

Into the dark hole her lover's parts had been tossed. And from down there, in eager receipt of the wet tumble, had come a scrabbling of great claws upon the rock.

Kat had screwed herself into a ball as the red people had fallen over each other in their haste to escape what bayed and leaped and circled from below their bemired feet. Only the elderly male figure in the doggish mask had stood firm. He'd appeared more upright: impossibly taller, erect, the head and shoulders thrown back. And into the air he'd shaken his staff and from his shabby muzzle he'd coughed and growled out more of the rough, unintelligible sounds.

Kat had seen no great beast with muscular flanks that rippled beneath a reeking hide. But she had seen something, or experienced its presence, though only behind her closed eyes and within her mind as the tremendous expulsion of hot, foul air had belched from the ground and filled the cave. A mighty bleat had resounded inside her skull.

Inside her mind she'd also seen a geyser of panic erupt in the wild brown eyes of an animal: orbs peeled by panic into the size of apples. These eyes had filled her thoughts as the creature's flesh had been torn into by spears and sharpened stones. She'd felt the great impact of a woollen side slammed against a snow-dusted earth. *Another victim from another time but brought here.* Reason had become irrelevant but she'd navigated those images as if dreaming. She'd been in the presence of the red. Known this at once, instinctively. There, in that place, had existed an impossible continuity from another time to this one.

And she'd seen these things behind her squeezed-shut eyes: the rough-faced, both young and old, male and female, their bodies stringy and dirty as they'd plodded into a fire-strobed darkness on unshod feet. Tatty-headed people herded by red devils. She'd seen their huddled forms dragged to the floor and sawn into. All in this very place, in other times. *Razor flint, black and iridescent, parting joints, separating limbs from . . .* for ever and ever.

Down there, under the barn, she'd listened to the consummation of the rite. Slippery bones had been crunched by teeth that must have been longer than thumbs. Devils that once clawed that very ground had pawed the fetid soil again: she sensed the steam-breathing snouts of black things that had once trodden the earth when it was much colder, those that had flowed sinewy from out of crevices and galloped the surrounding plains. And they had been returned for a terrible succour in that same darkness, partially illuminated by firelight.

Had there been words in that pit too? Voices? She'd thought so, but in no language that she'd ever recognise.

Eventually rough hands had pulled her backwards and away from the fire.

All who'd been summoned to that awful place had withdrawn from the lightless crevice in the floor, a fissure in stone, beneath the grate that had been Steve's final bed. Inside the barn, all had retreated save the elderly man who'd stood too tall and the smeared ancient woman who had risen from her wheelchair to prance and parade like a young girl before a bedroom mirror.

21

*O*utside, four dogs had kept pace with Kat and her captors. Hounds that had come and gone, milling, circling, walking point, pausing to raise their noses into the cold night as she was pulled to a second broken building. Rusting bars had gridded its solitary window.

That room's interior had resembled a workshop and had reeked of oiled steel, dust, damp wood. Amber light had fallen from bulbs collared by old tin funnels. A long rectangular table dominated, its timber surface scarred, vices attached to the sides. Worn drilling and sawing equipment had rusted in a corner. Dirty rendered walls thickly lined with metal shelves had been crowded with variously sized stones, lumps of rock and long bones.

The surface of a second workbench had been scattered with tools and open boxes, oily rags and dross. But upon that surface Kat had seen a great tusk: bigger, thicker and longer than an elephant's. *Mammoth*: she'd seen them at the exhibition in Exeter.

From the workshop two men had carried her through a connecting door and into an annexe, a smaller space with red walls turned powdery from damp. Inside, an elderly man had sat upon an old office chair: a red room with an old red man inside.

His withered form was no longer so straight. He'd wilted and re-aged. Sweat streaking his thin, whiskery face had made the rheumy blue eyes weep blood. Beside his foot, his evil-looking headgear had grimaced in silence.

The old figure had nodded at the two men gripping Kat's upper arms and they'd released her to the floor, where she'd shivered, gasping, her toxic shock lingering as a permanent electrification of nerve and sense. The liquor from her nausea had made her skin slick.

The old, ruined man had smiled. His teeth had been bad, missing in places, top and bottom at the front. Those remaining were deformed: whittled yellow pegs. He might have been imbecilic had his eyes not leered with such a frightful confidence and cruel intelligence.

'The red miraculous. You don't know yourself.' Like the elderly woman who'd worn an animal mask, his words had purred, a voice enriched by privilege. 'What comes to us is too great to know.' He'd said this while nodding his scraggy head as if sharing knowledge that Kat already possessed: a man merely retelling and reaffirming what was known by all present. 'So be thankful you never saw the pack.'

When the figure had winced and leaned to the side his eyes had lost focus, the smile dying. He'd slumped and sighed, wafting a bony hand in the air. 'How it comes and goes . . .' he'd said quietly to himself and she'd been convinced of his madness. 'There aren't songs. Why try?'

Kat had swallowed the burning sensation in her throat to speak. 'Willows . . . You're Tony.'

One of the old eyes had reopened and filled with a brief awareness of itself, then closed again.

'The recordings, Tony.' This new voice had originated from behind her shoulder, from the bearded man who had snatched her from out of her home and her life so that he could hold her down in animal shit while they'd *done that* to Steve.

'Yes, E. Ours. Bring our songs home,' Tony had muttered.

The bearded man had pressed his slimy face against Kat's, the sensation of his wet hair on her eyelids making her cringe. 'Her brother wiv the recorder we gave up to the red, yeah? You know what I'm saying. We don't have narks here. He found that out. That one whose just gone froo red jaws would tell you that too, if he could. But he's gone froo the walls, see. So this girl with the discs, you will bring to us. Your fella give you up easy. But you don't have to go where he's gone.'

Kat hadn't understood much of what he'd said and hadn't responded.

'Another life. All gone,' Tony had muttered and rubbed his sunken chest.

Against her cheek, she'd felt the wet beard widen into a grin. 'Guess how old he is, yeah? Nearly eighty. Shouldn't be here. Heart. His heart was fucked. And *her*, guess how old? Witchwife's even older. Cancer should have had her twice. The red bit it out. The red looks after its own, yeah? Some is favoured. You is not, nor *him* . . .' The bearded figure at her side had snorted a chuckle and Kat had known he'd been referring to Steve. 'You don't know nuffing. We's the ones who let the dogs in.' He'd chuckled to himself, his breath a wheeze, and tapped his hoary head before pointing at the floor. 'You wouldn't believe what's down there. But turn that word inside out and dog becomes "God". Yeah? Yeah? You see, hmm? I fink you might grasp a bit of it.'

Old Tony on the chair had merely shrugged and opened his old hands as if this business had nothing to do with him; as if he'd merely been a spectator, indifferent to the woman before his gnarled feet. Then he'd grinned like an idiot. 'Old Creel. Those pups hunger, what?'

The wet beard had brushed Kat's ear again. 'In times coming. Terrible it is, terrible times . . . There's what, seven billion of us? Who gives a fuck? *They* don't. You's all going. You is, yeah?'

His breath had been too foul for her to focus on much else. She'd not understood much of the idiotic jabber either and thought it a half-understood version of what the bearded oaf had been told by someone else: knowledge he believed fervently that had enabled him to perform such inhuman acts upon a stranger. She'd truly entered a land of psychotics and met its crazed inhabitants.

'All going. Going, going, going,' Tony had said. He'd seemed to think his affected sardonic air was funny; he'd been amused with himself. He might have been drunk, drugged or just deranged.

Kat's own mind had remained full to capacity with what the smoke had done. What she'd experienced her mind had quickly put from itself in order to survive the ordeal, leaving her unthinking, unresisting and numb. She hadn't trusted her thoughts since: her short recall was full of blanks.

'Please,' she'd said to stem the hysteria that had wanted to burst free.

'It's in the stones.' Tony had pointed at the floor. 'There's sound in the red earth. Music. Visions. Poems.'

Other bodies had crowded into the room. Another man had crouched beside Kat, taking the place of the foul-breathed oaf who'd abducted her. This man's hair was thinning and scraped over his skull. A thin rat's tail soaked in red ochre had fallen down his naked back. In one hand he'd held a joint and the smoke had seared Kat's eyes. When her discomfort had registered he'd deliberately held the burning weed under her chin.

'What Daddy and my associate are trying to tell you is that you are going to bring those recordings to us. All of her fucking gadgets. This girl that has them, some sister, yes, of that thief we put to the red years ago. She comes to us with what she has, yes? You understand? Dear Steve told us all about her. Helene. And her CDs. That music belongs here and shouldn't be above the ground, ever. So how this plays out is now up to you, yes?'

He'd then dropped his well-spoken voice to a whisper. 'You wouldn't believe what we can see. Backwards. Forwards. All about. Including right into every nook and cranny of your drab life. We're completely out of our heads right now. It takes time to readjust but I'm positive you get the gist, yes? So you've some messages to pass on to dear Helene.

'You know, she was even here. We had her here! She came here, like her brother. Nosing. Cuckoos. Neither of them had one iota of sense. They couldn't begin to imagine what they were fucking with. And if you never want to see us, or this place again, or come anywhere near what we have *down below*, then you've some *arrangements* to make.'

Kat had nodded her assent.

'You'll never forget tonight and don't try and understand it. Because you won't, ever. None of this is for you, yeah? I can sense that. You're bright enough to lay off. So play along and the big dogs won't bite.

'My associates will take you home now, so you can get the ball rolling with Helene. Once you've finished throwing up and all that.'

At the outer limits of her hearing, possibly from beyond the doorway, a voice had said, 'He's here. Five minutes.'

And then Kat's head had been re-gloved by the hood and she'd been taken outside. A car engine had rumbled in the distance and she'd been half-dragged towards it.

Voices and the sound of bare feet had come and gone within her blindness. Someone had wept. She'd heard an animal cough and had whimpered at the sound. When dog claws had scratched about the road surface near her feet and a wet snout had sniffed her crotch, she'd screamed.

Overhead lights had bathed the ground as she'd neared the idling car engine. She'd heard the roar of a plane's engine, too close to the ground.

Lying on the cold metal floor of the van, barely able to breathe, she'd then been taken home. Impossibly, unbelievably, they'd driven her home. They hadn't cut her apart and fed her to the devils in the cave, nor chiselled off the top of her skull. They'd just taken her home to its absurd light and modernity and possessions that meant nothing and offered no security.

Two uninvited guests had stayed with her and they'd not let her out of their sight since. Naked and sobbing, her hands flat against the tiles, she'd even showered before the eyes of the murdering strangers. But no amount of hot water and continual scrubbing had rid her body of the terrible stench that had dispersed from the cleft in their red earth. And nothing on the planet would ever scrub her mind clean of what they'd done to Steve.

22

is mum and dad. His bloody mum and dad.

Steve's mother, Delia, was coming apart on her sofa. Kat doubted she'd ever seen a body shake as much. Reg clutched his wife's hands as if to prevent her twitching free of the furniture.

Delia was barely recognisable. Naturally thin maybe but she'd recently developed a crippling stoop. Legs and hips at the point of collapse, she'd been led inside the cottage by her husband. Only one eye seemed to be functioning behind her glasses. While crisis pummelled her mind and set fire to her nervous system, all of Delia's focal power was concentrated into that one interrogative orb.

Kat's call to them, three days before, had fertilised the first seed of concern in Delia about her son. The seed had germinated into chronic anxiety and subsequently flowered into a panic that required sedation.

Over the last few days, Delia's periodic calls to establish if Kat had 'heard anything yet' had been her only contact with Steve's parents. Her petty estrangement from Reg and Delia had maintained a distance but it had finally been erased by parental terror: a fear now slipping towards grief. Mourning was the unavoidable conclusion to their plight, though Kat was unable to get them started on what she was suffering.

Reg had never entirely disapproved of their son's choice of girlfriend. Kat had shared the occasional bout of camaraderie with Steve's dad and they both read le Carré. At the handful of stilted dinners she'd endured with them, he'd found Kat's company easy enough when Delia wasn't micromanaging him and everyone else in the room. But little bread had been broken between them.

Now, Kat wondered if she'd ever experienced such desperate social discomfort. She was trapped by it, clueless about what to offer the couple by way of support. Hideously, what made things easier was her inability to share anything other than what the red folk had told her to say.

In a single, mad surge of excitement that nearly became action, she did consider telling his parents the truth. Just letting it all spill from her mouth. But she remembered the keen edge of the bearded man's flint against her soft throat and she assumed that if she confessed, the red folk would have no choice but to butcher all three of them.

When Steve's parents arrived, her two guardians had retreated to the kitchen. As she'd been instructed, Kat had meekly told Reg and Delia that the strange man and woman in her home were neighbours offering support. Steve's parents had accepted the lie without comment. They weren't interested in her arrangements, they just wanted their son back.

The red folk now stood near the kitchen door and listened to every word that was being exchanged in the living room. Neither Reg nor Delia seemed aware of them. Scrubbed of the red dye, her jailers were merely ordinary, scruffy people.

Reg spoke in taut specifics. 'It was a farmer out by Whaleham. He saw a person in the water. This was the same evening that Steve took his walk.'

The mention of 'water' quickly sent Delia into a fresh paroxysm of shudders.

'They think,' Reg continued, 'that he might have fallen. And with the tide going out and an offshore wind . . . The farmer reported it to the coastguard. They sent a boat from Divilmouth but couldn't find him. This all happened before we knew he was missing. Apparently it's happened before, with walkers. Out there.'

'But what was he doing there, at that time?' Delia shrieked, as if fatigued by her husband's soft voice and his considered words, so weary with resignation. For Delia, this was no time for polite reasoning; it was high time answers were thumped out of people. 'He must have told you! He was always here!' Her one sentient eye bored into Kat; she sensed it searching the interior of her skull, seeking insincerity.

Sheila's contact on the force, Lewis, had called Kat that morning to take a more official statement about Steve. That time, the levity had been absent from the detective's voice. Kat had assumed that the humouring smirk had also been stowed, chastened by the reality of an actual missing person, something he'd almost laughed off in Sheila's office.

During the call, Detective Lewis never mentioned Steve's Redstone Farm theories, nor anything of that nature that she'd recounted to him when they'd met at *L&S*. Nor did he refer to anything she'd said about Matt Hull. Kat wondered how thoroughly those details were being investigated, if at all.

Prompting the detective for progress on those fronts had been impossible because the bearded oaf who'd invaded her home had been holding a flint knife under her jaw. He'd also put the call on speaker and then confiscated the phone. She had no landline. Her laptop and tablet had been removed. As far as she knew they were no longer at the property.

Numb with dread now, Kat felt unable to do much but sit patiently and listen to Reg's account of how he and Delia had busied themselves with the coastguard, the police, the local hospitals and their son's extended network of friends: the windsurfers and old schoolmates, anyone who might offer some flotsam of optimism about Steve's whereabouts. As if Kat couldn't be trusted, she'd been cut out of this investigation through official channels. Had her own circumstances been different, she'd have been offended by the dismissal.

But they'd never know the truth. Never know why they'd never see their only son again, alive or dead. Kat was the only person in Steve's sphere who knew he wasn't coming back, not ever. There was nothing left to return.

Kat failed to stem the return of the vague, opaque state

of mind that Steve's parents had disrupted. Her attention drifted, musing on the fresh perspectives brought here by her dead lover's parents, these pale, hapless figures sitting on her sofa.

The news of a 'farmer's' report to the coastguard about a 'person in the water' offered chilling insights into those behind Steve's ghastly demise. This witness was clearly lying: Steve had never been in the water. So that would mean the farmer was covering for Willows's sect, this coven, cult or whatever it was that these 'red children' had formed near that stretch of coast.

This also served as endorsement of Matt Hull's claims that Redstone Farm had a long local reach. When she'd met Helene at the Redhill festival, her guardians had exchanged looks of recognition with others: the subtle slide or narrowing of their eyes that day had not escaped Kat. They'd also fielded numerous calls since occupying her home; people had come to the door with supplies, all part of the network.

Kat recalled the few farms marked on Steve's map, dotted between Divilmouth and Brickburgh; Redhill was the sole village. For all she knew, everyone living in that borough was part of Willows's operation. She and Steve had been clueless about what they were up against until it was too late.

Only Matt Hull had offered any vestige of the sinister truth. An insider who'd loosened the crust. Her boyfriend had knocked the scab off. Because she was a journalist with a connection to each man they'd unwittingly served her with notice of an impending, vile death.

She wanted to be sick again.

Steve's hunches had been right. And there also existed a lead to Lincoln, Helene's brother. The man at the farm with the wispy beard and rat face had admitted as much. She assumed the weasel was Tony Willows's son, Finn: he'd been mentioned on Wikipedia.

They'd murdered Lincoln Brown six years before. Helene's brother had gone 'to the red', not off a bridge in Bristol. As no body had been found, Kat had to assume that Lincoln had been slaughtered like Steve. His suicide and Steve's slipping from the cliffs in the dark were setups. Matt Hull was missing. The walker, the campers: no bodies in any situations strung across six years and counting.

The imminent slaughter of Helene, whom she'd lured to the coast with promises of news of her brother's last week alive, plus herself: the tally was mounting.

Was Helene even still alive?

Clothing folded on the shore and cars left at notorious sites used by suicides: easy to arrange. No evidence of foul play. The red people had form; the craft of *disappearing* someone was much practised.

This compelled her to wonder how many other souls had been disposed of at the farm, because this was serial murder committed by a group. Ritual murder. And maybe it even began when the young woman died in mysterious circumstances at one of Tony Willows's debauches in the late Seventies. Perhaps the abattoir had been open long before then. She'd never know.

Didn't killers often get away with their crimes for years? Many of them were never caught at all. Kat was aware of the theories, including the one that suggested that most missing people were the victims of serial killers. No witnesses, no bodies and the tracks went cold within twenty-four hours.

Unknowingly, she might have been living next to a cottage-murder-industry for years. It was preposterous. *Here*, where people took their holidays in caravans, where snowbirds retired with a sea view. Absurdity and improbability the best camouflage that Tony Willows could have asked for; far better than his masquerade as a recluse.

Right here, a broad slate was being wiped clean. Nothing was being left to chance. Every leak, no matter how vague, was being sealed. And when Kat considered the age of the caves and of what had been found inside them, the true length of Brickburgh's murderous legacy could only be imagined.

Heartbroken girlfriend of drowned man commits suicide: Kat experienced no difficulty writing the headline of her own obituary. She was next.

But the motives of the red folk? They didn't seem so simple.

Matt Hull and Steve had seen things; Lincoln had recorded weird underground noises on Tony's land. They'd been caught snooping. *Narks*, that's what the bearded oaf, earwigging from her kitchen, had called Steve: 'a nark'.

But were people dying because of the drugs or because they'd passed close to something else, something unnatural? Something that had been hidden under that farm for years? Something far worse than a crop of weed?

The implications of what she'd heard beneath that barn, while drugged by the intolerable skunk fumes, she'd barely considered since, because memories of the bestial sounds were always accompanied by vivid images of Steve's end: the jumbled, blurred and assorted stages of his butchery, murky yet poignant recollections that continually made her sick.

And yet everything she'd believed about the earth, the cosmos and the natural laws that governed it might no longer be the whole story.

With what mental capacity fear had allowed her to reason with, she'd struggled with that idea more than anything else.

The red man with the ponytail had advised her not to attempt an understanding of what she'd experienced. Enlightenment for her was an impossibility: that had been his message. But it was reasonable to assume that whatever had noisily consumed the son of the two people currently falling apart in her living room might not have been natural in the sense that she'd previously considered anything to be natural. When lying a few feet from that awful crack in the earth, what she'd heard from beneath the ground of an outbuilding did not easily occupy any 'normal' classification of animal that she could identify.

There was always a slim chance that Tony kept wild and savage beasts down there, inside a cave or pen – attack dogs, big cats. And there had been several things down there, a pack of some kind. Drug dealers had macho affectations. Weren't people always seeing odd things on the moors like big cats?

But other fragments of evidence did not support this wishful thinking. How had the two elderly and decrepit individuals in that barn assumed the stature, dexterity and strength of people aged a fraction of their years? Why had the wooden walls become stone before her eyes? How had rock walls painted with the prehistoric imagery of extinct animals become animated?

Might the effects of the burning drug have caused her delusions? Had everyone in that barn been hallucinating too?

Or did Tony Willows's farm maintain an unnatural continuity with the past? An era most bloody and cruel, in which survival was determined by the murder of others within a cold, harsh climate.

Relics from such a time, tens of thousands of years earlier, had littered the cases of the museum in Exeter. The dig was no more than three miles from Redstone Farm.

Kat was surprised at herself for even entertaining the idea. But how could it not be considered?

The ritual and ceremonial practices attributed to the Red Queens of Brickburgh and their homicidal shamanic successors might still be a going concern. Cannibals had occupied those caves, on and off, across sixty thousand years. Neanderthal children had been devoured a stone's throw from Redstone Cross. Human heads had been *capped*, bones splintered, then gnawed for their marrow by busy human teeth. The shelves of Tony's outbuildings had been crammed with artefacts.

While psychotic from LSD overuse, maybe Tony Willows had found something on his land and copied it? It seemed unimaginable, the stuff of fiction. But Kat knew the only things stranger than fiction were the people who inhabited reality.

'But why was he even there? On those cliffs. That's what I don't understand!' Delia shrieked, breaking Kat's preoccupation. Reg's muttered pleas for Delia to calm herself were ignored.

He was there because he was looking for a crazy story about an old folk singer who grew drugs on his farm, who made people disappear if they trespassed on his land. And your son discovered that his crazy, paranoid conspiracy theory was half-true, and that the whole truth was far worse. But he died with all of this knowledge. As I will too, with what I know. Soon.

Kat excused herself from the living room. She went upstairs to be sick. The old woman in the headscarf followed her. 'Juz seein' she's OK,' she said to Reg and Delia.

Delia was crying again. Reg remained polite and said, 'Of course. Thank you for helping Kat. You're so very kind.'

Upstairs in the bathroom, Kat fell to her knees.

23

*B*eing in the presence of open sea offers a unique perspective. Even when an onlooker is standing a few feet from where the foamy shallows lap the sand, beholding such an indifferent vastness can consume a mind. A fleeting comprehension conjures the sense of deep personal insignificance and an acute vulnerability before an insurmountable, barely knowable presence.

A belittling of the sense of self is even more apparent when you are afloat upon the surface of the sea, aware of those leagues of empty, lightless water below your frail body. Being beyond sight of land can electrify a mind with wonder but mostly with a great and suffocating terror. Helene only experienced the latter.

She spent a fair bit of her free time at home in water, swimming in the safe, chlorinated pool of a local leisure centre. Up and down, up and down, until she'd covered one mile, three afternoons each week before picking up her daughter from school. As an adult she'd swum in the sea too, during holidays in Spain and Portugal, but that was many years before she became a mother.

During her short trip to Devon Helene never expected to find herself so suddenly and intimately reacquainted with the heaving power of the ocean: the elemental vastness, the swamping pressure upon her mind shaping prospects too frightening to analyse, and promising to be the last thing she'd ever experience.

Even before they'd removed the hood, she'd smelled the brine and heard the slop and splash of the swell against the hull of the boat she'd been taken aboard. Below deck, she had become instantly aware of the immensity of unlit water surrounding the vessel, and of the depthless canopy of air above the sea's surging surface.

The three-man crew took her a long way out. As the motor of the boat chugged, even though she was hooded and without sight, she'd sensed the safety of land reducing to a thin strip of darkness behind her, twinkling with occasional lights, so far off and beyond reach.

The comprehension of what she was being ferried into had made her shudder bone-deep and she'd whimpered like a child. What was about to swallow her seemed far more frightening than the intentions of those who'd seized and bound her like an animal they'd trapped. But they were only people. Horrible, callous, cruel and psychotic strangers who'd painted themselves red for some bizarre reason known only to themselves. The threat of the sea was deeper, colder, less personal, impervious to entreaties or negotiation. The sea didn't even let you breathe beneath its monumental surface. The very idea of so much open water had accelerated her agoraphobic panic.

Earlier, in darkness, three men had boarded the boat with Helene. Two of them had carried her below deck. Prior to casting off, and for some time once their van stopped rattling down a steep hill, their feet had crunched on sand and pebbles. She'd heard their exertions, the gasps and grunts as they'd carried her weight and length through the night. Their feet had eventually sloshed through shallow water and only then was she reminded of how the temperature dropped like a stone once you were mere feet from the sea's surface.

Her legs had been tied together at the knee. That felt odd, her knees bound, with the twine wrapped around a towel. Her arms were secured at the elbow with a second towel slipped between her joints and the binding of rope. *But not secured by wrists and ankles?* She'd been bound at the guesthouse, on the floor of reception, as if her captors hadn't wanted the bindings to hurt her if she struggled. But concern for her comfort was the furthest thing from their minds.

The people with the red faces who'd come running through the house like excited hell clowns and then pulled her to the ground were not on the boat. But images of them had endured in Helene's mind the whole time she'd lain on the metal floor of the van that took her to the shore. Inside the closeness of the hood, her most vivid memory had been of Carol making that horrible dingo sound. As Helene was seized, from behind the reception desk the elderly woman had barked like an old lunatic mistaking itself for a dog.

Their job done, Carol had stayed behind at the guesthouse with her blood-faced comrades. The men on the boat weren't painted. Their eyes weren't swivelling, wide and messed-up on some kind of drug either. They'd been outside when she was captured and bound. Their van had been parked in a lane shielded by a hedgerow, near the guesthouse. The first wave of attack had involved the red lunatics; the second assault comprised three unpainted men in drab, ordinary clothes. The latter had been more methodical, silent, less aggressive.

Aboard the little boat, when they finally ripped the hood from her head, the crew didn't look her in the eye. Whatever they'd planned they wanted done quickly. They weren't drunk and she felt no sexual threat: the only upside she could scratch from the situation. Nor did they want to hear what she had to say. Onboard, the muffling rag remained taut between her jaws.

Once Helene blinked away the tears scalding her eyes, she was confronted by the confines of the small white cabin. She lay between a padded bench and what resembled a kitchenette counter in a caravan.

The boat appeared new, its surfaces shiny. No scratches, no signs of wear. A few cupboards, a little table supported by aluminium legs, a padded bench seat, three steps that ascended to a bridge and the broad back of the man who piloted the boat.

She guessed that between thirty to forty minutes had passed since they'd snatched her from the guesthouse. And despite her panic, there had been enough time for her to form some perspective on what was going down tonight. Kat made a lot more sense now. The state of the woman at the festival, the psychological collapse, was part of *this*. Kat had asked her to come to Devon specifically for *this* and even provided her with accommodation. She'd been set up.

What was wrong with people that they would do something like this? And to a stranger who has already lost her brother? That's what she'd asked herself self-pityingly and what she'd asked of God, who she dearly hoped was listening.

Kat's desire for Lincoln's discs was connected. But these men and those red horrors were welcome to them. There was no need for any of this. She'd have handed them over at the first sound of a raised voice.

There had also been ample time for her to suffer desperate thoughts of home, of her daughter and her mum. Recurring thoughts of Valda dominated and formed a heartbreaking loop. Helene had told herself not to cry, not to lose it. She had to keep her head straight to reason with the men who'd bound and gagged her and taken her out to sea in their boat . . . *out to sea, oh Jesus.* She'd faint if she thought about that part too closely.

Perhaps they only intended to frighten her. *Job done.*

But once the hood was off, she did lose it. Only a thin fibreglass hull now separated Helene and the sea, an alien region that you'd never see the end of this far out. And her terror of that immensity of water and sky returned. It was choking. No lifeguards, no shallow end out where she'd been taken. Not much natural light with the sun sunk below the horizon.

She cried upon the fibreglass floor of the boat that smelled of oil, bleach and the sea. Oddly, weeping helped, at first. But then crying tipped her into hysteria and she flipped about the wet floor of the boat like a big fish that her abductors had landed. She kicked both feet into the furniture, uselessly.

The pilot told the younger man, 'Hold her still. Don't want her chokin' on her tongue. Nor gettin' bumped about.'

With his long fingers that stank of tobacco, the younger man with the alert eyes and sallow skin pushed her shoulders into the fibreglass deck. 'I'll sit on ya if you don't stop,' he said.

They'd gently placed Helene on the floor before setting sail and had been very careful with any physical contact since they'd collected her from the naked aborigines at the guesthouse. A strange consideration.

The third man in the red baseball cap and sunglasses wouldn't look at her at all. His face was pale. He stood at the stern, above the motor's churn, and looked out at nothing: there was nothing to see but black water and a matching sky.

When the boat slowed, the engine thudding then whining like a food mixer, Helene nearly threw up. The winding-down of the motor implied a terrible finality. Only the rag between her jaws held nausea at bay.

'Gag's leavin' marks,' the younger man said. His fingertips were hurting her shoulders. The youth was so frightened or excited that he probably didn't know he was bruising her skin. If not leaving marks had been an objective, these men had failed.

'Get it off her then!' the pilot barked.

Surely they aren't really going to hurt me. Her head seemed to clear, momentarily. *This cannot be real. They're just trying to scare you. They won't . . .*

And why was she even here? She was a single mum who lived in Walsall, who worked part-time in an office. She'd never done anything to deserve this. She'd come to Devon for the weekend to see people who knew about her brother, who'd died years ago under his own volition. So why was she out at sea, lying on the floor of a boat, bound and gagged? Because of some old recordings that had been in her garage for half a decade? If the CDs accounted for her current plight, they already had them. One of the red things at the guesthouse, a woman with the hair oiled-out from her skull like a scarecrow, had hooted and scampered up the stairs to retrieve Lincoln's discs and the laptop from Helene's room. So them having those discs didn't make sense of her plight. Nothing did.

'Why?' she asked once the gag came off. 'What have I done?' Her tearful voice was both too young and too old for her.

The man in the red cap clutched at the steel railing that ran around the stern. Helene guessed he was struggling with the situation too: this plan, or intention, that had been devised to terrify her, or to achieve something far worse.

She remembered some of what she'd planned to say to them when she'd been lying on the floor of the van. 'People know . . . they know I was at that hotel . . . I've used credit cards down here.' She hadn't, but how did these men know? 'There are emails and phone calls between me and Kat. I told people where I was going!'

'You'll not have to worry about that bint,' the pilot said, as he came down the steps from the bridge heavily. His trainers expelled air as his weight thumped down, *whuff, whuff, whuff.* He was the only one present who seemed comfortable with the situation. A bald, stocky man with a face that looked like ham moulded into porcine features. He wheezed like an asthmatic but the suggestion of strength in his solid pink arms was intimidating. She suspected he was trying to generate confidence to bolster the resolve of the other two men. 'She wunt be found.'

Helene flinched when the younger man shrieked like an animal: the same sound the red people had made at the guesthouse. *Naked, barefoot, howling.*

'Not 'ere!' the older man said. 'That don't concern the sea. Only the red earth. She ain't for that.'

'Please,' Helene said.

The men still wouldn't look at her, not in the eye.

She swallowed. 'I have a little girl. She's only six. She needs me . . .' Her voice broke.

The man in the red cap in the stern dipped his head and spat over the side of the boat. His younger comrade grinned.

There were tiny spittle balls around his whiskery mouth. His pulse thumped inside his throat. The eyes in his thin face were those of a confused dog.

'Don't got ya sea legs, Phil!' the bald pilot shouted at the man in the red cap. Then he whispered 'Soft cunt' to Helene, grinning as if they were friends sharing an observation about a mutual acquaintance.

Helene didn't think the pig captain was sane. There was something wrong with his reaction to the situation, to her being so upset and distressed and frightened on the floor of his boat. He had no empathy or pity. He regarded her plight with an air of amused indifference as if he couldn't take her circumstances seriously. Job needed doing, that sort of vibe. He wanted the onboard atmosphere to be light and seemed disappointed by the lack of camaraderie.

'S'not right!' Phil in the red cap blurted. 'Not this!'

'Fuck off!' the ham-pilot shouted at his comrade. His piggy eyes reddened and he might have been on the verge of dispensing violence about the small craft. An unstable man, perhaps even more unhinged than the grinning, twitching youth. 'The red not bin good to you, aye, Phil? You was fuck-all when it crept round your door. Think we don't all sin you scratching about? A pisshead? Your dad woulda lost his farm, everyfing. You was no help to fucking no one. You tellin' me this ain't worth what you has? Fuck off. You do your bit same as all. Ain't that right, Richey? Don't see him puking when he's driving that Range Rover, aye. That bit he's happy with.'

The thin head of the younger man bobbed in agreement. His eyes were permanently startled now, unable to rest upon any single thing.

'You fuckin' enjoy it!' the man in the red cap roared.

'You watch your mouf. None a that. None a that. Or I'll put you over too.'

Oh God, they're going to throw you over the side. Arms and legs tied. At that moment, Helene sensed the excoriating froth of the sea in her throat. Saw herself coughing as a wave covered her face.

'Won't fool nobody, you stupid pig-headed fucker!' Phil in the red cap yelled. 'She just told ya. People knows she's down here.'

'Messing with your head. They'll say anyfing when they're caught. You seen them go into the red, ain't ya? Hear it free or four times more and it don't mean nuffing. They goes in the red and we is gifted. No more to it than that. Stop complicating fings. What's it matter anyway? You sin what's coming to all of them, aye? But not us. Who you wanna be, them or us? Old witch-wife opened your eyes, so why is you closing them again?'

'They . . . they got forensics and things. When she washes up . . . They'll know. They'll know!'

'Reason why others do the thinking in the red is cus you're a stupid cunt, Phil. You fink she's the first? The red'll keep us, no worries. We've coppers, councillors, twats and all sorts on our side. Red goes deep. You ain't breaking no rules when you is making them. Aye, Richey?'

Richey nodded along and added his own self-convincing spiel. 'Deaf by misadventure. Or suicide, like her brother. One or t'other. It's fixed, Phil. It's all fixed up.' But the younger man had wet himself. Near her face, Helene could smell urine soaking into denim.

'But if you wobbles, yeah? Yeah?' The pig pilot was directing his sole attention to Phil again, who would not turn around from the black sea, as if he couldn't. He just stood still and stared at where she *was going*. 'If I fink you're a liability, yeah? Then when it gets back to you know who, yeah, and it gets passed up to the witch-wife, yeah? Then when she gets queened up, you'll be capped. I promise you that. I'll do it meself. You'll be in the red before you know it and I'll piss on your bones too, or whatever the Creel leaves down there. You're a waste of space, Philly. Always was. I vouched for you but I'll be just as happy to see you go froo, yeah? Down there, yeah? Froo the walls. Cunt.'

Phil slumped at the railing.

'So git over here and fucking help out!' The captain of pigs then turned his attention to the youth, Richey. 'You grab her legs. We go froo the back and she's in, yeah? Don't let her bang the sides, like. Take the rope off her arms as she goes in, yeah? Last minute, like.'

Easy to believe that you'll have something to say at the end too, when all hope has gone. That you'll impart memorable last words. But it's not true. People become vague. They call for their distant mothers. Things like that. Helene understood this. The last of you was mostly useless. But she did briefly inflame from her toes to the ends of her hair. A bit of her former self that gave boyfriends hell resurfaced.

'No!' she screamed. The nonchalant way in which the swine captain had imparted instructions for her disposal into the sea had burned out an inner firewall between her fear and rage. Anger scorched, loosening her muscles. She swivelled on her buttocks and kicked both feet, as hard as she could, into the stout trunk of the captain's nearest leg. Right on the knee.

The hinge joint clicked back, locked and he roared, slipped sideways. One fat hand scrabbled across the table like a corpulent sea snail, failing to gain purchase. He thumped against the floor and found himself lying alongside Helene, sweating hard with his face so red his heart must surely burst.

'Fuck's sake, fuck's sake, fuck's sake,' Phil repeated as he walked up and down the tiny deck outside the cabin.

Richey grinned like the idiot that he most surely was.

The captain gasped, struggled to his knees but made sure to put his weight on the one that Helene hadn't kicked. 'Bitch,' he said, his mouth filling with saliva. 'Kill ya!'

'No marks, no marks!' Phil shouted as he finally ducked inside the cabin.

'I'll have ya. I'll have ya!' the captain shouted, clawing pudgy digits at Helene's hair.

Phil and Richey dragged her away, out and onto the deck.

Cold air drenched her body: mere warning that the ocean itself would be far colder. 'God, no. My daughter . . . No. My little girl needs her mum. No. Please. Please.'

Phil began to cry. 'Nothin personal. It's nothin personal,' he chanted.

Richey took control and was horribly strong for a scrawny youth. His hands passed under her armpits and he hoisted her upwards. Helene kicked her feet about the deck, her trainers squeaking without finding grip.

And there it was. Black, slopping, stretching for ever. The sea. The unfeeling, unseeing sea that would suck her down into non-existence, into the depths where she'd never see her baby again. 'No! Stop! Oh, God. Please!'

A lazy pummelling of small waves shifted the boat about queasily. Indigo patches the colour of her daughter's blackcurrant juice were spotted near the boat's lights. The reek of brine engulfed her. The cold bit her nose. Her body lost its strength and flopped limp. Feeling sick, weak and dizzy, she thought she'd pass out.

'Not yet,' she said, feebly, finally, her voice distant amidst the shock she was slipping into.

'Get her in! Get her fuckin' in!' the oaf captain shouted, his pig face a lather of spit and sweat at the mouth of the cabin.

Valda, running through a sunlit garden. Her face one big smile. A melting ice lolly in a small hand.

Valda: a baby on her zoo mat, little feet kicking at the mirror and bells, tiny hands whizzing with excitement.

Lincoln, smiling, his hair tousled.

Mum, Dad.

The binding was cut from her elbows.

One of them, Richey or Phil, was panting as if he'd run a marathon. She didn't want to see their faces.

There was no going back.

A hand grabbed her ankle and began to pull that leg from the slippery deck. A second hand scraped down her calf, trying to seize her second ankle. They meant to tip her in, over the back of the boat, headfirst.

Helene seized the railing and kicked her free leg backwards, blindly. Catching Phil's groin. He collapsed against a moulded bench. She raked a hand behind, found Richey's face. A cold, rubbery ear, wet lips, a stubbly cheek. He pulled away, out of reach, his dirty fingers releasing her hoodie.

But what happens now? *They going to take you back to shore? All a big mistake? Soz, love.*

No. The pig captain was on deck, with a limp and a complexion like roast beef. Clutched in his hateful swine hands was a long wooden pole that ended in an iron spike. Boathook.

Helene didn't consider what she did next. She acted before her conscious mind processed the impulse. Riding a surge of unreason, she passed into a weightless euphoria and she stepped up and onto the stern of the boat.

She turned her head and called the fat man 'Bastard!' through bared teeth. And without any further assistance from the crew, she plunged into the black sea.

24

When Sheila finally called, Kat's captors crowded her, their fingers whitening around the razor flints they held at her jawline. She still did not know their names. They were close to being as unfamiliar to her now as when painted red and pushing inside her home. Grief and horror and fear kept her compliant because they'd dehumanised her. All she could do was confer the same treatment on them, so in her mind and until this was over she would call them Beard and Headscarf.

Both of her jailers possessed a high boredom threshold: she'd worked that much out. They either watched her or watched terrible television, each activity undertaken without comment, and though it was never difficult to assume that they disliked her, they rarely conversed with each other and never smiled.

Kat suspected that old Tony Willows, or whoever called the shots at his unwholesome farm, had told Beard and Headscarf to dislike her. For the kind of people who could ecstatically dismember a living man and feed him to *dogs*, such a command seemed sufficient justification to hate someone.

Not once since they'd taken over her life and home had she seen a flicker of empathy in their hard eyes. They didn't *see* her. Not plainly. They didn't perceive her distress, and their absence of sympathy horrified her. She'd never met the likes of them before but she'd always known that they were out there.

As the uncomfortable cohabitation progressed through a third night, Kat's thoughts sank deep enough to become still, emotionless and blank. They'd periodically resurface in shallower cerebral water, then sink again. And so she'd slept, wept and slept some more.

They'd established a routine, the three of them. Kat washed in front of the strangers, slept in front of them, picked at food while they stared and even used the toilet in front of the woman. Beard let her close the door as if afraid of being disgusted. The woman put clothes out for her each morning. The man mostly watched television.

And when Sheila called, the bearded oaf had delivered Kat's phone and issued his usual crude warning. During the call even Sheila was uncomfortable and desirous of an end to a conversation she'd never wanted to be part of. Kat remained uncommunicative. Her mind blanking. What could she say anyway?

Acceptance that Steve had gone into the sea was growing out there beyond her confinement. *It didn't look good.* That was clear from Sheila, even if she balked at using drastic terminology. Her boss also mentioned work and told Kat that she should 'take as much time as she wanted in a difficult time'. Upon hearing that, Kat sensed that Sheila had not only written off Steve but her as well. She could afford to, and Kat might only be problematic henceforth in Sheila's rarefied world. Tragedy did not become the brand values of *Devon Life and Style*. Kat was never going back to work.

There'd be an obituary for her in the magazine, nothing depressing. Kat sniggered at that thought, which confused her captors. They'd never seen her laugh before and exchanged glances.

She was *losing it*.

Kat just didn't feel like herself any more. In what time she'd left she didn't expect to.

She'd often pondered how trauma incubated deep below the surface of the conscious mind to create transformation. Bits of the cerebral flotsam rising from wreckage repressed in the sea trenches of the head, buoyant fragments bobbing into more self-aware waters. Random floating signals were examined as shards from some greater puzzle. The debris offered an indication of how the mind was changing below.

Perhaps the mind altered to a more anxious state, or a less optimistic one, as it slid into a depressed period weighted by disappointment. It might find scant relief in wisdom or acceptance. But sometimes it became irretrievably broken. And maybe only then did it prepare itself to act in desperate ways.

In captivity, under house arrest, Kat also found time to think and to identify a connection between her ex's controlling moods and her current situation.

Damage inflicted by Graham was permanent but had been manageable over time. When they'd been together, his passive aggression had surfaced whenever decisions were made about their evenings out, or whom they would see as a couple, or what they bought together, or when deciding what to do on a Sunday in London before the pressure of work refocused their minds by late afternoon. Graham had always sulked or brooded Kat into submission. She'd detested that side of her ex, a manipulative man and, she knew, in hindsight, despite his undemonstrative manner, a selfish bastard.

Yes, he'd been conflicted for years and torn himself apart over the final act of betrayal but he'd still left her alone and forced her to reconstruct a life without him. That had taken a long time. He'd broken every promise he'd ever made. Annihilated her trust in others. Ruined her fertility and scorched her mental health.

But maybe Graham had done her one favour: he'd left Kat strongly averse to anyone who tried to impose their will upon her. Anyone who nibbled at the periphery of her life and attempted to appropriate her space, her freedom, her emotions, she quickly detested. She suspected she'd developed a phobia about commitment and a myriad other feelings of repulsion for the wilful, the ambitious and the self-interested. Once bitten in half, forever shy.

She'd only wanted to cruise down here by the coast. Yet here she was again, this time with her hatred of being controlled maximised, magnified and multiplied. A couple of thugs this time: deranged, degenerate bullies who'd taken part in the slaughter and butchery of her lover.

Beard and Headscarf controlled her completely. Everything she'd worked for was effectively theirs now. They'd just taken it from her and could end her life too: the very workings of her mind and heart could be gone any time they wished. That was their plan, assuredly, because her current circumstances represented only a temporary delay before they destroyed her tactically and purposefully. They had their reasons for postponing the inevitable. She had no say in the timing or the method.

By day three Kat was comforting herself with visions of Tony Willows's farm on fire. She fantasised about her guardians having their own red heads smashed in too. Cracked right open.

She also comforted herself with the idea of seeing them all sucked into the black crevice, that void under the dirty floor, a place she could not think about for more than fleeting moments. The stench of what had stalked below was still trapped inside her sinuses.

Over the years, she'd also fantasised about Graham dying. Many times. Usually first thing in the morning. Less so now, but in these fantasies he'd never been destroyed by her own hand. She'd favoured imaginary surrogates to claim her revenge: buses, accidents, muggings. Kat had sickened herself while entertaining these pipe-dreams, and her new fantasies about her jailers also troubled her. They stemmed from the damage her tormentors had already inflicted upon her mind. Permanent harm again, no doubt.

So what kind of person was she now? And what could such a person do unto others if given the chance?

Kat was finally thinking about herself, about what she might do – because unless she managed to extract herself from her current situation, she'd die like Steve. And this posed the questions: how could she escape? How was that done? The self-extraction: how was it possible?

Only on day four did Kat happen upon an idea she thought was feasible.

25

*T*he cold was sharp. It cut subcutaneously. It withered. The dive took Helene deeper than she'd anticipated, to where the cold seemed capable of peeling skin and hair from her head.

Underwater, the roar that came from breaking through the surface was deafening. A layer of ice seemed to form about her entire body, an encasement of aching cold that burned and thumped the breath out of her chest. Her insides shrivelled.

When the momentum of her plunge slowed, a terrible silence rushed in from the freezing darkness surrounding her.

You never jump into cold water.

She'd not had much choice.

Cold-water shock. Down here, the involuntary gasp was the killer. The drowner. Sea water chilled in layers. The surface layer was closer to the sun by day but that was only a few feet deep. Further down, the temperature plunged. A metre down the temperature might be zero degrees. At night, in early summer, even the uppermost layer racked a warm body with shudders. And she'd just arrowed a couple of metres into the black region that is home to panic, gasping and the strength passing from your blood and into the water. Half a pint of seawater inside your lungs and you're done. Dead in three minutes. Helene had punched into the black freeze with her eyes wide open.

She knew how it worked: you were supposed to gradually accustom yourself to cold water, one inch at a time, breathing quickly. She'd swum for years and never thought her local

236

pool warm enough, but in this ebon sea, kicking an iceberg would not have been unexpected.

Too deep.

Too deep.

Too deep.

The alarm in her mind chattered. Panic flicked a switch in her animal brain. Her mouth opened to inhale. The rapid beat of her heart sent out a distress sonar.

Anyone less experienced would have sucked her lungs full of the caustic brine and filled her tanks with the watery choker, the ice-cold killer. And as her dive bottomed, something, some nihilistic impulse, some internal nurse with a euthanising syringe stuck into an ampoule, even offered an alternative to her shrieking desire to survive. In an inappropriately calm but natural tone, the impulse had communicated the thought: *why not let go? Get it over with.*

She refused. Valda's small inquisitive face appeared in her thoughts, how it looked first thing in the morning. And she thought of her child's soft body strewn across her lap on the sofa once Valda had pried her mum out from under the duvet and made her go downstairs to watch cartoons. Helene even heard a small voice asking, 'Is the time six past twenty-five yet?'

Turning her fingers up and kicking hard, Helene had seconds to surface. Any longer and her mouth would widen and that would be that.

She clawed at the bubbles of her wake. They blossomed silvery in an eternal black. Employing her entire will, she overrode panic just enough to keep her lungs empty and broke from the cold, her face surfacing in lightless air that felt thirty degrees warmer than the sea.

Separate from her mind's stewardship, her body shuddered, her chest panted and heaved at the air. Her skull was a warehouse fire, a combustion of animal and childlike terror. She gulped the air her lungs were bruising for, then floated onto her back.

Her skinny jeans and hooded top were soggy and heavy and seemed far more cumbersome than they had any right to be. But she could float, yes, for a little while. And while she floated she told herself that she needed to calm down. *Don't think about anything, just calm down.*

At the edge of her awareness, the boat's motor grunted in the water and she heard a voice call out, 'Drown, you bitch!' The pig captain.

As if in disbelief at what they'd just done, the thin silhouettes of Richey and Phil watched from the stern in silence.

26

*K*at's red roommates would split her skull or slice her throat if she made a dash for the front door. And that's what they'd expect: her fleeing and screaming for the front. They were primed for it.

You go all or nothing for the door or a window and they'll make sure you never attempt it again.

They'd tie her down. She'd go from standard imprisonment to solitary confinement in bonds. So the front entrance was out.

For a few hours on the evening of day four, Kat clung to the thin hope that the disappearance of Matt Hull, Steve and Helene would draw the attention of even the most understaffed, underfunded and half-assed local police force.

She also drew some comfort from the idea that Tony Willows and his "witch-wife", who might even be the Jessica Usher mentioned in the Wikipedia entry, were both spinning an awful lot of plates. Their body count was unacceptable for the postcode.

Vague connections existed between each victim. And if Kat was to take a tumble from the coastal path mere days after her boyfriend, adding herself to a tally that included the two other people she'd recently associated with, Matt Hill and Helene Brown, then such a cluster of accidental deaths and apparent suicides was a risk that Tony and Jess probably weren't willing to take. Right now, she guessed she was more dangerous dead than alive.

They needed her to lie to Steve's parents and the police, to throw them off the scent. But for how long the stay of execution would last was the mystery. *Not that long*, her gut told her.

Her jailers were fanatics enthralled by a mad, bloodthirsty cause. But Headscarf was old and, judging by the headwear, seriously ill too. If the situation arose, woman to woman, Kat believed she could deal with Headscarf. She'd never overpower Beard though. He was a brute. When he wasn't looking at her, he was never more than a short charge from the front door. He didn't wash and she hadn't known him use the toilet with the door closed when she was awake. She'd never fight her way through Beard.

She couldn't open a window and scream fire either. The windows were locked and the small metal keys that unlocked them had been confiscated. In any case, she wouldn't have enough time to do it, and her one neighbour was half-deaf and pushing ninety. Escape was only feasible once her opponents had been dealt with indoors. An idea that was cause for much light-headedness.

Kat reviewed potential weapons, because one had to be involved. Her hands and feet would never be sufficient. And as her memory scrolled through what was still within her reach – tweezers, a hairdryer and hair straighteners, a crystal bowl filled with dried petals – she remembered *the spray*.

Once, while working in Germany for a few days, in Hamburg, Kat had purchased a weapon illegal in Britain. A small item designed for the defence of women if they were unlucky enough to be attacked by predatory men. This device was made of metal, painted yellow, cold to the touch and about the same size as a lipstick: a small yellow canister of pepper spray. She'd brought it back to London inside her luggage, stowed in the boot of her car.

Around that time, two of her friends in London had endured assaults: one inside a taxi, one at a bus stop. Back then, self-defence had been on her mind. But she'd never tested the spray. For years at a time, she'd forgotten that she still possessed it. Occasionally, when she was reorganising her possessions, or having a clear-out, or when she moved house, she'd come across the small metal cylinder. But she'd never thrown it away. *Just in case.* So the spray must still be in her possession, inside her property. *Somewhere.*

Where?

Kat had a vague memory of last seeing it in a wooden box she kept under the bed that contained her odds and ends, her bric-a-brac: a travel sewing kit, some old mobile phones, her passport . . . she couldn't remember what else. But the spray might be in that box.

If the spray was stored in the attic with the Christmas decorations and abandoned hobbies, then it might as well have been buried in Australia: she'd never get the hatch open or ladder down in time. But if it was in the wooden box under the bed and she managed to find an opportunity to locate it, Kat had to wonder whether the nozzle would work when she pressed it with her finger. *Did pepper spray have an expiry date?* She'd bought it ten years before.

When she'd purchased the spray, and whenever she'd come across it in the past, she'd vividly remembered her schooldays. This was the very reason why she'd hung onto it and why the idea of having the spray in her hand began to glow like a soldering iron in her thoughts. School had taught Kat what pepper did to human eyes.

In the dining tent on a school camp, an idiotic and immature boy called Nigel Baxter had covered her plate in white pepper. When she'd blown the pepper off, a dust cloud had filled her eyes and she'd been unable to see for twenty minutes. Her eyes and nose and everything behind her face had burned so fiercely that she'd secreted gloopy handfuls of clear mucus and a torrent of hot tears through her nose and eyes. Her mouth, one of her friends had said, resembled Geiger's Alien.

She'd been helpless, insensible and possessed by panic and shame in equal amounts. A true public humiliation she'd never forgotten, its memory still made her face burn. A trainee teacher had led Kat to the toilets to wash her face and eyes. They'd remained red and swollen for two days.

Nigel Baxter got away with it. She'd not told her teachers who had sprinkled the white pepper on her white plate. At her school, 'grassing' on the bullies and thieves guaranteed exile until the end of your school life. A rule engraved in stone that helped no one except the thugs. After all, it had been *their* rule: it was the bullies who had made secondary school feel like prison, not the harassed teachers.

Nigel had actually fancied Kat. That's why he'd laced her plate with pepper. He'd even asked her out one year after the incident and Kat had said no. But another girl, Olive Newman, had fancied Nigel and wanted him for herself. Olive had been so incensed at Nigel's attraction to Kat that she'd bullied her rival for the entire fourth year. Olive Newman's campaign of terror only ceased when Olive was expelled for stabbing another girl in the hand with a pair of craft scissors.

Back then, Kat had believed that if the dozen or so male and female thugs in her year, like Nigel and Olive, had been killed on their way to school, then the other two hundred children in her year would have been much happier people, then and now. Or even just happy.

But that kind of justice was rare. If such just deserts occurred they happened by degree and the reckoning was always too slow; it failed to restrict the number of damaged victims the bullies subsequently racked up. Justice should be far swifter, Kat decided, and the thought no longer troubled her.

There have been too many people like this in your life, girl. They're all still with you, inside. They're unforgettable. They like that. They like to make an impression and for their influence to linger. It's all they have of you.

You've run as far as you can.

Running was always a good option. When you cannot do unto others what they are doing to you, you have no choice: you leave, you run. But what happens when you can't run any further?

Kat told Headscarf that she felt unwell.

She and Beard had just opened a large bottle of cider.

Kat told them that she wanted to go to bed.

They seemed pleased with that.

She went to bed and stayed awake with her eyes closed.

Much later, Headscarf's bird feet descended the stairs, the sound muffling as the woman reached the ground floor.

At the edge of Kat's hearing came the squeak of rubber soles as Headscarf turned on the kitchen lino to open the fridge door. Neither of her captors had taken their shoes off indoors. Another black mark. Kat had always forbidden outdoor footwear indoors.

In the past, when one of her captors had broken their surveillance of Kat's bedroom to use the bathroom, or to smoke in the kitchen – those black marks just kept adding up – the other one had come upstairs and watched Kat from the doorway. By day four they'd stopped doing that. They never left her alone for long but the guard was no longer as vigilant.

The windows were covered and the kitchen doorway was close to the front door, so they were confident that she'd never get out that way. They'd also probably assumed that their prisoner was so devastated and cowed, and she was both of those things, that she was unlikely to offer resistance to their guardianship.

But time was ticking.

Kat shuffled to the edge of her mattress.

The bed was noisy. Movements upon it registered in the living room, directly below her bedroom. Even when moving slowly the bed issued protest.

Kat paused and caught her breath.

In the kitchen the kettle conveniently boiled.

She swung her head over the side of the bed and peered underneath. She saw a dozen pairs of shoes, lined up like a phalanx of leather-armoured troops, bristling with buckles, patent straps, tipped heels. Behind them were three opaque plastic crates. One contained bank statements and financial records. Another was filled with the equipment and clothes she'd bought for her sole camping experience with Steve. The third box contained notepads, her diaries and a collection of self-help books. There was a duvet under there too, a sleeping bag, three soft animals her ex had given her. She'd hidden those from Steve and been unable to decide whether to keep them or to give them to charity. *Perhaps you've hung on to the pain?*

But near the foot of the bed, in one corner, half-covered by a spare duvet cover, was the wooden chest. Not ideally placed: that part of the bed was closest to the door where her captors had positioned the stool. But at least the box was close to an edge. She wouldn't need to reorganise the stuff around it. That would make too much noise.

Footsteps on the stairs.

Kat swung her body up, turned about on the bed.

Once her head was on the pillow she made sure to face the other way. And breathed out slowly.

Headscarf resumed her position on the stool. Slurped coffee from Kat's *Elle* mug. A memento. Kat closed her eyes and thought of another memento from Hamburg.

27

*T*he great black canopy of night frightened Helene as much as the plain of water she floated upon like driftwood. The sky was vast. The stars frozen at an incredible depth. She pictured how tiny her body would look from far above. That didn't help.

Don't look up, don't look down. Don't think up, or down. Think straight ahead.

At least a minute had passed since she'd surfaced. Her heartbeat and breathing had slowed. 'Relax. Relax. Relax . . .' she said to herself through chattering teeth. She unbuttoned her sopping jeans and pushed them over her hips. Her pants went with them. *Who gives a shit?*

She went under twice. The jean-legs had turned inside out and she'd gone under water to pull at the denim with all her might to stretch and tug each leg from each foot. While under the water she'd seen nothing in any direction. All was black as pitch and she couldn't tolerate more than a few seconds below the surface, the cold immediately making her desperate to take a new breath. Her jeans eventually floated beside her like a pet with long ears that didn't want to be left alone.

Without jeans she felt especially insubstantial but at least her legs felt freed in the water and more agile. But they were much colder too and she wondered if she would have done better to leave her jeans on for the smidgen of warmth they provided. She kept her hooded top on just in case it might assist her survival. She kicked her feet to stay afloat.

The water's fairly calm. At least there's that.

Currents? We don't know about currents. Don't think about currents. You've enough on your plate.

Gotta move or you'll slow down. Slow arms, slow legs in cold water . . . no no no. Can't have that.

Once panic no longer filled her mind, her daughter inevitably returned to her head. It was as if Valda had just walked into the kitchen casually seeking her mum, or padded into her bedroom expectantly to see what mum was doing. Her little face smiled inside Helene as if an activity could be instigated, a treat negotiated from out of the cupboard above the microwave, or a hug received.

Helene started to cry. 'Baby . . .' she said once.

Then she was angry and screaming, 'You bastards!' into the sky. That felt better. Much better than thinking about her girl not having her any more.

She'll have to live with Mum and her arthritis until she goes somewhere else . . .

'No. No. My baby . . . She's my baby.'

Parents die all the time.

'Not this one. No, no. Not this one.' Helene spat out sea water. She'd sunk a bit and the gentle chop of the waves had lapped her face.

Helene looked towards land. In the far distance and in the direction the boat had gone (the vessel was now a trio of white specks in distant darkness), Helene could see a messy crescent of white light, maybe Brickburgh harbour. But where those lights originated was too far away to swim for.

South of the harbour, a few lights pinpricked the hills above a shoreline unlit and invisible. Maybe that was the stretch of coast she'd walked. A few farms dotted those hills. *How far across the water from here to there?* Two or three miles. Maybe more.

But swimming in the sea was not like swimming in chlorinated water. The sea was much thicker. It moved more, ever surging with waves and currents. Moving through it was harder work and it stole more of your energy. And there was the cold. In Britain the water temperature rarely peaked at twenty degrees in a hot, late summer. This was May. She reckoned she was treading water with a temperature nearer one or two degrees around her knees. If the cold overcame her, her blood would retreat to her core and her arms and legs would stop working and become sluggish. She'd drown. She already felt like she was wearing a shower cap and face-mask moulded from ice.

But once horizontal she'd be swimming in marginally warmer water, maybe by a few degrees at the surface: water less bloody freezing than it was around her feet and knees while bobbing vertically. A few degrees might make all the difference.

Swim steady. Not too fast.

Go.

Helene began to breaststroke to accustom her body to moving in cold water, to get the blood moving through her muscles again. She wasn't ready to dip her face and ears into the black freeze to do a front crawl. Backstroke was her third favourite stroke but a straight trajectory was hard to maintain and she couldn't, at any cost, afford to go off course while swimming on her back.

However she swam, if she hit a strong current she knew she was done. If the wind picked up and she was swimming up and down the chop she doubted she'd be able to swim for more than half a mile, and only that far if she didn't freeze first. Her extremities, her feet, hands and nipples, already ached. If a cramp crept into her feet it was over.

Don't!

Valda and the lights. Valda and the lights. Valda and the lights.

She chanted this inside her skull to quell the other thoughts that were as cold as the night. At the same time, stretching out her long body, Helene began a front-crawl in the direction of land.

28

*K*at continued to feign sleep. But wasn't Headscarf bored? For two hours she'd sat upon the stool outside the doorway, vaguely peering into the darkened bedroom where Kat lay. In an age where people were constantly wiping their fingers up and down screens or prodding them, Kat thought this remarkable. Downstairs, the television muttered. And how could anyone stand that much bad television?

The couple had been charged with an important task; they'd been chosen. Maybe the unimaginative made the best killers whether they sat behind a desk or held a rock in their red paws.

Only at midnight did Headscarf finally dismount the stool, with a faint creak, to use the bathroom. She didn't close the door, only pulled it to. *Bitch is good.*

Kat immediately slipped her body down the mattress to the foot of the bed, to get closer to the position of the box beneath the bed-frame. But the noisy chaos of compressing springs and squeaking wood soon brought the manoeuvre to an end. She visualised Headscarf tensing in the bathroom, with her pants round her ankles, listening intently to the distant percussion of the bed.

Kat pushed back to her former position.

Whether the two occurrences had been connected she didn't know, but after the bed creaked the taps briefly ran in the bathroom. Within moments of placing her head on the pillow, Headscarf's bony face was peering through the doorway, staring at her inert body beneath the duvet. The creature then resumed its sitting vigil.

So close.

Kat was dozing when the guard was changed. Without a word, Beard assumed ownership of the stool at 2 a.m.

At 3 a.m., when she was fighting hard to stay awake, he went downstairs. Moments later the kettle boiled, the fridge door opened, then a cupboard. As he looted her kitchen and made preparations for coffee, his phone rang. She didn't hear what was said but Beard's hoarse voice gruffly barked brief statements at the caller. He even laughed for the first time in four days.

Kat had to assume that Headscarf was asleep on the couch. The television had finally fallen silent.

She spread her body wider than before, face-down, and turned herself upside down beneath the duvet. She had to stay on the mattress, couldn't risk the sound of her feet on the old floorboards. When the coverings blocked her hearing, she pulled the duvet from her head to listen.

Silence in the kitchen, save the final gurgles of the electric jug approaching the boil.

She waited, motionless, fearing that if she was found in this position with her head at the foot of the bed, she'd struggle to convince Beard that she'd been having a restless night.

Another cupboard door was opened. *Even a cunt likes snacks.*

Kat reached over the end of the bed with one hand and found the wooden box, the hinged lid and the nickel-plated locking mechanism familiar against her fingertips. She swiped the catch free but the lid was too close to the bed-frame to be raised, ruling out a search. The box needed to be withdrawn from beneath the bed to enable a rummage for any toxic treasure it might yet yield.

Footsteps on the kitchen lino. The squeak of training shoes.

Like the big hand of a clock, Kat returned the top half of her body to the pillows, spreading her weight again. Still a noisy manoeuvre and the duvet caught underneath her body.

Stairs creaked under Beard's feet.

Kat fought the duvet, then straightened her body a moment before her captor reappeared in the doorway, holding a steaming mug.

She was now lying on the other side of the bed and holding her breath, hoping the new position merely suggested that she'd moved in her sleep, perhaps switching sides to find cooler, less wrinkled sheets.

Beard resumed his seat.

Kat wondered if her heartbeat was audible. She didn't know whether to be disappointed that she hadn't opened the box or relieved that she hadn't been caught with her head over the foot of the bed. They'd surely search under the bed if she showed any interest in what was down there.

Thirty minutes later Beard's buttocks slid off the stool again, heavily. Deciding to sit on the floor, he leaned back against the short railing at the top of the stairs. He closed his eyes.

Unsure if he was sleeping on the job or merely resting, Kat took stock: the box needed retrieving from beneath the bed to enable a search and the spray had to be tested. That process was asking for a lot of time. The bed would squeak. Steady hands would be required for the latter part of the procedure or she might blind herself.

Although Beard was the more formidable adversary physically, she'd have to make her move on his watch. He was less attentive, went downstairs more often and took longer to finish his business in the bathroom. Prostate trouble was a possibility: a long silence always preceded tinkling.

Time withdrew like a tide. Her stomach burned with frustration, so the next time the Beard went downstairs she swore to herself that she would open the box and then . . .

Whatever might happen *then* made her feel sick.

29

Helene must have been swimming steadily for fifteen minutes when she felt the first glimmer of relief: a satisfaction that she hadn't yet drowned by succumbing to the cold.

She couldn't fully feel her fingers and toes, her shoulders and neck had stiffened, but by forcing awareness of her fatigue from her thoughts she'd continued to chop at the water and to breathe steadily on the surface of the heaving black.

Twenty more strokes, she repeated to herself and counted them. Resetting her clock she then counted twenty more. With what capacity still remained for imagination inside a skull filled with the noise of her exertions, she pictured herself from above, cutting through the black water with the purpose and speed of a ship's prow.

For as long as she was able she refused to look up and ahead. The vast distance between herself and the lights on shore remained too demoralising to judge. She told herself that when she next checked she would be closer, she would be encouraged.

When she did finally look up, the lights seemed no closer at all. In fact, with nothing else to measure her progress, her mind tried to trick her into believing that her body was, more or less, still in the same place she'd entered the water. She suspected that a conspiracy of currents was pushing her backwards and that she was merely rising and falling on the swell.

But the natural world and water were full of illusions and little beyond the cold sea could make you feel so small, so futile and weak. She assured herself of this. Maybe only an astronaut adrift in space would know her dread.

When she'd been swimming for what she estimated to be half an hour, she became aware that she wasn't feeling as cold and was breathing more easily. She was no longer tugging at the air and gulping it and spluttering it out again. She'd reached a plateau, her optimum swimming time. She recognised this stage from swimming in a pool. For a dozen lengths she would feel ungainly, her strokes poorly coordinated and she'd swallow water. But a rhythm and regular breathing would always evolve, hinting that she could swim for ever. Only now would she truly discover how far and for how long.

Small waves nudged her from every direction but she adjusted her strokes and now inhaled on every third stroke rather than every other stroke. This made her believe that she was going faster, with better technique.

When she judged she had been swimming for about as long as she'd need in the pool of the leisure centre to cover one mile, she rested and trod water. That meant she wasn't doing anything but rising and falling with the swell. And once again she thought of her daughter. But it no longer helped to motivate her, because the lights onshore were still too far away and a paralysing feeling of futility made her sob. Another waste of energy.

She thought of the pig captain's ruddy face instead, grinning aboard his little boat, and of his stooges, Phil and Richey. It was not right that creatures like that could make her daughter an orphan. She wanted to believe that they would be caught and punished. Surely they would be. Her mother knew where she'd been staying . . . Carol would be questioned by the police . . .

Helene then considered the statuette that had been sent to her daughter in Walsall from down here. Kat had been the only person with her address but who had she shared it with to put Valda and her mum in danger? Lincoln's recordings were only on disc but her tormentors didn't know that. For all they knew she had the cave noises on the hard drive of a machine at home in Walsall. If they were prepared to go to these lengths for a handful of CDs, then what might they do to retrieve a home computer?

Her daughter and mother were at risk. They were known to the people who'd orchestrated her tortuous execution by drowning with added hyperthermia. This, and a fear that she couldn't feel her legs properly below the knee, made Helene resume swimming. Only now she wanted to kill Kat even more than the three men aboard the boat.

After each turn of her head to draw breath, Helene returned her face to the eternal cold darkness beneath the surface, trickle-breathing from her nose to expel air. Sometimes she grunted at the cold and she heaved at the water out of fury, but she also understood that it was now getting harder to think clearly, or to hold any thought in her mind for more than a moment. This was exhaustion: from moving one arm after another, again and again, from rotating her body from side to side, from remembering to kick both legs hard. All of this was consuming her energy while the cold sapped it.

But up and down the small waves she went, kicking her long pale legs, digging at the water with her hands. On and on. On and on.

Valda, Valda, Valda and the lights.
Valda, Valda, Valda and the lights.
Valda, Valda, Valda and the lights.

30

As the floorboards outside her room depressed beneath Beard's feet, Kat withdrew her hand from the disordered contents of the wooden chest. Her arm shook so hard that she dropped the spray.

Bending at the waist, she scrabbled for the small bullet, seemingly unable to retrieve it from the weave of the carpet. Angry with herself, at the pitch where self-harm probably wasn't far away, she lunged in desperation and seized the container. Finally, she cupped the cold lozenge inside her palm.

He'd been downstairs again, Beard. Had he not been so tardy and sluggish on the stairs, he'd have caught her with the lid of her box open. Kat inserted the metal capsule inside the pocket of her jogging bottoms.

With no time to enjoy the elation of retrieving the weapon she looked down at the box that was no longer beneath the bed-frame.

Outside the room, a coffee mug was placed on top of the wooden stool. Without having time to consider her action, Kat tugged the duvet part way from the bed so it slumped over the open box and her bare feet.

A bearded face appeared in the doorway. 'What you doing?' His words were thick with lassitude, boredom and sleep deprivation, his eyes red from lack of sleep, too much screen-time and alcohol. They dropped to the duvet on the floor.

'Toilet,' she replied, feigning a yawn to conceal the alertness that would be visible in her expression under the landing light.

She shuffled towards the door. Beard stood aside but for several airless moments Kat anticipated the rough leather of his hands on her arms. She could practically hear him shouting, 'What you got there?' and reaching for the bulge in her pocket. Was it visible? Kat covered it with a hand.

And then she was inside the bathroom with her back against the door and a towel across her mouth to stifle her panicked panting.

She had the spray now, in her pocket. *The spray!* Using it on a human face was another thing altogether but she'd got here little by little, inch by inch. She'd bloody done it.

Bastards, she mouthed at the door.

She'd have to spray that hoary bearded face out there on the landing and soon, at close range. The very idea made his body seem too large and dense. There was so much of him. The tiny canister, not much bigger than a lip-gloss tube designed for a woman's clutch-bag, seemed especially pathetic. What could it possibly do to that brute?

Even after all they'd done to her, what they intended to do, what they'd done to Steve, Matt Hull, the others . . . *Helene, they made you walk her into certain death . . .* she no longer seemed in possession of her previous resolve: her determination to defend, to avenge.

Where had the fantasies of destroying them gone? Maybe they had been nothing more than the desperation of the condemned.

Now she was frightened, not angry. Her muscles were boiled pasta gone cold. Her heartbeat thumped inside her ears. This is what happened when you'd been captive for too long, when they'd let you live for a bit. Hadn't she'd also begun to feel stupidly grateful whenever they brought her water or tea and when they let her use her own bathroom?

Calm down. She had to calm down.

Kat sat on the toilet but was too scared to pee.

Beard hadn't resumed his seat. She'd have heard the creak of his weight on the wooden stool, even through a closed door. She was familiar with these few sounds from her days and nights in captivity: her existence had been reduced to a few feet of space and a meagre selection of noises.

Maybe he knew something was up, that she was behaving differently. A weasel mind adapted that way. The merest alteration in a victim's eyes and they were alert, their instincts honed. They knew who to attack by the posture of a person's body. Murderers, kidnappers, fanatics: they thought differently and she was trapped in their medium. She had to do it now.

Oh, God.

Kat stood up and ran a tap so Beard could hear something he might associate with the innocent use of a bathroom.

The duvet was still on the floor of her bedroom. She saw it in her mind, like a betrayer, a feather-filled Judas. If Beard poked beneath the duvet he'd see the open box, a container full of old phones. Their batteries were dead, the services and numbers disconnected. But how would he know that?

Inside her mental parliament, each side of the house rose and jeered at the other's suggestions. Her head was too busy, nothing seemed clear any more. *Get angry.* This was her only opportunity. *Get angry and be quick.* Because if adrenalin didn't take her over, this plan would not work.

And then Beard forced her to act. Three noisy steps sounded on the landing before he thrust open the bathroom door.

Kat was nearly grateful to him for forcing the inevitable. She'd needed him to, or she would have remained pale, shaky and hopeless.

You're all head, girl, no gut. Gutless, a little admonishing voice said inside.

He had seen the duvet then. He thought she'd been up to something, her sleepiness unconvincing. His eyes peered all over her, took in her hands. Looked at the bath, the sink, the toilet beside her. He was looking for what she'd just removed from the wooden chest.

257

Beard stepped into the bathroom, his stare fixed on her pockets. 'Gimme that phone!' he roared. He'd seen the old mobile phones. There'd been at least four inside the box.

Kat visualised his rough hand on her wrist before she could bring the spray in play. *You never tested it into the sink like you were supposed to!*

The crevice in the dirty floor of the barn . . . Cap the bastard . . . that idle hand, lifeless, chopped from a body by a sharp stone and left amongst the spoor of livestock. A grooved human chin wet from feasting.

Kat backed into the sink. The rim indented her buttocks.

She thumped one hand outwards, fingers wide, into Beard's sternum.

Her free hand scrabbled at her hip until her fingertips found the pocket of her jogging bottoms.

Beard snatched her outstretched arm at the wrist. She pulled back with all of her might and sat in the sink. A sudden sharp pain from the taps pressing into her lower back stabbed some purpose into her mind. Kat dipped her hand inside her pocket and the canister slipped into her palm.

Beard grasped her weapon arm below the shoulder. He didn't prevent its range of movement because he wanted to see what she held in her hand. He suspected a phone, not a weapon.

'See,' Kat said. 'Lip balm.'

Beard moved his face closer, eyes wide to identify what lay inside her palm.

Kat's index finger slipped into the groove intended for a woman's frightened finger. The top of the can was black and made from rubber. She thought of how the pepper had burned her whole life away for twenty minutes at school camp.

Watch for blowback.

"'Tis that? What you got?' Beard demanded.

And then his ruddy, veiny face and bulging eyes were engulfed by the discharge of an aerosol. Small droplets cavorted in their thousands.

31

Mouth open to inhale, Helene caught another small wave in the face. Engulfed by the shock of choking on seawater, she flailed.

Panic brought immediate clarity to her vision, electrifying her awareness but failing to fully extend into her muscles. She was too weary, losing rhythm: practised movements were heavier, clumsy, slowing. Her half-closed eyes stung. The inside of her ears throbbed like thumbs beneath misjudged hammer strokes. Her nose burned and tendrils of pain threaded her sinuses. Her face might have been struck by a shovel carven from solid ice.

Helene floated on her back to regain her breath, to ease the terror of the wave flushing her mouth.

She calmed and discovered that the persistent anxiety about how long she could swim worried her less than it had when she hit the water so long ago.

She turned onto her tummy and began breast-stroking: slowly, her shoulders screaming, but at least her head was more out of the water than under it.

Ten minutes later she was sure she saw an object on the surface. A moment later it appeared to be another head, some distance to her right. She stopped swimming and trod water.

Peering about, she waited for a series of small waves to slope away and reveal the dark blur facing her: a shape different in colour and form from the surrounding air and water.

There. There it was again.

Helene struck out for it, losing sight of the object briefly before her frantic vision rediscovered the dark sphere.

She lost it again in a trough. Then found it.

The fact that she took so long to reach the buoy when it had never been far away was a fresh blow to her confidence about her progress. A fear of swimming against a current or tide from the beginning made her body seem twice as heavy. Maybe her sluggishness and the presence of the marker signified a current. She didn't know. She couldn't read the symbols of the sea.

Reaching the buoy, Helene engulfed the slimy sphere with her hands as if it were her own child.

By pressing it down and under the surface she attempted to rest her chest and chin upon it. At the first three clumsy attempts the buoy slipped between her stiff white hands, bobbed up and away.

Beneath the surface a rope disappeared straight down, so she coiled her legs around the mooring to keep the buoy still. Mussel shells encrusting the rope cut rough and sharp against her calf muscles and ankles, but she kept hold of the buoy.

Once clear of the water her shoulders and upper arms told her how much they ached. Oddly, she no longer felt cold. That couldn't be a good sign. Not after she'd been in the water for so long.

Looking to the land, she could see that the distant hill lights still appeared small. But the separation between the lonely vigil of one light and its neighbour seemed much greater now, wider. If the lights were further apart then she must be closer to land. These lights were not strung along the shoreline. They were shining from buildings in distant hills. The coastline must be some distance below and before the faraway beacons.

She had made progress. A lot of progress.

There was only a trace of illumination from the distant moon and no light pollution along the coast. By concentrating her gaze straight ahead she just made out the lumpy silhouette of a rocky coastline: an uneven line barely distinguishable in the darkness. The rocks of the shoreline were a lighter colour than the oily sea but still distant.

Helene pressed her face against the slippery buoy and wept for a few seconds. She'd come so far. She'd come so close.

Further ahead of her she saw another buoy: dark and bobbing like the head of another person in the water. Maybe twenty metres ahead.

Looking about herself she noticed another one behind her. Further to her left she thought she could see another two.

Why they were there was a maritime mystery but she'd just swum across two parallel lines of buoys anchored to the ocean floor by rope. And to place her numb and wrinkled hands upon something manmade almost kidded her, for a short time, that she was close to saving herself from the sea.

But how far out in the water these buoys were and how far away the distant, patchy suggestion of rocky land, she couldn't accurately judge. And what of her frozen body if she even managed to claw herself onto those rocks? She knew she had little strength remaining and would be unable to walk if she even made it ashore. Of that she was certain.

The end of her natural resources approached. The swim had kept her afloat and active but merely reaching the first buoy had sapped what felt like the very last of her strength.

She turned her weary face to the sky and then pushed herself away from the buoy. She swam on her side in the direction of the next one.

Valda . . . Valda and the lights . . .

Valda . . . the lights . . .

Valda . . .

32

*H*ands with skin as hard as old shoe-leather clapped the outside of Kat's shoulders. Great paws cupped, crushed and yanked her upwards.

Torn from the sink, the top of her buttocks caught a tap spout. Panic rioted inside her skull. Her strength fled, resolve following.

Had the canister only ejected a spraying agent and not a blinding chemical? *You're supposed to shake it. Did I?*

Beard had merely blinked under the aerosol's deluge but barely slowed. She must have squirted water from a dud. *Use by date*: the phrase screamed at Kat accusingly. The hairy killer was not for slowing down.

He hauled her like a child across the bathroom, onto the landing. Pulled about too forcefully to keep her feet, she went down. On her knees she said, 'Please.'

She wasn't sure what happened next but her attacker's hands unclenched, releasing her bloodless arms.

Looking through her hair at the floor, she was braced to receive a blow from above when a roar of animal pain filled the entire cottage, vibrating through timber and brick.

A glance up.

Not much of Beard's head was visible. Inside a halo of wild, greying hair and crispy beard, his thick-fingered hands clutched at his face. He bent double, bellowed again. Tears dropped from his chin and splashed onto his tattooed forearms.

Delayed effect.

Kat stood up.

Without giving notice of her approach, Headscarf appeared on the stairs. She peered between the banisters, the rat-face inquisitive. 'Wass wrong, E?' she said. 'Wass she done?'

Sprightly for a woman in her sixties, Headscarf skipped onto the landing and grabbed E by an arm. 'Lemme see,' she demanded of him like a mother before a son with something stuck in his eye. Maybe they were family.

'Bloody spray!' Beard roared, and spat gobs down his chin. 'Fuck! Fuck!'

Headscarf frowned, trying to comprehend, and Kat took two steps into the melée and laced the woman's face from close range. This time she wiggled her wrist like she was a graffiti artist with a spray can tagging a concrete bridge.

The woman stumbled back, lowering her face. 'Bitch!' She instinctively thrust out a knobbly hand in defence, arthritic fingers gripping a black hand-axe, before screaming from the agony engulfing her eyes and sinuses.

Kat dithered. Tried to remember her plan. It had been simple but her mind blanked amidst the screams, the tears, the screwed-up faces, the flying saliva.

Get past them and run.

She'd dosed them good but didn't know how long the spray's caustic effects lasted. To make sure, she positioned the can under Beard's covered face as he spat and grunted at the floor, his head almost between his knees, and discharged it again.

He pulled away violently and knocked Headscarf down. He carried on capering and wheeling until his back hit the wall outside her bedroom.

Something like hope merged with delight and surged like electrical current. Kat ran the last few feet of the landing. Tucked her body between the roaring oaf and the staircase. One hand on the railing, on legs unaccustomed to moving quickly, she padded down the stairs. The bright ground floor of her home reappeared in her vision. The sight was blessed.

Hesitation gripped her again outside the kitchen. Her legs were shaking. Her hands too. They had her car keys and her phone. That's right, she was supposed to retrieve those from her captors once she'd sprayed their faces. In hindsight, that part, the spraying, seemed to have gone too smoothly. Recovery of her car keys or phone, or preferably both, chimed new alarms.

Should she run from the house in the dark? How far would she get? She wasn't fit. Her neighbour was elderly and probably wouldn't open her door in the early hours. Further up the lane were another two cottages. Each owned by elderly widows. Though one of them, Grace, usually had her daughter staying over.

A quick survey of the kitchen counters and then the living room: the sofa, the coffee table, the bookshelves and counters, revealed neither phone nor car keys.

Kat returned to the hall and stuffed her feet into a pair of trainers. She looked up. Beard was ranting, his broad West Country accent more pronounced when in pain. The timbre of his voice alone was terrifying and he was fumbling his way down the stairs like a blind man. One eye kept trying to open before clenching shut again like a frantic red snail inside its shell. But if that bloodshot orb managed to remain slightly open and the pepper spray was too old to be effective for long, she'd be in all kinds of trouble again and fast.

Kat unlatched the door and undid the mortice lock. The door handle had little give. *Locked.* They'd removed the Yale key from the main lock.

The sounds of her scrabbling at the cottage entrance incited greater efforts from Beard. He thumped his feet down the few remaining stairs. If his cruel hands seized her now he'd just hang on. He'd make sure next time.

Half-finished job.

Kat side-stepped into her tiny kitchen. She glanced about: toaster, breadboard covered in crumbs and dirty knives, dirty dishes, microwave, dirty pans . . .

Panting, shaking his messy head, Beard angled his face down in case gravity offered relief from the sting and clawed at the front door. He pressed his hands against the wood and seemed relieved to find the door closed.

Clearing his nostrils onto her mat like a bullock, he realised that his quarry was still indoors. The cottage was small. Even blind he'd find the bitch.

With a clarity that made her grow cold, Kat understood that if he got hold of her now he'd probably kill her where she stood. At the very least he'd knock her senseless. *And then . . .*

Do unto others . . .

She opened two cupboards beside the oven. Food mixer, oven trays, bin bags, tinfoil on a roll, clingfilm, but nothing to weaponise.

Cutlery drawer next. Kat opened it so fast the drawer reached the end of its runners and snapped them. Beard must have heard the tinkle of sharp metal things. He turned from the door and tried to force that ulcer of an eye open. Kat stepped up to the kitchen doorway and re-sprayed his hoary face.

With a roar he tumbled backwards, escaping most of the fresh dose, but a few droplets must have entered the puffy slit of his parted eyelid. His hips struck the cabinet storing unopened post and racked shoes. A grasping hand tore two coats down.

The can's tiny load was nearly spent, the nozzle fizzing alarmingly during the last despatch. And now she'd made him even angrier. Once this conflict concluded one of them would not be getting up again. She swallowed this revelation like bile. But with her advantage the idea also excited her in a perverse, shameful way.

Kat retreated to the drawer that tilted out of the fitted kitchen unit.

Headscarf was washing her face upstairs. Kat heard the gush of a tap. The wrinkled rat must have sunk its burning face inside the basin to stop the pain.

Kat removed kitchen scissors from the cutlery drawer.

Dropped them. Snatched the small, sharp paring knife. Pocketed the weapon. Then grabbed the wooden rolling pin she'd only used once in a disastrous attempt to make pastry: a beef Wellington so dry and misshapen that she and Steve had been forced to order takeout. They'd eventually laughed until they cried. 'Can I watch it go into the bin?' Steve had asked. 'Bastard!' she'd called back at him, helpless with laughter.

'Bitch!' Beard roared from the kitchen doorway like a bee-stung bear, obliterating the brief echo of her dead lover. He knew she was in the kitchen and was aware of the room's tiny dimensions, its potential as a domestic killing bottle. He'd been foraging in there for long enough, making endless cups of coffee like a recovering alcoholic, and had smoked so many rollups the room was now fungal from tobacco fumes. He'd made her space his own and he would kill her upon its linoleum floor. Even with him blind, his monstrous hands would still inflict catastrophic damage: they were tree roots wrapped in moleskin capable of crushing a windpipe like a bunch of spring onions. She was cornered.

From the back pocket of his jeans he pulled a flint hand-axe. His hairy mitt cupped it, point down, as if he intended to hammer something hard.

Steve.

Kat remembered the sounds of Steve's body coming apart in the dirt.

Beard stepped inside the kitchen.

Kat stepped up to him. And brought the wooden rolling pin down so hard and with such a wild swing she clipped the kitchen light. It shattered. Glass and the metal casing showered the floor. But the arc of the makeshift club, this comedy weapon that seemed to have passed from a *Tom and Jerry* cartoon and into her hands, connected with Beard's head. She caught him where the simian forehead sloped.

He grunted, dropping his head, feet planted.

Vibrations passed along Kat's arms. The wooden pin had bounced off his skull with an almighty coconutting sound that made her feel sick, the impact suggesting his head was a hollow wooden vessel.

A bright streak of blood bisected his face, passing between his swollen eyes and around his flat nose to creep through the untidy moustache. Tributaries of crimson spread through his hairline. Kat's nausea slid from six to ten.

Beard clumsily swiped his arm through the air, the hand-axe at its end. Whisking the air, the weapon passed no more than a few inches from her eyes. It would have opened her face like a sandwich.

Dizzy, panting like a dog on a hot day, Kat's thoughts fell about inside her mind like drunks. She really wanted this to stop. *You made him bleed. Sprayed him three times. Why won't he fucking stop? Why won't they all fucking die?*

This is your house! They killed Steve . . .

Upstairs, Headscarf was sniffing and jabbering. *To herself?* No, because the old woman had climbed the stairs with a phone in her hand. But would she be able to see the screen and activate a call with her eyes clenched shut? Or maybe she'd already initiated a phone call to one of her colleagues before she'd run up the stairs?

Beard shuffled about trying to regroup his wits inside the earthquake Kat had just dropped onto his skull. He readied himself for another swing that would swipe deeper inside the tiny room. One of his big arms pulled back, a fleshy catapult, determined to tear her soft body apart with a primitive implement, the tool that had reduced her lover to wet pieces on a grubby floor that stank of animal shit. And that's all they were now: savages, swinging sharp stones and clubs at each other inside a soiled cave.

Kat stopped thinking, stopped informing herself, stopped hoping, stopped despairing. 'You dirty bastard,' she screamed and went at Beard.

The second, third and fourth blows were easier to deliver against his big head. Kat pulled down more of the light and some ceiling paint and plaster with her back swings but she caught the top of his head, the side of it above an ear and then the back of his skull.

Beard blindly thrust out an arm in defence and she battered that too, twice, until it was withdrawn. She only stopped swinging when she was too tired to raise her arms and when her horror at herself overcame what had felt like elation as she'd destroyed the intruder.

Beard's head was wet, darker, dripping. He was less vocal. Truly one of the red folk now, repainted by her and brought down by one of their own notorious techniques. It all seemed to fit.

Beard slumped against the washing machine. His mouth moved. Nothing much came out of it, nothing intelligible. As he'd turned from her blows she'd seen the oblong outline of a smartphone in the rear pocket of his jeans. He was now sitting on the device.

'E! E! You get her?' Headscarf shouted from the top of the stairs, in between sniffs and expulsions from her nostrils.

Not done yet.

Kat stepped over Beard's legs. One of his feet scraped purposelessly against the lino, his head leaking horribly. But Kat continued up the stairs to deal with the old woman who would still be half-blind. *No one gets left behind.* And then she'd need her phone and she'd need the police here fast.

As Kat jogged the last few stairs, Headscarf fumbled her way into the bedroom, slapping her hands about the walls, directing orders at someone she couldn't even see. 'Get away, bitch! Get away! I got the cancer. I'm ill. Don't hurt me!' She clutched a phone in one hand. The screen was glowing. She'd called someone.

Kat clenched her teeth and raised the wooden club in her hand. *We're all monsters here. We're all red now.*

33

As she closed the distance between the first and second buoy, the lack of sensation in Helene's arms and legs made her think of waterlogged timber.

Using one arm to slowly claw forward, she tried to swim on her side, but a scissor kick proved too much for her numb legs and they drifted like dead weight. A tourniquet of bruise now encircled her neck and her lower back. Halfway across, she went under, twice.

Slipping under shocked her enough to force her arms to reach and grasp the second buoy. When her head nudged the hollow plastic sphere she managed to cling to it with half-paralysed hands.

Valda ... Valda ... Valda ...

My light ...

She reached the third buoy, twenty metres from the second, on her back. Unable to kick her depleted legs, she merely wafted her arms at her side, drifting more than sculling. Repeatedly stopping and looking over her shoulder to keep its blob of a silhouette visible, she eventually bumped the plastic ball. Then hugged it.

Valda and ... light ...

A strident but thinning chorus of drunken thoughts urged an attempt to reach the next buoy. Each one would take her closer to the rocks. They seemed to continue in a line for ever.

Lights ... Valda ...

Helene set off for the fifth buoy while still able to move her shoulders. The ball joints were grinding dry sockets. Curiously warm from the chest down, she had more of a memory of her legs and feet than any real sensation in them now. Her body was too heavy.

The next buoy never materialised. She lost it in the darkness.

Too tired to lift her head much, she drifted on her back, arms stroking at the water. Undulating with the swell, the shivering returned and was far worse than when she'd first entered the sea. Water filled her ears and iced her feeble thoughts, her breathing sped-up but she might have been holding her breath. Gazing at the stars, the sea took her.

She thought the great black tide was returning her *out there*. And almost didn't care.

Valda . . .

34

*A*ll was silent upstairs once she'd finished with Headscarf. She'd truly *finished* her too.

Shaky but aglow with a strange satisfaction, Kat threw the rolling pin onto the bed, then returned to the ground floor. The warm, full feeling in her tummy was like the quenching of an enduring thirst. *But what had been so parched?*

Beard was crawling in the hallway, his head down, between his shoulders. He couldn't see where he was going and Kat had no fear of him getting to his feet again. The vibrations of solid wood cracking against his skull remained in her hands and forearms like trapped static, a sense memory.

Remaining cautious, she withdrew the paring knife from the pocket of her joggers and held it to the rear of his neck. Fishing inside the back pocket of his jeans with three fingers, she retrieved her phone and the front door key attached to the octopus keyring that Steve had won in an arcade. The screen of her iPhone was splintered.

In the kitchen, she stepped around shards of glass from the obliterated light fitting, turned on the bulb inside the extractor hood. She activated the handset.

Waiting for the software to load, she stepped over Beard and unlocked the front door, but she couldn't open her route to freedom wide enough to pass through, obstructed as it was by the directionless shifting of his body.

If she'd thought her anger depleted and sluiced away by her liberal use of the rolling pin and pepper spray, she was mistaken: there was ample heat left and it flared alight, hot and red and quickly, at this new obstacle. She swung the door from side to side rapidly, slamming the edge against Beard's ribs until he fell onto his side and cleared the exit.

On the front path, Kat hauled the cold night air to the bottom of her lungs. When was the last time she'd breathed so deeply?

She bent double and retched onto the paving.

Gathering her breath and wiping the hair from her face, she straightened. Her leg muscles had jellied. She'd wrenched tendons too and muscles in her stomach while battering her foe. But her mind was perplexed more than shocked at the idea of what she'd just done to two human heads. *Why the heads?*

Fifteen years of pain might have just discovered an outlet at the side of her bed and inside her tiny kitchen. Processing that might take a lifetime. *Join the queue.*

Without a tremor of pity, she wondered whether she'd killed Headscarf. *You must be in shock*, she told herself.

Back inside the hall, Kat unhooked the one coat remaining on the rack. Slipped her arms inside the jacket. Then left the house, shutting the door and its red-faced horrors inside.

She walked uphill, following the lane connecting her home to what serviced as a village centre, in reality a crossroads of two lanes. There wasn't even a shop up there any more. From there she would walk to Ivycombe, where there would be more light and more people.

Without much enthusiasm, she mused that she should call an ambulance for the red folk inside her home. But before she moved far, her body crashed, the trembling in her limbs unstoppable. Her thoughts diffused into irrelevance. Parts of the last few hot minutes slipped out of sequence in her memory and into vivid flashes of sound and image that she struggled to anchor in narrative.

Other thoughts were intent on digression, on scattering along pointless paths. She thought about selling her house, and her mind filled with a list of what she would need to do to relocate. Concerns about her deadlines at the magazine mixed themselves up with plans for her next meal. It had been cup-a-soup and plain biscuits for four days – when she could stomach them. Then she was crying hard and saying her mum's name.

The icons and text on the phone screen were as fractured as the glass. Thumbing through the call list, she found the number for the detective, Lewis: he'd called her. Steve was the detective's case. Her own case was now connected to Steve's. Lewis knew what she'd discovered about Redstone. He should be the first to know what had happened to her. She tapped the call icon. Her phone sought the connection.

'Kat,' Lewis answered quickly, his voice taut, breathless. He was driving.

'The police need to be here . . . get here.'

'What's wrong?'

'They killed Steve. I saw it.'

'I'm sorry?'

'Some of the people who killed him are in my house.'

'I don't . . . Where are you now, Kat?'

'Home . . . near there. They'll need an ambulance.'

A long pause ensued. All she could hear was his breathing. 'I'll get a car out to you. I'm on my way too. Stay where you are.'

And then she thought of the tall blonde woman, Helene. 'She was only looking for her brother. They took her too. They made me give her to them.'

'Kat, you're not making sense. I need you to calm down and to stay right where you are.'

'You have to find her. Helene. They have her too.'

35

A distant, muffled roar: the crash of water against rock. A sound Helene had not heard since being carried out to the boat, hooded and bound.

Stiff and racked with shivering, she righted herself in the black sea. Her feet and hands might have dropped away into the darkness below so she tipped her head back to keep her face clear of the surface. If she went under she'd never make it back to the air. There was too little movement remaining in her depleted, dragging legs.

Her eyes flicked around, looking for where the sea met the rocks to create the muted impact at its border, before the land began. Only then did she see the light to her right. Small, bright, not unlike a star in the far distance. It returned a sense of perspective to a mind lost in the watery expanse, amidst beacons that never drew closer.

She wafted her arms harder so that her whole head might break free of the water and see this light better. When enough water had run from her ears, Helene heard distant laughter. One man, then another. Wheezy, hearty laughter travelling through the stillness.

She called out. And she called out again. She called, 'Help'. Her voice was thin and even quieter than the slop of the small waves in the windless air. But she kept on calling despite the shudders shaking her jaw. She fluttered her hands at her side. She was beyond swimming and only wanted to stay afloat a little longer.

As horrid as the sensation was, at least she was shivering. The muscle convulsions had started when she'd left the last buoy. Her exhausted limbs had slowed and her blood had cooled too quickly. Her body's engine was no longer able to generate enough heat to combat the permanent, withering, debilitating cold.

This is the end of me, the end of myself. I just want it to stop.

The laughter stopped and Helene cried, 'No! Don't . . . go away!' She dipped under.

Fighting the water to get her head back above the surface; if she stopped moving she would go down fast. A pull from below, a freezing magnetism between her body and a black depth.

Overcoming the shaking of her jaw, she cried out, 'Help!' again, as loud as she possibly could. The cry doused one of the few remaining embers of life in her.

The voices returned. They were no longer laughing. She heard the voices talking hurriedly, as if they'd been frightened by something. Two more lights joined the first. The first was stationary. The new lights moved through the air, sideways, along what must be the shore.

'There!' a man cried out. A thin band of greyish light flicked over the black surface so near to Helene's face. A torch. Under its beam, the seawater looked like thin oil.

An uneven silhouette moved behind the light, behind the silhouette, the sudden outline of what might have been a hill. Dull glimmers of stone suggested themselves. *The shore.* She'd come in much closer than she anticipated. So long had she been in the cold water, the textures and idea of land had erased themselves from her mind.

She'd almost made it. A moment of fascination gripped her; a wonderment at herself. She'd been dropped into the middle of the sea and swum so far, so close to the land. She'd nearly done it all by herself. 'Valda,' she whispered.

A second tiny orb of light followed the first. More of the vague, greyish illumination appeared on the water near her head. 'Christ!' a voice said. 'There's someone in the water.'

'Can you hear me?' a second voice called.

Helene nodded. Then remembered she needed to keeping making noise. 'Cold.'

A new sound entered the worst night of her life, but one that offered an outcome she'd never considered. And it took Helene several seconds to understand that the noise she heard closing on her position was that of a human body wading through water.

'Baby. Mommy's coming.'

36

$\mathcal{A}$ car engine revved. Headlights appeared and disappeared as the road twisted beneath the vehicle. It sped along a lane shielded by stone walls and unkempt hedgerow.

As familiar as Kat was with the road, the speed of the vehicle hurtling in her direction forced her to retreat from the bend. A speeding car on a narrow, unlit, B-road could easily swing round a corner and destroy a pedestrian. It had happened out here. After all she'd been through, the possibility of being knocked down by a police car was ironic but too horribly plausible to dismiss. She pushed her body into the foliage.

She'd covered no more than half a mile since leaving the cottage. A few lights outside the distant houses of Ivycombe were visible ahead. If this car carried the police, she could easily return home and begin what would be the first of many explanations. But Headscarf had also managed a phone call while half-blind. The woman's phone had been active when Kat caught up with her at the foot of her bed.

I got the cancers. All over. Don't. Don't. They made me do it so I can have more time.

The screen of Headscarf's phone had been glowing, so Kat had smashed the device from the woman's hand, breaking her thin forearm with a muffled, sickening crack. So fierce had been her hate for the birdlike creature who'd watched her shower and use the toilet during her captivity that she'd proceeded to belabour the woman into total silence, knocking her about the head, shoulders and neck, before leaving her crumpled down the side of the bed and leaking into the carpet.

As Kat crouched inside the hedge, what was foremost in her mind was who Headscarf had called and notified of Kat's unexpected insurrection. She feared the swift arrival of brutish reinforcements before the police lights turned the night blue and red.

The red folk, she assumed, would travel from Redstone. Red country and thirty minutes away by road if a car was driven as if in a rally. But it shouldn't take the police more than fifteen minutes to get to her from Divilmouth, if they got a move on. Ten minutes had passed since she'd called Detective Lewis.

The vehicle whipped past Kat. The occupant hadn't seen her. But when the car braked hard for the corner she caught a glimpse of the driver. *Lewis.*

He must have been driving when she'd called him: maybe on duty and using local roads. Uniformed police and an ambulance would surely follow the detective once he'd looked inside the cottage.

Kat forced herself out of the hedgerow and headed back to her house.

The police would be forced to detain her on account of what she'd done to Beard and Headscarf and for using an illegal weapon. But no matter, she'd explain everything. She wouldn't be a criminal for long. She'd soon be labelled a victim who'd survived a terrifying ordeal. And the revelations that she'd hit the local authorities with would return this small plot of hilly land to the nation's headlines. The role and reputation of the Brickburgh caves would be revised because the horrors of its history were not the preserve of the distant past.

A new elation at simply being alive was matched by the prospect of telling the police all she knew. Together, she and the rule of law could put an end to the despicable scourge that emanated from Redstone Farm. She'd be instrumental in killing it before anyone else was murdered.

Kat's eyes moistened as she began to realise she had a future again, and how important a role she must play in the days ahead.

As she wiped away her tears and gathered her wits to explain the awful scene that Detective Lewis was about to discover in her home, Kat realised something else: she was a much stronger person than she'd ever known herself to be.

She smiled. The expression felt unfamiliar around her mouth, like sticky food or a tickling stray hair.

37

*T*wo night fishermen found her, fifteen metres out from the shore. Larry and Ian were local men who'd decided to fish that night because of the clement weather. With their tackle, stove and the live sand-eels they favoured for bait, they'd set up at a favourite spot accessible by foot from deeper inland.

Over the years they had walked from their cars to that same spot to haul flatfish, bass, mackerel and pollack from a pebbly shoreline, from spring right through the summer.

That night they had arrived at their preferred spot just before dusk's indigo light had vanished like a ghost. Two hours later they'd seen the lights of the boat that had taken Helene out to sea. Three white dots in the distance. They'd judged the craft to have left a beach half a mile down the coast from where they found the girl in the water.

Almost imperceptible to Helene as she'd ploughed headfirst and onwards and seemingly for miles into the black freeze, a northerly current had caused her to drift to where the men had chosen to fish.

Many other things had conspired to save her too, as if the natural world had compelled her to live: a calm sea; warmer than usual spring temperatures at play upon the surface during the day for the previous two months, following a mild winter; an incoming tide that had turned in her favour; and the presence of two fishermen who'd wanted to take advantage of the fair evening weather. It had all added up.

The stamina she had built up by swimming regularly to

avert her own melancholy, frustration and the anxieties that life seemed intent on heaping upon her shoulders had also made a significant contribution. Had she not swum so hard for so long she would have drifted past the fishermen. Had the buoys marking rows of crab pots not appeared, her sodden remains might have been picked over by the very crabs the pots were designed to trap. Every variable had coalesced favourably, fortuitously saving her life and her daughter's future.

But her love for her child had played the biggest role. If she'd believed in such things, and she was tempted to, Helene would have concluded that she was not destined to die that night, because of Valda.

When Helene's story was shared at the hospital, the fishermen were even more surprised at how far the pale woman must have swum than they had been when they heard her voice near the rocks where they'd been standing to cast their lines.

Ian was forty-six. He'd fished her out. Before walking into the sea, he'd stripped down to his underwear so that he'd have warm clothes to cover a cold body when he came out. Without much thought about his own safety he'd waded up to his shoulders, adjusting his body to the water's temperature to prevent cold-water shock. He'd then swum another few metres, slipped a hand beneath the young woman's chin and pulled her to shore, swimming on his side, scissor-kicking for propulsion.

Later, he'd said that just getting her to the rocks had taken most of his strength, but he added that his endeavour was truly put into perspective by what she'd endured and achieved on her own in open, wild water for so long. In her hospital bed, Helene had managed a smile. She'd said, 'You get used to it.'

She'd been moments from losing full consciousness and was only half awake when Larry and Ian pulled her out of the water. Had she lost consciousness and sunk any further into the hypothermia she'd already succumbed to, the two men would have needed to attempt CPR on the rocks, amidst their tackle, and continue the treatment until the arrival of an ambulance. During the time it would have taken an ambulance to reach that part of the shore and return Helene to the specialist unit at Divilmouth Hospital, she'd probably have passed out and sunk away from this life.

Even if she'd still been alive when she'd been admitted to the hospital, the doctor had told her, she wouldn't have been far from needing a cardiopulmonary bypass. This would have required the extraction of blood that would then have to be warmed before an emergency transfusion. *Extracorporeal membranous oxygenation*: that's what the doctor had called it.

But Helene had avoided that eventuality, just, and sidestepped weeks of convalescence, because the fishermen had acted so quickly following the miracle of hearing her crying out from the offshore darkness.

Ian and Larry had torn off her wet clothes and dried her with a blanket. Beside their camping stove, they had hastily hauled a spare fleece and the second fisherman's combat trousers onto her body.

Larry had forced hot coffee into her mouth after telling her to cough. She'd not known why, but had obeyed him and coughed. Larry told her later that he'd needed to make sure that she could still swallow before giving her coffee. When she'd coughed gently, he'd wasted no time giving her the hot drink from his flask. The coffee had streaked warmth through her chest like new blood.

The men had then tugged two hats over her head and pulled two pairs of socks over frozen feet that had begun to resemble new marble. Ian's extreme-weather jacket had covered the fleece when zipped to her shivering chin. Around the coat had gone their second blanket.

Their swift actions had begun the steady return of warmth to her body; they'd headed off the coma that had only been moments away.

Supporting her body in the crooks of their elbows like an injured athlete, they'd taken it in turns to carry her up a hill and along two dirt tracks to their pickup.

'She's a weight.'

'Don't say that to a lady.'

'She's tall is what I meant.'

And so it had gone, brief exchanges between the men's hard breathing as they'd struggled from the exertion of getting her up that hill.

Eventually, with her body between them – one holding her legs, the other her arms – they'd stumbled to Larry's Mitsubishi.

Neither man had stopped checking to see if she was awake, or telling her to stay awake. When they'd reached the vehicle, Larry had needed to sit down; he was pushing sixty-three and had exhausted himself getting her that far. Even in darkness, Helene had noticed the sickly pallor of his face against the dark vehicle.

An ambulance met them before they had time to leave in the pickup.

In that part of the country, people knew what to do when someone was pulled from the water. They weren't all bad, Helene had since decided. Three strangers might have taken her out to sea and thrown her over the side of a boat. But two other strangers had fished her back out again and saved her life. Odder things might have happened to a girl during a weekend away from home, but never to her.

38

*L*ewis came out of the cottage unsteadily and it appeared to Kat that he might be sick. His handsome features had no colour beyond an ashen grey. When he paused to grip the porch post under the carriage light, Kat stepped out of the darkness.

As if electrocuted, Lewis flinched. He seemed frightened of her. No one had ever been frightened of her before, but Kat sensed his struggle to connect the carnage inside the house to the tearful woman he'd met in Sheila's office.

'What the fuck did you do?' he said.

Kat didn't answer. As if to prompt a response, Lewis pointed at the open door. He was wearing a fashionable suit. Hugo Boss. She recognised the cut from a recent feature she'd written in *Devon Life and Style*. It looked like the sample they'd been sent that had been too small for Steve.

'I'd say the response was proportionate.'

'What?'

'They've kept me captive for four days. In there. My home. They were going to kill me.'

Lewis remained speechless. His eyes worked hard at her face. Comprehension was losing out to shock.

'Have you called an ambulance?' Kat asked. The unnatural calm in her voice surprised her.

The detective nodded.

'Where are the others?'

'Who?'

'The police.'

Lewis finally stood taller, straighter, as if she'd reminded him of his role. 'On their way.'

'I need to make a statement. I know what happened to Steve, my boyfriend.' She nodded at her house. 'They killed him. I saw them do it. They had to wait a while before they could fake my suicide as well.'

Lewis finally came out from under the porch canopy. He looked drained and sick. One of his eyelids spasmed. He was fairly young and Kat assumed he'd little experience of serious crimes.

'I'm afraid you've got your work cut out, Detective. For the next few years, at least. I'd say –'

'I'd say you've said enough.'

And Kat's arm was up and behind her back. He'd moved so quickly, turned her round and pressed her thumb so far into the palm of her hand that the pain immobilised her. 'Hey!'

Her left arm was snatched from the air and brought about to join the other.

Kat tried to kick her heel into the detective's shin. In response, he depressed her thumb further into the palm of her hand and she screamed from a lightning bolt of agony, shooting up her arm to dazzle her brain. Her strength withered as his muscular hands tugged her wrists to the small of her back. Aftershave engulfed her head as Lewis pushed her down, face-first into the tarmac.

Her ribs impacted with the unforgiving road surface. She moved her head to the side at the final moment and issued a thin scream.

A broad knee thumped between her shoulders and knocked the breath from her lungs. A bracelet looped her wrists. Plastic clicked. The band tightened, cutting into her flesh. A plastic tie.

As the knee was withdrawn from her back, his hand slipped inside the collar of her hooded top and clenched. Kat was yanked to her feet, choking as the fabric noosed her throat, bruising the cartilage.

'What? You fuck!' she managed to scream.

A hand squashed her mouth closed. 'Shut it!' A command that ended in a hateful hiss, hot inside her ear. Spun around, Kat was dragged backwards. Her heels scraped the road to the man's car.

The detective's hands remained clamped around her middle but someone inside the vehicle opened the rear door. Springs in the upholstery sounded beneath the weight of the passenger with whom she was going to share the rear.

The opening of the door activated the vehicle's interior lights and Kat was tugged about-face. What sat in the rear of Lewis's car grinned at her: a thing that seemed to have climbed out of hell's mouth to take a seat in a private vehicle.

Luridly white eyes, set in a face the red of blood drained from veins, expressed a sadistic glee. Two rows of pale teeth split the rust-coloured head.

Kat pushed back against Lewis. 'No!'

He picked her body from the ground and stuffed her inside the rear of the vehicle, headfirst. Right into the naked lap of the thing that reached out with its red arms to receive the new passenger.

39

'Would you recognise the place if you saw it again? Do you think you could identify the people with the dogs who confronted you?'

Helene nodded, though her eyes betrayed her discomfort at the idea of going back to the farm she knew as Redstone Crossroads.

The female police officer, WPC Swan, smiled. 'You'd be perfectly safe. You wouldn't even need to get out of the car. But if a search is required of that farm, and arrests have to be made, we need to be certain that we're looking in the right place. Redstone covers a lot of ground, mostly farmland. Your brother made the recordings in a quarry west of the crossroads?'

Helene nodded again.

The policewoman bit the inside of her cheek. 'A lot of old quarries there, that's the problem. Seven, in fact. They're dotted for miles around those crossroads and cover land owned by at least five different farms.'

'His disc was labelled Redstone Crossroads. He must have made the recording close to the farm I visited. And what about the men from the boat?'

'We have an idea who one of them might be. We're looking for him now.'

'But you don't have him?'

'Not yet. He's not home.'

Helene let that sink in, then sat up in her bed. 'My

daughter. You said you'd get in touch with the West Midlands police.'

'She's fine,' the policewoman said and leaned forward, one hand hovering close to Helene's arm. 'So is your mum.'

The police in Divilmouth had previously assured Helene that they would speak to the Midlands force to make certain that her mother and Valda were safe.

Once her body temperature had been sufficiently restored and as soon as she'd woken from a deep, exhausted slumber, the first thing she'd done was call home, at six o'clock that Sunday morning. Her mother had answered. She'd been asleep and the call had frightened her. No one called that early unless there was a problem.

Helene's feat of endurance had left every muscle bruised and aching. Even walking to the toilet had required the support of a nurse and a wall to lean on, but she'd felt she had no choice other than explaining to her mother why she wouldn't be home that evening. She'd told her that she was in hospital and being treated for hypothermia, dehydration and exhaustion.

Hearing that, her mother had become breathless. Helene knew that she'd pawed at her heart too. She always did in moments of crisis.

Helene had reassured her that she was much better. The doctors had said so. She might even be discharged in a day or two, depending on the need for her bed. But she wouldn't be able to drive and would need to convalesce for weeks at home. Her return would also be delayed while she helped the police with their inquiries.

Knowing no mother would have been satisfied with so little information, Helene confessed to Lincoln's connection to something illegal in South Devon. She didn't say much more beyond telling her mum that the horrible statuette of the dog-headed woman sent to Valda was part of this. Whoever was behind the gift had sent it as a warning for Helene to stop investigating her brother's last week alive. The people he'd interfered with in Devon had since interfered with her.

Mercifully, her mother's shock and disbelief had prevented her asking any further questions. Helene had made her promise to take Valda to her flat. She'd also extracted an assurance that her mother would not open the door to anyone except a police officer with ID. Local police would check on her and Valda that morning. Helene had then ended the call while she'd had a chance.

Since she'd come round, the idea that Lincoln might have experienced her own fate and been dumped in the sea to drown had filled her with rage: a fury recharging her strength more than the seep of vitality that came from resting in a hospital bed. She knew exactly how he would have suffered before succumbing to the water.

But there had been no body, so Lincoln being thrown into the sea didn't entirely fit. They tended to find them down here, eventually: that's what the doctor had said. Most of what she'd remembered of the conversation on the boat was about something the three men had called 'the red'. One of them had said Lincoln had 'gone to the red'. The pig captain had also used the phrase as a threat to motivate the man called Phil. But 'the red' made no sense to the police at her bedside.

Helene had also insisted to the officers that the attempt on her life had been carried out by three men acting on the orders of another. She was sure one of them had mentioned someone called 'the witch-wife'. The constables had tried not to smile.

At nine, the police had confirmed that her car and some of her possessions had been found on the shoreline of a cove near Plymouth. Her shoes and rucksack had clearly been placed on the shore to make her disappearance look like suicide, and she told the officers just that. It was obvious, but only to her.

At that stage, to her dismay, the police officers suspected she'd made up the entire story: that she'd entered the water of her own volition. Their eyes gave them away. The sea's currents were not in her story's favour: from that cove near Plymouth the current could have eventually washed her to where the fishermen had found her in the water, exhausted, freezing and close to unconsciousness. People who drowned further north, near Brickburgh, were even known to wash up as far away as Dorset. The current patrolled the shoreline.

Her blood-work had been checked for drugs and alcohol. A trace of the wine that she'd drunk in her room at the guesthouse had shown up. Helene insisted that had she been intoxicated she'd have made poor choices and died within minutes of entering the water.

'The men in the boat can't know that I survived.' Helene had blurted that out when the idea struck her. 'They can't know. No one can know that I survived. Don't you see, that leaves me and my family in danger?'

'They can't know you're here,' the WPC with the kind face had said. 'No one but us and the night staff who attended to you even know who you are. You're safe here, Helene.'

She'd succumbed to tears as she attempted to convince the police just how determined and serious her attackers had been. She'd also continued to insist the very same people had killed her brother six years before.

But the constables had struggled to accept the Lincoln connection from the start. In their defence, as she'd shared her assumptions, the connection she'd made between the sounds that her brother had recorded underground, so long ago, and the recent attempt on her life had seemed just as preposterous to her.

When two detectives arrived later, she repeated her story to them several times. Repeat tellings did not rid her story of its weird and fanciful character. In her statement she provided information about Carol, the guesthouse, the red people who'd assaulted her. An absurd story detailing abduction and attempted murder by people who'd painted themselves red. The more she insisted the less the police seemed to listen. By early afternoon she'd wanted to scream and to keep on screaming until they sedated her.

By midday the WPC brought news that no 'Carol' had been traced. The guesthouse had been empty for some time. The nearest neighbours were certain that the owners, a retired couple, were in Spain. And 'this Kat', the disturbed journalist who had lured her down for the weekend, had also vanished. A subsequent visit to Kat's home by a patrol car revealed the cottage to be empty and locked. They were still looking for Kat and no one that Helene had named was available to help the police with their inquiries.

Only when she'd offhandedly mentioned Kat's boyfriend Steve, did Helene detect a shift in the detectives' tepid reaction to her wild tales. All four officers had exchanged glances across the bed.

A detective had then furtively mentioned that the coastguard and coastal watch volunteers were currently looking for him in the sea. He'd been missing for five days. It was believed that he'd fallen from the coast path during a walk.

Kat's mental state at the fête quickly acquired a new and startling significance. Helene's mind whirred until it ached. The journalist's instability at the Redhill festival might not have been a sign of Kat's heartbreak but an indication of something much worse. If the same group who'd tried to murder her had taken Steve, then it was even possible that Kat might have been coerced into making Helene travel to Devon: as a means for *someone* to get Lincoln's recordings? Kat had been desperate to take the discs and now she was missing too.

'Kat,' Helene had insisted. 'You have to find Kat. Steve's girlfriend. She's involved. This is all connected. Steve. Me. Kat. My brother. His bloody recordings. I don't know why, or how, but Kat had information about my brother. Or claimed she did. That's the only reason I came down here. And Kat was so bloody desperate for those discs. Don't you see?'

Unfortunately the police didn't.

Frustration burning more fiercely as each rebuttal registered, Helene had eventually closed her eyes against the impossibility of her situation. 'How many of you will be in the car when we look at the farm?' she'd asked in resignation.

'Er, it'll be us two.'

Helene had looked them over carefully: a small, earnest woman, and a man who couldn't have been older than twenty-four and appeared to be more of a veteran of the rugby pitch than of murder inquiries. Neither carried a sidearm.

'Our colleagues,' the WPC offered, 'will also be checking the other farms in that area, backed up by what the neighbouring force can provide in support. It's a joint task. Once we've identified the owners of the land that is relevant, we'll make thorough inquiries. We'll be sure to get you home to your daughter too.'

This was said almost apologetically, as if the police were desperate to get her out of their jurisdiction. 'Can you have a look at this map now?'

On a tablet, upon which a Google map had been downloaded by the WPC, Helene traced her route on the coastal path and through each of the places where Lincoln had made the recordings.

The two constables then conferred with each other near the door until WPC Swan nodded decisively and said, 'We'll start with Willows.'

40

*I*n anticipation of her own slaughter, a palsy came to Kat's limbs. To be *here* again: the scene of Steve's butchery, the abattoir.

A highlights reel of stored grotesques ran through her mind: the shrieks, the crack of bone, the flecks of scarlet upon stone, a pale body glistening in thin light . . .

Stop!

Cap the bastard.

Bestial whines, cutting through the narcotic fog, that yapping of devils. Claws scrabbling upon rock below the barn, the haste for succour: such noises left echoes in the mind. *Feeding.* The feeding. As above so below. White eyes in red faces. All to be endured again.

Near her cell on the farm, that very metal grate where her lover's broken body had lain confused and delirious awaited her now.

Steve's torments were over and she envied him. Being conscious here was intolerable. With consciousness came its twin: awareness.

Kat felt ready to take her own life. Better to do it herself before she was torn apart and fed to . . . *dogs*.

'No. No. No.'

She rocked back and forth inside the fusty, unlit room she'd been dragged into by Lewis and the grinning red fiend. Her hands itched maddeningly, the circulation almost cut off by the plastic tourniquet about her wrists.

They'd left her kneeling on the dirty cement floor of an agricultural outbuilding where rank odours stained each air molecule. Maybe a wet carpet had once mouldered within the damp confines. A bare floor now served to signify the reduction in her status and her diminishing prospects, because the only way out of here was down there: into the red.

In a few hours the sun would rise, but until then the barred window, encrusted with cobwebs and grime, would reveal nothing but a black square of deep night.

When would they come?

When she'd been delivered to her final destination earlier that evening her captors had eschewed a hood. It had no longer mattered that she'd seen bits of the farm because she was never leaving it. And in a darkness raked by headlights, a communal expectation had thickened the atmosphere. Cars had been parked in a lane outside an old house, a few people had milled in the road, torches scything their haggard silhouettes. A small gathering. For her. *For the reddening.*

What she saw of the house had sagged about a weed-corrupted lane of holed tarmac. Dim yellow light, edging the windows of the ground-floor rooms, offering a glimpse of ragged hedgerows, long grass, a deck where motionless figures had gathered to watch the detective's car pass: the carriage driving her deeper into where it all began and her final destination.

Before she'd been interned in the grubby cell, her scant mental capacity, the fraction not consumed by fear, had grown aware of voices outside the detective's car: raised voices suggesting that everything might not have been going to plan for the red folk. She presumed she'd posed a setback, a thin pyrrhic victory, and the only satisfaction she might derive from despair turning into a permanent state of mind.

The torment of having been so close to freedom before it was snatched away was near-impossible to acknowledge. She'd come so close to evading a death that she'd not imagined possible in the twenty-first century. Any hope of escaping that was a mirage now.

What she'd done in her cottage had not been enough, because now there was *this*. As if marked indelibly during her first visit, her current dilemma appeared like destiny. She'd dealt with Beard and Headscarf in ways only conceivable in the psychotic fantasies of her lowest ebbs. Buried aggression maybe, stored up since secondary school, then embellished by bad relationships and terrible jobs and finally given vent? She didn't know. Though once she'd started down that path with weapons gripped in her manicured fists not only had her actions become uncomfortably satisfying but her will had seemed to surrender itself to . . . she wished she knew.

And Lewis, that false saviour, who'd assaulted her and carried out the second abduction she'd endured within a week, had been displeased with his hosts on arrival. He'd pulled up beside the row of dilapidated buildings slumped beyond the sunken house and ranted at someone near the vehicle. She'd heard some of what the Judas had said, his voice hissing with rage. 'There was fuck all on those discs. A few noises. What the hell were you thinking?'

Two motorbikes had passed then, the sounds of their engines hurting her ears. A car's headlights had followed the bikes.

It was Tony's son, Finn, that Lewis had confronted. Kat recognised the ferret's voice when he spoke. 'He got a lot from round here. Film too. All we know is that we don't have it all. There must have been stuff in his flat we couldn't get out. We didn't know what the sister had.'

'Too late now! And you topped that photographer? You bloody mad? Madder than I gave you credit for. You're fucking everything up for yourselves. Do you think you're invincible?'

'He saw *things*.'

'We had an agreement this wouldn't happen again. You swore no one else would go!'

'Sometimes shit has to happen.'

'Pay them off! But don't . . . for God's sake . . . What are you doing? What the fuck are you doing?'

'What's necessary. And it gets worse so you better get your head straight, Louie. We've also taken our local flyer, the one with the big mouth, on a journey he won't be returning from any time soon.' Willows's son had only found the detective's distress amusing. 'And your maths is way off too. Keep up, Louie. There's the sister who came south for the ghost of her rubbernecking brother. We picked her up as well. She was blathering about uploading the recordings. Can you imagine that? We'd no idea what else she knew, which wasn't much, as it happened. By then it was too late. She was in the middle of a red roaming. We put her over the side of a boat.'

At this news of Helene, Kat's head had dropped. She'd let the tears fall.

'This bitch of a hack's next.'

That news had swiftly returned her to the present.

'Jesus wept,' Lewis had said. 'This stops. Now.'

Finn Willows had spat on the ground. 'Have you seen what she did to E and his mum?'

'The journalist will make it four. Four! Missing in a matter of weeks? This isn't bloody Mexico. Two of yours need hospital. Enough of it.'

'Our own will be taken care of but listen carefully. Everyone's going to be keeping their heads down until we know what's in the wind. We're out tomorrow, we're leaving. And that's where you come in, Detective. You're really going to earn your keep now. Plenty of your esteemed colleagues not familiar with the enchantments of this red earth and its ways may soon be poking their beaks in. When this nosy bitch can't be found –'

'Enchantments? That what you bloody call this? It's murder. Multiple murder.'

'For your own preservation we'll need the inside track on everything. Every angle, every lead, so the red can deal with its foes in its own way. Like it always has done.'

Kat had heard the detective groan at that; a sound dragging itself from his belly. 'Jesus,' he'd added, the word weighted with the opposite of salvation.

'And remember your place, Louie. You're an associate, a lackey. *She'll* be here soon and I don't want you running your mouth round her.'

'You bloody morons,' Lewis had wailed, uselessly. Kat had sensed he'd never grasped the full vision of the red.

'Hindsight's a wonderful thing, Louie. I bet it was for you, after playing blackjack online and pissing away fifty grand.'

'I never agreed . . . not *this*.'

'You're in the middle, Louie, and everything's at risk. But in the scheme of things, nixing a few cuckoos is irrelevant.'

'The red demands.' An elderly voice had entered the conversation then and the atmosphere outside the car changed, a hushed tension seeping through the darkness. 'And protects itself. They've been at our door for years. We knew this time would come. But what can I tell you? The red thirsts. All our futures are red.'

'Tony, for God's sake.' Lewis had tempered the volume and tone of his voice, but barely, which had only served to increase Kat's sense of his desperation, his helplessness. 'Tonight alone I've done a hundred times more than was ever agreed. I got your people out of that cottage and I delivered the reporter. I was minutes away from being caught. She could have called anyone. And you put people in her house. Abduction? You can't. You can't do that. How was that going to end? You're out of control . . . This isn't the fucking Stone Age.'

'It's a shame you've always hung around the fringes, Louie.' Tony's lordly tone was mocking. 'If you'd shown a little more commitment, you'd be more than bent swine with gambling debts. You could've seen what we see, lad. You could have shared something remarkable. It would have provided you with more backbone than you're showing now. I'm disappointed in you, lad. Bitterly.'

Finn had laughed and sounded like a horse neighing.

Lewis's meagre restraint had finally melted. 'Save your mystical garbage for the nutters. And for the simpletons that you've got hanging on to every word of bullshit that drops out of your old lady's mouth –'

A foot had then scraped the tarmac and the assembled crowd had jeered. Kat had overheard the sounds of an enraged and screaming woman being restrained.

'You ill-mannered bastard!' That had come from Finn. Huddled on the backseat, Kat had sensed his anger building through the exchange: he seemed about as stable as his father. 'You say that *here*? You greedy, shitty pig! You want to be shown what we have here?'

'Finn! Get him out of my sight.' Willows's voice had risen amidst the standoff, the kicking and scuffling of feet, the confusion in the darkness outside the car, the convergence and collision of raised male voices. Kat had recalled an afternoon in a pub in King's Cross when football fans had exploded into violence near her table.

If Lewis, a police officer, was working for the family and the operation, or whatever it was, who else might be in league with the red? Sheila had introduced her to Lewis. The sudden sickening idea that her editor was involved had turned Kat's shock to concussion. *Not Sheila, surely. No.* Involved with these dirty, dyed devils? *Butchers. Cannibals.* She'd never live to disprove her paranoid grasping but the last few days had been sufficient preparation for Kat to believe anything.

Eventually, a sullen Lewis had returned to the car and yanked Kat from the rear seat as if she'd been a dog with fleas that stank and left stains on his upholstery. His mouth had been bleeding.

Finn Willows had appeared too: a scrawny frame topped by a thin ponytail and a scratchy beard. His ferrety face a mask of loathing as he'd lit her path into the cell of the condemned.

Others in the lane had tugged open the front passenger door and retrieved Beard. He'd lain slumped forward in the seat, ominously silent, leaking. Headscarf's remains had been dumped inside the boot by Lewis.

At her cottage, once the detective had secured Kat in the car, he'd dashed inside to remove as much evidence as possible. He'd come back out carrying Headscarf like a limp child before depositing her in the boot. There had been no time for the collaborator to administer first aid: the false protector had merely hauled the wounded red soldiers from her home so they wouldn't be found.

Her current prison cell adjoined the main barn, that place of murder constructed from vertical planks of wood, stained dark. Earlier, even when only partially visible from the road, the building's silhouette had declared its malign purpose, withering her spirits and chilling her flesh more than the night air. A black place on land from which all decency had long been erased.

Before the building's jagged silhouette she'd gazed as if hypnotised by a place of worship, where the god was still present. An improperly secured cap, that's what the building was. A fragile canopy above a pit so deep she could imagine an abyss carrying on for ever, through the earth and back through the ages.

Beneath that wretched barn perhaps even matter as she knew it, and all that her experience had taught her to understand of the world's rules, ceased. A brush with the very idea had paralysed her limbs. They'd needed to push her inside the cell.

A hand struck wood, palm down. The door of her cell opened and the bent figure of Tony Willows was led inside by a woman Kat put at around fifty years old. She had once been pretty, even beautiful, but the freckled skin of her face was grooved and etched by so many creases that her expression had re-formed into a misery mask. A Pre-Raphaelite princess whose noble features had slipped and sagged around eyes that still suggested kindness: a quality Kat forbade herself to hope could exist in such a place as this.

In better light, Tony Willows's skin now appeared treacle-brown, the flesh at his throat and sunken chest wattled, liver-spotted. Despite the timbre of his voice he looked like a man at the end of his life.

Kat found her own voice. 'This doesn't have to happen. I've no interest in what you're doing. I'm not that kind of journalist. Not a reporter.'

Tony raised a palsied hand to silence her, the fingers quivering like a plucked string. The other lumpy hand gripped a walking stick. His eyes were half-closed, his demeanour sombre like a judge silencing the accused who babbles for his grace and mercy.

The woman smiled. 'It's not an end, but a beginning.'

Tony's old eyes opened. They were filmed with tears. He clutched the woman's hand and cleared his throat. 'Nanna's right. People would flock here if they knew of the miracle. They'd give anything to be a part of what is here. What abides. You've no idea of the bounty, nor the vision we are blessed with. You can't understand. You're a vandal. Vandals destroy what they don't understand. It's what they do.'

'No.' Kat shook her head, emphatically. The woman was Nanna then? Willows's daughter, Finn's twin. She'd been mentioned in the first online article Kat had read.

Tony only sighed in exasperation as if she was a child displaying naivety on an important matter. 'This earth has been remade, lass. So many times. But through the endless freezes and great flooding thaws, a wonder far older than our species lingered. We can't expect you to understand, but you need to gather yourself. Make peace with your past. And then forget it all because it really is irrelevant. That should be a comfort. You're a spark. They go out, dear. Infinitesimal. Nothing. We're dealing with something our tiny minds aren't made for. I won't tell you any more because only one of us can truly see what's under here, where the red yawns. And may it always yawn so that some of us outlast the desolation that is due.'

Tony sighed, his chest a dry bag, deflating. He pitied her. 'But you're nourishment for a moment, lass. Nor are we much more. Meat and a few thoughts, a little heart from time to time. Again, again, again. It always comes back around. We're ready, are you?'

To Kat, it was a garbled scripture he must have canted before. 'Please . . .' she said, and yet she struggled to plead for her life. Horror choked her. Pushed its hot fingers down her throat. The profound weight of inevitability stalled her thoughts. A childlike misery persisted.

Nanna knelt before her and unpacked a fabric bag. She laid two items upon the floor. A small bottle of brown glass, the contents murky, and an object wrapped in a white cloth. Whatever was contained inside had stained the cloth the colour of iodine. 'You're strong,' she said to Kat, smiling sweetly. 'Your will has been demonstrated. It has made you even more delicious. Your strength, your hot spirit, will be wonderful nourishment. It's an honour, my love.'

'This doesn't have to happen . . . please.'

'Our red mother watched you. She caught scent of your lover too, the thief, who crept inside with us.' Nanna winked, her smile now verging on the salacious and chilling Kat with the suggestion of a deep instability that surged behind a seemingly affable veneer. 'But it's time to forgo the struggle. And we all thank you. We'll never forget you. We love you, Kat.'

'Love. Yes. We adore you, girl.' Willows's faded eyes misted with sentiment. He wafted a withered forearm as a mad king on a blasted heath would do to dispense wisdom to his last subject, or fool. 'You give so that others can abide. We must pass on, lass. To sanctuary. Conceal ourselves in this hostile wilderness. Once more, again and again, the red children take flight. But the black dog and her white pups must be fatted. A dry summer and a hard winter are coming, my girl, and you'll be the last for a while. The last to go down. We've made them . . . excitable. They need to rest in the dark now. For all our sakes let's hope they do, eh?'

He leaned forward, his eyes peeled with what she read as panic. 'We brought them up too far. Too far. You cuckoos are to blame.'

Kat moistened her throat. She didn't know what could be said in response to such lunacy, nor whether anything was worth saying. What words struggled through her shock seemed futile before they left her lips, even then as a whisper. 'Please. I swear on my life. This is sacred to you, I can see that. You've done something special. I see. I see that. I get it. I've seen it too. What's here. I have. I really have. But I have a life. In return for that, I'll say nothing . . . do nothing . . . help you even. I can be useful to you.'

Tony shook his grizzled white head. He was beginning to remind her of an old Native American chief, or a homeless man leathered by the elements who chatted druggy nonsense to those passing by his cardboard throne. Eyes twinkling, the smile benevolent, as if to a child he said, 'You've no calling. No. You're a bitch not a witch. But *she* is one and *she* decides. Our witch-wife. *She* found it. Buried, so far inside . . . years ago. Understand, if you're capable, that what was welcomed back has saved us, all of us here. And *she* who is greater than us decides who abides and who is swallowed whole. We follow a message. There's a receiver. Here. You didn't know? No words, no words. Pictures, in the mind. Never been wrong. And you've threatened the old grove. You're from *there* . . . that blasted place. Coming unbidden. All traipsing about. We saw you. We saw you. The red has seen you off many times. Left your bones in darkness for thousands of years.

'We watch the door, lass. We merely bargain, and you're blessed, the bounty. You're a full belly on a cold night, girl. Be strong now. That's all, lass. Be strong and be grateful for what you offer to what abides.'

Tony's daughter unwrapped the cloth from the object on the floor. 'Drink with us now. Close your eyes. And see. It's rising. Today. For us. The pack whines.'

'Blind dogs scamper through the red earth even as we sit here, sharing. Old Creel! Old Creel!' Tony shrieked with what appeared to be a private but powerful ecstasy. 'And thy thirsty pups!'

Kat flinched as the bowl was laid before her knees. She'd seen similar in the museum in Exeter and in the slide-show so many years before in Plymouth, manmade artefacts removed from Brickburgh's caves. Each time they'd made her feel sick.

What lay on the filthy ground before her was the top of

a human skull. This one pale and still moist inside. A more recent addition to the Brickburgh collection. A cup. A cup of special significance like the items buried alongside the red queens, preserved in graves for thousands of years. A receptacle: that's what it was, designed for purposes for which there was no written or spoken record.

Cap the bastard.

Kat whimpered and backed away from the horrid thing. Shuffling on her buttocks she reached the nearest wall but could get no further. In the corner her vision whited out. She spat out the bitter taste that gathered in her mouth.

Tony grinned. Changed his tone, his demeanour. The wise old man dropped the beatific act and stepped forward a few thousand years to adopt a fresher discourse. 'Good. Even better on an empty stomach. More potent. Doesn't get diluted. I'd know too because I've taken everything. So let me put it another way: you'll not want to venture one step beyond that door straight, woman. This shit'll take the edge off. No one can take Old Creel straight. You've gotta be messed-up, lass. So get your load on, girl, because this promises to be the most intense experience of your life. I'd even be tempted to consider this communion wine as a form of anaesthetic before surgery, if you follow, because you're literally going to come apart next door.

'You've squeezed us through the ringer, girl, so you must go, as all our foes are sundered. Who else can we give? And the dogs are out. Can't say fairer than that.'

'The red ways.' Nanna touched Tony's arm as if he were being uncouth and embarrassing a guest in their home. 'We'll share what you experience. Through your terror, Kat, we all share in wonder. Passing to the red is a great privilege.'

Tony pushed himself upright. 'Another era ends. Won't be the last. But we will remember your cries this day as you nourish sacred ground. So sup, lass. Sup your last. The red awaits. Your passage between the walls is booked.'

'The red abides,' Tony's daughter said, smiling. 'All we red children abide.'

Relics

41

athered in scarlet and masked and frightful, they made their journey down the lane: a mother and her dear son. The son pushed the wheelchair. Every bump and judder of the rubber wheels rolling across each crack, lump and fissure in the tarmac now so familiar to them, mapped by the vibrations within their thin, unclothed bodies.

'This will end where it began,' the hunched figure in the chair said to Finn, or to itself.

The odour of the black headpiece that wobbled on his old mother's head wafted under her son's nose: it was the musk of old dogs drying beside open fires and the distilled stock of sweat made caustic by age. Over and above the manure from the pony's paddock, the scent of rain on tarmac and the cold meatiness of upturned earth, the mask's fragrance proved resilient. Hers had been worn for a long time before she found it; the family had never been sure of its exact age. But the tatty mane of the headpiece had engulfed her pointy shoulders so many times, as it had covered others before her.

'Mother,' Finn said, sniffing. 'Quiet now. We've made arrangements. This is only a setback.'

The shaggy skull in the chair twitched. Though muffled, her outburst was strident. *"Did you see . . . It's . . . moving?"* That's what the girl said to me!'

Her son nodded as if only half-listening to something he'd heard so many times before.

Without any acknowledgement from him the woman's voice continued to whine through the ragged muzzle of the

307

shaggy helmet. 'Who could have known that it would move so much? Or come so close?'

'I know the story, mother.'

That great black helmet, bison-sized and carrying the face of a devilish ape upon its grimacing front, so ruffled and patchy and bristling, soon dropped forward as if the occupant of the wheelchair had fallen asleep. The toothy mouth grimaced and its eyeless sockets gazed at the road before the rumbling, rotating wheels.

Between the tatty jaws, inside the cavernous mouth, an impossibly wrinkled, red face had closed its eyes to remember when she first dropped out of time. The passenger in the chair had truly gone under, not to dream but to sink into a reverie of times long gone, appearing as vividly to her as events occurring the week before.

Forty years gone, she walked the halls of what was here before her. And had she not done so her life would never have been so long. 'I'd never have seen this day,' she muttered. 'Our last, as shepherds.'

Her son heard that. 'Mother. Not true. This is not the end.'

That girl, so long ago, had been right to think the walls below the ground had moved. A girl in a distant beginning had opened the Creel, but never lived long enough to understand what it was that had overcome her; what it was that she let loose with her terror.

'That was a long time before we knew their nature, son. Finn? Are you with me, my boy?'

'Right behind you, mother. Here.' The man stretched out an arm and stroked the teeth that protruded from the preserved gums of the headpiece: bumpy and dusty and the colour of tar. 'The turning. Round your column. It must be done as soon as we get there, mother. We've the numbers, just, and the Creel's right under our feet again.'

'She was pretty. Excitable. A child.' *She'd been nothing more, the first girl, the precursor. Sometimes, Jess even remembered her name, Maddy Gross, who'd played a decorous game too at her man's 'soirées' at the farm. That she remembered bitterly. So eager had been that pretty lamb for the dregs of Tony's entourage.*

Tony had caught young Maddy's eye in an inn out Divilmouth way. Men always had a use for a girl like Maddy. 'Tony. Troubadour.'

'He's here too, mother. See, ahead of us, with Nanna. We're all together. We'll do this together, like always.'

How he hobbles though. Bent over his stick. An old man who needs a daughter to guide him now. So old but still the twisted, selfish boy that she'd taken for herself in Germany a long, long time ago. 'They all heard about him here.' Tony had been the object of such fascination, her man: a fallen star who'd bought the broken-down farm at the crossroads.

'But beneath the ground, my son . . .' *Maddy's beauty had been of no consequence down there, only her helplessness proved useful.* 'Much more than our own past. Something much greater we've seen.'

'And much more we will see, mother. Together. Not right here. This is over. But we'll survive. Like the red. Always.'

'"How far are you prepared to go?" I asked the girl that. What was her name?'

The sky had been glowering to dusk that day too, forty years gone, but the girl called Maddy Gross had still followed Jess below the ground through the old door in the quarry. She'd worn red boots with Cuban heels and a special coat she'd found in the house. A suede jacket belonging to her, Tony's woman, Jess: the woman Maddy had betrayed in her own home.

Jess had picked out that jacket in Copenhagen when she was with Tull. It was purple, patterned with rhinestones. But back then, beneath the ground, Jess had been unsure how to confront the girl. Maddy, her rival, had made deep inroads, had become dear to Tony, so Jess had only wanted to intimidate Maddy in a place that was dark. Yes, in the dark. But that was all: she'd only wanted to frighten her. 'The matter was taken out of my hands, my son. The red came. It filled the air.'

'Aye, mother. And we can't keep it waiting now. It's on our doorstep.'

On that day, forty years gone, her old bones were not wheeled down a rutted lane in a hideous chair like a babe. Her son hadn't even been conceived. 'That sweet girl and I had stepped like nymphs through the meadow to the quarry. Our hair was so long, so black, son.' *By that afternoon, forty years gone, no one at the farm had slept for three days. Coming inside to escape the rain, they'd all crashed on the floors and couches. Nothing unusual about that but the others were asleep when it happened, or wrecked when the girl with red boots was lost below the ground.*

Someone from the record label had brought coke that weekend. His true purpose to inquire about a new album. Terry, a photographer, had come down from Kensington too, with a shoulder bag stuffed with marijuana. Sometimes Jess remembered them, the old crowd. 'Brian was your father's manager back then, son. He abandoned his Rolls-Royce in a lane. It was miles from the farm. It was stuck. He came on foot with a bottle of wine in each hand. Over one finger he had a carrier bag, from Harrods. It was full of pills. His car was there for a week until a real farmer towed it here.'

'Yes, mother.'

'Under the ground, I held the torch. Poor Maddy didn't have one.' *And it was Jess's light that found the paintings. They were inside the cave. So horrid were the designs, yet fluent and so elegantly wrought upon the stone. Jess had never forgotten them. An ancient work. Hellishly beauteous.* 'A map, a tapestry, a history. I only understood that later.'

'And how beautiful are your readings of it, mother.'

A work both abstract and figurative. Art that used the contours nature had fashioned into rock over millennia. How one texture augmented another had astonished her. How one thing became another when it was illumined . . . Was that not the nature of this land she'd come to know so intimately, transformation? 'It watched us, son. It still makes me breathless.'

A curving hollow of stone, coloured by hand, had formed a great bestial eye, to gaze upon the occupants of the chamber for ever. An eye drawn so artfully in pigments of ochre, powdered bone and charcoal. But for how long had that eye been open? She hadn't been able to guess. But after they'd stumbled from the chute and into the vault the eye had observed Jess and Maddy, closely.

The first great chamber, but never destined to be the last that Jess would find.

A much older version of that young woman now laughed gaily in its wheelchair. 'That girl . . . Maddy Gross stopped giggling then, I can tell you!'

'I bet she did. We've watched the faces of a few cuckoos straighten here, have we not, mother?'

The change in the register of Maddy's voice had been so abrupt. The purest darkness was the killer of levity. The sudden freeze had chilled their spirits rigid. Foes and rivals the women were, but how they had clung to each other upon entry, she and Maddy, and before paintings so dreadful that they were instantly sobered from their weariness and intoxication. A hangover that had lasted for days. There'd been such a party at the farm, the origins murky, its conclusion indefinite.

'Your father wasn't easy to live with, son . . . I'd been below before. To get away from your father. I'd gone inside. A crevice. But never so deep.' *Much further down that time, much further with the cuckoo, Maddy, who'd been wearing red boots and Jess's precious coat: the pretty oaf that her man had pawed. Maddy.*

'She was not blameless!'

Finn sneered. 'None of them are, mother.'

Maybe Tony was rich. The girl had surely had that on her mind. Inquiring but dull, a tiny mind. Though how could anyone have known there was no money left? The farm had been worthless.

'I'd only wanted to frighten her . . .'

Maybe back then, when she and Tony took it on, the dilapidation of the farm had been charming. For a while: those sombre ruins and the antiquity of the tools the real owners had abandoned. Tools that spoke of an austere, methodical use of the land lasting for generations.

The former tenants, a local family, had worked that earth and survived and watched the quarries open and close, their own fortunes rising and falling hard, their ranks withering to those two thin men who had sold the ruins to Tony.

The farmers: an elderly man and his son. The mother of the family had been in the ground five years. The son had no wife. Everything ended for that family in those two exhausted, heartbroken men of few words. And they let a hippy, wearing white cowboy boots, buy their home at a good price. That's what happened when you gave up the Creel for the cross.

But how the ghosts of those farmers had continued to make idiotic the bearded figures who'd been drawn to Tony from London, all of them in their unsuitable footwear, stumbling about the muddy pastures and churned yards.

'This. It was your father's idea.' *Tony's dream to live on a farm. Escaping the system, the suits, managers, accountants, taxmen, the serpents, usurpers, backstabbers, users, the false prophets, the manipulative, the hangers-on . . . away from them all, and Jess too. But she'd never let Tony go. He'd once promised her children, away from the transience, the fatigue and sleeplessness of a minstrel's existence upon the road.*

She'd wanted to free Tony from himself most of all, those tendencies for bedlam that flourished inside his delicate, boyish head. 'I wanted a home and children . . . we were going to adopt.'

'The red provided,' Finn said. 'It always has done.'

To be a young family on an old farm so far from the distractions that were destroying her man: that had been their dream. Together they were going to be children again, she and Tony, at the dawn of time, before history, before 'the man'.

After his stay in the hospital in Surrey, she'd kept Tony secluded and fostered his desire to sow and reap, to take food from the ground, to grow smoke, distil cider, to rise with the sun and sleep at sundown.

'I'd started to believe it was possible. Your father had seen others do it, buy farms in Essex. He'd envied them. But he couldn't change. He was incapable.' *Just like their son, Finn, who'd sowed the new crop and made them so wealthy. But all Finn's father had longed for was a lazy kingship. From afar on tour and in London he'd wished for a smaller fiefdom, surrounded by admiring subjects. One simpler, easier to govern, his plot in Devon a Garden of Eden: no tourists and only a few local farms clinging to the red earth.*

But what strange music would he find in a part of the world so left behind and stuck between the wars? The Sixties had passed by Brickburgh and Redhill. They promised perfect isolation, but for Tony it was only ever going to be morbid and depressing. The silence in the valleys, the power of the sea beyond the cliffs, had soon swallowed them and made their days boom with loneliness.

How he'd drunk again and picked up his old crutches that he rolled into cigarette papers: as trapped inside his own labyrinth as he'd been before. He'd never asked for desolation, never obscurity. He couldn't coexist with the highs or function without them and so the darkness had reclaimed him. His light dimming month by slow month, he'd performed pastiches of who he'd been. 'Moving here was the worst thing for your father.' *His instruments had gathered dust. Ghosts of his enemies had consumed him. He took to remonstrating with them in loud whispers. He was sick and yellow. Only the prospect of a party and a girl half his age roused him. Until that day.*

'The red land was not for repose, my dear Finn. It had to be worked.' *Was not for owning either but it allowed stewards, for a time.* 'We've had our time.'

'It's been worked red, mother, our most precious wife.'

And below the red earth that afternoon, when so far from the weak and watery sun, most fearful was Jess's recognition that so little had altered down there. All that was below the ground had remained unchanged for more years than she could imagine stacked together. How long had those paintings been on the wall and who were the artists? She asked this, but who was there to answer her? That worn old man and his quiet son with the yellow eyes had said nothing when they sold the farm to Tony. Only due diligence had revealed the existence of the disused quarries and the overgrown, unstable ground that was once used to extract iron oxide for paint. The tunnels she'd found had never been mined. They'd formed naturally and been kept clear. Their old doors had been smothered by ivy or packed with earth. But they were still open.

And surely those pictures upon the walls were important, valuable? And without the music from where would their future prosperity come? Farming? All this had turned in her mind. But in that chamber, without even knowing it, she was granted her three wishes. 'The future was decided, my bright boy. Right here.' *As it was, as it has been, as it will be for others. Always.* 'We were claimed by the red earth.'

Under this bloody soil she'd seen it. The evidence of the former tenants was revealed. Ancient occupants who'd left their own mark upon the earth as her family had done in their time. The etchings suggested ideas she'd never entertained before.

Others had come later, after the original artists, and settled and felled the trees in the valleys and left them bare and ploughed the earth into furrows. In time, she saw it all. Livestock trampled and clomped the hills shorn and barren. Gouges wounded the land for the extraction of minerals. Battered and scarred: the place, its people. They'd all inflicted damage and became damaged upon the soil that clotted like blood. But once it had all been wild. Like her man and all who came to be with him. And here, beyond the red crossroads, was a place that had always longed to be wild again. She'd known at once.

Jess remembered keenly how she'd felt before those paintings. She'd felt like a mere grain, occupying a place of mystery and wonder for less than a moment of time.

'He put me underground, your father, with that idiotic girl. It was his doing. What was her name?' *His mistress? Maddy. That was her name and Jess had taken the silly girl deep.* 'I even held her hand as my own daughter holds his hand now. It was so pale, Finn.'

Final journeys. That had been the last path the girl in red boots had ever walked. And this was the last one for her own family. 'My children.'

'Don't cry, mother. Don't upset yourself. Hush now. Hush. We're here. Now turn the red, mother. Turn the children about you now, beloved. You are our column.'

That first summer. There had never been another like it.

42

*O*ut at sea the sky darkened and the wind buffeted from the east, skimming the distant water and carrying cold, watery pins in its gusts.

The patrol car had stopped at the top of the valley where the land re-formed itself into an unpleasant familiarity. Through the windscreen, Helene recognised the holed tarmac and overgrown borders and bitterly recalled her relief at finding the crossroads that first time. Breathless and ragged from the steep ascent up the valley, it was here that she'd come upon Lincoln's last clue, scribbled on the side of a compact disc.

The steel gate blocking the lane had been open and concealed by the overhanging trees. Now it was closed. To reinforce the boundary, two idling men leaned against the metal rungs of the gate as if in expectation of unwanted visitors.

The guardians at the gate wore green Wellington boots and waterproofs in preparation for the rain now pattering on the car's roof. The hoods of their raincoats were raised and they wore hats beneath. Fleeces were zipped up and pulled over lowered chins, obscuring their faces.

Beyond the gate unruly grass and weeds tangled with the hedge and trees, forming the impression of a narrowing chute burrowing into the farm. Merely peering down the lane awoke the dogs in Helene's memory; they leaped and crushed her into the hedgerow. *Kent.*

The two police officers alighted from the vehicle and a

discussion began at the gate. Helene cracked the rear window but was unable to overhear what was said.

She was stowed safely inside a police car but that failed to allay the bustle of anxiety that shortened her breath. As soon as they'd arrived she'd wanted to get out of the car and walk away. *Here* wasn't safe for her. Lincoln never recorded anything again after placing his microphones here. *They'd* put him into the red.

She'd allowed herself to be talked into returning. The police didn't believe her story.

Only one of the men at the gate spoke with the officers, his slouch transmitting an air of irreverence in the presence of authority. Inappropriate and no doubt tiresome to the police. The male officer's arms were folded, tightly.

The WPC did the talking from their side of the barrier, expressing herself with hands that never stopped moving: two white flickers in a grey world, hurriedly working the air. This was a murder investigation or would be soon.

The second figure's hood was tight around his head. He looked at the ground. Hands in pockets.

Helene's eyes probed that oval head bound in Gortex. She couldn't make out the face inside but the spiky proportions of the man's thin body seemed familiar. *The prick on the boat who'd knelt on her shoulders?* She needed the police officers to make him show his face.

The male police officer returned to the vehicle and climbed in. He smiled reassuringly. 'Right pair here,' he said, then spoke into the radio on his shoulder.

A crackle of static and a voice electrified the air. Helene marvelled how anyone using two-way radios understood anything transmitted between them. But the police officer made a brief report to the radio operator and mentioned 'obstruction'.

'Bit early to be off their heads,' he also confided. Perhaps he wanted the operator and Helene to find the situation and these men amusing. 'But I'm not smelling drink on their breath. And they're not for letting us in.'

Another connection stirred her back brain. *Drugs.* That's what the police officer was referring to. It triggered thoughts of Lincoln. Substances had handicapped his development through his teens, his early twenties too. And where there were drugs criminal elements and tendencies abounded.

The officer finished his call with 'We're going to take a look around inside.'

He turned to Helene as the radio operator's voice buzzed meaninglessly. 'We're going to make this pair of likely lads understand that we're pursuing some serious allegations.' The young officer was confident and that worried her.

'I don't like it,' she said. 'The skinny one, I don't know . . . he looks familiar. I can't see his face. Make him show it. Then maybe we should go? You can come back without me. I'm feeling very uncomfortable.'

'Sure. In a minute. But we need to do a recce first and we need to speak to the landowner, this old rock star, about what he's got on his land. See if this quarry is near and if he saw your brother. We've got your description of the couple with the dog as well but we can't take the car any further. They're claiming they haven't got the key for the padlock.' The officer rolled his eyes. 'So we're going to hop over, find old Tony Willows and where this quarry is and come right back. They're hiding something. See it a mile off. We'll be quick.' Before she could raise any further objections, the officer alighted from the car with an athlete's grace.

When she'd traced her route on the pad for the police officers, one of the plainclothes detectives had said that an old musician owned the farm by the crossroads. 'An old hippy. Harmless but nutty.' Helene and the uniformed officers had never heard of him. Tony Willows was his name. Helene thought that was what the detective had said. Willows, like a tree.

Now they were going to leave her inside the car and enter the farm: a notion that made her feel terribly exposed, just like she had been in the water the night before.

Helene shivered inside the coat loaned to her at the hospital. The sea's chill was far from thawing from her marrow but she wound the window all the way down to try and hear the discussion.

In the distance a motorbike spluttered, its echo adrift in the valley. As it died away, a faint sound of what might have been a whistle was issued. Several long notes followed.

No, it wasn't a whistle but piping. Yes, pipes. She could hear pipes, soon accompanied by a murmur of raised voices as if a choir was warming up or a small crowd jeering. The sounds reminded her a little of Lincoln's recordings.

At the gate, between the officers' heads, she gained better sight of the other men's faces. They'd raised their chins, alert to the pipes. The overweight man had a boozer's ruddy complexion. Helene had also seen him before, though where she couldn't yet grasp. She heard him say, 'As I told you, no key, like. And you still ain't give us no reason why you want to come in.'

The WPC leaned in closer to him, her voice too low to hear. But whatever she'd said brought a reaction from the second, thinner man in the hood. He moved his head towards the car as the WPC's voice rose. 'I'm not going to ask you again to move away from the gate.'

As the portly, red-faced figure grinned at this rebuke, Helene remembered where she'd seen him before: he'd been bellowing into a microphone at the Redhill village fête.

She also saw the face of the second man more clearly as he peered at the police car. *Trying to see who was inside.* Cheeks hollowed out as if sucked in, a broken nose, acne scars: *Richey*, the rat from the boat. And no matter how indistinct, the very sight of him conjured the ghosts of his bony hands around her ankle as he'd raised her leg to tip her into the sea. She'd scratched his face: he'd be marked.

Helene sat up straight. The wind about the car seemed to pause. As she cleared her throat to call out to the police officers, a distant female scream tore the taut atmosphere apart: a far-off but urgent cry.

The police officers cocked their heads at the distant trees. 'Right!' the WPC shouted, then dipped her head to the radio at her shoulder.

From somewhere near the origins of the scream a group of dogs barked a noisy chorus and Helene wished that she was lying in the hospital bed again.

The two men at the gate broke away and began running in an ungainly fashion down the private road. Their rubber boots flapped noisily. Richey made yards on his portly, intoxicated comrade.

Helene scrabbled at the car door, her muscles and arms unthawed and slow.

The male police constable climbed the rungs of the gate first. The metal barrier wobbled, shaking in protest, but once on the other side, he held it steady as his partner ascended the rungs. *They were going in.*

Helene's heartbeat thumped up her windpipe and beat inside her ears. She clambered from the car and shouted, 'Him! From the boat! Skinny bastard wearing the hood!'

The police woman looked at Helene and nodded. 'Stay in the car!' she called, before angling her mouth to her radio. Her colleague was already gaining on the portly oaf.

43

*T*he pyre crackled and snapped. It was only half the size of what had been ignited for Steve. Regardless, like her lover Kat knew she would die here: inside a ruined, reeking barn, tied to a grate encrusted with his blood. She would depart this life from a miserable patch of dirt enshrouded by the stench of animals.

Shivering upon the dirty cement of her cell for hours after refusing the Willows' drug, Kat had listened to the preparations for this event in the barn. They finally came for her around noon.

All morning the dogs had raced in the lane outside her cell. Motorbikes had growled past before roaring away to the valleys where they'd grunted like excitable animals set loose. A commotion had agitated Redstone Farm.

She'd sensed that something was being collected and removed in great haste. Hydraulics had wheezed as if freight transport had squeezed itself down the rat-run. There had been much clanking of metal and screeching of roller doors. What sounded like a van had repeatedly bumped up and down the tarmac on incessant journeys.

When Willows had arrived with the skull-cup to offer his anaesthetic, he'd cryptically alluded to 'exile': her death the last 'nourishment' of the red earth. At least for a while. From this she could only assume that her demise would serve as a last hurrah before the red rats deserted their bunker.

She assumed the red folk were engaged in a tactical retreat. Perhaps Willows and his band of red murderers had been found out. They'd been on a spree for sure, confirmed by the argument Lewis had chaired that she'd overheard. Maybe they'd killed beyond their ability to conceal their scarlet tracks through these hills and inside their neighbours' homes. The detective had been furious at their profligacy with the blood of strangers. And when Tony and his daughter had performed for her, and recited their mystical, apocalyptic script, she'd known enough anxiety in her own life to smell it on others.

Inside the barn, the hooting and the shrieking of the man-apes was less intense than it had been for Steve. The piping came less shrilly from the two red musicians holding lengths of antique bone. Each was elderly: a bony man and a woman not far shy of eighty. They formed a shabby ensemble. Their notes and overtones were tunelessly piped into a space that seemed too airy and bright for what was intended.

Partnered by the wet, grey weather, a desultory, subdued aspect had dogged these proceedings from the start. Her own spirits had waned to the same hues of the watery, washed-out light that made the world outside the barn so drab. She could see some of the sky through the crack left in the barn doors: it was as murky as a dismal seascape that vanished into mist. Rain had speckled the roofs all day.

Not nearly as many of the 'red children' had gathered for her slaughter. She counted only eight including the pipers. Naked one and all, daubed in scarlet dye, but tucked against the walls like shy pensioners at a dance in a community hall. Their voices were smothered by the roar of the vehicles outside in the lane and barely reached the blackened rafters.

Perhaps the wrong atmosphere produced such muted effects. Maybe daylight was interfering with the environment requisite for murder. Kat imagined the red was best accessed at night: the traditional time of nightmares, criminal deeds, Sabbats and the sundry unwholesome acts of the depraved. That made sense but brought no comfort, because here she was again where the imminent actions of these people promised to match the very worst incidents in her country's criminal history.

Braziers had been lit and they issued a familiar, sickening pungency. Keeping her breathing shallow, Kat plugged her nose with her grimy hooded top and spared a thought, which seemed gigantic inside her skull, for how many others had also lain upon this altar before passing to the red.

'Oh, dear God,' she occasionally muttered and had little else to offer the grubby air of the barn. This sign of her trauma went unacknowledged.

She'd thought for a while that she should try and knock herself out. She also feared that her refusal to sup the brown fluid had been premature. But drinking from her boyfriend's wet skull had stalled any thought of swallowing the filthy medicine. She'd kicked the horrid container across the floor of the cell and watched it skitter, spilling its contents across the legs of Tony's daughter Nanna. But not before father and daughter had each taken a good draught. And if they'd required medicating before exposure to Creel then she'd need a double dose.

Victims were drugged here, dismembered, partially consumed, the bulk of their parts cast into darkness. That's why they'd wanted her stoned, to assist her end. This was no mediaeval practice but an abhorrence culled from much earlier times, before civilisation tempered the bestial urges of her species. 'Dear, dear God. Dear God,' she repeated, though she didn't know why: the last time she'd been in church was for a wedding.

They would remember her demise, cherish it: that's what Willows had said, and at the memory of those words Kat stared down and through the grate, seeing only empty darkness. An absence. A steady stream of air that reeked of wet stone and animal rot passed over her face.

The Black Dog. The White Pups. Her recall of the names made her jaw wobble like a child's. But the drugs and ceremony, the wretched but carefully wrought atmosphere, might be nothing more than a ruse for when wild dogs flowed over each other down there in the black pit. Fighting dogs. Animals conditioned to consume what was thrown down still warm and wet.

Perversely, the prospect of real animals was less awful than what she'd imagined rising from the earth during her previous visit. And that was all she could hope for now: that she'd been wrong about *something else* inhabiting the black space beneath the floor of the barn.

Oh, Steve.

The sounds the creatures had made that last time, and the movements of the earth, and the transformation of the old wooden walls into painted stone before her eyes: for these strange and hideous things she had no answers. The sense that she'd been returned to another time, where she'd seen beasts and rough-faced people crudely put to the flint inside a cave: how could she explain that?

Her shaking worsened.

Kat sipped the toxic air. She'd pretend she'd succumbed to the fumes when they came to remove her bonds . . . *to move you into position, face-down* . . .

She'd fight like before when trapped like an animal in her own home. That would be her only chance. There would be a moment *and then* . . .

Suppressing the image of a hand-axe, the blue flint glistening in red light, Kat squeezed her eyes shut.

All here might change again, soon, *transform*: the building, the very earth she lay upon destined to alter and welcome what pawed hither, across the moist ground. This notion she could not suppress. It persisted. *Now*, right *here*, would soon combine with *another time*. One place would become the other.

'God!' As if her cry acted like the bleat of a tethered goat, her distress finally received its acknowledgement from deep below. A thunderous rumble, as if great stones had just ground together, created a tremor across the very surface of the world. A subterranean groan followed by a bustling, or a burrowing through the red earth.

44

The woman in the distance issued another scream. It ripped apart the drizzly air. A chilling resonance lingering about the police car Helene stood beside.

Somewhere deeper inside the farm, farther down that potholed lane, a mind had snapped, its terror insufferable: a distress signal confirming that the police presence was no longer a matter of merely making inquiries.

Wailing came next, as if from a sparse crowd of agitated lunatics. Coordinated cries rose in unison to form a shrieking chorus, one that repeated in waves. A woodwind instrument piped in and out when the wailers paused for breath. No discernible tune, just random, blurted, reedy notes. Male voices barked. Their contributions too distant for words to be distinguishable but the tone implied anger, or even exultation, structured into a crude rhythm.

Smoke billowed beyond where the lane turned: a dirty trail of charcoal vapour disappearing into the low grey cloud. But the deep rumble that thrummed the soles of Helene's feet was the most frightening sign of how the world around her appeared to be altering.

Perhaps it was only her vision and not the light dimming, but night appeared to be falling prematurely. She peered up at vestiges of watery sunlight leaking through the thin cloud: a veil of ashy vapour oppressed and gradually swallowed by an advancing shelf of black sky, ushered from the sea by a strong, new wind. Rain pattered on her coat and her face. She shivered.

An earthquake, or its aftershocks, or an earth tremor, registered again in her ankles and knees. She imagined that great gears of rock were churning within the earth. The thud of her pulse drew the blood from her legs. She rested her weight against the patrol car and cowered behind the rear door.

A motorbike's roar broke from the distant chaos of human cries: a bike approaching the gate. The engine's grunt set her teeth on edge, her instincts anticipated violence. Helene's need to get inside the car and lock the doors competed with an urge to run.

Behind her, two thin lanes cut the fields and led away from the farm: tarmac crowded by hedgerows that offered no cover. And how far would she get on a B-road with a motorbike in pursuit?

The path that had first brought her here from the Brickburgh Caves was closer. That track ran into the valley below, the wood beneath the farm topping slopes of pasture. She could hide in the trees until the police were reinforced.

Helene fled along what her guidebook had called an 'ancient green track' connecting the caves to the crossroads.

Alongside the righthand side of the track, trees and vines marked the wood, underpinning the sly grin of the private road like a tangled beard. At the first possibility of ingress, where the blackberry vines and nettles rose no further than her knees, she stepped off the track. Arms up to protect her face from the whipping branches, she yanked her knees high and clumsily stepped through the spiky undergrowth, cutting inwards, parallel to the lane. Moisture soaked her calves, nettles stung her ankles.

The roar of the motorbike drew level with her off-road position. At the gate the bike's engine coughed to idling.

Helene couldn't see through the wet tangle of tree branches but heard the rider dismount.

Stepping a few feet further inside the wood she came upon a boundary fence: three strands of wire strung in line with the gate. And almost sobbed with frustration. If the motorcyclist followed the track and spotted her at the edge of the wood he'd reach her before she could clamber over the wire. Nor was this terrain she could move across in haste. Unmanaged, the thorny vines and deadwood created a perpetual tangle as far as she could see. She'd tear her legs to ribbons.

Where were the police?

Up on the lane, the gate jingled and a chain slapped the tarmac. Hinges groaned as the metal barrier swung wide. The motorcycle was remounted, the engine revved. The vehicle roared away.

Helene exhaled, sagging with relief, then attempted to climb the fence in case anyone else came down the lane.

It was not easy to get over; the wires dug into the palms of her hands. Supporting her weight, the length of wire shook, wobbled and seemed determined to pitch her over into the waiting nettles. By clinging to the nearest wooden post she eventually managed to get over, falling more than climbing.

As she squatted in the nettles and brambles on the other side, perspiration prickled icily across her scalp.

The motorcyclist had been in a hurry: his bike now subsided from full throttle to a whine in the damp distance. He must be making a run for it. With the arrival of the police, that made sense.

Helene looked deeper inside the wood ahead of her, to where the bracken eventually thinned about a haphazard arrangement of trees.

She strode between the thick, thorny stems to better conceal herself. She'd crouch and hide here. More police would be arriving in support. She'd seen the WPC use her radio before giving chase to Richey and the purple-faced clown.

But that scream: ripped from a throat while others, inexplicably, were playing musical instruments and singing? What in hell was happening here?

Muffled by the trees and thick undergrowth, the piping and the wailing continued in the distance and Helene couldn't quell a suspicion that she'd arrived as an event ensued at the dreadful farm. Even the wood maintained a peculiar, unnerving stillness as if it had paused in its wild business to observe her ungainly entrance.

From the very start the area encompassing Brickburgh and Redstone had struck her as peculiar: enchanting, weird, sinister, hostile. In this environment she couldn't have expected to be more than a city girl out of her depth. But her deepest instincts conveyed to her that this place was just not right in a more fundamental way. Its strangeness was about more than psychotics painted red and murderers on a boat.

She waited, biting her lip, her eyes those of a hunted animal. About her the canopy dripped water. Mulchy and damp and dank: an atmosphere failing to offer reassurance to those desiring concealment. It was hard to imagine this ground ever being dry. From the fields of the valley drifted the aroma of animal dung and, with the new ceiling of storm cloud, dusk had surely arrived at midday. Beneath the treetops the light thinned further. She needed a torch and fought a childish panic that the land was cursed in ways she'd never understand.

Legs buried to the knee in nettles and dead wood, she passed deeper, from one lichen-slippery tree to another, to better hide herself, then ducked at the approaching roar of a second motorbike on the private road.

This bike didn't stop and only slowed to pass through the open gate before turning west like its predecessor. She saw nothing of the bike or rider save flashes of yellow between the boughs and verdure. But *they* weren't looking for her.

More vehicles followed the bikes. One, two, three cars passed through the gate, including a four-wheel-drive. A white Luton van shuddered out soon after. The police had routed something. There'd been too many people down there for the law to control or subdue: a significant number of people must now be fleeing arrest.

When the noise of the straining engines dimmed, other sounds filled the empty grey atmosphere above the farm. A muffled male voice ranted in a sequence of gruff sounds: a sentence of sorts that was rhythmic like a chant. A woman wailed as if engaged in a Middle Eastern lament. Dogs maintained a perpetual barrage of angry barking.

Two police officers were down there so why weren't they stopping this?

They'd be outnumbered.

Helene imagined the neat, trim, young constables being overwhelmed. *Though by what?*

Still weak from her ordeal in the sea and only declared fit enough to sit in a heated car while continually hydrating her body, she could do little to assist them. Her role had been to identify a place while fingering anyone she'd suspected of involvement in her abduction and attempted murder. She'd done that. Even if her core temperature had stabilised that morning there was no fight in her.

She listened to the rain on the leaves and the harsh sound of her own breathing against the hood of the coat. *What to do?*

A compulsion to know why she'd been thrown into the sea and why her little brother had been murdered competed with caution.

She needn't risk exposure by getting too close to the shouting and the smoke. If she watched what was happening while concealed by the wood she might at least act as a witness. The police officers had tried to help her. They'd also run to help the woman who'd screamed: they'd risked their own safety without a second thought. She had to do something. Helene moved on through the trees.

Another thirty metres through the tangle and she saw the top of the grimy, sprawling farmhouse, near where she'd been stopped by the scruffy poshos and their dogs.

Creeping closer to the lane she established there was no one out in front of the building and no dogs. The commotion was occurring much deeper along the private road, somewhere out of sight, perhaps at the epicentre of whatever continued to rumble beneath her feet.

Soon she found herself struggling to see much further than a few metres in any direction, and feared the sun risked being totally obscured. She looked up, remembering the eclipse of 1999 that she'd seen on holiday: the vast sweep of cold air that had hushed the earth around her in Cornwall. Momentarily epochal, that quickening of night. The eclipse in Falmouth had pierced her with a pang of cosmic terror and she'd been left breathless. Lincoln had been entranced by the spectacle: a minute of darkness during the day.

But unlike her experience in Falmouth, within Redstone's sudden and unnatural darkness Helene now heard the sounds of Lincoln's final recording.

Inhuman shrieks. And much louder this time: a distant yapping that was almost a voice before it laughed horribly. Never quite human yet garbling a message that made her visualise wild apes. The volume of the horrid chatter obliterated the human cries and the pipes as if all before the exotic shrieks had been muted in shock.

There were several of these animals down there. And such cries could only be uttered by beasts of considerable size: powerful forms with a tremendous lung capacity. Perhaps a breed of giant cat that they kept on the farm?

Or maybe she was hearing an ape after all, a great ape, and its cries were suffering from acoustic distortion and amplification in the valley below. Helene hoped so.

The rapid laughter beyond the wood degenerated into a sustained growling, wrung deep from a throat wet with mucus.

Helene's shaky confidence withered. Instinct or imagination again connected the cries to giant savage cats: she effortlessly pictured them rolling across the ground engaged in desperate combat. The alteration from the unpleasant yapping and demoniac giggling to the roar had been so sudden.

Amidst the signs of bestial outrage human screams rent the air.

Horses too? Surely those were horses that now shrieked amid the rout of people? The sudden equine cries split the air not far ahead of her, piercing the gaps between the trees.

A hound yelped itself into an unnerving silence. Then another squealed horribly and fell quiet.

Helene crouched deeper within the sopping undergrowth, the ferns and dead wood.

A malefic snarling spiked her ears. An idea of muscular jaws worrying and shaking prey set her teeth on edge and she finally clapped her hands to her ears. Had she been on a safari in Africa or beside a zoo, she'd have been better able to accept the presence of such ferocity. Even then, what kind of animal could it be and what kind of zoo was equipped to contain such savagery? But she was certain that something bestially dangerous was now running amok on the farm.

The earth beneath her feet grumbled in the grip of an aftershock.

Distant but rapid bangs against wood followed the monstrous shrieks of rage. The irregular, sickening thuds made her think of bodies flung against walls. A few human screams managed a final, desperate crescendo, one voice so full of terror that Helene stuffed her index fingers inside her ears. She'd never heard anything as awful as that cry.

In wet air astir with such violence the only noise that offered a shred of reassurance was the distant police siren emerging from the north. She couldn't judge its distance, but as if cowed by the distant wail of the siren, the desperate struggle on the farm muted.

The maelstrom of screams could not have lasted for more than seconds, though to her those hateful moments had seemed to elongate time, to trap her in a turmoil that, had it continued for longer, would have sent her mad. And whatever had just occurred seemed far worse for this abrupt, unnatural subduing.

Obscured by the trees ahead, a man's voice soon called out in torment to break the temporary silence.

A second male voice chattered continuously, the words undecipherable yet incongruously calm. Perhaps he was asking questions that no one would answer. The animal cries had ceased. *Thank God.*

Beneath the ground the rumbling had also concluded, though her senses had been so paralysed by the awful animal sounds that she'd not noticed when the tremors had stopped.

A woman now wept as if in desolate answer to the groaning man imprisoned within a tremendous suffering. The second male voice still talked incessantly but drifted away.

No dogs, no horses and no vehicles could be heard at all. This new absence of all save a few sounds of human distress, and the rain against the leaves of the bent and tangled trees, created an eerie vacuum. It settled amidst the wet wood like the uncanny silence over a well-used battlefield.

Helene's fatigue equalled what she'd felt lying in the hospital bed. But at least the air beyond the wood was perceptibly lightening and filtering back to the watery grey of only moments before. The fall of rain was now more refreshing than confining.

She crept on through the undergrowth as noiselessly as possible, certain that she was approaching an aftermath.

Her hunch was confirmed when she reached the paddock.

45

our weary figures hobbled along the tunnel, their descent enclosed by wet walls. They scurried further, deeper, away to where lights were embedded in the rocks in a widened passage. From darkness they came back to the light. From siege to freedom.

Bare feet scuffled the rock. The old man's tortured wheezing competed with the sibilant whispers passing between the mother and her son; he now carried his mother within his sinewy arms, her wheelchair left far behind.

'My boy. We shouldn't go on. Take me home, Finn. Take me back home.'

Finn sniffed and swore under his breath. He'd been crying over the loss of his dogs and for the abandonment of the precious crop he'd raised from the rocks like John Barleycorn. 'Police. They're at our place. They must have seen it. I doubt it was pretty. The old Creel was wide open. We're for sanctuary, mother. There's nowhere else for us now.'

'Sanctuary? I don't trust him. Adrian's no true neighbour.'

'He owes us. The arrangements stand. They were made for this day.'

'Am I heavy, son?'

'We'll be out of here soon. We've a car, waiting. We're safe. I promise.'

'"They moved." You know, the girl said that to me, son, when I was this far down the first time. Maddy. That was her name. Maddy Gross. Have I ever told you that? Finn?'

That was the last time Jess had been so frail and frightened down here, but not as frightened as Maddy. Her torch's light had revealed the face of the girl in the red boots whom she'd lured into the quarry. And by torchlight Jess had seen the child the girl had once been and the child she'd remained. She'd been so young.

The girl, Maddy, had seen the movement in that chamber too, on the walls.

It was all so long ago now but Jess remembered being tired and hungover. Her mind had not been as it should have been. She'd been taking things, smoking them, for a long time. They all had at the farm. She'd been open to the suggestions of the darkness. But, without a doubt, she'd seen something similar to the movement of bodies beneath a blanket at the corner of her eye, where the torch's light had thinned across the painted walls of the cave. A disturbance, a shudder.

'Can we go back?' the girl had asked, eyeing the torch.

Yet, despite the unnatural motion inside the chamber and how it had frightened young Maddy, Jess had continued to hate that pretty face beside her. How fresh the wound of betrayal had been. A cut reopened by a memory of the girl's flushed face when she'd stumbled back to the fire they'd had in one of the fields, after Tony had had his way with her, up at the house.

So like some foolish, jealous peasant girl in one of Tony's old songs, Jess's hatred had flared, the old green burn. She'd already entered the red. She'd just not known it at the time. The red made her see things differently.

The animals on the wall had moved again. The girl hadn't lied. Jess's own eyes hadn't deceived her either. A ripple creased the striped flanks of the painted herd. Their heads rose and fell. The movement was natural. Their white eyes rolled; they were alive.

Yet when Jess looked again at where she'd seen the movement, the figures all became stationary, as if she'd merely seen apparitions of charcoal sliding over the stone.

The girl had screamed.

The air had smelled of iced turf.

Then they were cold, became colder, were shivering.

From where had those piped notes arisen? From deep in the tunnels beyond the chamber, or from behind the walls? Had their presence coaxed out the fine notes? And how, down there, had so many come to move about them in the darkness? Maybe the girl's screams had woken the earth and the restless ground was no longer asleep. What was not seen was sensed, parting the black air, their faces buffeted by curious wakes and slipstreams, a slow breath moving their hair. They might have been standing at the edge of an underground platform anticipating the roar and rush of an approaching train.

Where had the walls gone, upon which the lurching herd had been etched? The torch's light had failed to find them. The walls had disappeared or been removed like stage sets. Same above their heads: the space had become big enough to know no boundary.

That was the first time Jess had seen in the dark and the first time she'd seen what had panicked the herd into flight.

In the cold darkness, strong, dirty teeth had chattered close to her face.

The laughter of dogs had broken above her head.

The herd of animals that could not have been there had jostled and then broken into a rout.

The feeble glow of her torch had flicked across an upright devil. The first one. The trembling beam unveiling it from out of the dark and for no more than a moment. But there had been an indistinct face. A white muzzle. Most horrible. Wet. Snouted. And dear God, the eyes. Pink like a rat's. A pale breast matted red. Big and white it was, up on two feet and drenched down the front from what it had been eating. It had made Maddy scream. She'd seen it too.

The torchlight had shrunk from the form as if of its own volition and the beam had crossed the great eye to reveal a second stained muzzle, atop another long, white, furred thing with a distended belly that also moved about on two legs. And yet its body was fashioned for walking on four. They'd been on the walls of that cave, those albino terrors, but weren't any longer. It was as if they'd climbed down.

Insensible, a hysterical child, Maddy had stumbled, fallen.

And Tony's young mistress had cast about for a way out on her hands and knees. Poor Maddy never stood up again.

And so briefly, yet so clearly, through that pall of darkness had slowly grown a great white sky, spread so wide above the frozen ground they had smelled at their feet. A tundra. So little grew: the earth had iced to stone and had rumbled from the hooves of a stampede.

They were no longer inside the cave? Or was that new place purely inside Jess's mind? All that was painted upon the rocks was animate, alive. And that raw eye, painted upon the stone wall, was far too moist.

The first time.

The babble. The terrible babble that had approached from a crevice that Jess had seen on the far side of the cavern before everything changed. Out of that wet, black slit had burst the sniggering, the baying, the awful whining. It had echoed through her mind ever after.

The girl, Maddy, had taken to whimpering.

The origin of the new shrieks was not visible, but a doggish snout was easily imagined, like those of the two white bitches with fearsome eyes that had tottered past on their hind legs. Yet, in comparison to the sounds that had barked from the crevice, the white things must have been the young. Because another, much larger presence had arrived in the cave.

An apprehension of its presence alone had further panicked those animals upon the walls. And all around Jess had raged the bellows and the frantic kicking of hooves as the herd ran blind.

What on the earth could have produced that stench? Her mind had been consumed by the most powerful presence, many carcasses strewn in its wake.

Heavy unseen forms were slammed against the frozen ground as the cave's purpose opened, though not wholly. The paintings were mere impressions of where the herds had once been stampeded: into a pit where they were splintered like timber. A vision from the dark.

Maddy in the red boots finally fell silent. That had been worse than her hysteria.

Something hunted there, in that cave, always. The paintings on the wall were only understood by the terrified when inside such a darkness. Up and down, north and south, what was far and what was near, made no sense when your mind became a spark dropping into cold space. Jess learned this the hard way. And only at the brink of a mind being extinguished, when so deep, was such vision granted without light.

Jess had run. She left the girl behind: the mewling girl on her hands and knees, wearing red boots and a jacket that hadn't belonged to her.

Jess had fled among the red people. Those who'd appeared around her and who scrambled away after they'd driven the herd into the killing cave. A hungry fury was gibbered in the dark as the red folk ran wild. And down a tunnel she'd stumbled with them, panting, maybe back the way she'd come, her ears filled with the piping and the screams. The coughs of bullocks. Dying cattle.

The red people had worn masks. They'd grunted through headpieces made of bristles and sticks and hair. Inside the eye sockets their white eyes had bulged. The red-limbed folk had stunk, all fouled by the corrupted flesh from the tatty remains in the pit of bones, the place where they offered succour to the terrible laughing dogs. But Jess had run with the red folk and run red with their rage, their eternal rage. She'd reddened and run past nightmares mapped upon the walls. She'd run with the past, she'd run into the future.

The torch was long gone, knocked from her hand, but it wasn't needed when a moon's silver light gave the land below new form and showed faces not seen by day. She ran from there and back to here, crossing a border, a boundary beneath the ground.

Eventually, a late sun, coin-sized at the mouth of a tunnel, had led her to the surface and returned her to where the ivy cascaded over the scraped walls of the quarry; where buddleia splashed the greenery purple with heavy flowers nodding. And there she had lain until the sun had sunk and the world above the ground was as dark as it was below.

She'd returned to the farm and Tony had wanted to know where the girl was. Her man's first thought had been of Maddy, his peasant mistress: the girl whom Jess had left under the ground with the great frighted herds that had been run by the red folk unto their gods in the pit of bones. Jess had understood this instinctively.

The red folk had formed a circle beyond the herd to guide it inwards, before fleeing, lest they too became quarry.

She'd fled with the red people from a place where all had shown the silver moon their devil faces.

The girl, Maddy, was back with the upright white bitches. She would still have been amongst their busy, wet muzzles and below the sharp pink teats of their pregnant bellies: those pale hounds that had walked upright like men whose words had opened Jess's eyes so wide that she'd seen in the dark and so far back in time. And their jabber had opened the ground wider to summon another too. She'd not seen that one, but had heard it; though poor Maddy may have laid her pretty eyes upon what had come out of the crevice.

At the farm, Jess had told them all of this.

There was an argument about the drugs, about the gear being bad. The manager and photographer had gone into the ground with torches, where she'd been, and they'd returned with no blood in their cheeks. The manager had been sick all down his bottle-green gabardine trousers.

'I told you. I told you,' she'd cried at them. 'Isn't it incredible?' But all they'd found was a dead girl, Maddy, who'd crawled a long way in terror until her young heart had stopped beating. God knows what had crawled alongside her because the look on her face had made the photographer sit down, unable to speak for the rest of the evening.

Dead and stiff, Maddy Gross had been cold in a way none could account for, her final thoughts clearly crippled by what she'd seen: that had been frozen onto her face like a mask. Her eyes had been filled with it. All the guests, save Ade, left the farm. Ade had loved Jess.

Tony had then gone below with Ade, whom he thought he could trust and who'd played in the band longer than anyone, and they'd brought the dead girl above ground in a wheelbarrow that Ade had fetched from the old barn. And like a couple of schoolboys suspected of stealing, they'd dumped the evidence at the edge of the farm and then stayed up all night muttering and drinking to get their stories straight for when the time came.

Later that summer, Jess found the masks.

46

*T*rees sheltering Helene's hesitant progress through the wood ended at a wooden fence, the railings encompassing muddy ground before a black barn with no doors.

Inside the paddock's rectangle of churned red soil three farm animals lay on their sides. All were motionless save a weary flick of a single black tail.

An equine head then reared, the eye of the animal wild with agony. The creature's ears were flat, its mane matted with soil. *Ponies.*

Three black ponies. Two full-size, one smaller, maybe a foal. Two of them were dead while the third had little life remaining. From what she could see from behind the fence, Helene doubted that any animal would survive the injuries inflicted upon the tortured statements of their bodies.

From the still moving pony, purple and ruddy coils, rubbery and moist, spilled from a once rotund belly and steamed in the mud beside what looked like a fleshy bag the colour of an aubergine. Part of the second adult pony's throat was missing. A red sash of soft tissue gaped where the underside of its neck should have been.

Her legs threatened to give way. Helene slumped against the top rail of the fence. Whatever had done this might be nearby. She thought of the police car outside the gates and suddenly craved being locked inside it. Though was a windscreen sufficient defence against what had slaughtered these animals so rapidly? Their terrible wounds suggested a killer wielding a power as swift as it was tremendous: and what size of mouth could remove so much of a pony's throat?

Helene peered into the dilapidated wooden barn behind the paddock. Nothing moved inside the dim interior but she could make out the lifeless shapes of at least three dogs. They appeared to have been squashed or pressed into the soil. *Kent?*

Dangerous animals had slaughtered the ponies and dogs: the very things she'd heard in the distance cackling and growling and yapping so horridly while engaged in this dreadful butchery. And there had been people at this despicable farm. So where were they? Where were the two police officers who'd accompanied her here?

A second police vehicle, an estate car, screamed down the lane towards the paddock, its blue light casting an icy swirl over the treeline.

Helene moved up to the lane, both hands gripping the fence's top rail to support her bloodless legs. As she handed herself along the top rung, her spine tensed at the prospect of a terrible form rushing out of the barn's gloom. None came, but only then did she realise that the third and smallest pony was missing its head. That she spotted near the body: a black, shaggy lump, red at the breach where it had been sundered from the neck, the black muzzle grinning at the moment of destruction.

The police car passed as Helene arrived at the verge of the lane. The presence of more police officers was reassuring, and the part of her mind that still functioned beyond shock compelled her to seek out the two constables who'd brought her here. They could explain her presence to their colleagues. But more than anything she found herself desperate to know that they were safe: they'd been so young. They'd rushed into this dreadful place to apprehend her tormentors. Though, given the state of the ponies and dogs, she did wonder how they could be safe.

Beyond the ponies' paddock the police car's siren pipped and fell silent. Car doors slammed, one following another.

Neither officer who climbed from the vehicle spoke until one of them muttered 'Jesus.' A name carrying more weight when uttered in such despair.

Somewhere beyond what was visible to Helene, the groaning of the injured man finally concluded. But the man talking kept up his strange, interrogatory monologue and the solitary woman continued to weep. There were survivors. At least two. The police must have found them.

In the wake of the patrol car, Helene inched closer to these sounds of human distress. Further inside the farm, if she could stand to look, she'd get a better idea of what had just happened. For Lincoln, for the painfully obscure reasons why three men had tried to drown her at sea, for why the landlady of a guesthouse had painted her naked flesh red and shrieked like a chimpanzee, she *had* to see, to understand, to know. The need was now maddening.

From her vantage point in the middle of the private road the roofs of several other buildings emerged from tree cover: uneven rows of grey slate scales topping a row of ramshackle structures. During her first visit she'd seen them in the distance. Men had wandered out of them and idled in the road.

Maybe there had been a detonation of some kind because the agricultural buildings were damaged. Smoke drifted from out of the largest, a stained, rickety barn.

Silently, Helene walked past the stationary, empty police car. It was parked outside the gaping doorway of the smoking barn where a red man sat slumped. He either spoke to himself or was speaking earnestly to the mess of innards gathered in his lap. His entire body was red, both from the blood that had escaped his torso and from the same pigment she'd seen on the skin of her abductors at the guesthouse.

The two police officers who'd just arrived stood motionless on either side of the slumped, disembowelled and, impossibly, still living form.

Ten metres in front of their car, another body lay in the road. Black trousers, boots, utility belt and a white shirt marked the body as belonging to one of their own: a police officer. The body of the male constable who brought her here, and who'd raced into the farm to investigate the woman's scream, was now headless.

The two living police officers weren't sure what to address first: their decapitated colleague or the muttering figure sitting outside the barn, who'd been opened down the front like a cardboard box but who somehow remained alive, though his mind must have blown like a fuse at the sight of what now glistened between his legs.

Down the lane, about twenty metres further, Helene spotted the thin scarlet form of an elderly man. He was missing an arm and paced slowly, his destination inexplicable, as was the thin flute-like object he clutched in his remaining hand.

Only when this slowly walking figure collapsed sideways did the police officers move. They'd seen him too but been unable to react. One officer hurried back to the patrol car and ducked inside to operate the radio. The second officer moved to the boot. He rummaged inside then raised a shelf from under the vehicle. With a lid propped open Helene saw the dull shapes of firearms fixed by Velcro straps.

Such was their preoccupation and her mute, motionless shock, they never noticed her standing on the other side of the lane.

Inside the barn the embers of a fire glowed upon the earth. What appeared to be another scattering of bodies lay about the soil floor. The parts that Helene could see of the corpses were unclothed, the bare flesh darkened. Incongruously, a wheelchair lay on its side at the mouth of the barn.

Armed with a small submachine gun one of the police officers returned to the carnage. The second officer retrieved a pistol from the boot, produced a torch and joined his colleague. Silent and immobile in disbelief, they stood in the fetid, smoking mouth of the dilapidated building for a moment and then entered.

Helene sat down on the tarmac. She wouldn't shout in case the police officers shot her.

Weariness engulfed her body. She listened to the sounds of the policemen inside the barn. One of them came back outside. Hands on thighs, his face as pale as cream cheese, he bent over and was sick into the mud. Smoke trailed after him and Helene's sinuses identified the intense pungency of burning cannabis.

Three dead ponies, three dead dogs. Dying or dead people who'd suffered catastrophic injuries. She recalled the distant sound of what might have been a rumbling explosion, transforming into a sustained grinding of stone below the ground, like an earthquake.

If an explosion had occurred under the earth's surface then how did the male police officer end up in the lane, missing his head, and why had those dogs been flattened into the soil? There was no sign of the WPC.

Helene's imagination wanted to envisage, and believe, that there *had* been an explosion, one that had laid waste to the occupants before a shockwave tore through the lane and paddock to inflict such horrific injuries upon people and animals.

Though why were the ramshackle buildings still standing? And how would an explosion account for the bestial baying and the cries of blood-lust she'd heard?

Confused and sickened by it all, Helene felt a sudden need to be at home, holding her little girl tightly. It was so sharp that the desire made her dizzy.

The slumped man against the wall of the barn moved. His tattered head fell over his rouged chest as if he were taking a closer look at the foul spillings coiled upon his thighs.

47

A few minutes earlier.

*F*umes tinged blue billowed from the braziers, fogging the air, clouding blackened rafters.

Woozy, cold with nausea, Kat scrutinised the darkness below the grille. Her fearful survey only broken by the slow procession of the two shamans, or whatever the animal-headed psychopaths believed themselves to be and their red acolytes assumed they were.

As before, the couple's thin bodies were weighed down by shaggy, oversized headpieces. Their stringy forms were naked, painted red. Tony Willows weaved about, greeting his followers, withered and spindly, his arm held by his daughter, Nanna, who was unmasked. They'd emerged from somewhere in the back, beyond the pyre, but Kat couldn't see a door in the smoke. The second elder was rolled into the barn in a wheelchair, through the front. Jessica Usher.

Jessica's wheelchair was pushed by her weasel-faced son, Finn. He was unmasked. The wheels of the chair carved soil and dung.

Raising a shrill handful of notes inside the stinking wooden cavern, the pipers heralded the entrance of their degenerate leaders.

Kat craved a free arm and a weapon. She wanted to have a go at them: the resulting violence would be as much about escape as taking pleasure in retribution. Something of that

343

nature moved too easily about her mind now, like a hound, sniffing and probing on a lower storey of her consciousness. It shied from the scrutiny of reason, but she detested these signs that she was similar to these people, even if her motives differed. At least loathing offered relief from terror and the sickening cramps of anxiety that had been squeezing her stomach for hours.

Six red folk, who'd backed against the walls, stepped forward and raised reddened arms. Ululating to the roof, they seemed like tatty-head imbeciles, beggars from a distant age who'd drunkenly failed to incite the primitive ecstasy that once brought them such pleasure. Even if their efforts were reinvigorated by the arrival of the two elderly figures, who were unable to enter this place of ancient slaughter unassisted, their cries stopped short of achieving the intensity conjured at Steve's sacrifice.

Tawdry, psychotic, hideous and wilful: all of it. Designed to put an end to everything she was and had hoped to be. Was any murder less glorious to its victim?

From beneath Kat's soiled knees, the earth rumbled again, distracting her from the rickety performance of the mad folk in their shack. Down below, great mounds of rock were surely shifting. Something had shaken loose. Perhaps a fragment of the very earth was parting to reveal sinuses best left blocked. But whatever resided below was on its way up and closing fast. Through the grate, a long breath developed into a warm breeze befouled by charnel fumes and unseen mouths festering with canker.

Kat screamed. Then attempted to stand up to relieve her choking terror. But the red folk were only thrilled by her desperate cry. They knew what neared the same surface they walked with unshod feet. Their piped notes skirled anew to pierce their captive's thoughts more deeply: thoughts immediately scattering like unaccompanied children frightened by growling dogs.

Outside the temple, voices continued to bark. Men, shouting, breathless in their urgency and with efforts and tasks unseen within the fume-smothered barn. Engines growled as accelerators were depressed to the floor.

Old man Willows shook off the arm of his daughter that he'd leaned upon. He began to croak in a strangled tongue, from the throat. Maybe the communication was part animal, part human. Whatever the frightful sound communicated, the caterwauling of his folk followed at exultant volume.

At either side of his mangy black head, old Willows's arms rose and tensed. Within the open maw of the mask, between canine teeth, his mad white eyes caught the firelight.

From her wheelchair his mate became animated, unsteady for only a moment before a miraculous renewal of vigour and posture took hold of her decrepit form and brought her upright.

Coquettish, the emaciated and stained form of the withered matriarch minced from the wheelchair, wailing a falsetto that quivered at its highest point. Such was her excitement that she slapped arthritic hands against her doggish headgear, the knuckles red lumps, the fingers cramped and unmoving. Then she turned round and round on the spot, horribly, like a starving child, blood-mired and participating in a Satanic party game. Her bony feet pranced upon the dirt.

A skull-cup was carried down the grand chamber, held aloft by Finn, the weasel son. Nodding, he passed and offered communion to each of the eight red fools who still screeched or piped, their grotesque noises old strings designed to draw a most unspeakable company from out of the earth.

All supped deep from the cup to dull the arrival of what was scampering through the hidden shafts of rock below: more than one beast, rising from the tunnel in haste to reach the grille upon which Kat paced and peered into the darkness between her feet.

Had the barn door been closed? Had the rags of the feeble sun finally passed behind rain clouds? Maybe the anticipation of what unfolded promised to be unbearable for a celestial body of light and warmth. Darkness turned the barn into a hollow vessel and a void poured between its shanty walls, from above, from below.

Beyond her head and at ground level the edges of the wooden structure disappeared from sight. Only the fire cast a radiance, and those weak flames offered feeble reassurance in such abject darkness: there was no protection or warmth otherwise in the stinking barn or the human skulls that wailed about her. Perhaps the fire's proximity to the grate was even a form of protection to those who conducted the ceremony. Maybe this light and heat were intended to keep one thing from another during a hideous interaction: to separate the worshipped from its worshippers. Instinctively, Kat drew as close to the fire as she was able without catching alight.

White pups. Was it those she could now hear? Grunting through the earth, then yelping and yapping and laughing as they scampered closer, until, directly below her feet, a whinny issued from pitch darkness. Long did it warble before descending the scales to a mocking snigger: a monstrous giggle underwritten by a wet growl.

Claws raked stone in the chute below. Large forms leaped and scratched at the grate. Kat's bonds kept her in place so that her terror could be inhaled and her succulence surveyed by what frolicked under her toes.

The fresh stench from the pit was withering, a slurry of old blood, the choking ammonia of dung: a gust of rot distilled and fermented by age in an airless cavity. She was sure the red earth's foul breath alone would suffocate her and she desperately wanted to be overcome by the gas so that she would not endure the sight of what had produced it.

As two pairs of hands grasped her limbs and tugged her to the side of the grate, Kat screamed so hard she matched the idiotic, primitive cries of the two shamans and the cacophony of their shrieking red folk.

Facing the soil with her toes scraping the ground, her body was pulled forward. One of her hands risked dislocation from the wrist as the rope pulled taut.

Through locks of drooping hair, she saw firelight battle

with shadows in a narrowing circumference of light. Where it flickered, hoary feet and creosoted shins staggered about her. And then she was in position upon the killing floor.

Inappropriately sleepy, she wondered if her body had issued an anaesthetising drug of its own to dull panic. Then she recalled a particular image that she'd suppressed for days. It snapped her alert: a glimpse of an old mouth, the chin deeply lined, suckling on a wet jawbone to extract nourishment. *Steve.*

Kat screamed, but this time she screamed until she thought her lungs would tear like paper bags.

From her wrists and ankles the bindings were severed. She kicked herself to her knees. Only two of the red folk were restraining her while a second pair made a drunken attempt to raise the grate. Once open, they'd throw her parts down or discard her whole unto whatever yapped and growled so impatiently inside the pit.

Kat reared and threw her body around in an attempt to free her arms, limbs gripped by the insistent claws of two men who swayed like addicts.

'No!' she shrieked.

The two fools raising the grille ignored her and continued to heave the trapdoor free, their arms trembling from the weight of an iron cap designed to keep *below* separate from *above.*

From the near distance, perhaps outside the barn doors, a man shouted, 'Filth! Pigs is fucking here!' It was repeated by another two voices, raised, breathless.

Within moments, a motorbike was kicked into grunting life. Car doors slammed. But those who held her seemed unaware of the commotion outside. The two pipers were seated now too, their eyes turned inwards as if the elderly musicians were succumbing to long overdue comas.

Beyond the widening aperture in the floor Kat glimpsed the witch-wife. She was being carried like a thin child that had injured itself. In cowardly haste, Jessica Usher's son Finn was removing his mother from the scene, away from the raid but also, surely, from what was contained within the pit. The couple vanished into darkness at the rear of the building.

Tony Willows's former frailty reclaimed his scrawny form and he clawed at his daughter's arm pathetically. A sudden desperation to flee the barn had gripped him while his distracted and intoxicated underlings still toiled about the hole, to get it open and her inside.

The last two members of the family vanished into the murky rear of the building where Tony had first emerged so pompously. The family were leaving her in the clutches of their dazed but committed congregation, an aged and motley assemblage that appeared unaware of their priesthood's retreat and the alarms raised in the lane outside the building. The substance in the skull-cup must have been potent, its effects increasingly evident in the clumsy stumbling around her body. And if the grate moved any further she was no longer destined to be the only victim here. 'No. They're leaving. Look! For Christ's sake, look!'

Amidst the chaos came the most piercing animal shriek from below, one so full of inhuman excitement that Kat's theories of fighting dogs and great cats collapsed with no possibility of revival.

As if finally coming to their senses about what they were almost certainly going to set free, the two men released the grille partway open and stumbled back from the hole they'd opened in the ground. One of them peered about the smoky darkness like a child seeking direction from its elders.

Inside the pit, the scrabble of what tore at the underside of the metal seal, now only covering one third of the aperture, intensified, as did the chorus of snarls. Those who'd raised the gate must have been out of their minds and yet they seemed too stunned to completely uncover the pit, or re-cover it. Her jailers had become entranced or paralysed by what bayed at a deafening volume inside the black hole.

Before she could see what they'd seen, with a surge forward Kat found her knees and tugged one arm free. She caught a face with a fist, punching up and through a tarred fringe of dishevelled hair that haloed hollow cheeks.

The eyes of the man she struck were glassy. She drove her fist into his eye-socket and he went down without a sound. Yanking her other arm with sufficient power to pull the second man down and onto his front, she glimpsed his bewildered face as it struck the soil. Her eyes met the eyes of an old, confused man.

Kat ran at the fire. She ran *into* the flames. Within that infernal darkness, instinct alone insisted that the fire might be the only thing at hand to preserve distance, no matter how narrow, between men and what had so recently appeared in their modern domain. And she'd have run through lava in bare feet to escape what burst from the earth behind her.

The desultory piping and the calls for those beneath the ground were over: swiftly replaced by other noises, like the ripping of the first torso, a sound of moist cloth tearing.

The rending emerged from behind Kat's head as she skittered through the fire, her legs kicking up a shower of embers and a flurry of sparks. Multiple stabs and sudden sears penetrated the jogging bottoms she'd lived in for days. Burns pierced the soles of her feet. Hair crisped around her face, crackled inside an ear. A vile smell swamped her sinuses. She was on fire and she screamed and launched herself at the absolute state of darkness beyond the pyre, landing on all fours, not on earth but on stone that rubbed the skin off her knees.

As she turned about and slapped at the searing agony on her ankles and feet and behind her knees, a shockwave of stinking air blew the fire flat.

Kat never saw the men who'd raised the grille come apart. Nor did she see what it was that removed their heads, but she did hear two human carcasses thump the walls where they'd been flung. And when the fire briefly righted and tongued a ceiling of rocks the colour of blood, two incomplete bodies dropped to smack the ground.

The stampede of hooves through the darkness was

heralded by a roar of shrieking animals. A herd, their rout a deafening thunder. Nothing of the creatures was visible but the force of this rushing multitude buffeted her face: heavy, powerful shapes plunging through the void. Had she been an inch further out from the fire she was sure her body would have been broken apart by trampling hooves.

Inside the black space the herd was massacred. And beyond the carnage distant dogs squealed and horses screamed as they too must have fallen beneath the same claws and teeth.

Devils laughed through it all and aloud, and they growled on the blood they gulped in the way of hounds assuaging desperate thirsts in puddles. Beyond the fire's tiny borders, in skirts of dim light, the feeble silhouettes of the red folk were tossed back and forth like puppets, limbs flopping. A throat was opened far above Kat's head and a warm broth washed her face. She tasted salt.

A damaged figure crawled: an intoxicated piper in possession of enough sense to realise that something had gone amiss. Kat watched this woman's bony back opened like pastry. The straggly head then vanished under what might have been a great hand or a foot; it pressed her skull as flat as fresh putty. Perhaps the limb that crushed the skull was clawed; a suggestion of a matted leg held the remnants of her head in place so that the body could be ribboned. The sorry carcass was swiftly peeled and emptied before Kat could look away.

A length of timber burned beside Kat's grubby toes. She seized it. Its end glowed white and red with heat and ash and burned her hand. She dropped it. Patted the length of wood for the cooler end and reclaimed the short plank. Then turned, arcing the flame through the darkness at an arm's length.

The meagre light of her torch was momentarily reflected in eyes as wide as headlights: amber amidst a jaundiced yellow, stricken with capillaries. A silhouette found scant definition, only for a moment: a broad shadow with great haunches that trembled behind a dipped head, the small ears pressed flat before the shape withdrew, or vanished.

She tottered from the pyre, swinging the burning plank at waist height. Pushing onwards, she moved in an ungainly lurch to where the world dropped into complete darkness. There should have been soil yet stone pressed the burned soles of her punished feet. *Impossible.* But curiosity had no place in such an abattoir, nor did hesitation: the mauling and scattering of the red folk the only testimony she required.

Savage grunts, the slopping of heavy, wet carcasses in rank air. Quarry thrashed frenziedly against the ground, then flung against the walls, repeatedly. A rapid scuffling of large feet. Inert forms were tugged and fought over anew, between jaws she was blessed to never see. Kat doubted that anything survived behind her burned heels.

About where she guessed the entrance must have once been, she heard new voices. Distant, urgent cries of 'Police!' But these voices seemed to be too far away and at the mouth of a stone tunnel. They were lost in the reeking wind. A human voice was incapable of much besides unwisely announcing itself to what growled about this hell; either that, or it could scream once its presence had been acknowledged. As these new voices briefly did.

A rumble below the ground passed away; a vast wave chased by the bestial screams that had arisen from the pit. The whinnying, terrified herd retreated with the tremor. Their cries rapidly subsided and withdrew to an impossible distance as if swept from where the barn had been. The noises of the devils going about their butchery were no more, the screams of their quarry ended. The earth beneath her feet was dense and silent once more. The departure of the unnatural atmosphere and whatever had scampered through it had been as swift as its coming.

Murmurs from the ordinary world, birdsong or traffic, however, remained absent. Kat imagined the earth breathless and mute with shock. Only the moans of the dying and the inexorable pattering of the rain upon the roof tiles disrupted the silence.

Keeping her feet, she followed where Tony and his invalided wife had run. This had been an endgame that had only spared the perpetrators. Maybe they'd lost control of what they'd directed onto their property. Once it was out, she didn't believe anything capable of holding *that* back.

The kindling she clutched still glowed and what remained of the pyre flickered against walls of wood once more, timber walls instead of stone. She'd been returned to a recognisable place; her smarting feet stumbled on damp soil, the coolness a sudden balm.

Against a far wall a faintly lit rectangle of thinner air suggested an exit: the aperture through which the Willows family had made their undignified escape, leaving all behind to be mauled in a sudden manifestation of horror.

Traumatised but still functioning, carried by unsteady legs, Kat passed through the door and entered a cement room, its weak light celestial in comparison to the barn's unnatural darkness.

48

'*M*uch further?'
'Not far, mother. We're out soon. The seventh door is close.'
'You're tired, my boy. I've been such a burden. I can't breathe in this. Take my face from me.'

When she finally found the farmer's son so many years ago, that dear boy with the yellow eyes, he'd told her what the masks were for. In his wild tales, he'd explained how Redstone was a path and he'd helped Jess follow it.

Mottled, black, bristly, made from dogs but fashioned to resemble other things, the masks had always been old. But how old even the youth couldn't say.

The masks had the smell of smoke and damp stone, dust and layers of dried fear. Their scent filled any space they were brought into, grinning. Jess had found them in an outbuilding, inside the drawer of a scuffed bureau: an article of furniture exiled in a stone building you could only enter through the barn nearest the house. Her nose had led her to the headpieces as she'd searched for poison to kill the rats that had scampered the living spaces of the farmhouse.

Instead of poison, she'd found the masks, the flints and the little figures: knapped stones shaped like big teardrops and figures shaped from clay, laid beside the masks. They'd all been folded inside a piece of antique silk with a lace border.

The three figurines were additionally wrapped in newspaper. She'd known at once that they were associated with the cavern and the paintings on its walls: she'd seen similar walking below the ground.

After the night when she'd been so deep with the cuckoo girl, Maddy Gross, and for the next seven months, what had followed her from the ground had clung to her mind like a strange spell, infesting her sleep with pictures and scenes that were someone else's dreams: she'd watched much transpire under vast, white skies far younger than those beyond her bedroom windows. Sometimes she'd stood with others in a darkness flickering red with firelight and the red had flourished in her, surging through her heart like a new blood.

She was thrilled by a sense that there was a flowing without a destination or an end in the cool silence of the quarry tunnels. Waking from strange dreams she was tempted to dive again into the black spaces beneath her home. Only the death of the girl, and her fear, bade her keep her distance from the old burrows.

But Jess had removed the treasure from the bureau and carefully placed it inside a bag. She'd taken it to the youth with yellow eyes whose father had sold the farm to Tony. The farm should have been the boy's inheritance but there had been so many debts.

Jess had looked for his father first but learned of his passing from a woman in a guesthouse outside Divilmouth. His son had drifted to Plymouth where he'd occupied a single room in a grimy subdivided house. A place for the poor and the broken.

When she'd found him, the boy wasn't surprised to see her, and Jess had suspected he was simple or mentally handicapped and should have been in care. He'd sat alone on a fusty bed as if waiting to be collected by a relative or guardian who'd not arrived. What few clothes and possessions he owned had been folded neatly inside a suitcase. Empty jugs of cider had lined the scuffed furniture. Windows closed, curtains drawn, smoke from his pipe had coated everything in the dismal room with the smell of his father: the same pervasive, enduring odour of the sitting room at the farmhouse.

This sweet, gentle youth with yellow eyes had said nothing other than 'Come in' when she'd knocked at his door. In a room at the end of an unlit passage that had reeked of gas, he'd watched her with a steady, bright gaze while she'd asked her questions about the place under the farm. He wasn't moved to offer answers but his expression became grave.

Unpacking her bag as carefully as it had been filled, Jess had asked him why he and his father had left the artefacts at the farm: the masks, flints and figurines. She'd laid them upon the threadbare carpet of the dismal room, but still the young man had offered nothing. His silence had only made her frantic to know what the things were used for. Everything was connected: the youth, her, the dead cuckoo girl Maddy, the crude objects, the painted chamber.

Eventually the thin young man had turned his slow, yellow eyes to the window. A gaze containing no emotion, judgement, respect or contempt: the look in his eyes the same as they had been the day they'd exchanged contracts at the farm, while the slow father had showed Tony his new fiefdom. Because the youth was simple and clearly unfit for the world beyond the farm that he'd left behind in the patient, resigned manner that he'd taken from his father, Jess had decided to leave.

She'd gathered the foul masks, the blue-black flints and the three carvings of the big-bellied women with the heads of animals. The thrill born of mystification about where she was living, exciting her more and more since the day the girl had died, prompted her to take the objects back home where they'd always been. Each piece was shiny with wear.

Once the objects had been cleared away, the youth with yellow eyes had finally spoken. 'The dead lass they found was down the red.'

'She . . .' Jess hadn't been sure what to say. The incident had been in the newspapers. Everyone involved had lied, consistently, to the police about where the girl had died and about who'd given her drugs. But reporters had amassed outside the farm. Tony was facing charges of manslaughter and possession. There was going to be a trial. His panic and despair had reached levels she'd never seen before, and now he was back in the hospital and she was alone at the farm.

She'd tried to sell the land but local buyers had offered far less than they'd paid for it. There had been no serious attempts at farming since they'd been there. They didn't know how. The buildings were falling apart. With the last of the money, she was paying local men to tend what was left of the flock. But if she'd admitted that the girl had died underground then she might face charges too. No one would ever believe her story about what she'd experienced, nor what had stopped the girl's heart. They'd think her even madder than many claimed she already was. And Jess wasn't sure that she hadn't gone mad from her time at Redstone.

She was frightened and lonely and expecting twins within two months. She didn't know where they'd be born and Tony was so heavily sedated that he'd stopped speaking. So she did what all do in uncomfortable positions: she'd offered more questions to those questions asked of her.

'What is the red?' she'd asked that thin head, haloed by the light passing through the water-stained curtains to sift the dust and curling wisps of pipe smoke. And what the youth said made her sure that if anyone was mad then he was. His father must have been mad too. Anyone who'd been isolated at that farm would lose their way and never rediscover it.

The young man told her that she'd 'made the earth grow dark'. He'd then pointed at her swollen tummy and said that she'd 'wet the dark earth and taken two babs in return'.

He told her not to enter 'the grove' again, unless she'd 'showed their faces back'. Bending over he'd taken a mask from her bag with his dirty, slender fingers and she'd imagined the dirt under his nails was from the farm and would never wash away: that he was so darkly stained with it, like she'd become, and as marked as the scruffy sheep that ambled about the valleys chomping the grass flat.

He'd asked if she'd been in a church and she'd nodded. 'Same thing at the grove,' he'd said, as if correcting her about something she should have known. 'Cover your head. Go wiv your eyes down.' He'd reached out, without a trace of amorous intent and tugged at her dress. 'You don't wear nothing in the grove.' Then he'd asked for her makeup, clicking his fingers to hurry her up, to get past her frowning and puzzlement.

From the makeup bag he'd selected a red lipstick. Then gently cradled her hand palm-down upon his own and smudged the greasy salve in long streaks across the fine bones of her hand. 'And all over if you're going to stand up in the middle of what comes round you.' *Carefully, he'd smudged lines of lipstick into more of her skin like a salve and as he'd rubbed her hand she'd squeezed her thighs together, her face flushing hot.*

'You's right to take lads in the spring if you want more of them,' he'd said, pointing at her tummy. 'You's taken the shape.'

All of the blood in her body had eddied into a weir, a tumult, then surged for the boy with the thin head and yellow eyes, passing its force through him and further still. The feeling had made her giddy, yet filled her with wonder at a future she couldn't understand. Tears had marked her face.

He'd known, this man, just by looking, that she was carrying twins. Yet she'd been infertile, her womb scarred by an abortion in her teens. But she'd come out of that tunnel on the afternoon that the girl died, pregnant with twins. They weren't Tony's. She'd let Ade have his way like he'd always wanted to, in revenge for Tony's fascination with the girl whom she'd lured below the earth. Maddy Gross. Maddy Cuckoo.

'What shape?' she'd asked.

'What comes after you give more to the red. More than we ever did you give already. Me mum and dad wouldn't ever give a girl or a boy. Folks used to. They'd give it what it wants. You're to use these for any giving.' He'd tapped a finger on the wrapped flints. 'And you need to be red for them.' The man had stroked her hands as if they were precious. 'All over. Red as the earth, your skin. You need a fire, else it ain't safe. You've to hide your face so you don't drown in the red like the lassie in the papers done.'

His mad words had left her hands trembling in her damp lap.

'The black mother and her white pups. You called them up. They'll abide cus of what you done. They've given you the centre where all gets shaped round you. What's done is done.'

And without a hint of mockery or sly humour or deceit in his face, he'd told her, 'You's inside the old Creel now. They'll take things from out of it that you put inside.' And as he said that he'd looked at her tummy.

'What are they?' she'd asked him, desperately, but he fell again into the familiar deep silence and was no longer listening but thinking on what could be done for her, as if he were a mechanic and she'd taken a broken car into his garage.

'They pawing the ground now?' he'd eventually asked, tapping the side of his slender head. 'Up here?'

And that had made her think of how often she'd run in her dreams to fright the herds, shepherding the herds alongside the red people with their stinking heads of beasts: some with horns, some with feathers, but all with the black muzzles that their wild eyes peered through. And she'd recalled what walked the darker edges of the pit on its hind legs, their dirty white bibs clotted scarlet. The pups would shock her awake before she ever saw more of them in dream, or of what came roaring up from the ground behind them. And she recalled how she would lie, panting like a dog, and shaking with relief at not having seen more than the end of the larger one's thin, black legs protruding from the crevice in the pit . . . yet always wanting to go to it, like it was her lover, her sex nearly cramping and opening.

'I think so,' she told the farmer's son, who was much more than that. And he'd nodded, sagely, as if what had been discussed between them was a subject of consequence to him.

'Nuffing is written down. It's all in pictures,' he'd said solemnly. 'Don't work without a witch-wife in the middle who shapes it all about her, you see? Takes time.'

'Can you show me how?' Jess had asked him with tears in her eyes, stroking the miracle thriving in her womb. And she'd knelt before the youth, which had troubled him. He'd asked her to stand and instead had knelt before her, placing his mouth on her feet.

The boy with the yellow eyes came home with her afterwards, and they'd taken his old dusty suitcases that had never belonged anywhere but upon the red land that few wanted. And he'd shown her what his mum had done with farm animals in the grove to fill the old Creel and what she'd been shown by the other wives and so on, before his dad had gone for Christ and stopped it all.

She'd learned how the sacred weapons and the music underground had always led others to the grove of the oldest red columns, the witch-wives. And she saw the patterns of witch-wife bones curled in the dusty nests where they'd lain a long time. She went below with him, many times, masked and unclothed and red and with great reverence so as not to drown in her own blood, and she'd let the maps upon the walls fill her with knowledge.

In the sacred grove she made the earth grow dark, from time to time, giving succour to the pups, who fed first, to resume the old bond. And in the parts of the earth that were still open enough and close enough to what paced below, the youth with yellow eyes taught her how the five-fold kiss worked and what it could do once the Creel was nourished. The first girl who went into the red was sufficient explanation as to how she'd given birth to the twins, Finn and Nanna, and why so many other mothers were soon blessed too, and how the flocks had doubled in size on the farm and on the land all around the crossroads.

The counter-clockwise steps around the red column with the sun's low light setting in the West allowed her to see much farther than the sea. The rite was used when something needed to be built or planted. That movement always stirred the pipers and opened Creel's door.

Others came and helped with the farm and with the rites and they settled her as witch-wife with kisses on her feet.

In the red places, once her cut flowers were bringing in an income, along with the lambing and calving and dairy farming, across all of the farms where the Creel was nourished and her tracks became visible again, Jess's place as the red column was accepted without question.

Before Finn was old enough to replace him, though his slaughter of the youth with yellow eyes she'd thought unnecessary, she'd asked the youth for the names of what it was that came and went beneath the earth – if called in the right way and when carefully provisioned with ponies, lambs and sturdy rams, all being the hue of night – and he'd said his mother had called her Creel. Her milky pups had names you never did more than whisper. There were other names, but those in the red grove were mostly referred to as a pack, or a trinity: the Creel.

They had been given that name, or the name of 'Old Creel', many years before, and all anyone knew now was the song about a giant in the West who'd kept his hunting hounds in a basket *filled with bones. But his hounds were devils and had escaped and devoured the giant, as well as anything living they'd come across, before returning to their basket.*

Only the cleverest tribe of men who'd hid their delicious scent by taking on the likenesses of the devils in the Creel, through the fashioning of their heads and the staining of their flesh, had survived the devil hounds of the Creel. Those men had learned to fill the capacious bellies in the Creel and to freshen the dread basket with new bones. The hounds had then hunted with the men as they'd hunted for the giant, and the men had fed on the scraps.

She'd learned the song and others still known in the oldest tongues of the West; some that could still be heard beneath the ground at certain times along with the pipes. Soon, she'd sung them all proudly and loudly in the old tongues that came from the back of the throat. Tony was next to useless so Finn took the role of John Barleycorn not long after he'd been caught offering black lambs in the grove independently of tuition. No school would hold him so she tutored him at home until he introduced the new crop that would sustain every red child for miles.

And by learning to see in the dark, as witch-wife she too saw that the past was red and that the future was red for certain. That the red abided and that all was truly red in the world and was destined to be red again.

She'd seen how red the world was at its end, which wasn't too far away, and she'd learned that even though much could conceal the red in every heart, those that didn't abide by the red were never saved.

49

*S*tatic crackle from police radios inside the barn, then a voice said, 'Christ. Here . . . Jesus, look at that.'

Helene kept her distance from the gaping, smoking doorway. Sickened by what lay strewn and ruined about the dirt floor at the mouth of the building and on the road, she remained on the lane in the drizzle, feeling delicate and useless inside the oversized coat from the hospital's lost property box. Though the next time one of the constables came out of the barn, she'd try and attract his attention. More police would be here soon too. Ambulances. *Please. Please come quickly.*

She struggled to put one thought in front of another to complete short bursts of comprehension. But disbelief and confusion mingled with the relief that it was over. She'd survived, again. Soon she would be reunited with her family. That's all that mattered now.

Until a woman staggered out from between two of the decrepit farm buildings. A person with bedraggled hair swaying in clumps about her face. A woman stumbling on bare, grubby feet, but not painted red or naked. She wore a hooded top and jogging bottoms: her clothing smeared with grime and inappropriate to the weather.

In her hand she dragged a long piece of timber that smoked at one end. She seemed intent on reaching the scrawny red arm that lay upon the lane's surface: an arm severed from a body.

The woman bent at the waist, emitting a gasp, and pulled something from out of the hand at the end of the crudely amputated arm. The object looked like a stone and the woman examined it until something in a tree beside the lane distracted her.

Scraping a dark lug of hair from her forehead, the dishevelled woman peered into the overhanging branches, then studied the drainage ditch at the side of the road. As if sensing scrutiny she turned her head and looked at Helene.

Even from a distance, recognition dawned in the mind of each woman.

The scruffy figure was Kat, the journalist.

They stared at each other some more. Inside the smear of a face, smudged with dried blood and soil, Helene watched the awareness of who she was dawn in the other figure's too white, too wide eyes.

Kat shuffled about to face her. 'Helene?' she asked in a dry voice close to a croak.

Helene didn't reply. This woman had given her to the red people. She'd lured her to this dreadful place where there had been an attempt on her life. She'd implicated her family in this unnatural business, her little girl, her old mum. The police in the barn needed to know that Kat was here and that she was part of this: part of the outlandish story that she'd narrated in a hospital bed to unbelieving police officers and detectives. Helene looked to the barn and parted her lips to call out.

'How did you . . .' Kat never finished the question but said enough to distract Helene. 'What are you doing here? I thought they'd . . . I'm sorry,' she said. 'I'm so sorry, Helene.' Kat wiped her eyes. Her body was shaking. The hand about the wood was white, the clenched knuckles defined. 'I had no choice.'

Helene pointed at her, moving towards her. 'You. I'm here because of you.' Her throat briefly closed with emotion, her jaw trembling, her eyes smarting with tears. 'Because of you . . . You did this!' She cast her arm in the direction of the barn. 'The police are in there. So you stay the fuck away from me. Don't you bloody move, bitch.'

Tears glistened on Kat's cheeks, diluting the filth around her eyes. The frustration of what she wanted to say creased her face as if she was about to cry. 'Steve,' Kat blurted, her voice shaking. 'They killed Steve. In there.' Kat pointed to the barn with her wood. 'They cut him open in there.' She nodded her head rapidly to add emphasis to the memory. 'They tried to do it to me. In there.' She looked at her dirty burned feet. 'I had no choice. They came to my home. They made me call you. Because of the recordings. I'm sorry.'

'Tell it to the police.'

If Kat heard that she paid it no heed. 'They killed your brother. And Steve. So many. I was next. The . . . *things* that did this . . . the murderers at this farm brought it here. They called it.' Kat looked up at the tree. '*It* was just here. Out here. Oh God.'

Helene followed Kat's gaze and saw that a dark, irregularly shaped object was caught in the tree. At first she assumed they were empty clothes, snagged on twigs. But when she moved to better see what was strewn through the branches, she made out a murky human form, criss-crossed by sticks.

At a glance the figure might have passed for a scarecrow with poorly constructed limbs, made from poles broken at odd angles inside its sleeves and trouser legs. Moving closer, she recognised it as the body of a man. He either had an arm missing or it was twisted behind his back.

Before she could look away, Helene saw the thin head, half-concealed behind the leaves, the facial expression contorted with displeasure. It was Richey, from the boat.

Kat pointed her stick into the ditch. 'The police have been helping them. You can't trust the police.'

Helene looked to where Kat now directed her attention and flinched. 'Oh, Jesus Christ,' she muttered, on seeing the body of the female police constable. She recognised the woman's petite shape and uniform but not much else. Headless, like her partner, her body had landed on its front in the weeds. It was also missing part of a leg, beneath the knee.

Richey now watched over the woman's body with his sightless eyes, while dripping from the tree in which he hung.

'No,' Helene said. 'No. She was helping me. The police brought me here. To catch the men who tried to drown me.'

What she'd said seemed absurd. But ever since her arrival in the village of Redhill to meet this woman, and to learn about her brother's final weeks alive, her life had been implausible. The trend was set to continue. Helene pointed at the tatty remnants of a man in the tree. 'He was on the boat.'

Kat wiped at her eyes using a sleeve. 'They were going to kill all of us. It was the sounds from the cave. Whoever heard those recordings, or came here and saw things, was finished.'

Hadn't she suspected as much? That those dim, awful sounds, recorded in a cave by her brother, were connected to this massacre? 'How . . .'

Eyes blinking rapidly, her stained face now quivering white with anger, Kat said, 'Steve came here. And they butchered him. They . . . they're not getting away with it. They're not.' And with that, Kat had reminded herself of some undisclosed purpose. She hobbled up the lane, away from the barn. 'They came through here.'

The police officers were still preoccupied inside the outbuildings. Helene could hear them searching one of the adjoining workshops made from bricks and cement blocks. Kat had said they couldn't be trusted, that the police were a part of this. Helene found that too hard to comprehend. She would not believe it of the two constables who had driven her here and raced towards the smoke and the screams, only to die so horribly while doing their duty, unthinkingly. She stepped after Kat. 'The police. They're here to help.'

'They're not getting away with it. They left us all to die.'

Helene followed Kat at a safe distance, her mind working hard at what the journalist had confided. 'Kat. The police brought me here, to help me. Now they're dead. Both of them.'

'A policeman brought me here too, to die. The red folk were going to give me to *it*.'

When Helene drew closer, she could see that Kat's eyes weren't right. She looked unhinged, the blood staining Kat's face only reinforcing Helene's sense that the woman was in shock.

'Did you hear *them* too? Mmm?' Kat muttered. 'They came from the pit and did this.' Kat pointed her short plank, the charred end still smoking, in the direction of Richey's motionless body.

Helene followed Kat to where the lane curved from view, the tarmac increasingly concealed by outgrowths from the hedgerow. 'It doesn't make sense. Kat! Stop! For fuck's sake, Kat, stop. Where are you going?'

And before Helene received an answer, both women saw the white house at the same time. Its front now visible through the unruly verdure at the side of the road.

'They went in there,' Kat said, and staggered on, in the direction of the big house, wincing with every step as the broken tarmac stabbed her swollen feet.

Helene followed her to the building hidden deep within the decrepit farm. Large and modern, the mansion's outer walls were resplendent with bright magnolia. Dark panes of glass caught the weak light and returned reflections of what declined about itself: the dereliction and wild, unruly growths. But nothing made sense any more to Helene about this land, or those who danced in red across it, or what had emerged from beneath it. Nor did she know who to trust or what to do any more. But was Kat suggesting that someone, the people responsible for so much bloodshed, had escaped from the barn? If so, then this mad woman with a stick in one hand and a black rock in the other appeared to be pursuing them.

50

This tunnel, if Kat was to follow it any further, would take her deep underground, where *it* lived. From down there the horror had burst. The realisation was sobering. For the first time since she'd escaped from the barn, her determination to pursue the Willows family cooled.

Rough walls of limestone led down, evoking a grim carousel of memory, of living forms flung through the dark, the thud of their falls. A sense of what might yet roam here, the inhuman strength of it, kept her at a standstill.

The wooden staircase she'd not long ago descended connected a utility room on the ground floor of the big white house to this subterranean level. Whoever had fled down here had left the connecting door ajar: someone in a hurry or with their hands full.

Kat fingered the black rock in her hand. Outside the barn, she'd scooped it from a dead stranger's fingers: an implement insufficient to the task of defending herself against those *things*. And she knew of no weapon that might offer reassurance if she should meet again what the red folk had called Creel, let alone its young.

Kat wiped a wet hand against her trouser leg to better grip the hand-axe.

Behind her, at the top of the staircase, Helene stood in silence. She wasn't coming down: wasn't going beneath the ground in pursuit of those who'd tried to end their lives and destroyed those they'd loved.

Helene was a survivor but the girl had suffered enough. That was plain to see. A drawn face, the manic expression and the palsy of her bloodless hands were sufficient evidence of a woman at the end of her tether. The red had tried to exterminate her by drowning. That's what she'd said.

But Helene's limbs were probably aquiver now from the shock of witnessing what Kat had so recently done to a living man, the man with the bad leg whom they'd found inside the big white house.

They'd come across him in one of the spacious living rooms: an enormous area with a fireplace the size of the bathroom in her cottage. The room had opened onto a brushed granite kitchen; the terrazzo eating bar could have seated eight people.

The mansion had revealed itself to be a place of atriums, roof beams, viewing walls, vast indoor plants, enormous sofas that slotted elegantly into corners, wooden staircases inlaid with cherry, and private decks offering a view of the distant, angry sea.

The incongruity of the house's existence at the farm had startled them both. How did such a palace occupy the same land as the other dilapidated, unkempt and aged structures, all leaning earthward, at Redstone Farm? The sale of sheep had not built the house nor its indoor pool.

Kat had glanced around as they'd shuffled inside, her raw and seared feet cooling on the marble floors, her professional eye absorbing the lavish interior as if it were a spread in a lifestyle magazine. Only the wealthiest people owned places like this. Not those with moribund music careers who'd taken to farming sheep.

She began to think differently about the nature of the land, the properties upon it, where it all began. The buildings at the front were mere facades, old ruins, concealing the guttural calling and the bloodletting, the dog masks, the horrible piping, the red skin and this magnificent house. What else was hidden here?

Redstone was not a working sheep farm in any meaningful sense. It probably hadn't been in years. And this gleaming palace was the headquarters of something else, another kind of business: private, exclusive, detached. This luxurious home was the heart that serviced the blood vessels of a criminal network that Matt Hull and Steve had alluded to. *Drugs.*

There appeared to be much more evidence of the operation: these hidden tunnels. Perhaps the burrows of the depraved even reached unto the far cliffs and caves. But what had sustained and seemingly just destroyed part of the very tribe that serviced it must also exist *below*. One thing had crossed over into another: hadn't Matt Hull said as much?

The authorities would never understand her story because they hadn't seen or heard or dreamed of what bayed and jabbered below this farm. Those who'd encountered it first-hand had either lost their heads or were also in league with the red but escaped the slaughter, like the man on the sofa had been.

'Who's that? Who's here then, aye? That you, Richey? That you, lad?' Mere minutes before, the chubby man with the bad leg in the living room had repeated himself, nervously, on hearing the entrance of Kat and Helene into the great white house.

He'd only stopped asking questions when she and Helene had passed through the grand atrium and discovered him propped up on a long settee, upholstered in white leather. One of his feet had been raised by three cushions.

No one else had been home. But when the man on the couch had seen Helene, his round face had transformed from a hopeful yearning to something purple-black. 'Bitch,' he'd barked, spraying spittle all over the glass table. He'd known Helene. 'You's should have stayed drowned, cunt!' the man had bellowed.

Wincing and wheezing, he'd struggled to his feet. Unafraid of the two women who'd appeared before him – one covered in dried blood and dirt, the second swamped by an ill-fitting coat and unable to stop shaking – he'd come at them, hobbling and spitting, his short arms wheeling for balance.

Helene's pretty blue eyes had opened wide with more than fear: she'd been terrified. She'd turned immediately, intent on fleeing the mansion they'd only been inside for a matter of seconds. She'd whispered, 'He did it. Tried to kill me . . .'

And Kat had known that like Beard and Headscarf, this man was one of *them*; and he was injured. His ruddy forehead was beaded with sweat, his leg stiff: any weight he put upon it caused him great pain.

Somehow, he'd escaped the morning's massacre. Maybe on account of his injury he'd remained inside the vast house. Or maybe he'd limped inside to hide while his colleagues fled or died. Kat doubted he was a Willow: they were whippet-thin, ferrety, anxious and posh.

At the sight of him, Kat had also remembered her own cowardice. How she'd wronged Helene: the woman who'd trembled beside her, the young mother whom she'd sacrificed hoping to save herself.

So Kat had grasped an opportunity to protect Helene. She'd recognised a chance to avenge the wrongs that this man and his kind had done to a frightened girl who'd already lost her brother: two more innocent victims of the red.

Her entire body had suffused with a special energy. Molten and red it had been: the red of fury, the red of a wordless rage, warming her muscles to perform acts of unfamiliar strength and agility. A great and unwieldy freedom had taken possession of her limbs. Engulfed by the surge, this awakening of the blood, her conscious mind had slid, sunk away. And with its passing had vanished the possibility of restraint. Her mindlessness had resembled sexual arousal. She'd bathed in a nourishing glow that had beat behind her face and she'd gone to work.

Kat had raced to meet the challenge of the wounded underling, the agony of her burned feet briefly forgotten, and she'd punched him backwards with her outstretched hands.

The man with the purple face and chubby, grasping hands, with the silly childish thumbs that bristled with black hair and made her think of a pig's trotters, never made it past the show-home table. She'd never struck anything so hard before; the balls of her hands caught him on the sternum and instantly deflated him.

Bending over his half-collapsed form, with the tip of her flint knife pointing down, she'd then hacked and felt the plates of his skull move beneath her fist. She didn't stop there, but aimed at his temple and his throat and the hands that he'd raised in defence. She'd pierced them all.

Then she'd gone for the ham of his shoulders and the gammon of his flanks. Even when the swine was down on all fours and bleating, she still hadn't been able to stop and she'd beaten his back like a drum. Made him boom until his inner softness had sucked at the flint, forcing her to rip the blade free, time after time, which had flecked her face with warmth and patterned the white ceiling with long arcs of bright scarlet: graffiti she'd fleetingly found beauteous.

She'd only stopped when she'd been too tired to hammer the man any flatter or wetter against the marble tiles and the rug that he'd drenched red.

Kat had spared a few thoughts for the woman in the headscarf and how she'd ruined her too, in the cottage, down in the tiny space between her bed and the wall of the bedroom. The woman's toothless mouth had cawed like a baby bird's but Kat had felt no sympathy. Crushing the foul-mouthed, chubby man had been a fuller experience: then she'd felt something more like joy, her mind half-blinded with a searing scarlet light. If she'd so much as brushed her sex with the beautiful blue shard that she'd used to smash open her foe, she'd have climaxed.

She'd turned to Helene after she'd finished and for a while Kat had struggled to put a name to the woman's face. She'd not even known herself.

Beyond the kitchen in a utility room Kat had then found a door operated by a silver keypad, as if it concealed a safe. Before the door, the false front of a tumble dryer and a cupboard had been left ajar.

Helene had followed her from the living room, at a distance, like a child who'd not known better.

Despite their haste to escape, Kat had judged that the Willows family wouldn't have gone down if it was dangerous. That's why she'd followed them.

Still panting hard from her exertions in the living room, and smiling oddly between lank laces of the dripping hair bootlacing her face, she peered up again at the tall woman in the doorway of the cellar. In Helene's face she saw shock, revulsion and sheer incomprehension. Helene, Kat decided, had not tasted the red as much as she had. Proximity was contagion.

Without another word to Helene, Kat followed the underground path.

Below the earth the temperature plummeted, a vague eddy of dank air making her shudder. Natural refrigeration.

The burrow smelled of soil and wet stone. Lights glowed orange along the walls, all fed by a wire stapled into the moist, limestone walls. The passage was too smooth to have been wholly formed naturally.

As if she were on ice, Kat walked slowly in a shaft that tunnelled south of the barn. Her feet were burned in several places, though how badly she wasn't sure. She'd not wanted to inspect her wounds until her journey was over. But as the adrenalin had drained from her muscles, her feet had begun to throb with an agony that interfered with her ability to think clearly.

And the further she travelled beneath the earth, the more the madness seeped from her mind. When the tunnel curved from sight, she again reflected upon being in the realm of the abominations that had burst from the earth to dismember anything within their terrible reach.

She unwisely recalled the skull of the piper in the barn: how it had been squashed flat like a melon under a truck tyre. She felt the cold air of the passage along her prickling arms more keenly then. She thought of Steve too and the horrid goblet from which the red folk had supped their murky brew. Her footsteps shortened, became hesitant. The idea of being lost below the ground took hold of her mind.

Avoiding whatever this ancient ground had kept hidden was her priority and yet the jeopardy she faced was equal to her need to avenge herself against Willows and his brood. Only the weasel son would pose any serious resistance and she calculated that he was a risk worth taking. So she carried on, her hearing groping ahead of her.

They would receive no mercy either, because once the red holes in their faces had been shut they'd not be calling *it* into the world again.

The tunnel turned once more. Around the bend there were more walls of stone: a rough ceiling, a worn floor, mined and levelled. She doubted that Tony could hobble much farther than this. He'd needed his daughter to support his feeble progress in and out of the abattoir above. Last seen, his queen had also been carried by the rangy stoat she'd sired. Such were the burdens and the haste of their children, they'd failed to seal the door behind them.

The deeper Kat journeyed, thicker power cables bracketed the walls, attesting to a greater demand for electricity. When the tunnel forked, she found a metal door buried six metres inside the rock. An annexe.

The main tunnel curved out of sight, disappearing into an unlit void. Down there, the lights were off.

Kat listened, sniffed the air. Her instincts balked anew at the idea of being drawn deeper inside the earth.

Instead, she returned her attention to the steel door. Perhaps she might get lucky and find them all cowering behind it. She tugged the handle and the door swung wide.

Opening the door was akin to drawing blackout curtains from windows bright with sunlight.

At first she thought the door was an exit, opening onto the outside world. But there was no rain. No diesel sky or grey air when Kat looked up at where she thought the sun must be, where such warmth radiated to bathe her face.

Instead of the sun, great yellow bulbs hung inside black umbrellas. Cables looped from the rig on the ceiling and reached walls covered in white rectangles of insulation: walls padded with what resembled floor mats in a gymnasium. And what she mistook, at a glance, for a glade of small ferns, carpeting the floor of a wood, were thick rows of identical green plants.

The bright foliage grew to the height of her knees. From stalks, spiky, blade-shaped leaves protruded. She recognised the serrated shapes of the leaves from her time in London: silhouettes that were often printed on merchandise and smoking paraphernalia in places like Camden Market. Cannabis plants, their aroma overpowering. A perfume she now associated with delirium and terror, with bloodshed.

Kat stepped inside the room and looked about herself in astonishment. The rumours Steve had heard about Brickburgh's illegal crops were true. When she hadn't wanted to listen, Matt Hull had hesitantly tutored her in the same local criminal mythology. Redstone Farm was a drug plantation: it concealed a vast cannabis crop beneath the ground. A red harvest grown close to a ghastly slaughterhouse.

Whoever threatened this subterranean crop was despatched. Steve, Matt, Helene's brother, walkers and campers who'd strayed too close: they must all have been deviously or ritually murdered.

This cavernous room explained why so much of the crop was incinerated in braziers during those rites in the barn, to facilitate the disordering of minds committing acts of such savage degeneracy. They had produce to spare.

Had Kat suspected that nothing would ever shock her again, she'd have been mistaken.

She recalled the sounds of the large vehicles and motorbikes that morning and of a small aircraft landing at the farm the night Steve had been butchered. Here was an established business. The neglected farmhouse and dilapidated outbuildings containing makeshift cells, abattoirs: all a functioning camouflage.

Matt Hull's claim of local corruption was no exaggeration either and she considered the smarmy detective, Lewis: he was on the payroll. Others would be too; perhaps those in local government and business. How deep did the scarlet roots of Redstone Farm reach? She could only guess but they'd extended deeply enough to keep all of this hidden for years.

The discovery of this crop, the sheer industrial scale of the operation, would summon everything that law enforcement commanded, near and far. No wonder the red folk had killed with impunity to protect it. The multiple murders, masquerading as cases of missing persons, would now require fresh investigations. Every local report of a missing person would have to be pursued anew. Willows's entire operation would need unravelling.

Kat's head hurt at the thought of what this tiny part of the world now faced.

Uniformed officers were already on site. Soon they would be everywhere: cordons and perimeter guards established; men in white suits painstakingly picking across the ground, inch by inch; grisly leavings in the barn encased in polythene tents; samples subjected to forensic scrutiny. This would become another dig and one to rival that of the Brickburgh Caverns: two sites of mass murder from different periods existing on the same land.

But even here, her instincts as a journalist prevailed: she knew she was on the brink of a monumental story. A story with a final chapter that she'd been instrumental in writing. And she vowed to find every last red tendril that twisted above or below this ground, because she was part of this. Unwittingly, she and her dead boyfriend and poor Helene must have contributed to the sudden demise of the red folk and their operation.

The Willows must also have known that the end was coming. They'd panicked at the sound of the siren. Perhaps they'd also been losing control of whatever it was that they'd fattened below the ground. Isn't that what Tony had alluded to? That they'd brought *it* too close to the surface? Who or what had been in control here?

How could the forces of reason ever conceive and accept what she'd witnessed in that barn, twice? Surely her narrative would be dismissed as the ramblings of a lunatic, a woman in deep shock, a woman who'd killed. Her own hands were no longer clean.

Kat recalled, and so brightly that her memory glistened, what she'd recently done in the living room of the house above. *An execution.*

Did I?

She squirmed with revulsion at herself. Squeezing her eyes shut, she forced herself to blank her mind. She leaned against the nearest row of plant beds until the wave of nausea passed.

Then moved through the crop, desperate for fresh air, her old self reviving and waking from that half-sleep: moment by moment, she felt as if she were breaking from a trance she'd occupied with her eyes open. What she'd seen and done were merging, dreamlike, with the artificial sunshine that warmed her face.

Between the parallel beds, her fingertips trailed through the spiky fronds until she reached the door at the far end of the subterranean greenhouse. The cave was at least thirty metres long by twenty across and as large as the Grand Chamber of Brickburgh, hidden beside the sea.

Passing through a connecting door, where the plantation's rows came to an end, she entered a second chamber. The walls were darker but it was lit from above with the same lights as the greenhouse.

From black wires, looping like skipping ropes to the far wall, great bunches of what resembled brewer's hops or bunches of drying oregano hung upside down in fat bushels.

The wires on the far side of the room had been cleared of their harvest. Detritus, similar to dried spice, littered the floor and stuck to her stinging feet: fragments disrupted from a crop partially and hastily gathered.

At the far end of the second chamber a metal ladder ascended to the ceiling. Kat saw it but didn't go to it. Instead, she gaped at what was crafted upon the chamber's walls.

She'd seen similar murals at the exhibition in Exeter and the illustrations here told a similar story to those on the walls of the Brickburgh Caves. Between two dense bushels of drying weed, a squashed, doggish snout, fashioned from haematite and charcoal, stained the wall. Red-eyed, jaws open, the hideous jackal-head was supported by human shoulders and the voluptuous body of a woman curved below the creature's hirsute throat. A figure that might have grimaced upon these walls for forty thousand years.

In their time below, had the most recent dwellers found something? A thing timelessly vile that former inhabitants had also known intimately? A thing they'd fed each other to, from one frozen era into another?

The scale of such a thought made Kat dizzy, and she felt the full effects of her fatigue more keenly now than for days, and in every part of her body. Her head teemed with horror: images of shattered bones, the tiny skull of a child, a row of flint hand-axes, a lined mouth suckling a wet jawbone by the red light of a pyre . . .

All of her waking thoughts and her dreams would lead here, to this farm, and to these caves, always, for ever. And to what she'd seen.

At the foot of the ladder, before she climbed out, Kat turned and took a final look of startled disbelief. The cave system must be truly enormous. The coast was three miles away but the archaeologists were tunnelling towards the farm. A physical connection between the two places must exist. The dig had slowly and meticulously followed a route inland for three years, moving from one buried cave to another, excavating a hidden story, but always unwittingly heading towards the Willows clan and into the present.

51

'Tony, Tony, my old friend.' The voice was muffled by a mask concealing most of the speaker's head, a visage incompatible with the elegant room in which the man sat.

Through the hairy black jaws of the headpiece, small blue eyes glittered within two fleshy beds of tanned skin, transmitting a cold, excited gaze. Perhaps a grin was concealed by the mask, one that was mirthless.

Four ragged, breathless figures gasped and panted beneath the small dais that the beast-headed man's chair was raised upon.

Strong light greeted Tony Willows and his family and it made them blink like moles; such an illumination hadn't existed in the passages they'd traversed for miles to get here. The natural light and white walls also invited an unflattering scrutiny of their stained and dishevelled bodies. They'd fled their home of decades without coats or shoes.

'An old friend. That is exactly what I am, Adrian,' Tony called in a jovial, chummy tone, despite his wheezing.

Tony's face was waxy and moist beneath what stain remained on his features. The journey had nearly killed him but his rich voice managed to summon itself and fill the room. A chamber tiled in white and blue from floor to ceiling, save where long rectangular windows were divided by Doric columns. Classical Grecian in style, this odd hexagonal space might have been an ostentatious conservatory with a sea view.

There was no furniture in the chamber beside the two seats on the dais, each upholstered in red velvet. Only a floor that discreetly sloped to a metal grate in the centre suggested the chamber's function: a form of wet room.

A hazy grey seascape existed soundlessly beyond its rain-speckled windows. Outside and around the curious chamber, a great white building crowned the cliffs. The impressive structure was visible through the glass roof: a *schloss* perched on a cliff edge like a forward observation point.

Tony smiled, spreading his arms. 'And to this old friend I have come to request that an agreement be fulfilled. A pact made in better times. Old dogs know how times change. So quickly. But there you have it.'

'All over, is it, Tony?' The masked figure asked.

'Aye, all over.'

'No time for a last encore?'

Tony bristled at that remark as if he wanted no reminder of his musical past.

Finn held his mother in his thin arms like she was his babe. He grimaced, his ruddy face streaked with sweat. 'Would a chair be too much to ask for? You can see who we have here!'

The masked figure turned his attention to the younger man but only for a moment did his stare linger. All four guests tensed. The eyes within that doglike maw had ratcheted from spiteful mirth to something even less appealing, like wrath, before relaxing. 'A chair for the witch-wife of Redstone,' the masked figure called out, his tone droll, irreverent, dismissive. 'She's missing her throne.'

From the rear of the room, one of the two men who flanked the closed entrance opened a white door and stepped outside.

A second masked figure sat beside Adrian in an identical chair. A woman who turned her head and muttered something to him. She was dressed in white jeans and an expensive print blouse, her pampered feet strapped into jewelled sandals of golden leather. The fingernails of her idle hands were painted red. Adrian wore a blue cotton shirt, tan chinos and leather loafers without socks.

Had the couple not been wearing the mangy and frightful animal masks, which seemed to have been plucked from a props wardrobe in an unappealing theatre, or from the basement shelves of a museum of curiosities, they would have passed as a wealthy couple relaxing before a private view of the sea.

One of the chamber's doors opened and closed, readmitting the retainer who'd gone outside. He returned with a patio chair and carelessly dropped it beside Finn and his mother.

'Taken by surprise, eh?' Adrian asked, grinning through his black muzzle. 'News travels. But how much did you get out, Tony?'

Tony looked to Finn, who answered. 'Enough.'

Tony shrugged. 'They came sooner than we anticipated.'

Adrian sighed. 'You trust imbeciles with a job and you get an imbecile's work. She swam, Tony. From way out. That girl with the recordings. The woman whose brother managed to instal microphones on your land in broad daylight. And from where you dropped her in the water, she swam back to shore. All that way by herself. Can you imagine it?'

'Impossible,' Finn said.

Ignoring him, the masked man continued to address only Tony. 'Fishermen yanked her out near Slagcombe. She's been in Divilmouth Hospital overnight. From there she was taken by the police to the gates of your proud establishment earlier today. That beating but much exposed heart of your operation.'

Tony and his son exchanged glances.

Adrian's eyes twinkled with competitive, triumphant amusement. To increase their embarrassment and misery, the man in the mask continued to explain their failings. 'We had word from the hospital early this morning. I doubt you were even awake when the news came in. And I assume you wasted valuable time today, preparing one of your barbaric rites for the journalist. The one you also failed to deal with. By all accounts, she escaped from your care too. You had her on a platter and yet she escaped. Our mutual friend Louie brought us up to speed.'

'We got her again,' Tony said.

No longer encumbered by his mother in his arms, Finn stepped forward. His fists were clenched. 'You knew. You knew the girl we threw in the drink survived? You never warned us?'

Tony touched his son's arm gently to bid him be still. 'She's gone now, this hack, to the red. She won't be coming back.'

The shaggy head upon the throne nodded sagely, the motion grotesque. 'Yet you waited until this morning to deal with her. You felt it prudent to wait because of your recent profligacy in matters of the red. You couldn't risk another death so soon after that photographer and the paraglider and the girl in the water. Have I missed anyone, Tony? Hmm? How many people have been taken on your land, or near it, by those painted chimpanzees up at that landfill that you call a farm?'

Finn took another step at the little dais. 'The fuck! Who are you to question us?' His voice was shrill, verging on unpleasantly feminine.

'Son!' Tony said, reaching for his arm. The father's hand was evaded. Beside the door the two men stood straighter.

The figure on the throne ignored Finn's aggressive posturing and kept his eyes upon Tony. 'Who knows what these bitches know or what they've jabbered to their confidants? Who can truly say what is known and what is not known now and by whom? It's always been the way with you, old boy. Insecure. And if the events of this morning are anything to go by, I imagine all of us will suffer the consequences sooner rather than later. The whole area, every crop will have to be erased. Scorched earth. All of it.

'So I've given this some thought, Tony. I've been forced to, even though I'd rather have been doing something else. But I arrived at an interesting conclusion. Hear me out.

'We've paid off our debt to you, by protecting your *situation* for as long as possible, given your errancy, your indiscipline. I don't think I'm being unfair. We've done more for you than you've ever done for us. You connected us but we've carried you for years, particularly on distribution. So it is you that has accrued the real debt and you no longer have a pot to piss in, do you? Your accounts will be frozen by teatime. Assets seized.'

Tony's jaw trembled. He tried to swallow whatever had blocked his throat but didn't seem able to raise the strength. He appeared to be paralysed by a sense of injustice, by the terms of an imminent betrayal. He'd never liked Adrian. The man had expanded the business but he was a detestable snob. He'd always been dangerous too and a tricky bastard, but he was their most powerful neighbour and had guaranteed sanctuary if ever they'd needed it.

Finn suffered no qualms about his behaviour as a guest. 'What the fuck! Sanctuary has been requested! You don't question it, you grant it! We want somewhere where we can clean up, before any decisions are made about what happens next. You've no fucking idea what we've had to do to keep *it* in the ground.' He pointed a thin red arm at the elderly woman he'd placed on the chair. 'My mother is exhausted. You haven't a clue how volatile it's become, or what we've given to keep it down. To placate it . . . We must have just lost another eight people. You talk to us about heavy lifting? You haven't any idea, fucking around the harbour with your toy boats while we take the risks!'

Sitting upon what increasingly resembled thrones, the two masked figures merely appeared amused by Finn's outburst. They laughed, though humourlessly. Adrian even slapped his thighs and when he next spoke it was to Tony again. 'You honestly believe that your shanty town is some kind of mother country? Hmm? And that we all look up to it? That being closer to the queens of old endows you with some divine right? Did you presume that we are your subjects, old man?

'They're digging their way inside your fetid bowels from those caves at Brickburgh, day by day. Coming right at you through the red earth. You've trespassers all over your farm, like ants because you left the sugar out. You're careless. You lost touch, Tony, a long time ago and you let this psychotic run things.' He indicated Finn with one lazy hand, without deigning to look at him.

'To be so careless at such a time when things are so good for all in the red, near and far. The ecstasy must be contained, channelled. You've always over-indulged. It's in your background, excess.

'There are times and places for the red. And you've been warned, Tony. Plenty of times. You listened to that mutt of a son too much. And your wife is senile. To be frank, I'm disgusted.' Inside the doggish, hairy snout of the mask, the little tanned nose wrinkled to emphasise its point.

Too angry to speak, Finn Willows turned and gazed at his mother. He shook his head in exasperation as if the man's temerity in criticising his family defied belief.

'We know how to run *this* business,' the masked woman at Adrian's side said, with an air of self-satisfaction.

'Shut your mouth, tart!' Finn cried out, his voice breathless with exasperation. 'You employed that bitch and the dickhead with the camera. They're on you!'

Adrian beckoned those at the door with a flick of his wrist. The two men stepped forward on command. Each man was stocky with a weathered face, over fifty, dressed in expensive yachting slickers and jeans. Besides a sullen determination, their eyes were blank.

Neither man said a word as Tony's son turned to face them. 'What's this? Are you fucking crazy? Adrian!'

A few feet from Finn the two retainers lurched. The struggle was short. Before Finn managed to raise an arm he was snapped over. Whining in pain, he was separated from his family.

Adrian stood up. Rotated his shoulders, stretched his back. He stepped from his chair and came to stand before

Finn, who spat at him as much as spoke. 'You bastard. You bastard.'

'No, I think you'll find that you and your sister are the only bastards here. One can only guess at who it was that mounted your mother back in the day, amongst the fucking sheep.'

'Adrian!' Tony stepped forward.

Nanna looked to her aged father beseechingly, as if she expected him to bring this scene to a swift end.

Adrian ignored Tony. He spoke to Finn directly, though still casually as if he were merely discussing sports equipment. 'You always stuck with the *bout coupé* up at your place. The original Neanderthal hand-axe. Traditional, you'd probably claim, when used for butchery. But when I feel the red, I tend to favour a leaf-shaped point, with a razor-sharp edge. I like to go deep, Devensian deep, you could say. I'm not a bludgeoner, Finn. None of us are, over this way. We've more restraint, more precision. Qualities that you baboons have always lacked.'

From the small of his back Adrian produced a long piece of dark flint chipped carefully into a spear blade.

'Cease!' Jess finally called out from her chair, her voice frail yet imperious. 'You don't know the red. You never did, Adrian. You only know what I've shown you. The shallows. The river bank. Not the depths where your blood would run so cold. We're in the depths now. All of us. The cycle was started when you were but a baby. So enough, or you'll know a rage as red as this earth. It's so close now. It never abates. It abides. So don't you go thinking that I can't bring it here.'

Adrian looked up, grinning. He raised his voice to be heard over the woman's snarling son. 'What did you tell me, Jess, right at the very beginning? How did you explain it? Let me see if I can remember. Ah, yes, it was when you set an example with that druggy, the one with the microphones. You said that the only thing that mattered, the only thing that counted, was survival.

'You said the tribes must always be pitiless to survive. *Survive.* And did one ancestral people not always succumb to another? Over and over again, right here? It's our story, dear. You said so yourself.

'And this is a time of plenty, not struggle. Or it was. None of this should even be happening. But some of us have not reached the end yet. We won't, not for some time either. Your sources are imprecise.

'You see, you're not alone, Jess. Not as *the* wife. There are others. The red favours strength, nothing else and it's been reaching out, further west, while your glorious era approached its sell-by date. Problem is, you never recognised it. You entered a most typical period of . . . degeneracy. Alas, history just repeats itself. We've all seen the writing on the walls, down below.'

Adrian seized strands of Finn Willows's hair, wisps clotted together with haematite, and raised the head as if he were holding a lamb in a slaughterhouse.

The action of his arm beneath Finn's ear was swift, the sawing back and forth. But the sound of the practised despatch was lost beneath the screams of his twin, Nanna Willows, which filled the elegantly tiled room to the rafters.

Tony fell to his naked buttocks, his old face aghast, his eyes glassy, and watched his son's blood stream hotly and splash brightly onto the tiles. Scarlet tributaries rushed for the grate.

As Adrian worked, he spoke through clenched teeth. His porcine eyes within the doggish maw were truly awful to behold as the red came upon him: vicious and bestial but alight with an intelligent purpose that eschewed compassion.

The cutting process seemed to last longer than it actually did and the Willows family beheld it with only the dregs of their earlier intoxication serving to dull their communal horror. And when the head of the heir of Redstone Farm was entirely severed from his bony shoulders, it was raised aloft by its sodden pony tail.

Finn's one good eye remained fixed upon his folk with a look of surprise. His bearded jaw feebly twitched at the air but he'd already said his last.

From the chair his mother wailed. A terrible sound that might yet reverberate beneath the earth to echo through hidden, lightless spaces and vibrate along the old stone walls tunnelling below.

Tony Willows tried to join her in this old lament but lacked the breath to form the customary chorus. He looked winded and broken at the death of his son, an act he hadn't imagined possible until only a few moments before.

The men who'd held Finn released his spent form and took his sister, pulling her away from her elderly parents. She looked no further than her mother for help. The terrible wear grooving her once beautiful face she earned anew in a heartbeat, her silence serving as perverse acknowledgement of a fate long anticipated. She never made another sound.

With Tony on his bare, red backside, and his daughter held at the side of the chamber, Adrian wasted no time and moved to the witch-wife, dropping Finn's head on the tiles behind his speckled heels. The thump of the skull on the ceramic surface was far more sickening than the preceding sounds of flint carving through a spinal column.

Adrian clamped a tanned hand over Jess Usher's mouth to silence the gruff baying of the elderly woman. 'You've served us well, you old jackal. What you brought here was marvellous. I can't thank you enough. Though that bit with the marrow? I know you're one for tradition and for an exactitude drawn from what you *see*, but I've always thought that detail unnecessary.

'You should have moved with the times. You never did and look at you now, you old fool. You've not long left as it is. You can't even walk. When your legs went, your folk should have nested you in stone. That was when the trouble began. You kept on going. On and on and on and now the wheels have come off your chair, lass. The red has taken its toll. I know, I know. We've all watched it happen and it's been sad to see. But we've another queen. All will be well under new management.

'I promise you'll be well cared for and placed in a good nest, deep in the floor. Our descendents will honour your bones too, those that survive us. Your remains are going deep too, where no one can dig 'em up. There will be reverence, tradition, all the rites at your funeral. You have my word. We know how it's done.'

Adrian moved further behind Jessica Usher and cut her wizened throat, scything his flint from beneath one shrivelled ear to the other. When her tatty head flopped to the side of her shoulders and lolled, spilling warmth from a new mouth beneath her jawbone, Adrian pointed his blade at Tony.

'Old boy, you and Nanna are going to run. Not very far, I expect, because the sides of my combe are steep. But over here the grove isn't a cave. We intend to make our provision of what must be given above the ground. You brought it up this far, way too far, but we'll take it from here upon the red earth. There are other ways of managing *them*.'

He nodded toward the windows. 'It's incredible. You'll get to experience it first-hand too. We've a nice moon due and providing there's no cloud, the old Creel will fall upon you in sufficient light so that we can watch it happen from up here. Personally, I cannot wait.

'And even though you've fed the red like it's a favourite hound, I don't expect you'll be shown any favours. You've noticed how boisterous they've become. That's on you. All the other clans are in agreement. You've had this coming, old boy, and we need to get those bitches back on a leash.'

Adrian paused to follow Tony's horrified gaze: he wasn't listening and only had eyes for Jessica Usher's carcass.

Adrian's expression turned to disgust. 'I don't think she had long. What do you think? Sooner or later Creel would have had the lot of you in that shack and left you in bits. You brought them far, far too close. They should never have left the grove. You overfed them. You must have been fucking insane.'

'You don't understand,' Tony gibbered. 'You think we wanted to? You don't know what they demand –'

'Yes, yes, Tony. But I want you to recognise this judgement as a kind of penance for endangering the rest of us. We've been the poor cousins but we're absolutely *pitiless* when it comes to *our* survival. So out with the old, aye? Has ever been thus.'

Adrian then took a moment to look down his front. His trousers and shirt were wet through. 'Darling,' he said to his wife. 'I need to change. We've guests coming.'

Rising from her chair, Sheila nodded. She stepped off the dais, moving carefully on shaking legs.

52

*H*elene's nose nuzzled Valda's hair and inhaled the aroma of cherry shampoo. Under it the fragrance of infancy was still strong, a scent unique to small people.

Slumped across her lap, her daughter was concentrating on the cartoon flashing on the television screen: a scene hectic with pink explosions, glamorous fairies and what resembled toads.

Helene had watched the news headlines while Valda took her collection of toy squirrels through complicated social routines, before changing the channel so that Valda could watch a show before bedtime.

Valda stayed up until 8.30 now. An extra hour granted each night since her mum had returned from Devon. And even when her daughter was tucked in, Helene still sat beside her bed, or lay alongside her until she fell asleep. Five months before, she'd come close to never being able to do that again.

She anticipated no end to the bad dreams either. At night, Helene often returned to Redstone before awaking with a jolt, her hair soaked.

Those nights, she'd always get out of bed to check on the small sleeping figure next door because in most of these dreams she and Valda were in the water. Black water beneath a lightless sky and no matter how hard Helene swam towards the distressed cries of her daughter, towards glimpses of that small, pale head that bobbed between the waves of night, she never reached the girl, or even moved any closer. Instead, she'd drift further away.

In other dreams the two of them were chased by what might have been large dogs, across the very land that she'd once wandered to find the place where her brother had made recordings in a quarry. In those dreams, the big muscular forms that she never saw clearly would laugh and chatter and gabble along the valley floors. Valda's little legs were never able to move fast enough, so Helene would be forced to carry the child in her arms, while her heart thumped fit to burst and her legs turned numb and clumsy.

Other nights, she'd dream of Lincoln. And she'd most often see him before the pitch-black opening of a cave, or a tunnel, or a gap in some rocks. Apertures all covered in long vines and purple flowers that made her nervous.

Lincoln would smile and talk to her in these scenes about things she could never recall on waking. But he'd chat innocently and she would awake with a strong sense that he knew everything about her and Valda.

Sometimes he'd be a small boy, appearing as vividly as anyone can appear in a dream, and he'd be wearing clothes that she'd long forgotten he'd ever worn. The boy Lincoln would play a thin flute inside the mouth of a cave and she would run to him, only to watch the small figure begin to cry and reach for her hands as if she was his mother. But the boy was never able to prevent his own slow progress backwards and into the dark where his voice would fade. No matter how hard she begged him to stay with her, no matter how hard she cried, he'd always walk backwards until his small freckled face vanished from sight.

Helene felt grateful for any night, or afternoon nap, when she woke without remembering her dreams. On waking, she was happiest if she hadn't dreamed at all.

She also swam more than ever before. She would not let her terror swamp her when she looked at the clear blue water of the pool in the leisure centre. She would force herself to get in and she would swim hard and only stop once her shoulders burned and her breath grew ragged.

The others at the local self-help group she attended in Sutton Coldfield, and the counsellor she was seeing for cognitive behavioural therapy, all thought her swimming was a positive sign of managing her trauma.

Valda giggled. Something in her show had amused her. Her mother tried to smile but her attention was mostly consumed by what she'd seen on the evening news. *And when was the farm and what existed below it, not in the news?*

Seven million pounds: that was the value the police had just revised and affixed to the annual yield of the drug crop discovered in the four underground plantations on Redstone Farm.

She had difficulty keeping track of how many councillors had resigned from the Brickburgh council and in the neighbouring boroughs. But another two had just gone from their positions in local government amidst the usual allegations of payments of dirty money into their bank accounts, large sums they were struggling to justify being earned from 'consultancy work'.

Five police officers, including two senior officers and the Police and Crime Commissioner for the county, had been suspended or had resigned ahead of facing charges. A detective was being investigated for his involvement in several murders and abductions.

Further down the food chain, a stream of electricians and builders, assorted tradesmen, every employee at a food distribution centre, the owners of four large yachts and even a headmaster had all been arrested. A holiday camp and four new hotels were implicated and had been closed.

The investigation was in its fifth month. The harbour town and the surrounding farmland had been turned over: every barn and boatshed searched from Brickburgh to the banks of the Divilmouth Estuary. The man Helene had briefly known as Phil, a crew member from the boat that had ferried her out to sea, was found pretty soon after the police had 'rescued' her and Kat. She and Kat had been found wandering towards the outbuildings of Redstone Farm, not long after Kat had discovered the first underground plantation. Phil had since proved very useful to the police.

At Divilmouth police station she and Kat had been separated and Kat was kept in custody for a long time, because of what she had done to the man with the bad leg, the pig captain, who'd taken Helene out to the channel in his new boat so that he could drown her.

That boat had been another asset purchased with illegal earnings and was also being held as evidence in a police yard, in preparation for another trial that she would have to attend as a witness.

Kat had also killed an elderly woman during that red and frantic time that they'd both endured. A woman who Kat claimed had been one half of a couple who'd kept her captive at her home: a mother and son whose real names she'd never known. But though the woman's identity had been established, her body had still not been recovered. The woman's son, a local man implicated in the criminal organisation at Redstone Farm, remained in a coma, brain-damaged from the injuries the journalist had inflicted upon him.

The news channels no longer showed the picture of Lincoln, the photograph, sourced from their mother, of him sitting in her garden, taken a year before he'd disappeared. In the picture he had been smiling. Maybe he'd just cracked one of his quips or jokes. Her mother couldn't remember exactly, but he'd dropped in for a few days after exploring some canals in the centre of Birmingham, where he'd made recordings of echoes and other noises. She had taken a picture because he'd grown a long reddish beard. She'd thought he'd been the spitting image of her father.

That had been one of seventeen photographs shown of those who'd gone missing, or whose apparent suicides in parts of the South West had been called into question and were being reinvestigated, as far back as the 1980s. Helene had only recognised the pictures of her brother and Steve, the photographer.

Some remains of the missing had been found in the myriad tunnels and caverns beneath the area referred to as Seven Quarries. Bone fragments and teeth had been connected to six of the missing individuals, though what had reduced the human remains to such a deplorable state had not been caught, or seen, as the police and forensic investigation had continued below the red earth of Redstone.

It was believed that the family at the head of the criminal organisation had escaped shortly before the police had arrived at Redstone Farm, the morning after Helene had swum for her life and for her daughter's future to reach the shore.

The very family that Kat had been looking for when Helene came across her in the aftermath of the slaughter at the farm, the now notorious Willows family, had comprised two elderly people and their middle-aged twin children. Helene had briefly encountered the twins but not the parents. None of them had ever been caught.

The father, Tony, had once been a famous musician, but Helene had never heard of him before that interview she'd given the police in a hospital bed in Divilmouth. Nor had she ever before seen the clips from *The Old Grey Whistle Test* and the festivals. Broadcasters kept showing a performance recorded in the Seventies of Tony Willows playing a mandolin and another of him dressed as a Morris dancer at Knebworth. He didn't look at all capable of becoming the head of a vast, organised, ruthless criminal gang and Helene understood why so many people for so long had found the whole story difficult to accept.

The 'attack dogs' to which this family had fed their victims had remained the greatest enigma. They had killed the first two police officers on the scene and dismembered eight members of the strange, ghastly cult that had served the drug empire. But the animals had never been found. They'd either been destroyed and hidden or removed by the fleeing Willows family. Like their owners, they'd remained at large. The police were currently looking for the family in Spain and Portugal.

The journalist, Kat, whom she'd known so briefly, had remained in hospital for a long time. After they'd been picked up outside the still-smoking barn, Kat had remained under police protection while she'd helped with their 'inquiries'.

The charges against Kat had been dropped but there were many rumours about her mental health and she'd been transferred to an institution somewhere up north. She and Kat had not spoken since that afternoon at Redstone Cross, where Helene had watched the woman – a lifestyle journalist whom she'd struggled to recognise during their second and third meetings – destroy a human being by hand with a sharpened rock.

Eventually, Helene turned her attention away from the latest news and from her own grim memories. She checked the time.

'Bedtime,' she whispered, squeezing her daughter gently and drying her moist eyes in the little girl's hair.

53

The room reminded Kat of her room in her halls of residence at university: a single bed, a laminate desk combined with a shelving unit, one chair, blue carpet tiles as rough as a scouring pad, terrible curtains. She'd felt comfortable and safe there.

Despite a growing desire to leave, swelling over the last month, her mood was maudlin on the eve of her last night in the room. Her feelings were strangely akin to the day she'd left university, over twenty years ago, to start anew in the world without a job or much money in her bank account.

Kat had since decided that anyone might benefit from time out in an institution, now and again, to be sealed from what was hurting them *out there*. The idea was no longer as crazy as it might have sounded to her five months before. With the right medication, gallons of tea, much time spent talking to people who listened and the space to actually think her life through, her time at the hospital hadn't been so bad. Time, distance, more sleep than she'd ever had in her life and not giving a shit about her weight for once had all been good medicine. All of it.

She placed her hand on the bed covers and smoothed then out. Her tummy cramped from nerves and she wondered whether she should visit the bathroom.

Reg and Delia would arrive the following morning: she imagined they'd be prompt too, bang on ten. She imagined their faces whenever they saw the hospital's sign at the end of the drive, branded by the NHS Trust. What came next would not be easy for them. They'd been kind.

With a smile, Kat imagined what Steve might have said about the situation that she was about to enter, alone with his parents.

Well, you did kill two people, Kat. With a rock and a bloody rolling pin. Mum's bound to be a bit nervous about having you in the spare room. She'll avoid discussing specifics in any situation but will sleep with one eye open. Trust me.

Kat looked at her bump, took her hands from the bed and stroked her tummy, caressing their unborn child. A little miracle she often talked to. Steve did too, in her head.

Through Delia and Reg's desire to help her with this child, she'd accepted how much they'd loved their son, unconditionally. And now she was carrying their grandson, the sole factor in the entire debacle that brought joy to any of them.

The forthcoming battles she imagined waging with Delia, a woman who'd be unable to restrain her proprietary tendencies with the baby, Kat vowed to manage with the same techniques she'd learned through her CBT sessions at the hospital. Those skills would help her understand how she'd feel whenever Delia crossed the line. Severe feelings of victimisation and powerlessness still occasionally swamped her, but the aggressiveness that grew from that distress she managed much better now. The red part of her, that's what she called it and that was how she would always refer to it. She'd always had the red inside her, always. She'd even come to believe that everyone did too. But she'd never imagined that it was limitless.

Kat would continue her therapy. She liked it. Delia had already sourced a Mind group in North Devon, close to where she'd eventually be living. She'd meet others in her situation, just like she'd done here: people who'd suffered psychotic episodes and been the victims of the violent, of predators.

Steve's mum and dad had sold her cottage and found a new flat for her, where she'd eventually live with her son.

They'd also paved a smooth path from the door of her room at the hospital to their holiday cottage in Cornwall, where she'd spend her first few weeks outside, with them, before going to her new home: her flat, west of the moors. It looked nice in the pictures they'd shown her.

At times, Delia even held her hand now. She'd finally entered the inner circle of Steve's family. Steve would have appreciated that irony too.

Kat dabbed her eyes with the back of a knuckle.

With her books and computer all packed away and awaiting Reg's Range Rover in the morning, her thoughts returned to her first night at the hospital, the last time the room had been so Spartan and empty.

Kat had been detained in the secure hospital for five months. Initially, she'd been taken from the farm to Accident and Emergency in the big hospital in Torbay, where they had a room for conducting psychiatric assessments.

Her criteria had quickly been established as 'high risk' and she'd been judged as someone suffering from a 'severe psychotic episode'. Under the Mental Health Act of 1983, she was deemed to have presented a 'significant danger' to 'others' and to herself, because of the 'profound degree of violence and aggression' that she'd displayed in her cottage and then at the farm.

She'd told the doctors and nurses that it was just as well she had been able to summon such a 'profound degree of violence', or she'd never have been around to be assessed.

She'd consented to the treatment the doctors advised, both in A&E and at this hospital, even though they hadn't needed her consent. That's how bad a case she'd been in their eyes. And even after all she'd been through, their judgement about her mental health still upset and shocked her. This was how other people saw her now, including Reg and Delia, even though they were careful to hide it.

The idea that she posed a 'risk of harm' to others shamed her more than it hurt. But the diagnosis was not one that she found herself able to convincingly argue against for long.

No physical restraint had been involved when they took her into care, into the system: she was merely led to a secluded room beside A&E where anti-psychotics were injected to reduce her agitation and the distress that had consumed her outside the boundary of the farm.

Dry-mouthed, restless and twitching, then drowsy and uncommunicative, often dizzy, constipated, she'd been brought to this hospital and that's where she'd stayed.

Her anti-psych medication was soon stopped because of the side-effects, once it had been established that she was pregnant.

The worst of the side-effects passed within a few days after she was clear of the medication but the taint of her 'delusional disorder' had meant she'd needed to be kept in this room. The thoughts and hallucinations about the farm's barn that she'd persisted in sharing had guaranteed her confinement. Her medical records hadn't done her any favours either.

Last night.

Kat went and sat at her desk and recorded her feelings in her diary.

She'd done a lot of writing at the desk: enough to require massages to ease her lower back pain. From what she'd gathered online and from newspapers and magazines (which never stopped running features about the Willows family, the murders and the drug farm), she'd already produced a pretty good structure for the book she planned to write.

Her own story would form the narrative spine. The prologue she'd already written and augmented with excerpts from her diary in a psychiatric hospital. From that point, she'd take the reader all the way back to the press conference in Plymouth, where the contents of the first cave were officially shared with the world.

She had contacts in publishing and knew there would be significant interest in her story; she'd even fantasised about a newspaper serialisation. And she would include the story of what it was like to be a new mother who'd barely escaped death several times, but who'd emerged a survivor blessed with a child that she'd been told she was incapable of conceiving. A miracle baby.

When she closed her diary, Kat checked the corridor outside her room. All was quiet so she returned to her desk and opened her makeup bag. She'd not worn cosmetics for months, not even when Sheila or Steve's parents had visited. But she'd go out there tomorrow with her face on.

She began applying her favourite red lipstick and her fingers trembled enough to irritate her. As she applied the cosmetic to her mouth she also felt a curious, reckless impulse to allow the slippery head of the stick to skirt her mouth: to go out of bounds, to slide beyond her lips.

The colour of the lipstick must have excited her imagination because when she closed her eyes, she acknowledged a now familiar idea that another red face existed behind her own.

When Kat opened her eyes she wiped at the lipstick on her top lip to produce a crimson streak at the side of her mouth. She smeared the cosmetic further, across the pale skin of her cheek.

This made her whole face and scalp flush, her throat too. She felt hot all over and absurdly guilty.

Her limbs loosened.

Restless, she leaned back and placed her hands upon her womb and acknowledged what had been a rare and sudden episode of arousal. There'd not been many of those inside this room. And again, so strangely and unexpectedly, she'd also recognised a need to run. A compulsion born of a body that seemed to have discovered a trapped source of energy. These sensations were not unpleasant; they were the opposite.

Out of curiosity, Kat wiped a little more of the lipstick onto her cheekbones, on both sides of her face. Then she leaned forward in her cushioned seat and, using the pads of her fingertips, rubbed the cosmetic into her skin with more purpose, circling the bones below her eyes: slowly, sensually, applying a rouge with fingertips, reddening her pale skin.

When she sat back, the sight of her face in the mirror made her breath catch.

Closing her eyes, she calmed herself and this time she didn't repress the images that appeared inside her mind. She let them form, let them grow.

And so clearly did that land, beneath the white sky, appear to her: a long pale place, so open and so wild.

Story Notes:
About This Horror

Although I set most of *Lost Girl* and *Under a Watchful Eye* in South Devon, the part of England where I've been living since 2014, *The Reddening* is the first story in which I sensed the landscape, climate, atmospheres and tones were finally settling at a more meaningful depth in my imagination and thoughts.

By the time I began writing the book in late 2016, during the shoot of *The Ritual* in Romania, I was over two years into walking the local stretches of the South West Coast Path, swimming the coves and beaches near my home and exploring the fabulous estuaries and valleys, or combes. By the time I said 'enough is enough' and signed off on the final draft of this book in August 2018, I'd walked from just under Topsham near Exeter to East Prawle in South Hams, was swimming further afield and for longer, and kayaking Torbay's coastline, and the Dart from the sea to deep inland. I spend a lot of time outdoors and what never fails to surprise me is how the landscape, and its flora and fauna, changes dramatically (as does its geology). Within a few miles I can walk from the sub-Tropical to the volcanic and forbidding. I've taken hundreds of pictures and studied the light and atmospherics, the coast, valleys, woods and open expanses, the skies, cliffs, caves and farms, before trying to define and recreate it all in language. Feebly, I'll admit, but this story was the formal start I needed to make in recreating a particular landscape. If you decide to visit Brickburgh or Divilmouth, or anywhere that lies between these two harbours, you won't find them on any map save the one in my imagination and this book: they have been fashioned anew from the places that I've spent four years investigating.

The Eureka moment that became a compulsion to vividly capture a sense of the place in which I live, as well as the vast passages of time that have acted upon the landscape, occurred underground, in a cave: Kents Cavern, in Torquay. This happened in late 2015. Until that descent beneath the surface on a guided tour, I had only wandered around down here, in something of a daze, marvelling at the trees, rocks, the colour of the water, while reading Geopark signs about fossils, geology, the changes occurring in Devon across hundreds of millions of years. Though I'd experienced an expansion of my imagination out to the horizon, across the landscape and back in time, my inspiration had remained formless and had yet to yield more than a couple of short stories that incorporated much of what my senses were continually reeling from when outdoors. I lacked a specific image that might lend itself to horror – though time itself, and a sudden revelation of one's insignificance within a vast landscape, or before an enormous body of water, can be pure horror of the most sublime type, that involves equal parts terror and wonder. But, for a novel-length story, I needed something localised, specific, more tangible, a kind of metaphor for time, our origins and those incomprehensible stretches of time existing before we stood upright and systematically rid the planet of its mega fauna and flora.

The penny dropped inside Kents Cavern, on the guided tour, and in a few moments of sensory deprivation when the guide turned the lights off to return us to a world without electric light. This occurred shortly after we'd heard the recorded shriek of a hyena; an animal that once topped the food chain here. The guide had also informed us that early Homo Sapiens cohabited within the cave with these very animals, then the size of African lions, as well as giant cave bears, cave lions and the great scimitar cats. Each species used a different entrance and our ancestors would probably have huddled near the surface and around a large fire that was never allowed to go out. The earliest remains of modern humans (us) in Northern Europe were also found in that cave: part of a male jawbone that I have seen. And, we were told on the tour, the fragment of bone was either torn from a human face or scavenged from a grave by a giant hyena.

And I had my 'in'. My imagination latched onto a sense of the cavern's horror in a heartbeat and the legend of The Old Creel and her White Pups was born right then, underground. Not an un-Lovecraftian theme because the nature of the very material imposed a cosmic dimension.

Amidst my persisting claustrophobia and desire to get back above ground, away from the dank, dripping walls and infernal sinuses of Kents Cavern, burrows forming naturally in the Pleistocene epoch, that terrible hyena scream lingered in my imagination too. In it, existed the horror that endured for at least a million years for early human species, before the last surviving human race, Homo Sapiens, found itself in the current Anthropocene era. But the scream was also a reminder that despite the best efforts of industrialisation and urbanisation over the last few centuries, animals we remain, ever a part of nature and ever beholden to our ancient nature too. From that point, so much more of this story evolved while I was out walking and using my feet to cross rural landscapes and coastal vistas, some not much changed to human eyes since The Younger Dryas mini ice-age, 12,000 years before. And at times I have felt myself walking back into prehistory and my imagination would crowd with scenes, ideas and characters. So this story came out of the land and sea itself, while I was mobile. As a result, the circumstances of its creation make *The Reddening* my least sedentary story; it was imagined as I moved, apart from my own kind and the developed world, even more so than *The Ritual*, its closest relative in the circumstances of its imagining.

The folk elements and characters steadily appeared as I went along and fashioned my own alternative history of this tiny part of the earth. At times, while out walking, I have also blundered and trespassed. Though once my ineptitude as a hiker had been established by landowners, the farmers were always kind and helped me find my way to where I needed to be. But from such encounters, and from the many abandoned buildings I've found along the way, the Red Folk were given life. A tribe further embellished by what I discovered in books about prehistory.

Anyway, I have let lose the hounds and I hope that the Red Folk will sing loudly out there and catch the ears of all willing to follow me back underground.

Thank you for your time and patronage.

Manes exite paterni
Adam L. G. Nevill
South Devon
December 2018.

Acknowledgements

*I*n my stories, fact and fiction often merge and get lost within each other. And my intention to create a sense of prehistorical authenticity in this story was greatly helped by Chris Stringer's fascinating works: *Homo Britannicus*, *The Origin of our Species* and *One Million Years of the Human Story*. Timothy Darvill's *Prehistoric Britain* and Dr Alice Roberts's *Evolution: The Human Story* were also key texts for expanding my feeble knowledge of the earliest years of our species. Devon County Council's website was very useful in enabling me to correctly name the rocks I often walk across or scramble over, on my explorations of this wonderful coastline.

The creation of this artefact and the other editions wouldn't have been possible without the managing editorial skills of Tony Russell and Robin Seavill, the text design of Peter Marsh (Dead Good Design Company) and the artwork and designs of Simon Nevill. The wisdom, expertise, knowledge and mentorship I have received from Brian J. Showers of Swan River Press remain priceless.

Ritual Limited's publications to date have been kindly championed by a long list of reviewers and signal-boosters, to whom I am indebted again, not least: Tony Jones and Gingernuts of Horror, This is Horror, Des Lewis at Dreamcatcher: Gestalt Real-time Reviews, Lovecraft eZine, The British Fantasy Society, Ramsey Campbell, Pop Mythology, Ellen Datlow, Stephen J. Clark, Postcards from Asia, Diala Atat and Blogging from Dubai, Oddly Weird

Fiction, The Eloquent Page, Carmilla Voiez, Dark Musings, James Everington at Scattershot Writing, Horror Novel reviews, Confessions of a Reviewer, Bookaholics Refuge, The Grim Reader, Reluctantly Freaky, Terror Tree, Sci-Fi Bulletin, Writing in Starlight, Literature Works, Amazon, Facebook, Twitter, WordPress and BookBub.

For their eyes, time and thoughts, I sincerely thank my first readers: Clive Nevill, Anne Nevill, Mathew Riley and Hugh Simmons.

Of the highest possible value to me and my literary frights, are you readers, who make it all possible and worthwhile. Thank you for allowing me to haunt you again.

About the Author

*A*dam L.G. Nevill was born in Birmingham, England, in 1969 and grew up in England and New Zealand. He is the author of the horror novels 'Banquet for the Damned', 'Apartment 16', 'The Ritual', 'Last Days', 'House of Small Shadows', 'No One Gets Out Alive', 'Lost Girl', 'Under a Watchful Eye' and 'The Reddening'. He has two collections of short stories: 'Some Will Not Sleep' (winner of the British Fantasy Award for Best Collection, 2017) and 'Hasty for the Dark'.

His novels, 'The Ritual', 'Last Days' and 'No One Gets Out Alive' were the winners of The August Derleth Award for Best Horror Novel. 'The Ritual' and 'Last Days' were also awarded Best in Category: Horror, by R.U.S.A. Several of his novels are currently in development for film and television and in 2016 Imaginarium adapted 'The Ritual'into a feature film.

Adam also offers three free books to readers of horror: 'Cries from the Crypt', downloadable from his website, and 'Before You Sleep' and 'Before You Wake', available from major online retailers.

Adam lives in Devon, England, and can be contacted through www.adamlgnevill.com, @AdamLGNevill on Twitter and Facebook.

Adam L. G. Nevill

More horror fiction from Ritual Limited, available in print and audio book at all major book retailers and in eBook at Amazon (including Kindle Unlimited).

Some Will Not Sleep
Selected Horrors

A bestial face appears at windows in the night.
In the big white house on the hill angels are said to appear.
A forgotten tenant in an isolated building becomes addicted to milk.
A strange goddess is worshipped by a home-invading disciple.
The least remembered gods still haunt the oldest forests.
Cannibalism occurs in high society at the end of the world.
The sainted undead follow their prophet to the Great Dead Sea.
A confused and vengeful presence occupies the home of a first-time buyer . . .

In ghastly harmony with the nightmarish visions of the award-winning writer's novels, these stories blend a lifelong appreciation of horror culture with the grotesque fascinations and childlike terrors that are the author's own. Adam L.G. Nevill's best early horror stories are collected here for the first time.

Winner of the British Fantasy Award: Best Collection 2017.

Praise for *Some Will Not Sleep: Selected Horrors:*

"An outstanding anthology of career spanning short stories." *Gingernuts of Horror*

"Beautifully crafted, original and complete works." *This is Horror*

"In *Some Will Not Sleep* nothing is sacred, nothing is safe, and goodness me, if you like horror fiction you're going to absolutely love every damn minute." *Pop Mythology*

Limited Edition Hardback available from www.adamlgnevill. com. Available in eBook (and included in Kindle Unlimited) at Amazon, Paperback and Audio Book from all major online retailers.

Adam L. G. Nevill

Hasty for the Dark
Selected Horrors

The hardest journeys in life and death are taken underground.

No blackmail is as ghastly as extortion from angels.

A swift reckoning often travels in handheld luggage.

Once considered inhumane and now derelict, this zoo may not be as empty as assumed.

A bad marriage, a killer couple, and part of a wider movement.

No sign of life aboard an abandoned freighter, but what is left aboard tells a strange story.

The origin of our species is not what we think.

In destitution, the future for revolution and mass murder is so bright.

Your memories may not be your own, and your life nothing more than a ritual that will compel you to perform an atrocity . . .

Hasty for the Dark is the second short story collection from the award-winning and widely appreciated British writer of horror fiction, Adam L. G. Nevill. These selected terrors range from the speculative to supernatural horror, encompass the infernal and the occult, and include stories inspired by H. P. Lovecraft, Robert Aickman and Ramsey Campbell. The author's best later horror stories are collected here for the first time.

Praise for *Hasty for the Dark: Selected Horrors:*

"His stories weave their way inside of your head and plant seeds of doubt and terror. He is a master of creating oppressive, creepy atmospheres and of taking your imagination to places you would rather he didn't." *The Grim Reader*

"For a genre fan, there can be little better than reading the work of an author at the top of their game. I can't fault a single story in this collection." *The Eloquent Page*

"The nine tales are cleverly varied, exhibiting varied pace, chills which deal with the supernatural in both every day and altogether freakier situations, and other curve-balls which drop feet into other genres." Tony Jones, *Gingernuts of Horror*

…ed Edition Hardback available from www.adamlgnevill.
. Available in eBook (and included in Kindle Unlimited)
.mazon, Paperback and Audio Book from all major online
.ilers.

Free Download

A book of shadows

If you like horror stories, missing chapters from an award-winning author's novels, advice for writing horror, articles on horror fiction and films, and much more, go to adamlgnevill.com and register to summon your Free copy of

Cries from the Crypt

Made in the USA
Middletown, DE
14 May 2024